Love Marks

Rachael Harriet

To the girls with paper hearts and stars in their eyes.

Content Warning

Please note that this book has content warnings for adult language, adult content, sexual assault, and sex work

Chapter 1

Quinn

Sometimes the best thing you can do is listen to signs from the universe.

Take tonight, for example. All the signs were telling me to stay home. It started this morning when I woke up with a pounding headache. Things only got worse when my last clean pair of tights ripped halfway up my legs as I was getting dressed. When my most comfortable pair of heels broke, I should have taken the hint. Forgetting my metro card, subway doors closing in my face — all of it, I simply chalked up to bad luck.

In reality, they were signs from the universe, warning me that a storm was brewing. But instead of listening to those signs, here I stand, in the world's tiniest black dress, a smile plastered onto my face. My shift is about to start — a shift that will last late into the night. Oh joy.

As far as jobs go, working at The Phoenix Lounge isn't half-bad, so I probably shouldn't complain. I didn't imagine being a waitress at this point, but here I am. Technically, I'm not even a waitress, I'm a hostess. At 28, I thought that by now I'd have achieved all my dreams and then some. Life had other plans, though, and if there's one thing I've learned, it's that the myth of realizing all your dreams before 30 is just that: a myth.

The Phoenix is one of the most elite spots in New York City and I managed to land a job on the host staff. Ian, the maître-d and my boss, likes to remind us that our jobs are precious gems every chance he gets. Like we should kiss their feet for employing us. The truth is, the hours are terrible, most of the staff is rude, and I have to dress like Manhattan Barbie every night. But all of it is worth it when I get even the smallest glimpse into the kitchen.

I've always loved restaurants. When I was little, my mom and I would make our escape to the Sunset Park diner for donuts and burgers, always in that order. She let me get whatever I wanted off the menu even though money was tight. More importantly, I'd start with dessert before my main course, a tradition I cherished deeply and still practice myself at times. I can't help it; I have a sweet tooth. Dentists hate me.

Standing beside the hostess stand, I glance around at my surroundings. The Phoenix Lounge is the antithesis of the Sunset Park Diner. Sleek black countertops, extravagant chandeliers, and velvet-wrapped booths. It is the essence of elegance. When I was a kid, I didn't even know places like this existed.

I still remember my first fine-dining experience. Shortly after my dad disappeared, divorce papers appeared in the mail. Within a few weeks, my mom was set to go to court over child support. I don't remember much from those days, but I do remember my mom's lawyer. She wore a navy-blue pantsuit and waltzed into the courtroom like a FiDi Wonder Woman. After the case was closed, she offered to take me and my mom out to dinner. I'd expected another round of donuts and grilled cheese, but instead, she took us to a Michelin-star private dining room in Soho. It was at that moment that my dream of opening my own restaurant was born.

Until that happens, I'm stuck at The Phoenix. Even though I don't make much as a hostess, it's worth it because I get to shadow different staff members, so my job doubles as both a source of income and a training course for restaurant management. The Phoenix provides a private, intimate space for everything from romantic dinners to business deals. The owner, Pierre, a French expat and Forbes Fortune 500 business owner, opened the place 25 years ago with the mission of creating a space where business, pleasure, and food meet. I admit that when I first started here, I resented the fancy attitude of the place. I've been here almost a year now and I can say with certainty that it's something special. Just like the Sunset Park diner, there's no place quite like it. Extravagant displays of wealth aside, the restaurant is *cool,* and Pierre, with his bright colored scarves and his sharp eye, is at least nice to look at.

Tonight is a busy, booming Friday night. We have back-to-back reservations booked until 2:30AM. Another thing that sets us apart from other fine dining, luxury establishments — we're open late enough to accommodate video calls with Chinese partners or an after-work drink for those who work 100-hour weeks.

"Give me the run-through for tonight," Ian barks from behind me. I have never seen Ian smile. He's all business, but I don't mind. I'm always up to the challenge and I'm used to it with him. He's friendly enough, but we've never been friends. I pick up my iPad and swipe it open, reading the details for tonight.

"Mr. Parker is meeting with the Deloitte team at table six. They've requested four bottles of Clicquot and are expecting a phone call at 11:00, so they'll need a private line. Ms.

Stevens and Mr. Brighton are coming in for their weekly cocktail hour, but it's Ms. Stevens' birthday, so he's ordered flowers and a soufflé, already confirmed with the florist and the kitchen."

"Confirm again with chef."

I nod and continue going through the reservations for tonight. Once I'm finished, Ian takes the iPad from my hands, swiping through to make sure everything is in order before we open the doors for the night.

"We just got a last-minute addition from a major VIP, so I'm moving Mr. Parker to table four up front."

"But he prefers—"

"I know what he prefers, Quinn. Mr. Marks has an important business meeting tonight and he's chosen us to host said meeting, so he'll be getting six. It's our most private booth."

Samantha, one of the other hostesses, chimes in from behind me.

"Benjamin Marks?" she squeaks out.

"No, his son, Wesley," Ian replies, hardly looking at Samantha.

Wesley Marks.

I've only heard his name tossed around this place like some urban legend, mostly drooled off the lips of female patrons. Not that I know any of the women he associates with — mostly models and actresses, according to the tabloid magazines that frequently write about him. Samantha has a habit of reading said magazines aloud to me during slow shifts, which is how I know a disturbing amount of information about the eligible bachelors of Manhattan. Broad-chested, chiseled jaw, perfectly tailored Tom Ford suits, Wesley Marks the embodiment of new money in New York. His father, Benjamin Marks, went from rags to riches when he founded the Marks Group, one of the largest hotel chains in New York.

"Oh my god. He's so hot. He's like, a Greek God." Samantha's eyes are wide and she's pulling her dress down and pushing her chest out. I roll my eyes and take the iPad from Ian, putting the finishing touches on the evening.

"Just keep it professional, Sam." Ian's eyes cut down to her low-cut top and she smiles that sweet, saccharine smile of hers.

"Of course. I'm just, a little nervous. Aren't you guys nervous? He's like, Mr. Intimidation. I heard he doesn't even eat. He just drinks whiskey and black coffee."

I roll my eyes, "There's no way that's true."

She shrugs, unfazed. "Just saying. I read it in like, Forbes."

"If you two are done gossiping, it's 5:00. Let the show begin." Ian smiles his signature Cheshire cat grin, and we're off.

Eight hours later, and I'm exhausted. My feet are killing me in these heels. It's almost midnight and all the reservations have been seated for the night except for Mr. Marks. The asshole's reservation was thirty minutes ago but of course, time doesn't matter for the VIPs like him. When you're gorgeous, young, and rich, the world is your oyster.

If Ian can tell how tired I am, he doesn't say anything. The servers are rushing around, eager to close. Most of the staff gets off at 12:30, except for the closers who can't leave until the last patron leaves, which really could be anytime. Samantha left thirty minutes ago, much to her disappointment.

"I'm happy to close tonight, really. Please? I don't even need to be on the clock. I'll just sit at the bar — just one peak. Please?"

Instead, Ian and I are the lucky ones saddled with dealing with Mr. Marks and his confidential business meeting. Ian left me to finish the floor while he deals with office stuff with Pierre upstairs. I always wonder what it'd be like to get to Ian's level — maître'd just has such a nice ring to it. Maybe then they'd let me wear flats instead of heels.

My eyes are half-closed when the door finally opens. I go to put on my award-winning smile, but it drops quickly from my mouth looking at the man standing in front of me. If the wobbly feeling in my knees is any indication, this is Wesley Marks. He waltzes in and *oh god* Samantha wasn't kidding. I try to remain unfazed by his presence, but I swear I'm swooning a little bit and I never swoon. Never.

He takes up the whole room as he walks towards my podium, his sharp jaw jutted forward as his dark eyes sweep the room. Finally, his gaze lands on me, no hint of emotion behind his eyes.

"Marks," he barks out, his voice gruff and hard.

I nod, as if I didn't already know it was him. I manage to bring him over to his table without turning completely to mush, but each step feels like a mile. My legs feel like jelly as he slides into the hidden booth.

What the hell is happening?

"Whiskey neat and an old-fashioned."

Please, I add mentally. He may be hot as all hell, but jeez, would it kill the guy to throw some manners into the mix? I don't know why I expect it from any of them, honestly. My ass has been grabbed so many times at this job that I've learned to push down the anger. Deep down. For some reason, though, it grates me that he won't meet my eyes when he commands me to serve him.

"Right away, sir." I smile like it's my greatest pleasure in life and swing by the bar before returning to my podium and swiping his name off my iPad. I take a deep breath. One (not so) short ride on the N train and I'll be back in my apartment in my fuzzy pajamas with a cup of hot cocoa, extra marshmallows.

A few minutes later, a man in a suit sweeps into the room and asks for Marks and I walk him over to table six where the whiskey neat and old-fashioned sit, untouched.

"Anything else I can help you gentlemen with?" I ask, sugar coating my words.

"No. You're dismissed." Mr. Marks waves his hand, still hardly glancing in my direction.

The rejection stings in an unexpected way. Why did he have to say it like that?

You're dismissed.

Next, he'll be ringing a bell and I'll be singing a ballad from *Annie.* Does that make him Daddy Warbucks? I suddenly have a new fantasy.

Frustrated, I head back into the kitchen, hoping for an opportunity to chat with our head chef and my favorite person in this place.

"Manny!" I call out.

"QT!" he calls back, smiling and bringing me in for a hug. QT is his nickname for me — Quinn Taylor. I'd never tell him, but I actually love it. Luckily, when it's late like this, Manny lets me taste some of the gourmet dishes and even gives me copies of some of the simpler recipes to try at home.

"Aren't you a sight for sore eyes?" he twirls me a little bit. "Isn't she a stunner?" he asks Tina, one of the line cooks, who shakes her head and keeps clearing her station. He pulls me over to the dessert station to try the latest sorbet flavors and I nearly moan when they reach my mouth. I didn't realize how hungry I was, but it's been almost 8 hours since I ate anything. He makes me a little goodie bag of leftovers to take home as the kitchen finishes their closing routine.

When I get back to the host stand, Mr. Marks' guest has left and he's sitting alone, sipping the last of his whiskey. He's the only one left here but he doesn't seem to notice; his eyes are completely focused on the drink in front of him. Next to him, a folder rests on top of his briefcase. He knocks back the rest of his drink and swipes his belongings off the table. I'm about to wish him a goodnight and finally head home when he stops directly in front of the stand and for the first time tonight, he looks right at me.

"Hello."

Again, his voice betrays no emotion. I stare into his dark eyes and find nothing there, either.

"Hello. I hope you enjoyed your evening," I say, hoping my voice doesn't sound as shaky as it feels.

"Yes, it was fine," he answers. It's quiet for a moment and the silence seems to stretch between us like a rubber band. I go to ask if he needs anything else, but he cuts me off before I get the chance. "What's your name?"

The question sounds more like a demand coming from him and images rush through my mind, other demands he would make from me.

God, I need to get laid. How long has it been? Six months? Seven? A twinge of disappointment fills me remembering the last time I tried to have sex. Tried being the operative word, since I was so far gone inside my head that I was barely there at all.

Answer him, you idiot!

"Quinn. Quinn Helena Taylor."

Holy shit. Why did I say my middle name? I hate my middle name. It's what old ladies at Bingo are named, not hot, mysterious women. I think my face must be red because it feels like it's on fire with the blush I'm sporting. If he notices the middle name thing, he doesn't say anything, but I swear the corner of his mouth twitches. Just a little.

"Quinn, I'd like you to do something for me. In about ten minutes, a Mr. Adleman from Hyatt is going to come and pick up this folder." He holds it out to me. "The information in here is very sensitive. Do you understand?"

I nod, dumbly, and reach out for the folder.

"You're to hand this folder to him, and only him, yes?"

"Alright."

Both our hands are still on the folder. He hasn't released it. His eyes are staring into mine, searching. It's intense. I clear my throat.

"I understand, sir. I'll wait for Mr. Adleman."

He finally releases the folder and I almost stumble back. I hadn't realized I was gripping it so hard. I suddenly want to know what's in the folder. What is so important to the illustrious Wesley Marks.

"Thank you. I'm trusting you to handle this with discretion."

"Of course, Mr. Marks."

"Wesley."

My heart flutters like a damned butterfly. Those, too, in my stomach. I feel like a schoolgirl with a crush. I'm like a walking embodiment of the heart-eye emoji.

"You can count on me, Wesley."

I smile and he does not. His face is a mask, betraying nothing. With a single nod of his head, he turns on his heels, and walks out the door.

I stare down at the folder. Why didn't he just wait and give it over to Mr. Adleman himself? Better yet, join the rest of us in the 21st Century and shoot the guy an email. Whatever. I don't bother questioning the business deals that go down here. I assume some of them are shady, otherwise why would they need to be so private?

I pack up my bag and say goodnight to the kitchen staff. I put my coat on and watch the clock on the wall.

Come on, Adleman. Some of us have a long train ride home.

My eyes are drooping when a heavy hand drops on my shoulder. I scream a little and my eyes fly open. Ian is standing right behind me, one eyebrow raised at my little outburst.

"I thought you left!" I shriek. "You scared me."

He rolls his eyes at me. "What are you still doing here? Everyone else has left, right?"

"Mr. Marks asked me to wait and deliver this to someone coming by for it, a Mr. Adleman."

He eyes the folder in my hand and nods.

"Oh, don't worry about it. I got it. You can go." He reaches for the folder, and I take a step back.

I don't know how to explain Wesley's intense request. "Well, he asked me to do it."

Ian furrows his brow a little and shakes his head. His impatience is written all over his face.

"It's fine, Quinn. Head on home. I know you've got a long commute ahead. I have a few more things to handle anyway and could be here a while."

I stare down at the folder. It suddenly feels very heavy in my hands. Very significant. But Ian is already reaching for it, and I feel weird gripping it, remembering the strange battle between Wesley and I when he handed it off to me. So, I let go. Ian shuffles the papers on the desk and doesn't look up at me, even though I'm still standing there, staring down at the folder. Finally, he looks up.

"You good? Need me to call you a car or something?" He asks.

I shake my head.

"No, yeah, I'm fine. I'll see you tomorrow night."

Ignoring the pit in my stomach, I pull my scarf around my neck and head down to the subway. I feel kind of bad that Wesley asked me to handle it personally and I passed it along to Ian, but it's not like I could tell my boss I can do his job better than he can. Whatever. It's fine. It will get done no matter what.

Still, the whole train ride home, I remember how terrible my day started, the storm cloud of bad luck that seemed to follow me around. I can't help this sinking feeling in my gut, can't stop replaying the image of Wesley's sharp, dark eyes boring into mine, his words seared into my memory.

I'm trusting you.

Chapter 2

Quinn

When I wake up the next day, my mom is still fast asleep in her room. I'm thankful. Sometimes in the mornings, she's up with her head in the toilet. It's the chemo that makes her sick. She was diagnosed with breast cancer nine years ago. She was in remission for a while when I was in college, but last year it came back, and she's been in chemo for the last few months.

Our two-bedroom in South Slope is quiet except for the sounds of the traffic outside. We live right across from the expressway. Last week I woke up at five in the morning and heard a drunk driving accident out front. It was unnerving, but I'm used to it by now. In fact, I don't mind it much. At night, the sounds of cars whooshing past my window is the only way I can fall asleep.

I'm starving and still exhausted from last night, so I pour some cereal into a bowl and scarf it down in record time. Then I make the mistake of checking my bills for the month. Between mom's medical costs, my student loans, rent, and utilities, my salary at The Phoenix barely leaves anything left for food. Mom used to work at the Home

Depot nearby, but she had to quit when she got sick, which leaves me.

I went to school for a few years at CUNY but eventually ran out of money and couldn't afford the tuition any longer, so I left. I didn't want to quit. I wanted to see it all the way through to the end, but I failed.

So here I am. It's times like this, staring down at the stack of bills in my hands, that I hear a voice rattle around in my head.

Useless.

I curl my hand into a fist, shaking off the memories that threaten to break through. No time to wallow. I have a million things to do today. Laundry, groceries, mom's medications. Saturday is one of the few days I don't work my second job, so I have to squeeze everything in. Slipping on my coat, I scribble a note for my mom and slip out the door.

"Well, well. Why do you always look like you're sneaking out?" Sheila's no-nonsense voice rings out from behind me.

"You're seeing things, old lady." I turn and smile at Sheila, my neighbor. She's standing across the hall, trash bags in hand. She's lived across from us since before I was born when my parents first moved into the place. She's always been old in my mind. In reality, she's a spunky 70-year-old.

"The ghosts of teenage rebellions past. I seem to remember catching you sneak out of that door once or twice in the middle of the night." Sheila holds her arms out and I take the trash bags from her. In the last few years, it's gotten harder for her to get down the stairs, so I take her trash and bring her mail up for her.

"And you'll never let me forget it," I groan.

Sheila chuckles. "Glad I caught you. Never even see you these days."

"I'm just working a lot," I offer, squirming a little.

"At that gentleman's club?"

"No, a gentleman's club is a fancy name for a strip club. It's just a restaurant that's open late."

"Sure, sure." She brushes me off and puts her hands into the pockets of her nightgown. "How's your mom?"

I sigh and shift the trash into one hand. I'm no good at conversations like these. Ones about...well, feelings.

"She's fine. She sleeps a lot. I'm taking her to chemo on Monday. You probably see her more than I do these days."

My attempt at a joke falls flat. Sheila just tuts a little in approval, the awkwardness hanging in the air as it always does. Thankfully, she doesn't ask anything else. I know she'll go over soon to keep her company.

Sheila pulls her mail key out of her nightgown pocket and hands it to me. "I'm expecting a very important letter from a long-lost lover looking to reconnect," she says, her voice light.

"Really?" I ask.

"Charlie Reynard. Left me behind to serve in the war. He had no idea I was pregnant with his brother's baby."

My jaw drops. Sheila simply raises her eyebrows at me and turns swiftly, slamming the door behind her. Chuckling to myself and shaking my head in disbelief, I bring the trash down the stairs and shove it into the cans outside the building. Pushing my headphones into my ears, I head out to face the day, keeping my head down and thinking about Charlie and Sheila.

* * *

I get back to the apartment around five. Climbing the stairs with bags of groceries slung over my shoulder, I flip through my mail. I'm getting close to defaulting on my student loan payments. They sent me a letter about it last month. Something-something debt collectors and bad credit. I just can't pay them right now with mom's hospital bills taking priority. That and rent. I shove the mail into my bag and slip Sheila's letters under her door. Nothing from Charlie. If he even exists.

When I step into my apartment, it smells amazing — like basil and bacon. I smile a little.

"Carbonara?" I call out.

"You know it!" My mom calls back.

I get into the kitchen with the grocery bags and drop them on the floor and start unloading. She stands in front of the stove, a scarf around her head and an apron around her waist. I've always thought she was so beautiful, my mom. People say we look the same, but I think I look like my dad. Sometimes when my mom looks at me, I know I look like my dad. He left when I was a kid. Too young to really remember, which I suppose is a type of blessing. I don't really think about him, but I know it hurts my mom a lot.

"You shouldn't be up and about like this," I say, putting eggs into the fridge.

"You're right. I should just do nothing all day and let you head off to a nine-hour shift with nothing but a grain of rice to hold you over."

"Hey, I had a granola bar earlier," I defend myself.

She grabs a bag of rice from the grocery bag and chucks it towards my head. Luckily, I grab it before it smacks me across the face.

"You need to eat," she says.

"And you need to relax," I challenge. We stand across from each other, arms crossed. Finally, she rolls her eyes and brings me in for a hug. I sigh into her arms, and she rubs my back and it's just us for a moment in time. Then she releases me.

"Go sit. I'll finish dinner and unpacking the groceries," I say, shooing her out of the kitchen.

"Fine. You're a better chef than me anyways." She sulks off into the living room and I finish unloading the rest of the groceries. The sauce is basically done so I put the pasta into the boiling water and set a timer, chopping some more basil.

"Sheila came over today. Says she's thinking of moving out," my mom calls out from the couch.

"What?" I almost drop the spoon right into the scalding hot sauce. Sticking my head out from the kitchen, I find my mom reclined on the couch.

"What do you mean, moving out? She's lived here forever."

"Well, she can hardly function in her condition, stuck in that apartment. She's moving to Nevada so her son can take care of her."

"Nevada? What, like, Vegas?" Bright lights flash in my head. That pyramid hotel. Sand. Strippers. "And she accused *me* of working at a strip club," I scoff.

"I knew you'd be upset." She shakes her head.

"I'm not upset," I protest, going back into the kitchen and stirring the sauce.

"Well, don't tell her I told you. She said she wanted to tell you herself, but you know I can never keep a secret."

Straining out the pasta, I realize that my mom is right, as usual. I am upset. I guess Sheila has always been a constant here, so it's weird to imagine life without her.

Dinner is a quiet affair. My mom twirls the spaghetti with her fork for so long, I know that she feels nauseous and doesn't want to eat.

"Just try to get some of it down," I encourage her, bringing my bowl to the sink and washing up.

"You should go, or you'll be late," she says, gesturing towards the clock. It's almost 6:30.

"Shit. I still need to shower," I groan.

"Too bad. You'll have to go smelly." She smiles at me and takes a bite, chewing slowly. I run into my room and change into the same dress I wore three nights ago. Spritzing myself more perfume than usual, I toss my hair up and grab my bag.

"Don't forget the pepper spray!" My mom calls out to me from the living room.

I grab the pepper spray from my dresser and stick it at the bottom of my bag just in case. I kiss my mom's cheek on my way out and she gives me her best smile, but I can tell that she's not feeling well.

"There's a joint in my room," I say, giving her a knowing look, and she nods. It's been an ongoing debate with us, me trying to get her to give THC and CBD a chance, which she finally has. She still won't admit that she actually *likes* getting high, but I know bliss when I see it.

I run to the train and miss it by a second, letting out a string of curses that I'm glad nobody is around to witness. On the train, I listen to music and wallow for most of the ride. The news about Sheila has put me in a mood that even my pump-up music can't cheer.

We're sitting on the bridge when I peer down at my phone. Shit. I'm late.

Why isn't this train moving?

The conductor comes over the intercom and apologizes for the delay, citing an unmoving train in front of us. The joys of the MTA. Finally, five minutes later, we start moving again. When I get to work, I am a whopping twelve minutes late. It's not that bad, except that Ian is standing at the hostess stand as I try to slip in the front hoping nobody will notice.

"You're late," he says.

"Sorry. Train issues," I offer, hoping he's in a good mood. No such luck.

"Pierre asked to see you," he replies, his voice a little colder than usual. Now I'm nervous. Ian may be kind of a hard ass, but he's usually more pleasant than this.

"Oh, cool. Maybe he wants to switch scarves!" I laugh awkwardly, holding up my bland, brown excuse for a scarf and Ian eyes it with disdain. I take the hint and move past him into the back, heading up the stairs to Pierre's office.

I knock lightly on the mahogany door and Pierre calls out from behind it. "Come in!"

He's sitting behind his desk with an orange scarf wrapped around his neck, his hand rubbing his chin in slight thought.

"Please, Quinn, sit." He gestures for the chair across from him.

Now I'm really freaked out. Pierre is being too serious. He's usually Mr. Light and Breezy but he's not even smiling. I cross the room and sit across from him, trying to calm my shaking hands.

"Is everything okay?" I ask, my voice quivering a little.

"Honestly, Quinn, no. It's not."

My heart is pounding in my chest. Is this a joke? I wait for his charming smile to return but instead he picks up the newspaper in front of him and drops it right in front of me, his expression disappointed.

I stare down at the headline before me.

Drunkard Dick Marks Nearly Drives Marks Group to Bankruptcy, Forced Merger with Hyatt Estates

"What is this?" My voice cracks as I start to skim through the article.

It's an exposé about Wesley's father, Richard Marks. I read further as it details his battle with alcoholism that has led his company to lose money and near bankruptcy. Now, Wesley is taking over as CEO and merging the Marks Group with Hyatt Estates while his dad goes to rehab.

Jeez, and I thought my family was fucked up. This is like an episode of Succession.

I read it again once through trying to make sense of the business deal here before I realize I still have no idea what this has to do with me. Just as I go to ask Pierre, he stands.

"Ah, Ian, thank you for being here," Pierre says, and I look up to see Ian striding into the room to take his place flanking Pierre.

"Quinn, I'm sorry, but we're going to have to let you go." Pierre says. I look up and they are both towering over me.

"Go...where?"

You know where, idiot.

Pierre sighs a deep sigh and looks at Ian, letting him take the lead.

"Wesley Marks has personally requested your termination."

Wesley? Wesley personally requested me?

"The Phoenix prides itself on creating an environment of confidentiality and luxury. It's our brand. Unfortunately, the evidence suggests that you are responsible for this breach in confidentiality and as such, a breach in your contract outlined as a fireable offense." Ian gives his speech like a robot and Pierre sighs again, that damned old man sigh like a British villain in a movie who says *what a pity* before killing a puppy.

Wait, backup. They're firing me? For leaking this story to the press?

Say something! Defend yourself!

I look up at Ian's smug expression.

"I did not do this," I say, my voice shaky but steady. I move my eyes from Ian to Pierre. He always liked me, right? He'll understand that this is a misunderstanding. "I gave the folder to—"

"Clause seven of your contract gives authorization for termination for any reason." Ian's steely voice interrupts and when I look into his eyes, they are mean. Meaner than I realized.

"You're lying!" I stand, pointing my finger at Ian.

"Quinn, please don't make a scene," Pierre says, his eyes pleading. I take a deep breath and meet Pierre's gaze again.

"I did not do this," I repeat, my voice firm.

Pierre shakes his head and has the decency to look upset as he leans forward and meets my gaze unflinchingly.

"We'll mail you your last paycheck. I'm sorry, Quinn. Your employment at The Phoenix is officially terminated."

* * *

My goodbyes with the kitchen staff are the hardest. Ian stands towering over me the whole time, rushing me out the door as fast as he can. He's like the Grim Reaper, minus the scythe. Pierre tries to hug me as he kicks me off the premises, but I refuse his open arms, sending a pang of guilt into my stomach. Why should I feel bad? He's the one who fired me.

Meanwhile, I've never seen Manny as fired up as he is when he finds out I've been sacked.

"Nah. No way. This is outrageous! Where's Pierre? Let me talk to him. He can find another head chef if he wants to fire one of our most hardworking employees for no good reason!"

He's standing in the kitchen, waving his spatula around and pacing back-and-forth like a madman. My heart grows a little from its shrunken hole seeing him go to bat for me, but I shake my head. He can't. I push him out of the kitchen and into the back alley.

"Manny, no. Don't — please don't try and defend me. They might fire you too," I plead with him. It's one thing for me to leave, but The Phoenix wouldn't be what it is without Manny.

"I'd like to see him try. Him and that evil twink." Manny smirks and I giggle a little. "Boy tried hitting on me once before, as if he's my type."

"Of course not. Richard Burton only, right?" I raise my eyebrows.

"Or a lookalike. I'd settle for a James Dean, but not a James Charles."

I laugh again, already feeling lighter in Manny's presence. He pulls out a cigarette from his apron and offers me one.

I don't smoke but I take one anyway. Why not? I just got fired after all. I stare down at the grimy pavement as we smoke in silence.

"So, what are you gonna do now?" Manny asks, glancing over at me.

"I'm thinking maybe petty theft, a little drug dealing on the side," I say, shrugging.

"Ha ha. No way. We'll find you a job. Plenty of other nice ass restaurants in this city. You'll be alright." He inhales and crushes the cigarette butt beneath his food. He brings me in for a tight hug, bumping my back with his fist, and for the first time today, I feel like crying. I feel like fucking weeping in Manny's tattooed arms.

I step back and take a steadying breath. I can't believe this is happening. What am I going to tell my mom? How am I going to pay my rent? My impending crisis looms over me.

"Thanks for everything," I say, feeling the weight of this goodbye in my chest. Manny shakes his head, smiling a little.

"This isn't the end, sweetheart. It's just the beginning."

Chapter 3

Wesley

Staring down at the New York Post headline in front of me, I feel numb. I'm not even angry. Some other feeling has lodged itself in my chest and burrowed deep like it lives there now. Something close to apathy but hurts a lot worse.

Fuck.

My mind is racing. There are a million things to handle. My mother, first off, who is probably calling me at this moment sobbing about her reputation and our reputation and my father's reputation. My younger brother, Ben, prepared with either an emotional support speech or some alcohol. Adleman. Dammit — did he leak the story?

There's no way. It's a breach of contract and the whole merger would be null and void. Then again, now that this is out, perhaps my negotiation skills won't be enough to save our asses. If he didn't leak it, he's going to be pissed. More importantly, if he didn't leak it, then who the hell did?

Fuck.

Deciding I can't wait for Ben, I make my way over to the liquor cabinet in my office. I pull out a bottle of Glenlivet and pour some into my glass. Just as I'm bringing it up to my lips, a knock on my door interrupts me.

"What?" I bark out. My assistant, Beverly, steps into my office.

"Your mother, brother, and Mr. Adleman are all on the line," she informs me, answering emails on her phone. I know she's working but I hate the way she taps on the touch screen with her acrylic nails.

"Tell them all I'm busy. Tell George I'll call him back in ten minutes. And get me a coffee, black."

"I know how you like your coffee, Wes. You don't have to be so dramatic." She rolls her eyes and closes the door. Luckily, she makes no comment about the scotch. Beverly's a good assistant. She puts up with my shit and gives it right back to me. As much as she annoys me, she organizes my whole life so I can't complain.

I knock back the scotch with a grimace. My fucking life. What a goddamned mess. Suddenly, a pair of round, blue eyes flash into my mind and there it is. Of course.

I know who leaked the story. I remember her.

Quinn Taylor.

The numbness in my chest isn't quite so numb remembering the way she looked up at me. The doe-eyed wanting in her expression. The rumblings of desire in my stomach that I haven't felt in ages.

My hand curls into a fist and finally the numbness is gone, replaced with anger. I feel rattled. What had I said? I think my exact words were *I'm trusting you.*

God, what a fucking idiot I am. Here I thought I'd acted perfectly by leaving it in her hands instead of waiting on George myself. I'd insisted that an innocent third party was the best way to ensure the paparazzi that had been trailing my ass for the past two months wouldn't spot Adleman and I in the same room together. My genius plan was biting us both in the ass.

"Mr. Adleman is on line one waiting for you," Beverly calls out from behind my door.

"Got it!"

Polishing off my drink, I lift the receiver to my ear.

"George," I greet him.

"What the hell is going on, Wesley? Is this some kind of scam? After your mysterious call last night, I drop the papers first thing, and this is what I see waiting on my desk?"

Shit, he's really pissed.

"No, George. You know as well as I do this is the last thing I wanted — news of my father's...condition getting out," I reply, running my hand through my hair.

"I should call off this whole deal. You're lucky to even be getting our offer with the state of your finances."

"I'm aware of the situation overall, George. I'm sure you're also aware of Hyatt's desire to acquire our properties on Park Avenue and the deal that has already been signed, so our predicament remains. We're in this together now unless you want a legal nightmare. Hyatt Marks Properties."

He sighs heavily and I hear papers shuffling on his end. Then it stops and it is quiet for a few moments.

"We need to meet to discuss how to handle PR," he says, finally.

"My assistant will send through my availabilities for tonight and tomorrow." I rub my fingers against my temples, trying to fend off a growing headache.

"Wesley?" He prompts, his voice tired.

"Yes?"

"You better fix this. For the future of *our* company," he says, and the line goes dead.

I slam the receiver down.

"Your mother's on line two!" Beverly calls out. Taking a deep breath, I lift up the phone to my ear.

"Mom?"

"Oh, darling," she sobs. "What are we going to do?"

I'm glad she's just on the phone and not standing in front of me. I could never stand to see my mother cry. Even hearing it, my throat feels like it's closing. I want to reach through the phone and comfort her.

Fuck.

I cough, clearing my throat.

"Everything's going to be fine, Mom. We knew there was a risk of this."

"The things they're saying about your father — it's so awful," she cries out.

"Well..." I trail off. I want to tell her that they aren't saying any lies, but I don't want to make things worse. She's never been good at confronting my father's shortcomings, numerous as they are.

"I just—I feel like I've failed. As a wife...as a mother."

I feel so tense. I need to get to the gym now. Beat a punching bag or run for six miles until I can get to work. Until I can figure out how to fix this.

"You haven't failed and you're not alone. Dad's going to get better and I'm going to fix everything with the company. Don't worry, Mom."

I hope for her sake that my words are convincing. The truth is I have no clue what I'm doing and even less faith in my father's ability to do anything other than think of himself.

"Oh, Wesley," she sighs. "I love you, darling."

"I love you too, Mom. I have to go deal with this," I say, choking down the growing lump in my throat. I slam the receiver back down and try to stop my hand from shaking. This rage is new. I've never felt out of control like I do right now. I glance over at the scotch and think of my dad in this office, one scotch after another. I can't have another glass. I can't be like him. Where the hell is my coffee?

Just then, the door opens and Beverly sweeps in. She sets the coffee on my desk.

"The vultures are circling."

Leaning back in my chair, I take my glasses off and rub my eyes.

"Who?"

"Forbes, Variety, Bloomberg, New York Times—"

"I got it. Fend them all off until I've met with George and talked to my father."

Beverly nods and heads for the door.

"Get me my brother," I say out to Beverly as she exits.

Might as well finish the rounds and get everyone out of the way. Besides, he'll make me feel better, at the very least. He's the good boy between us. It's why he's married with the cutest little girl in the world and I'm drinking scotch alone in my office.

"He's on line one," Beverly calls out to me.

When I pick up the phone, Ben immediately tells me to wait because Luna, his daughter, is pouring her yogurt all over the floor.

"Hey, sorry," Ben says. "Jamie's got her now. So, what do you think? Top five worst days ever? Top ten?"

"Hard to say. It's hardly noon. Could get worse," I reply, grabbing the stress ball off my desk and rolling it around in my palms. I squeeze it once, hard enough to destroy the atomic foundation of the ball itself.

"What the hell happened?" He asks simply.

"A girl, that's what," I say, despite myself. Quinn Taylor's expressive face flashes through my mind again and I'm filled with that deep rage, that twisted feeling in my gut.

"This should be good," he chuckles.

I take a deep breath.

"You know how the paparazzi have been following me for the past two months? Ever since we started the transition of me taking over. Well, I realized they were tailing me last night. They were waiting outside The Phoenix to see who I was going to meet."

"You sound paranoid," Ben says.

"Don't gaslight me, bro. They were there."

"Alright, jeez. I forgot you double majored in psych. What happened after that?" He asks.

"I called George and told him I was going to leave the contract signed at the restaurant and leave so they'd follow me, and he could pick up the final contracts. He dropped the copy of the signed contracts first thing this morning, before the story broke, thank God."

"So, the deal's still on?" He clarifies.

"Yes. Hyatt Marks Properties are a go. George as CFO and me as CEO," I sigh.

"How the hell did you manage that?" Ben asks.

I hear Luna yell out from behind him and he shushes her. She's learned to scream even louder than she used to, which I didn't think was possible.

"Basically? He has majority shares, and he's making more money," I reply. "Anyway, that's not the point. I left it with her — the hostess. She leaked the story."

"Who cares? The deal is still on. Mom will move on. A new scandal will replace this in two days. You're golden," Ben says, his voice light. He always was the optimist of the two of us.

"I'm in a lot of shit with George. Plus, the press is going to be even more on my ass now," I argue.

"You know you love the attention, big bro. Gotta go — the

demon child is calling." Ben hangs up on me and I stare down at the receiver.

A voice in my head tells me that Ben is right. This could certainly be worse. At least the contracts were already signed and filed before George could try and pull out of the deal. Still, my mom's voice rattles in my mind.

I feel like I've failed.

Squeezing the stress ball, none of my anger seems to dissipate. In fact, it just grows. The feeling of betrayal stings all over — of Quinn Taylor's betrayal. One girl thinks she can destroy my family. My legacy. My life.

"Get me the owner of The Phoenix in Tribeca. Now," I call out to Beverly, my voice hard.

I know what I have to do.

Chapter 4

Quinn

I don't remember much of the rest of the day. After I say my not-goodbye to Manny, I wander around the city in a haze. I walk all the way from Tribeca uptown, stumbling around for blocks before I finally realize where I am. Union Square. I sit at one of the benches and watch an elderly couple play chess. Should I start being one of these people now that I'm unemployed?

At least I still have my second job cleaning for the Milton's uptown. I consider calling Mrs. Milton and asking for extra shifts cleaning but think better of it. I just need to get another job.

I finally make my way to the train and start my journey home. On the ride back to Brooklyn, my anger starts to set in. How could Pierre fire me just like that? I thought we were friends. Or as close to friends as a boss and employee could be. Why would Ian set me up to take the fall? He must have been the one to leak the story, but why? I roll my eyes at the dramatics.

They really just fired me, just like that. I loved that job, and they didn't give a shit about me. I may not have had

Chanel shoes like the other hostesses, but I showed up and I did my job. If I'd actually done the thing they accused me of, I would have quit myself, but to simply be wrongly accused of something I didn't do...it's not right. It's not fair.

Life's not fair, dumbass.

I know that. I guess it's one thing to know something on a rational level and a whole other to experience it on an emotional one. The latter has my blood boiling. I suddenly remember what Ian said — Mr. Marks specifically requested your termination. He must mean Wesley. I drop my head into my hands. As if this day couldn't get any worse. Not only am I unemployed, but my closest thing to a Prince Charming hates my guts.

I take solace in the fact that I'll never see him again. A pang hits me in the chest at the realization. I don't know why — it's not like I even knew the guy. Still, his words ring in my ears like a children's taunt.

I'm trusting you.

Why did I give Ian the damn folder? I should have just done it myself like I promised I would. I guess it really is my own fault. If I'd stood up for myself and told Ian that it was my responsibility, none of this would have happened. If I'd stood up for myself with Pierre, maybe he would have believed me over Ian.

Who am I kidding? It's not like this job would have really lasted. Nothing ever really does. I guess I learned that when dad left. What the hell am I going to do? Another pang hits me, this one deep in my stomach. Guilt, settling itself neatly into my body, all the way down to my bones. Without the money from that job, there's no way I can afford mom's medical payments.

I get off the train at Atlantic and wait to transfer to the R, which, of course, is thirteen minutes away. Settling on the bench in the center of the platform, I take out my phone and open up my notes app, typing out a To-Do List.

1. Update resume
2. Print resume
3. List of references
4. Job spreadsheet
5. Kill self???

I delete that last one and pocket my phone with a sigh. I spend the rest of my ride imagining Ian choking on an olive from a martini. I get back to my apartment five hours earlier than usual. Nothing could prepare me for the sight in front of my eyes when I open the door.

"Oh my God!"

Ass. Bare ass. Bare man ass on my velvet green couch.

I love that couch. My mom and I carried that couch almost twelve blocks. I slam the door shut and squeeze my eyes closed, willing the image to leave my brain. I try to picture something else, but the image is permanently tattooed onto my brain.

"Quinn, what are you doing home? You're supposed to be at work." My mom's frantic voice calls out from behind the door.

I hear the sound of clothes being put back on and stifle a laugh. Now that the initial shock has worn off, I have to admit this situation is pretty damn ridiculous.

"I got fired," I deadpan to the door, which swings open, revealing Melanie Taylor in all her glory: hair strewn, lipstick smeared, and shirt on backwards. I quirk an eyebrow at her, but her eyes are sympathetic.

"Fired?"

"Fired," I repeat.

I stomp into the apartment to greet the mystery man standing in my living room. Thankfully, he is fully dressed now, but the image of his saggy ass is likely burned into my memory forever.

"Hi. I'm Joe. You must be Quinn, Melanie's daughter."

He reaches his hand out and I look down at it, wondering where those fingers have been recently. He seems to have the same thought as he peels his hand back and brushes it through his graying hair.

"Nice to meet you, Joe. Are you my mother's boyfriend? Fuck buddy? The new mailman?"

I drop my bag on the floor and plop into the oversized chair in the corner, avoiding the couch at all costs.

Joe struggles with how to label himself as my mom quietly pushes him out of the apartment, whispering reassurances. He finally hangs his head, resigned, and puts his shoes on.

"Nice to meet you, Quinn. I hope I'll see you again."

"I hope to see a little less of you next time."

I go into the kitchen and get my Chunky Monkey out of the freezer, hoping one pint should do it. If one more thing goes wrong, I might need to buy out the whole Ben & Jerry's franchise. Or at least rob the bodega freezer section.

Joe leaves, kissing my mother on the head in a sweet gesture that makes me wonder why she hasn't told me about her new beau. It's been a long time since she's had a boyfriend. My mom sits on the couch with a spoon in her hand, reaching out for the ice cream. I pass it to her.

"So, Joe, hmm?" I wiggle my eyebrows, teasing.

"Before we get into that, you got fired? Honey, what happened?"

Pushing down the sadness that threatens to bubble up, I force an uncaring grin, hoping it looks more convincing than I feel.

"Pierre sacked me. Whatever. The point is I need to find a new job, ASAP. Unless our luck has turned, and Joe is a Moroccan prince of some kind?"

"I don't think they have Moroccan princes in Long Island," she says, handing the ice cream back to me. "We met at chemo. His brother has prostate cancer, stage one."

"How romantic. I bet the IV fluids really turned him on." She throws one of the couch pillows at me and it hits me smack in the face.

It's quiet for a moment as we eat our ice cream. I wonder what my mom is thinking. Is she upset at me for getting fired? I think about telling her the whole story but if there's anyone to get fired up about injustice, it's my mom. Melanie Taylor is a fighter through and through.

"I really like him," she says, almost too quiet for me to hear.

"Why didn't you tell me about him? Didn't you want me to meet him?" I ask.

"Well, definitely not like that," she replies, a slight trace of humor in her voice. Her gaze turns thoughtful. "I did. I do. I just didn't want it to be too soon." She shakes her head. "C'mon, let's go on Glass Window, or whatever it's called."

"It's GlassDoor," I groan, knowing what awaits me.

Job applications. Nothing worse than the constant stream of rejections from jobs I don't even really want.

Why me? Why did evil Ian have to ruin *my* life? Couldn't he have blamed it on Samantha, or Jodie, or Elise, the new girl? I doubt he even knows her name. I'm the only one who ever took the time to get to know the new hires, and this is how I'm rewarded. With a proverbial kick in the nuts.

"Stop sulking. There's a million restaurants in this city, and one of them is about to gain the best hostess around," my mom says, jostling my shoulder a little as she picks up the Chrome Book that we share.

Sighing, I reach out to take the laptop from her and force a smile. My mom is right, I don't have time for a pity party. Time to buckle down and figure this out. I'm sure I'll find a new job in no time.

Chapter 5

Wesley

This is shaping up to be the most stressful week of my life. Even Ben took back what he said on the phone and declared last Saturday to be in his own top ten worst days, as well as mine. After I got off the phone with Pierre, the owner of The Phoenix who informed me that Miss Taylor would be terminated from her position immediately, the day somehow got even worse. My mother called back and informed me that my dad had checked himself out of rehab and was on his way to the city to talk to me.

Since the leak included the name of the rehab center where my father was a patient, the paparazzi showed up on the front lawn. He got a heads-up from one of the nurses and managed to sneak out the back and had his driver pick him up in his private car — a Honda Civic. My father may be an asshole, but he's smart when he needs to be.

I spent the rest of the day finding a new upscale rehab center that would take my father in on such short notice with him sitting across from me, insisting that this rehab business is "unnecessary."

"This is a blessing in disguise, son. Now that everyone

knows I'm a drunk, I can resume my rightful place at the company and put this all behind us."

His denial was truly incredible to witness. Still, I was in no mood to get into it with him about his alcoholism and the fact that he wouldn't be returning into his old position anytime soon, or ever. I eventually secured him a spot at Golden Lakes, another premiere rehab center in the Hudson Valley.

Since then, I've hardly seen my family. George and I should have direct brain transmitters at this point. I'm on the phone with him every waking minute figuring out the details of the merger and our rollout plan with the staff. The botched announcement caused a few higher-level staff to quit on both sides, so it's been an HR nightmare too.

Thankfully, it's almost settled. We're moving into their offices in Midtown next Monday. I don't like it but it's not like I have a choice. I like being downtown; plus, it's much closer to my apartment in Dumbo, where I'm currently sitting at my office desk.

Staring out at the Brooklyn bridge, I suppress a sigh. Ever since we confronted my dad about the drinking and found out about the company's losses, my life has been turned upside down. It started with me taking over as CEO, a decision he still resents me for. Sure, the company was always meant to be mine — but in ten years, not now. I'll be the youngest CEO of the Marks Group at the ripe age of thirty-two. As if things haven't changed enough, in a week, I move into the Penthouse suite of the Midtown Hyatt. Permanently.

It was George's idea, and I couldn't really say no with the current circumstances. He thought me moving into the Hyatt would truly show my dedication to this merger. Plus, our first joint property will likely be uptown, and my commute will be cut down to a thirty-second walk across the street to the office.

Obvious advantages aside, I don't want to do this. Mostly because I love my apartment. Ben doesn't get why I would choose to live in Brooklyn and not just get a high-rise closer to the office and all my so-called friends. He also hates that he's on the Upper West Side and our distance gives me more excuse to avoid babysitting duty.

The truth is I just like Brooklyn. Something about sitting in the backseat, driving over the bridge and out of the city each evening and coming back to my quiet apartment. I spend every waking moment in the city. My apartment is my sanctuary. Perhaps that's why nobody ever comes here. Not even the women I've dated.

Not that there haven't been women. I just never brought them here. We'd usually stay at a suite at one of my hotels, or I'd go to their place. Most of my romantic arrangements have been casual and mutually beneficial in nature, so there's not much need to bring them into this space.

I grew up on the top floor of a gorgeous, classic building in Soho, my mother's favorite of our properties. She's still there, alone now with my father gone. When she found out about my temporary move to Midtown, she tried to convince me to split my time at the Soho apartment, but I managed to avoid it. I hate to think of her all alone in that giant penthouse, but us living together in any capacity is a mistake.

My phone buzzes with a message from Ben:

Want to get dinner?

Just ordered sushi. Feel like coming to BK?

Definitely not. We still on for Sunday brunch with mom?

Unfortunately. Bringing the spawn?

Anything to distract mom.

I chuckle and put my phone face-down on the coffee table. Sipping my beer, I close my eyes and let my mind wander. Despite my attempts to avoid thinking about her, Miss Taylor's bright blue eyes fill my mind again. After Pierre informed me that she would be fired, he called back to inform me that she'd listed The Phoenix as a reference on her resume, and as such, wouldn't be getting hired at any restaurant in the city. The news should have filled me with satisfaction. Instead, I just want to see her again.

I want to see her reaction, that must be it. See the look on her face as she faces the consequences for her poor decisions, the punishment for inflicting pain on my family.

It doesn't matter. She doesn't matter. She's just some girl. Some girl that I doubt I'll be seeing again anytime soon.

Chapter 6

Quinn

It's been two weeks since I was fired from The Phoenix. I've applied for hostess positions at forty different restaurants in Manhattan and none of them have hired me. Yesterday, after another rejection came rolling into my inbox, I decided I have to expand my search and consider working in a different field.

The Miltons were nice enough to give me a few extra cleaning shifts when I told them about losing my other job. Still, I'm only there a few hours a week cleaning their apartments and it's not enough to sustain me and mom for much longer. I'm left with no choice but to browse other cleaning jobs in the city. It's inevitably going to be a pay cut from what I was making at The Phoenix.

Through all of it, I've had to stay strong for mom. If it were just me, maybe I could curl up and avoid the world forever until I rot. But I have to take care of her.

I can't let her down.

Scrolling through LinkedIn, I decide to give up for the day. I need to make dinner before my mom gets home. She's been feeling more active these days. She's been knitting hats and selling them to a few friends and locals. Just as I submit on one final application, my mom comes through the door.

"Quinn! Guess what?"

She's using her sing-song voice, which means good news.

She doesn't give me a chance to answer. "I found you a job!" She sets her bags down on the floor and comes to sit across from me.

"I ran into Eva Gonzalez while delivering a hat to her mother. She's been working as a maid at a hotel in Midtown and said they're hiring. I told her you'd come first thing tomorrow to talk to the manager."

I should be ecstatic. It's the first real opportunity that's come my way since I was fired. I guess I've just been living in denial about not being able to go back to The Phoenix. The thought of cleaning rooms at a Marriott doesn't excite me, but I feign an enthusiastic smile.

"That's great, Mom. Thank you."

"Isn't it? I'm sure Eva will be able to help you out."

I start on dinner while my mom talks about how good this job will be for me. I still don't know how to make up for pay decrease. I was barely making ends meet at The Phoenix. How the hell am I going to keep up with student loan payments and mom's medical bills on a maid's salary?

Shaking off my worries, I take a deep breath. Tomorrow my life changes.

* * *

When I get to the Midtown Hyatt, I wait in the lobby for Eva. The hotel is huge. Gold-plated crown molding and a giant fountain in the center of the oval room. I find Eva waving over at me from behind the reception desk. I thank her profusely for getting me the opportunity, but she's already strutting forward towards the back offices, swiping us into a long, fluorescent hallway with her keycard.

"Pay is shit, but it's \$18 an hour, which is \$3 more than my brother makes cleaning the pool, so count your blessings. Marguerite is the hiring manager, you'll like her. She's decent."

I struggle to keep up with her pace as she explains the job and stomps ahead of me. We get to a doorway where she stops.

"Locker rooms. I need to change for my shift. Door at the end of the hall is Marguerite's office — just tell her I sent you. Good luck!"

Just like that, I'm on my own. I go to the end of the hallway and knock on the door lightly. A voice calls out from behind and I step inside, where a slim woman sits behind a desk.

"Hi, you must be Marguerite?"

"The one and only. You are...?"

"I'm Quinn Taylor. Eva sent me. I'm looking for a job." I step all the way into her office, and we shake hands.

"Nice to meet you, Taylor."

I don't bother correcting her. She spends the rest of the meeting reiterating Eva's speech, adding more information about expectations, hours, and asks me to fill out some paperwork. All in all, it only takes a few hours. She tells me that I can start next week once my paperwork clears.

Standing on the street outside the Hyatt, I call my mom to tell her the news. She screams for a solid minute before announcing that we need to celebrate tonight.

"I'm going to cook eggplant parm!"

She sounds so excited about it, so I agree. Her eggplant parmesan is great. I tell her I'll pick up the ingredients on my way home. Heading to the subway, I spot a sleek black limousine parked outside the Hyatt. How the other half lives. I notice a man in a crisp black suit striding out of it and into the hotel, his back to me. He almost looks like...

"Watch where you're going, lady!"

A cab driver honks at me for five straight seconds before I realize I'm standing in the middle of the road staring at the man in the suit. I run forward with an apologetic wave, but the driver just shakes his head and speeds past me. I turn back to walk towards the subway, trying to muster some enthusiasm for my new job, but all I find is a sinking sense of disappointment.

Chapter 7

Wesley

I have officially moved into my new penthouse suite. I didn't bring much with me, mostly just clothes and a collection of books that was impossible to select. George came to greet me after the bellhop finished bringing up my last suitcase.

"Not too shabby, huh?"

He was bragging. Floor-to-ceiling windows with views of the skyline surrounding us, a giant kitchen with an island and a bar, a living room with a fireplace and multiple bedrooms — the place was fantastic, no doubt about it.

"It's perfect, George."

"Come, look at the office."

He gave me the grand tour, pointing out specific art pieces selected by Hyatt's on-staff collector. After about thirty minutes of detailed presentation, he finally left. I had that unsettled feeling in my stomach that I always get the first night in a new place. In my early twenties when I worked for our international division, I travelled all the time, staying at a penthouse in almost every major city, and I never lost that feeling. It's part of why I came back to New York for good.

Stepping into the master bedroom, I take off my tie and throw it onto the chair in the corner. I pull on a t-shirt and lie on the bed. I feel restless, bored. So, I do what I always do — work. Our first project as a merged company is the Park Avenue development. It's essential that this go well. My family's legacy is on the line.

I grab a water bottle from the well-stocked fridge and retrieve my briefcase from the foyer before I go into the office. The space is nice enough, but I still prefer my home office in Dumbo. With a teal accent wall and books covering almost every surface, it's got more of a personal touch than this Restoration Hardware catalogue lookalike.

Settling into the chair, I pull some papers out of my briefcase and fire up the computer. I check through my emails and send Beverly a few action items and notes for tomorrow. Monday will be our first day at the Hyatt offices across the street and we launch right into development of the Park Ave hotel on Wednesday.

I pull up the plans for the new development. We're still going back and forth about a name. For now, the project remains Untitled Park Avenue Project. The property's been purchased, and renovations are underway. Now, it's mostly in the architect's hands as he works with our interior designer, Lindsay, on getting together the plans for the hotel.

My phone buzzes with a message from Ben:

How's the penthouse, playboy?

I shake my head and type out a reply.

Strippers on the way.

What? I stand up from the desk just as the phone rings. I pick it up and the cheerful voice of Anne, the receptionist, greets me.

"Hello, Mr. Marks. Your brother is here to see you. Shall I send him up?"

"Yeah, go ahead. Thanks."

Ben loves to check in on me at unexpected and uninvited times. It's incredibly annoying.

The elevator doors open and Luna comes barreling in straight towards me. Her tiny arms wrap around my legs.

"Uncle Wes! Daddy said we're going to surprise you."

"Surprise," Ben smirks.

"Can I go exploring, daddy? Please please please?" Luna gives him her best pleading face, her brown eyes almost welling with tears, and he's defenseless against her talents.

"Sure, but don't go too far. And only for a little while."

She takes off like a bat out of hell as I yell after her to be careful. Ben sits on the stool behind the kitchen island.

"Driving me crazy." He shakes his head.

"Luna or Jamie?"

"Both, if you can believe it." He sighs. "I was thinking... did Mom seem a little, I don't know, out of it at lunch yesterday?"

I consider Ben's words and my mom's happy-go-lucky attitude at Giovanni's yesterday. I had expected more tears from her after the story and dad's move to the new rehab center. This whole process hasn't been easy on her. I know she wishes she could do more.

"I guess. She didn't seem as down as I was expecting."

"You should talk to her. You're the favorite son."

"That's not true and you know it," I argue. He's always saying shit like that, even though he and Mom spent a few years living in London while I was stuck in New York with my father. I was only eight at the time, and Ben was six, but I still wish I'd gone with them those three years.

Ben's kind enough not to pry about that time, but I think even he knows how hard it was on me. He and my father have never had much of a relationship. When we were kids, I relished in the attention my father gave me, thinking that it made me special, but almost as soon as mom and Ben left for London, I learned my lesson. Time spent with my father was time I'd never get back. Years of my life where every word, every move I made was subject to his harsh criticism. Nothing was ever enough for Benjamin Marks.

"Alright. I'll talk to her."

"Daddy, look what I found!" Luna comes bounding into the room with a piece of chocolate. I have no idea where she managed to find it, but if there's sugar somehow, I swear she'd sniff it out from a five-mile radius.

"Can I have it? Please?"

"Sure thing, sweetie," I say.

Eventually, Luna gets cranky so they head out. He reminds me about mom again before bringing me in for a hug, thumping my back with his closed fist. I sweep Luna up in my arms and twirl her around, attacking her with kisses.

Once they're gone, I give up on working for the rest of the night and settle into bed with a book. I read for a few minutes before my eyes start to feel heavy. Just as I turn over to turn the light off, my phone buzzes with a message from George:

Bad news. Construction delays on the office.
Looks like we can't get in until next Monday.
Hope you like the penthouse office — we'll
work from home this week.

I groan. Another setback. I knew I should have been supervising the planned expansion of the Hyatt offices. George assured me over and over that he had it covered, but this is the second construction delay and I'm getting a little sick of bad news.

I plug my phone in and turn off the light, staring into the silent, dark room, praying for some good news on the horizon.

Chapter 8

Quinn

I t's my first day of work at the Hyatt. I'm in the locker room staring at myself in the mirror. When I'd signed up to be a housekeeper, I guess I forgot about the whole uniform part. The pastel pink and white two-piece set clings to me in all the wrong places. Maybe I should have gotten a size up. Do they purposefully make the top so low-cut? I feel like I should have a feather duster and learn to say 'Oops' a lot.

Just as I get my hands firmly down my shirt, Marguerite comes through the door. I drop my hands but she's not even looking at me, she's rifling through the stack of papers in her hands.

"Alright, Quinn."

She's finally got my name right, at least.

"You've been reassigned to the Penthouse."

"The penthouse?" I repeat back to her.

"I have no idea why. They usually save the cushy jobs like that for experienced team members."

There's a little bite in her tone, like she's the experienced team member that should have gotten the job. I don't say anything else because the last thing I need is the person who got me this job hating me on day one.

"Here's your special key-card for access to the private elevator. Your hours might need to change now that you're only cleaning the top floor. This position is a step up in a lot of ways. Do you know how to cook?"

Cook? What the hell?

"Yes."

"Well?"

"What?"

"Do you cook *well?*"

"Yes. I actually...food is my passion. I want to open my own restaurant one day."

She stares at me like I'm an idiot. What am I thinking? *Food is my passion.* This isn't Zeke's verse in Stick to the Status Quo. Sure, it's been my dream to open my own restaurant for as long as I can remember, but it's not like she cares about that.

Food is a haven for me, an escape. When I realized that food could be more than mom's favorites, that it could actually be a whole *experience,* that's when I knew I wanted to open my own restaurant. I'm still trying to figure out exactly what the vision is, but my idea is an elevated restaurant that mixes fine dining with mom's classic recipes.

I shake off the *High School Musical* playing in my head and look at Marguerite.

"I don't understand. Why are you asking about my cooking skills?"

"The penthouse position is usually reserved for a single individual who cooks, cleans, and acts as a sort of liaison between the guest and the staff at large. It's kind of a combination of concierge and housekeeping."

I wish she'd stop using fancy words to say simple things. I

also still don't understand why I'm not just working with Eva on the regular floors.

"So, I'll have to cook and clean?" I clarify.

"There's a pay increase. 24 an hour."

Sign me up! Give me the frying pan and I'll whip something up right now, Marguerite.

"Okay. What else do I need to know?"

"I'll set you up for a meeting with Sharon from front-of-house staff to explain everything on their end of things. For me, you're good to go. All your cleaning stuff is in the closet, you'll clock in and out the same way."

I nod, overwhelmed. Why does it feel like I'm being thrown to the wolves somehow? This is a good thing, right? Marguerite gives me the special keycard for the penthouse private elevator, which I find after some searching. It's tucked behind the restaurant like a speakeasy entrance. I'm clutching my mop and rolling cart to my side like it's a life raft as the elevator rises to the top floor.

When the doors open, my jaw drops. I'm looking across at the skyline and can even see Central Park further off. With the floor-to-ceiling windows, it feels like I'm floating on top of the world. It's a little disorienting so I step all the way out and look around the suite.

It's *huge.* Suddenly, three hours isn't nearly long enough to get through this. How many bedrooms are there? I rush through the whole place, scanning it up and down and calculating what needs to be done. I go back into the living room and see a small note on the kitchen island.

Hello,

Welcome to your new position as caretaker of the penthouse suite at the Hyatt Estates. Each day you'll sweep, mop, clean down all surfaces, and prepare dinner for the guest. Laundry on Mondays and Fridays. Usually, you'd come in and replace for each new guest, but the current guest will be staying long term. You can discuss any specific preferences directly with him.

Sincerely,

Sharon Jackson, Head of Concierge
Hyatt Estates

I read the note twice over. Seems easy enough. I realize today is Monday — supposedly laundry day. I wonder if his hamper will be gold plated. My eyes catch on the last sentence.

You can discuss any specific preferences directly with him.

I have to talk to Mister Moneybags himself? I bet he wants me to order specialty water from some colonized river and pick up his dry cleaning every day.

I start on the sweeping even though the place is basically spotless. The whole room probably has as much dust as a single corner in my apartment. Once I finish sweeping, I fill up my bucket with soap and water and start mopping. It takes me a long time to get every room.

Just as I'm bringing the bucket back towards the sink, my foot catches on one of the stools and I go tumbling forward.

Water spills from the bucket and coats the entire floor, making its way slowly towards what I can only assume is a rug that costs more than my life itself.

"Shit, shit!"

I go to stand, but slip on the pool of water, my chest landing straight into the puddle. I'm now covered in soapy water. Helplessly, I grab one of the small kitchen towels and try to mat the mess. The corner of the rug is soaked. I pull the paper towel roll out completely and shove a giant handful onto the ground. It's pathetic. Just as I think I've finally got a grip on it, I slip one more time, landing firmly on my ass.

The door opens.

A man in a sleek black suit steps inside, holding a briefcase in his hand. His hard eyes meet mine and my jaw drops. There's no way. It can't be.

Wesley Marks.

Holy shit. What is he doing here? I scramble to stand up and grip onto the kitchen island like it's the last life raft on the *Titanic*. His eyes scan the scene in front of him with disdain. Water all over the floor, clumped up paper towel in a small pile, and me, sloppy and wet, clinging onto the counter for dear life.

"Oh my god. I'm so sorry. I'll clean it up."

Wesley Marks!!!

He steps into the apartment and sets his briefcase on the other counter, making no move to greet me or help with the mess. He doesn't speak.

Right.

His back is to me as he gets a bottle of water from the fridge and brings it up to his lips. He hasn't said anything, and I don't know if I should introduce myself.

Does he really not recognize me?

Of course he doesn't recognize you, idiot. It was one night weeks ago.

I step forward.

"Um. Hi. I'm Quinn. Your new...maid?"

He turns at my voice and stares straight into my eyes. His face is a wall of stone, and he says nothing. He just gives a little hum at my words, somewhere in between a murmur of approval and a judgmental smirk.

"You must be...?" I trail off, waiting for him to finish for me, but he still just stares at me. Finally, after what feels like an eternity, he steps forward and puts his hand out.

"Wesley Marks."

I put my hands into his and his eyes narrow at me as he tightens his grip on mine. My stomach drops and I feel hot. He just stares at me with that studying gaze.

How can he not recognize me?

I step back, overwhelmed, and force my eyes away from his. The corner of his mouth ticks up like he's trying to hide a smile, but he covers it quickly. He turns away from me again.

"Nice to meet you," I mutter.

He still doesn't turn back. I think of the note that Sharon left and clear my throat a little.

"If there's anything I should be aware of or anything I can do for you, just let me know."

"The water off the floor will suffice for now." His voice is sharp and I'm slightly taken-aback. If he doesn't recognize me, then why does it seem like he hates me so much? I can't be imagining the bite in his words.

I feel slightly woozy. How the hell did I get here? I feel like at any point someone will pop out and yell that I'm on candid camera.

Bing, bing, bing, you're a loser!

I blink a few times and try to nod.

"Right. Yes."

I kneel back down and start picking up the pathetic clump of wet paper towels. I feel like that clump of wet paper towels. At the sound of his footsteps echoing down the hall, I lift my head as he strides down the hall.

"Miss Taylor, was it?"

I lift my head and he's stopped mid-stride, his sharp jaw turned towards me. Seriously? He doesn't even remember my name? I told it to him like, five seconds ago.

"Yes. Quinn. You can call me Quinn, I mean. If you want."

God, why am I turning into a bumbling idiot? It's like I've forgotten how to speak.

"Is there anything else you wanted to tell me, Quinn?"

What kind of question is that? It's so cryptic. I'm starting to feel slightly dizzy. Maybe it's the bleach.

He knows! He knows it's you.

I search his eyes for any recognition or hint that he knows who I am. No way. It's a big city but a small world. It must just be some twisted coincidence. After all, if he recognized me, wouldn't he have said something?

"No, sir."

He gives a sharp nod at my response and turns, continuing down the hall, but before he disappears into his office, I swear I catch of glimpse of his hand at his side, curled into a fist.

Chapter 9

Wesley

When I saw her name on the list of new hires, I thought I must be imagining things.

Well, my first thought was that it must be another Quinn Taylor. After all, there's millions of people in this city. But then I saw the middle initial column with an H and somehow, I knew it had to be her.

My next thought was to have her fired. I don't need a money-hungry, disloyal employee sniffing around my hotel for the next big story, and I definitely don't need any distractions while I'm focused on the Park Avenue project and easing into the merger.

What is she getting at, trying to get hired at one of my hotels after what she did? What's her plan?

That's when I realize I've been handed the golden opportunity. A gift, even. I asked the universe for some good luck, and this is what I got. I've spent the last few weeks trying to get her out of my head, but she's stuck there. Her betrayal still stings every time I think of it — the dull sort of throbbing pain that I don't dare press into.

Without thinking, I call down to Sharon at the Concierge

desk and ask her to shuffle some things around. If she finds my request strange in any way, she doesn't say anything. She simply agrees to make the necessary changes and inform Marguerite.

I tell myself I need to keep a close eye on her, figure out what her angle is here. Another darker part of me wants some retribution for what she's done, payback for what she did to my family. And then there's the part that simply wants to see her again.

Still, nothing prepared me for the sight of her standing — no, slipping — in my kitchen in a maid's uniform. God, did they have to put her in that tiny outfit? A better man than me would have ignored the way it clung to her skin in all the right places, the soft curve of her ass in that miniskirt. On top of that, she pretended she didn't even know me. She'd introduced herself to me like we were perfect strangers.

"You must be...?"

Was I supposed to fall for that act? I even gave her a chance to redeem herself, to come clean and tell me the truth, and she chose to remain silent. She chose to lie.

"No, sir."

She's infuriating. Absolutely infuriating. Those round, doe eyes and plump lips are still haunting me. All part of her little act, no doubt. Still, I hadn't anticipated her being a distraction around here when I had her moved to the penthouse. How the hell am I supposed to get any work done this week while she's prancing around in that outfit?

I flex my hand out of the fist it seems permanently curled into. Groaning, there's a knock at my door, and there's only one person it can be.

"Sir. Um. Mr. Marks?" Her soft voice calls out from behind the door.

"What?" I bark.

"Can I come in?"

I don't want to see her. Why is she knocking on my door? What can she possibly need from me?

"Fine."

She pushes open the door tentatively and steps in with a small smile in my direction. She's still sopping wet, her hair clinging to her forehead and her shirt more than a little see-through. I force my eyes downward, ignoring the outline of her dark bra.

"Hi, sorry. Me again. Your...maid. Right. Just wondering if you wanted me to do laundry today. Or if there's anything else you needed. I'm heading down to meet with Sharon, but if you wanted me to do your laundry, I could do it now, or come back later. Also, I guess I'm going to cook dinner for you tonight? So, I was wondering what you like and if you're allergic—"

Jesus, does this woman ever stop talking?

"I don't need anything from you."

The words sound harsh even to my ears and her smile falters. For a second, she looks as though she might cry. My stomach drops at the thought, and I have the sudden urge to reach out and comfort her.

Get a grip.

"Have I done something to offend you?" Her voice is shaky and betrays her nervousness.

I tilt my head, studying her. "I don't know, have you?"

It's her last chance. Third strike, you're out. I meet her gaze head-on.

"I'll just...come back later." She shuffles backwards out of the room before I can say anything, slamming the door behind her.

Three chances. I gave her three chances to come clean to

me. I don't know what games she's playing, but whatever it is, I'm all in.

Game on, Quinn Taylor.

Chapter 10

Quinn

I cannot believe my luck. God must be punishing me for something. I must have been a serial killer in a past life. There's no other explanation for why I am currently Wesley Marks' personal lackey.

I bet he designed these skimpy maid uniforms himself. Sicko.

I can't stop thinking about the way he looked at me when I walked into his office. Like I was the gum on the bottom of his shoe. I was just trying to help! Sharon's note said I was supposed to ask him about stuff. The situation is clearly awkward, and I was simply trying to be polite. Something he obviously knows nothing about.

Whatever. He clearly doesn't want to talk about anything. Good. The last thing I want to do now is speak to him again.

When I get down to the lobby, Sharon is waiting for me and gives me the lowdown on everything I need to know. She also provides me with a list of groceries and Wesley's dietary restrictions and other specifics. I don't know why the hell she told me to ask him when she clearly has it all figured out.

Why doesn't she just do the job? I want to ask her why I was assigned to the penthouse, but I hold my tongue.

"Most importantly, Mr. Marks values his privacy above all. Don't bother him unless absolutely necessary."

Okay, so admittedly the knocking-on-his-office-door thing may have been a mistake. Maybe that's why he seemed so pissed off at me — the other staff usually don't bother him. Don't bother him. Got it.

"You can start with the laundry today. We'll check in tomorrow morning if you have any other questions."

I manage to avoid Wesley completely when I get back to the suite. I can hear him on the phone in his office, so I work quickly, stripping all the beds and grabbing dirty towels from the floor. While the laundry is running, I look through the papers and study Wesley's preferences. One note catches my eye.

Please continue leaving chocolates on the pillow.

Mr. Cold Shoulder has a sweet tooth. Good to know. Maybe that's the way I can get him to like me — I'll bake my signature brownies or some banana bread. By the time I finish with the laundry and other cleaning, I'm starting to feel dead on my feet from the long day, but I still haven't made dinner. I think Wesley is still in his office, but I can't be sure. I thought I heard him on the phone again while I was folding laundry but then I put my headphones in. It felt weird eavesdropping on his conversation.

I go into the kitchen, swaying to my music. Looking through the fridge, I decide to make enchiladas since he has all the ingredients. I crush up some peppers and jalapeños, hoping he's not averse to spicy foods. There was nothing in his notes about it.

Just as I'm putting the enchiladas into the oven, Wesley

crosses through the kitchen to the other side of the apartment. He scowls in my direction and disappears into his bedroom.

Would it kill the guy to force out a pleasantry every now and then?

I try to breathe through my anger. Only thirty minutes left until the food is finished — then I can go home and complain to my mom all about my new boss. I can't believe I thought he was sexy. I can't believe I thought he was *nice*. That night at the restaurant, when he looked at me, I'd thought for a moment that he had kind eyes. Gentle eyes.

Now when I look into his eyes, I see nothing.

My phone buzzes in my pocket and it's my mom, calling me. I glance around but don't see Wesley, so I pick up the phone.

"Hey, Mom, I'm at work. I can't really talk."

"Sorry, sweetie. It's just so late, I got worried. I thought you were done at 3?"

I glance around, paranoid. Why does it feel like an echo chamber in here?

"I kind of got promoted. I'll explain it later. I'm almost done here, and I'll pick something up on the way home for dinner."

"No need. I'm making enchiladas."

I gasp louder than necessary. "No way! I'm making enchiladas, too!"

My mom gasps back. "You're cooking? For who?"

I think I hear footsteps coming back down the hall. Or am I imagining that?

"I have to go!"

"Alright. I love you."

"Love you too." I hang up and slip the phone in my pocket, but it's too late. From behind me, Wesley clears his throat.

"Was that a personal call?" His cold voice drawls from behind me.

I turn around and meet his hard eyes. "No," I lie.

He raises his eyebrows at me. "You say I love you to all your business associates?" He challenges me, smirking.

"Sure. Yes."

What are you doing? He knows you're lying!

I can't help it. I know I'm being stubborn and digging my heels in, but he's infuriating. It was a thirty-second phone call, for God's sake. I haven't bothered him all day. Why does he have such a stick up his ass?

"I don't appreciate my staff lying to me. Or taking personal calls on my dime. Don't do it again."

His smirk is gone, and he frowns down at me again. I have to physically stop my eyes from rolling.

"Won't happen again, *sir*." I sneer the last word and turn away from him.

Luckily, I'm saved by the bell. The oven timer beeps, and I grab the oven mitts, opening the door and taking the enchiladas out. I was going to plate it and make it look nice, but I'm out of here. He can do it himself. It's almost 6:30 and I've been here for over 12 hours, running back and forth trying to make the devil smile. I'm going home.

I leave the food on the kitchen counter and grab my bag. I press the elevator button over and over, cursing under my breath for it to arrive. When it finally does, I step inside, fuming.

I hope he burns his mouth on my damn enchiladas.

* * *

No amount of complaining to my mother prepares me for the next day with Wesley. I spent all of last night bitching and moaning about him — which I never do. Eventually, my mom got sick of hearing about it and told me I needed to "chill out."

Believe me, I have tried to chill. The whole train ride over here I listened to a meditation playlist on Spotify and repeated mantras about my inner power. Still, the second I got onto the elevator, I felt the rage resurfacing again.

Luckily, Wesley isn't home when I get upstairs. At least, I don't think he is. Part of me is scared he's going to pop out of nowhere and tell me I missed a spot. My mom's words from last night echo in my head.

Take the high road. Show him you're going to be the best damn maid, cook, cleaner, whatever — that he's ever seen.

She's absolutely right. From now on, I vow to prove to him that he's wrong about me. Starting with the floors. I scrub until I can see my reflection in them, which, to be honest, looks kind of pathetic. I look like if Cinderella were from Brooklyn — big tits, crusty brown hair, and no fairy godmother.

The dish I made enchiladas in is sitting in the fridge with a piece of aluminum foil over top. It looks as pathetic as me. I transfer the remaining ones over to a Tupperware and scrub the glass dish, wiping it dry. There are a few other dishes in the sink that I do, too, and wipe dry and put away.

I finish all that by noon. I don't have to do laundry. I don't have to mop. Can I just go home?

The door opens and I grab the dish rag, wiping the counter to appear busy. Wesley walks past me and down to his office without a word.

Well, hello to you too. Yes, my day is fine, thanks for asking. And yours?

I sit on the stool, thinking. What else can I do? I glance around the apartment. It is kind of bland in here. Not very homey. I get an idea. I call down to Sharon to make sure it's okay and she gives me the information for the company card to use for purchases.

"I don't have a computer," I tell Sharon.

"Come down and I'll lend you a company laptop. You can keep it for the duration of your employment for expenses and such, if needed."

I go downstairs and get the laptop from Sharon and bring it back up to the penthouse. Then I start shopping. I buy a six-pack of candles from a small business that my old college friend Sannika runs in Bedstuy. I browse on three different specialty chocolate websites before ordering some variety packs and small bowls to put them in and place around the apartment. I call a floral shop in Chelsea and set up a bi-weekly delivery for a few different bouquets to place around. Then, just for fun, I get some extra cooking supplies to spice up meals and help with plate presentation.

I feel giddy once I'm finished. Who knew spending money could be so fun?

Wesley comes out and eyes me sitting at the kitchen counter. He grabs a Nespresso pod from the drawer and pops it into the machine. I close the laptop and take a deep breath.

"I was just ordering some stuff for the place. Candles, flowers. Just to spruce it up a little. I hope that's okay?"

He doesn't spare a glance in my direction.

"Sure. Fine."

Jeez, who pissed in your coffee?

I nod, pushing down my annoyance, and make a move to grab my bag from the coat rack where it hangs. I can feel him watching me, so I turn back towards him.

"Are you about to leave?"

"Yes. Unless you need me to stay?"

Please don't make me stay. Please don't make me stay.

"I haven't...well, you know what? It's fine. I'll just eat the leftovers from last night. Or order something up from downstairs."

"I can make something. I don't mind," I say, and I find I'm actually telling the truth. "Did you like the enchiladas?"

"They were fine," he says.

Fine?

They were *fine?*

I'm fuming. He couldn't have insulted me any worse. I've perfected that recipe a million times over and those are more than *fine*. When my mom ate those enchiladas last week, she nearly had an orgasm.

Wesley's voice interrupts the rage coursing through me. "Like I said, I'll just order in. You should go home."

I might have protested if I wasn't currently trying to hide the steam coming from my ears. I manage a jerky nod and shove my new laptop into my bag with more force than necessary. I can still feel his eyes on me, but I can't bear to look at him. I might just punch him right in his stupid, smug face.

"Great. See you tomorrow," I grunt, slinging my bag over my shoulder, and storming back towards the elevator, wondering what I did to deserve the boss from hell.

Chapter 11

Wesley

She's everywhere.

No matter where I turn, she's there. It's like she's invaded my home and my mind. Even when she's not here, I find my thoughts wandering to her, the nervous way she bites her lip when she wants to ask me something.

Worse, the place sort of smells like her. All around the kitchen island where she was just sitting, it smells incredible. Floral, like freesias and lavender.

Freesias? What the hell?

I shake my head. I can't believe I thought this was a good idea. My desire for retribution seems to shrink with every interaction we have. Why the hell is she being so damn nice? Asking me my preferences and what I like? Ordering specialty candles to brighten the place up? Cooking one of my favorite meals?

So maybe she had no idea about the enchiladas thing. Holy shit, though. They were amazing. I wanted to ask her where she learned to cook like that. Instead, I told her to go home. I simply couldn't stand her presence another minute, especially with her perched on my kitchen stool in that little pink skirt.

Jesus Christ.

I know I've been acting like a dick. But it's not like she's a beacon of honesty. She's still pretending she has no idea who I am, that we haven't met before. She's still playing the innocent act, as if she isn't just waiting for me to turn my back so she can snoop in my office for her next big story.

I realize now it's just a waiting game. I'll keep leaving the door open, leaving out breadcrumbs for her to follow until she reveals herself. It's not like she can keep up this facade for much longer. I can already see that I'm getting to her. She thinks she can hide it, but I see the sparks of rage behind her eyes when I speak to her. It's just a matter of time before she cracks.

Meanwhile, thanks to Miss Taylor, I'm still dealing with the fallout of that damned story. Mainly my mother's decline. She's on the verge of giving up completely. I went over to the apartment last night to check on her and she was asleep when I got there. The place wasn't in great shape, either — empty wine bottles all over the place. I plan to go over there again tonight. Hopefully I'll be able to talk to her and figure out what's going on with her, because I can't have two parents in rehab.

I'm sitting in my office enjoying the view when my phone buzzes with a call from George.

"Wesley. How's the penthouse treating you?"

"It's great, thanks. What's going on?"

"Well, I hope you like working from home, because it looks like our renovations are continuing into next week. But Gomez has assured me that the space will be ready by next Friday at the latest."

I take a deep breath, not wanting to explode at George. It

wouldn't be so bad if *she* weren't here all the time. I mean, how much cleaning does one suite need?

"Are you sure you don't want me to speak to the contractors? I can be very persuasive."

That's business-talk for *you're fucking this up and should let me handle it*. George just chuckles on the other end while I suppress a growl.

"Don't I know it. It's fine, just focus on the new development. Your meeting with the architect is tomorrow."

"I'm aware."

"Great. Let's connect tomorrow morning."

George hangs up. The more I work with him, the more he gets on my nerves. I wish he'd take this a bit more seriously. People rely on us for their jobs, and I don't take that lightly. Still, everything seems to be setting me on edge lately. The stakes are too high right now, with my parents both falling apart and everyone looking to me to save everything.

I decide to screw work for the rest of the day and go visit my mom. I call my driver, Pete, to pick me up downstairs and he says he'll be here in ten minutes.

I put my dish in the sink and change out of my suit into casual clothes and wait for Pete in the lobby. A few minutes later, he rounds the corner of 6th Ave and pulls in front of the hotel. I slide in the back and greet him with a smile.

"How's your sister?" I ask, breaking the quiet between us.

"She's good. Just hit seven months. She's got us waiting on her hand and foot."

I smile a little. His sister, Amira, is pregnant with her first baby. Pete tries to hide it, but he's thrilled to be an uncle.

"Did she get those prenatal vitamins I sent?"

"Yeah, and she told me to tell you that you shouldn't have." His eyes flicker back to mine.

"They're important for the baby's health," I say simply.

"Well, thanks for looking out, Mr. Marks."

The rest of the ride we stay quiet. Pete's been my driver for the past two years. He knows when I'm in the mood to talk and when we can sit in silence. I'm grateful for that.

We get to Prince Street and Pete pulls up to my mom's building. As I make my way up the stairs to the top floor, I hear jazz music coming from inside the apartment. I let myself in with my key and slip inside.

"Darling!"

My mother throws her arms around me, squeezing tight. I return the hug and step backwards to look around. The place looks better than it did last night.

"How are you? Want something to drink?" She's in caretaker mode, busying herself around the kitchen for something to do.

"Water's fine." I sit on the couch, and she brings over two glasses of water, sitting across from me.

"To what do I owe the pleasure of this visit? Come to lecture again?"

"Do you need lecturing?"

She rolls her eyes and tucks her feet underneath her, wrapping the blanket from the chair over her shoulders. "I know you're worried about me. I just get lonely. I don't know what to do with myself these days."

"I'm sure there's a social club you could join."

"Kicked out of all of them, thanks to your father."

"How about a hobby? All the old women are knitting these days."

She scowls at me. "I'm not old. Knitting, really? How utterly cliché," she sighs. I'm grasping at straws here, trying to cheer her up.

"Think of this as an opportunity. You've been given all

this time, free away from me and Ben and dad to do whatever you'd like. Why don't you go on a trip somewhere?"

She sighs and looks out the window.

"I guess you're right. I just didn't expect my life to turn out this way. I look around and I don't know where all the time went. Like my best years are behind me and I'm just staring into the abyss."

My stomach lurches. I didn't realize her thoughts had gotten so dark. She's starting to sound like me.

"Hey, don't talk like that. It's going to be okay."

She nods and it's quiet. I don't know what else to say. Luckily, my mom, like me, doesn't like to dwell on tough conversations, so she changes the subject.

"How's the new development coming? And the merger?"

I spend the rest of my visit filling her in on the construction delays and my new living arrangements. After a few hours, I call Pete to pick me up and kiss my mother on the cheek.

"Don't worry about me. I'm meeting Tina at a gallery opening later and tomorrow I'm going to the spa. I'm keeping busy."

We say our goodbyes and I wait for Pete out front. Wrapping my coat around myself, I try to rid my head of the image of my mother, staring out the window, trapped in the abyss.

Chapter 12

Quinn

It's been a week since the Enchilada Incident, as I've been calling it. Thankfully, Wesley and I have managed to avoid each other almost entirely. He's in his office all the time. We've interacted exactly twice since the Enchilada Incident. On Thursday, he nodded at me as we passed each other, and on Friday, he even managed a single *Hello* when I arrived.

Sheila has started packing her place up. It's downright depressing and I'm in total denial about her departure. She's leaving in two weeks. My mom keeps trying to talk to me about it, but she can tell that I'm not ready and she tries to respect it. The whole thing makes me feel very childish. I should be happy for Sheila. Getting out of that apartment will be good for her and she'll have someone to take care of her. I guess I thought we'd always take care of each other.

With my new hourly rate, I've stopped cleaning on the side for the two families uptown. The Miltons were understanding and even offered to be a reference for me, should I ever need it. I've been working for Wesley for almost two weeks now, so I've developed a routine that works for me and have figured out how to use my time wisely. Yesterday, the candles and flowers arrived, so the apartment is in tip-top shape. I talked to Sharon about my schedule and now I work weekends instead of Tuesdays and Thursdays, so I can take my mom to her chemo appointments.

It's Friday now and I'm making lunch for Wesley. He never eats enough, even when I leave food for him, so I've gotten into the habit of labelling my meals with post-its, providing witty commentary to inspire him. Really, I think he hates it. I finish making his panini and salad and put it on a tray, headed towards his office. I knock lightly at the door, and he calls out for me to come in.

He's leaning back in his chair, the phone pressed to his ear. I set the tray on his desk, avoiding his eyes.

"No, that's not what we agreed on. Don't try to yank me around."

Uh oh. Somebody poked the bear.

His eyes flicker towards me and the food. I smile in his direction, but he just looks away from me and returns to his phone conversation.

I don't know why I expect anything different. It's like I think that one day he'll suddenly start saying please and thank you and make an effort to get to know me. Instead, he just acts like I'm not there.

I slip out of the room and clean up the kitchen. The only thing I have left to do today is take the trash out and scrub the floors. I'm pulling the full trash bag out from under the sink when I turn and find him standing in front of me in gym shorts and a t-shirt. I've never seen him in casual wear before.

Holy shit, he looks good.

"Thank you for lunch."

My jaw almost drops. Did he just say thank you? I blink a

few times, trying to discern whether this is real or my imagination.

"I'm going down to the gym for a run. Need to burn off some steam. I'll be back in a bit. Will you still be here?"

I must look like a fish out of water. I think my mouth is just opening and closing like one of those animatronics singing *it's a small world* at Disney. This is the most he's ever spoken to me. More than that, he doesn't seem angry. He seems...neutral. Polite, almost.

"I'll be done here in about an hour," I manage to squeak out.

He nods.

"Well, I'll see you later, then."

And he's gone again. He grabs his gym bag from his room and steps onto the elevator, leaving me gaping after him.

What the hell was that?

He didn't smile, but he also didn't frown. He seemed to settle somewhere close to indifference. Indifference is good. Better than dislike, at least. Progress! We're making progress!

Shaking off the strangeness of our interaction, I fill up my bucket with soap and water and get to scrubbing. Realizing he'll be gone for a while, I call my mom to check in.

"Sweetheart! Is everything okay?"

"Everything's fine. The devil boss is gone so I thought I'd call. How are you feeling?"

"I'm fine. I'm over at Sheila's helping her pack some stuff."

Another pang hits my stomach. I hate that I'm handling this so badly.

"Cool. How's it going?"

"Slowly but surely. We're making our way. Who knew one woman could have so many tea sets? How's work?"

I sigh and dump the sponge into the water. I squeeze it out and plop it on the floor.

"It's fine, I guess. He was weirdly nice today. He even said thank you. Still, he's such an asshole. I swear he might be heartless. He's got me on my hands and knees, literally scrubbing his floors, and he still treats me like I'm not even here. One of these days, I'll tell him what I really think. Right to his face."

"Is that a promise?"

My blood goes cold. The next few seconds go by in slow motion. I turn my head, inch by inch, as if by moving slowly I can prevent the inevitable. But when I turn, Wesley is standing there, sweat dripping down his brow, jaw clenched.

I drop the phone, hanging up. How do I salvage this? Maybe I can convince him I was talking about someone else. Some other guy whose floors I also happen to scrub. He's staring right at me, his smirk fading into a glare as he watches the wheels spinning in my head. I land on apologizing.

"I am so sorry."

"What did I say about personal calls on the clock? Talk shit about me on your own time. In your own home, preferably, instead of mine."

"I wasn't...I mean—"

"I could fire you. I already warned you once. Besides, I'm an 'asshole', right? That's what 'heartless assholes' do — they fire people."

My heart lurches. I can't lose this job. I really can't. I think of the stack of medical bills waiting on my counter at home.

"Please don't."

I bark the bitter words out, hating the way they taste. The words are pleading but my tone is hard, almost angry. His eyes snap up to mine as he switches tactics.

"Well, now's your chance. Right to my face, you can tell me what you really think about me, hmm? Come on. Let's hear it."

He's baiting me and I can't rise to it. He's just trying to get me to say something worse so he can fire me. I hold my tongue, staring down at the floor. Rage burns within me. The angry words are out of my mouth before I can stop them.

"What's your problem with me?"

It's so quiet you could hear a pin drop. He narrows his eyes at me.

"Excuse me?"

I think he's as surprised as I am that I spoke up, but I'm already too deep in this to stop now. "Ever since I met you, you've been completely rude to me. What did I ever do to you?"

My words are steady as I try not to betray my emotions, but my anger burns stronger than ever. We're crossing the point of no return and I can't find it within myself to care. I know I should stop pushing and just let this go, but I can't.

"Seriously. What's your problem? Why did you hire me if you're just going to treat me like shit?"

He looks me dead in the eye, his chest heaving with an anger that matches mine.

"Oh, I don't know, it could have something to do with you leaking the story that almost destroyed my family?"

Chapter 13

Wesley

"What?"

She rears back her head like she's absolutely shocked by my confession. *Shocked.* Why the hell should she look so surprised? She's blinking back at me, her eyebrows bunched in confusion, but her face is still a mask of anger. She sputters for a while before she finally manages to speak.

"You knew who I was this whole time?"

Her chest heaves up and down in anger and I roll my eyes. It was almost satisfying to watch her mask of sweetness fall as she put her hands on her hips and demanded to know my *problem* with her. Standing in front of me with her jaw tight and her breath heavy, this is the Miss Taylor I've been waiting for.

"Of course. You think I'd forget the woman who almost single-handedly took down my family's legacy?"

She stares back up at me with those big, round eyes of hers, blinking in shock. I wish she'd say something — it's as if she's afraid to respond to my accusation.

"Why do you keep saying that?"

Is she serious right now?

"Do I need to refresh your memory?"

She still just stares back at me. I take her silence for a yes.

"One month ago, I went to The Phoenix Lounge, one of the most prestigious restaurants in the city, admired for their commitment to *privacy*."

Her face pales as I continue.

"I sat at my table for a little over an hour before I approached the host stand and gave a folder containing private documents to the hostess standing behind the desk. A woman named Quinn Helena Taylor."

An indiscernible emotion flashes across her face at the mention of her middle name.

"I instructed Miss Taylor that the folder be left with a business associate of mine and left the restaurant. The next morning, I woke up to my father's face on the front page of the New York Post."

She shakes her head and wrings her hands out. She still looks angry, but a nervousness has taken over her.

"Then imagine my surprise when the same Miss Taylor applies for a job at *my* new hotel and somehow gets hired. Now, I don't know what game you're playing here, but I'd tread carefully if I were you."

At this, her head snaps up and she meets my gaze unflinchingly. It's very quiet now. The only sound is my heavy breaths from my speech. She waits a long time to speak, and her voice is quiet when she finally does.

"I'm not playing any game. I'm here to work and that's it."

"Under false pretenses," I snap back.

"I never lied to you!" She points a finger in my direction. "You pretended not to know me, too!"

She's struggling to keep her cool. I can tell because I threw mine out the window when this conversation began. Her eyes are swimming with a million unspoken thoughts, likely insults she'd like to hurl in my direction. I wish she'd let them loose. The word *heartless* rings in my head.

"I wanted to see if you'd tell me the truth. Give you a chance to be *honest,*" I sneer the word at her.

"I am honest!" She throws her hands up in frustration and starts pacing, refusing to look at me. It's the breaking point. I want her to look me in the eyes while she lies to me. I take a step forward, invading her space, and she takes a step backwards, stumbling.

"Tell that to my brother who had to call in every legal favor he had to prevent my company from investigation. Or my mother who spends most nights crying. Or me — stuck dealing will the fallout at work and a business partner has all the fucking power now all because I trusted a stranger. Because I trusted *you.*"

She shakes her head and at least has the decency to look apologetic as she meets my gaze.

"I'm sorry that's happening, but none of that is my fault."

I take a step back and yank at my hair, needing something to do with my hands besides make a fist. I'm close to putting one through the drywall if she keeps lying to me.

"You're the only person who had that file besides me and my associate," I point out. "When I called The Phoenix, they assured me that you'd been fired."

"I did get fired."

"For leaking the story."

"I didn't leak the story! I don't even know *how* to do something like that," she cries out. "It was somebody else."

"Who?" I demand. She doesn't say anything, just looks back at me with a mixture of anger and indecision. "Who, dammit?"

She says nothing. She looks so earnest that I almost believe her. Then I remember that she had that same look that night at The Phoenix — open, warm, trustworthy — and I feel like a fool all over again.

"Fine. Let's try it this way. Who do you work for?"

"Excuse me?" She snaps back at me.

"Who. Do. You. Work. For." I growl each word. "The Post, obviously. Anyone else? Should I renew my *Bloomberg* subscription?" I force a light tone to mask my rage.

"I already told you — I didn't tell anyone! I didn't even open the folder. I had no idea what was in there until I saw the news myself."

God, she's good at this.

"If it wasn't you, then who was it? Like I said, it wasn't me, and it wasn't George. That only leaves you, and this conveniently unnamed person you claim is responsible but who you refuse to give a name for."

"It was—"

She looks like she's about to say more, but she stops herself and looks down. She's still raging, I can tell, but she looks thoughtful. Almost...disappointed somehow. She shakes her head and drops her shoulders.

"Yes?" I prompt impatiently.

She shakes her head, still avoiding my eyes. "You're wrong. You're wrong about me."

I unclench my fist, flexing my fingers, and throw one last glance in her direction.

"Well, unfortunately for you, Miss Taylor, I keep my office drawers locked."

I can't stand to look at her for another second, so I turn on my heels and storm back to the elevator, needing to burn off this anger coursing through me. I thought that I'd feel better after confronting her, but if anything, I feel worse. The tension swirling in my gut is raging stronger than ever.

I should feel satisfied, but I just feel empty. Pushing my feelings down, I vow to move on. She won't find anything on me, and I won't waste another single thought on Quinn Taylor.

Chapter 14

Quinn

I'm so angry I can hardly contain it. The revolving subway doors I just walked through are still spinning with the force of my shove. I didn't mean to take my anger out on them, but I can't help it. I always walk with a purpose in the city, but the way I'm hunkering down the subway steps, it seems that purpose is now to destroy anything in my path.

I can't believe him. I can't believe I thought that underneath that hard exterior, he might be hiding some semblance of softness. The only thing underneath all that muscle is a hunk of metal where his heart should be.

The way he looked at me!

The false accusations he made!

The disgust dripping off his words!

I tap my foot impatiently, waiting for the train. I've never felt so out of control as I do right now. I'm stuck between wanting to scream, punch somebody, or just curl into a ball and cry. I haven't felt this out of control since—

Don't go there.

He really thinks I'm some sneaky journalist or PI trying to infiltrate his life. What an egomaniac! I couldn't give less of a shit about his family, his legacy, or whatever bullshit empire he's trying to build. I don't have time for his *Wolf of Wall Street* drama. I'm a little busy over here trying to pay my mom's medical bills and not get evicted this month.

What the hell has my life become?

I replay the last hour's events in my brain, trying to figure out what went wrong. Admittedly, I shouldn't have said those things to my mom, but how was I supposed to know he was standing right behind me, listening? In fact, he shouldn't have been listening in on my conversation.

It is his apartment.

Whatever. Besides, he proved all my comments right today — he really is an asshole.

Maybe I should have told him about Ian. There was a moment where I almost did. I wanted to. It's obvious to me that this story has done real damage to Wesley's life. Underneath all that harshness and anger is a plain hurt that I know he's trying to hide. Still, when I opened my mouth to tell him the whole story — how Ian took the folder from me, how it was his word against mine when I was fired — I felt an endless sense of despair. Like, what's the point?

It's not like he would have believed me. Nobody believes women, not where I come from. I was naive enough once to think that if you told the truth, people would listen. That if you needed help, you'd get it. But I'm not a child anymore and I'm not naive. I learned my lesson years ago.

Besides, Wesley has clearly already made up his mind about me. I had the chance to give him Ian's name, and maybe he would have looked into it, but then Ian would probably get fired, and it's not like I'm going back to The Phoenix now. I know how hard unemployment in this city can be and I don't wish it on my worst enemy, which I guess Ian might be. Even if I had told the truth about Ian, nothing I could have said would have dimmed the burning hatred in Wesley's eyes.

The thought makes me inexplicably sad.

I spend the whole train ride home listening to my most emo music — a combination of Car Seat Headrest and Phoebe Bridgers. It does nothing to calm my bad mood and by the time I stomp into my apartment, I'm still fuming. Still, the sight of my mom sitting with Sheila in the living room brings a smile to my face.

"Hey, guys," I say, throwing my bag onto the floor and slipping my shoes off. "What's up?"

"Banana bread in the oven. I'm doing Sheila's toes." My mom waves the nail polish brush in the air.

"She forced me into it." Sheila shoots me a side glance.

I trudge past them towards my room, pulling my hair into a bun and suppressing a sigh.

"I can do yours next?" My mom calls after me.

"Okay," I call back and change out of my jeans into sweats. I put on a tank top and wipe the smudged makeup under my eyes. I go back into the living room and curl up on the floor across from Sheila.

"What's wrong?" Sheila asks. "You've got that look on your face."

"What look?"

"I think the kids are calling it the 'I'm-gonna-cut-a-bitch' look," Sheila says.

"Yeah. The stank eye," my mom chimes in.

I never should have set my mom up with a Twitter account. She's now in the habit of constantly sending me nonsensical memes and using internet slang to describe every situation.

"It's whatever. My boss is a dick."

"Every day you come in here complaining about this man, sweetheart," my mom says. "Why don't you just quit?"

"Not an option," I say flatly.

"We can figure something out. You shouldn't be unhappy."

"You always were too selfless for your own good, girl," Sheila chimes in.

I'm not going to quit. Not only was it nearly impossible to find this job, but I won't give Wesley the satisfaction of scaring me away. If he wants me gone, he'll have to fire me himself.

"I'm fine. It's one bad day. I'll get over it."

My mom raises her eyebrows at me, clearly not believing me.

"I'm fine," I repeat. "Now do my toes." I wiggle my feet in her face, and she smacks them away.

For the rest of the evening, I manage to put my burning hatred for Wesley aside and enjoy my time with mom and Sheila. We decide to throw a going away party for her next week and I set off immediately with planning and spreadsheets. I can't help it. I'm a Virgo.

Sheila eventually heads across the hall, much to my disappointment. Luckily, tomorrow is one of my days off. Unluckily, that means that my mom has chemo, so she tucks into bed early, leaving me cleaning up the apartment with nothing to distract from my fight with the devil himself.

The image of his broad chest heaving up and down is burned into my brain. His tight jaw and tussled hair. Hard as I try, I can't get the asshole out of my head. That night, as my head falls against my pillow, I'm still thinking about his dark eyes burning into mine.

* * *

I hate hospitals. The first time I was here was a night I've tried over and over to forget. A night that nearly took everything from me. Each time I come here with mom for her treatments, it's a brutal reminder of a period of my life I swear never to return to. It's a place of nightmares. Every time I walk through these sliding glass doors, I'm facing my mother's mortality. I'm facing my own inadequacies.

Ellen, the oncology nurse, comes in and gets my mother set up. I feel so useless during these visits. My mom says it helps just to have me sitting beside her, but I wish there was something I could do.

"Hello, Taylors! How are we this week?" Ellen greets us cheerfully.

"The family of rats that lives on our corner has grown. Saw a new baby this morning," my mom chimes like it's the best news all week.

While Ellen chats with my mother, I go down to the cafeteria to get some snacks for her. I'm paying at the cashier when I hear a throat clear behind me.

"Miss Taylor?"

I turn and meet a pair of icy blue eyes. Shit.

"How are you?"

It's Perky. Little Miss Take-Your-Money. Her curly blonde ringlets and cat-eye glasses set off my fight-or-flight. What's her real name again?

"It's Hannah. Hannah Dwyer from billing. I've sent you a few emails and letters."

All of which I have ignored.

"Yes, of course! Hannah. Hi." I force a smile to match her tight, forced one.

"I'm so glad I ran into you. Maybe we can finally sort out the card issue. The one you have on file has been declined for the last three payments."

I know, Perky.

"Oh, really?" I feign indifference and turn back to the casher, handing over some cash. I scoop up the snacks in my arms and turn back to her. "I'm actually on my way back to my mom, she's waiting for me, so..."

I walk ahead, but Perky follows me, matching my steps. "No problem. I'll walk with you."

Can't the woman take a damn hint?

I pick up my pace a little and she does the same. We're speed-walking down this hallway like we're racing.

"So, like I was saying. We really need to get the card sorted out. I contacted your insurance company and they've fulfilled their portion, but—"

"Yep, yep."

I speed up again walking as fast as I possibly can without breaking into a literal jog. Perky's fast, I'll give her that. We're almost at the cancer ward chemo area. It's the finish line. Just as I'm approaching the door and almost in the clear, Perky grabs my arm and halts.

"Miss Taylor. You really don't want this to go to the debt collectors. Whatever the situation is, come talk to me about it, and we'll figure it out."

"Sure. Yeah. Will do."

I force another smile and hold up the granola bar like it somehow absolves me from this conversation.

"Gotta go." I slip past her back into the chemo room, where my mom is finishing up. She looks tired. She usually is afterwards.

"How are you feeling? Hungry or nauseous?"

It's always one or the other.

"Nauseous."

Damn. I frown and help her stand. It's a good thing we've got a joint waiting at home. I just hope she'll be okay on the commute home. Picking up my mom's bag, I catch Hannah watching us from the corner of the room, pity in her eyes.

Chapter 15

Quinn

My mom spends most of the rest of the day with her head in the toilet bowl. When she's not throwing up, she's curled up on her bed, moaning and groaning. It's awful. I clean up the apartment and check on her occasionally, but she never really lets me hold her hair or anything. She says she doesn't like me to see her like that. If there's one thing we have in common, it's our stubborn sense of pride.

Finally, around dinner time, she feels mostly better. We settle in the living room, sipping ginger-ale and splitting a joint between us. I don't like to smoke that much, but this week has been too stressful to turn it down.

"Cancer sucks," she says through her exhale.

"Yep," I reply.

It's a familiar exchange, one we've had at least three times before. Sometimes it feels as if there's nothing else to say, really. I miss the days when we could talk without any weight between us, without the tension of wondering if this conversation will be our last.

"How's it going with Joe?" I ask, taking the joint from between her fingers.

She shrugs, matching my yawn. "I'm not sure. We're keeping things casual."

Oh god. When did my mother's dating life become more exciting than mine? Whatever. I've never been in a relationship before, and I don't really see that changing any time soon. It's not like I wouldn't like to have someone special in my life. The truth is I really would. I just feel so...broken.

Don't think about that.

Suppressing memories that threaten to break through, I say goodnight to my mom and hide in my room for the rest of the night.

The thought of seeing Wesley tomorrow hangs over my head. I have no idea what I'm going to say to him. Should I apologize? No — I can't apologize. He'll take that as an admission of guilt.

If anything, he should be apologizing to me!

He doesn't even have any evidence! He's just basing his accusations off assumptions. Where is the jury of my peers? Where's the court-appointed lawyer to defend me? Nope, no sixth amendment here. Wesley has decided that he's judge, jury, and executioner.

I toss and turn in bed and hardly get any sleep. By the time my alarm clock goes off, I've managed maybe three hours. As if this day weren't going to be bad enough, I'll have to face Wesley looking and feeling like a zombie. I somehow manage to shower, get dressed, and get to the train on time. The last thing I need is to show up late today.

Turns out it doesn't matter. When I get to the penthouse, it's empty.

"Hello? Mr. Marks?" I call out.

Silence. Nobody is home.

It doesn't stop there. For the rest of the week, when I show up for work and all day while I clean, Wesley is nowhere to be found. I hate that I'm curious about where he is and his sudden departure. Without him around, things are...well, boring.

I think he must be deliberately ignoring me. Why else would he suddenly disappear from his own apartment? I stew on that for about thirty minutes before realizing my ego is clouding my judgement. It's silly of me to think that our disagreement would run this man out of his own home. He must just be busy.

Finally, after almost four days of no-contact, I hear his voice from his office. The sound of it engages my whole body. My heart is racing and my eyes dart around the apartment for an escape route. I'm keyed up like I'm preparing for a fight. I tiptoe closer to his office, realizing the door is slightly ajar.

"Hey, hey. Don't say that." Wesley's soft voice is barely audible from here. "I hate to hear you like this"

Whoa.

My heart drops. He sounds completely different. His voice is soft and cajoling, like the way you'd speak to an injured animal. He sounds...vulnerable.

"I told you, everything's going to be fine, Mom. Just please don't cry."

His voice is tired now and he almost sounds on the verge of crying himself. I can imagine exactly what he looks like right now. Leaning backwards in his chair, running his hand through his hair in frustration. The image jolts me in my place and I suddenly feel awful listening to this private conversation.

What the hell am I doing? Snooping around, exactly as he expects me to?

I flee from the hallway and back to the kitchen, my

stomach churning. I have to wait for the delivery drop off this evening and make dinner, otherwise I'd leave right now.

I was planning on whipping up something fast and easy, but I feel the sudden urge to do something special. My mom is babysitting tonight for the downstairs neighbors, so I'm in no real rush to get home. Rummaging through the kitchen, I decide to go for a three-course meal of shrimp ceviche, glazed pork chops, and a chocolate caramel torte. I work quickly, throwing together the salad and glazing the pork chops. The delivery arrives and I pop the torte in the oven.

It's a whirlwind of an evening and I lose track of time entirely. It's almost 8 o'clock when I'm putting the finishing touches on the torte. I'm practically salivating over it, proud of my work. The kitchen is a mess, so I throw everything in the dishwasher and wipe down the counters, doing my best to leave it in fine condition. I'll clean the rest tomorrow.

"What are you still doing here?" Wesley's harsh voice pipes up from behind me.

"Sorry. I lost track of time with dinner. I'm almost done," I reply, tucking the rag into one of the drawers and untying my apron.

His gaze moves to the feast sitting on the dining room table and he stares at it.

"What is this?" He asks, his brow furrowed.

"Dinner."

His jaw ticks.

"I can see that. What's with the three-course meal? Is that cake?" He points to the dessert.

"It's a torte," I reply, a little indignant. He's the fancy one. He was probably raised with eight different types of forks — can't he tell the difference between a cake and a torte?

He nods and still stares down at the meal in front of him. I start to back up slowly. Any sudden movement might anger the beast.

"Anyway, enjoy your meal. Sorry again for staying so late." I wipe my hands off and grab my bag and coat from the coat hanger.

"Miss Taylor." He moves closer and stops me with his hand, the contact sending a jolt through me. He must feel it too because he retracts his hand almost immediately.

"Thank you," he spits the words out like they are nearly impossible to get out.

No smile either, but I'll take what I can get. I shrug like it's no big deal and offer an award-winning grin of my own, hoping it might catch on, but nothing.

"No problem. Bye!"

I run out of there like a bullet. My arm is still tingling from where he touched me. It's warm. In fact, my whole body feels flush.

Get a grip!

This is worse than the anger from before. I try to bring some of it back up, replaying our conversation from last week. It tugs at me, still, but the rage is gone, replaced with some weird uneasiness. Somewhere between angry, sad, and wanting. But most of all — confused as hell.

I miss my rage. Come back, rage!

It's no use. As hard as I try, my fire-burning anger has fizzled out a little. This time as I ride over the bridge back to Brooklyn, all I can think about is Wesley's soft, pleading voice and the way his hand felt wrapped around my arm.

Chapter 16

Wesley

I stare down at the feast in front of me, which looks incredible. I glance around my empty apartment, my thoughts wandering yet again to the blue-eyed vixen who is apparently a chef in her own right.

I sit down and dig in. Everything Quinn makes has been amazing. I'd never tell her that, of course. I can't give her the satisfaction of knowing her tricks are working. But this is next level. I'm shoving food in my mouth so fast I almost forget to breathe.

Where did she learn to cook like this?

I shake my head. Why should I care? It's a nice meal, sure, but there's nothing more to it than that. She was probably bored and thought it'd be fun to make. Still, it's exactly what I needed. Today was another tough day.

I've been having too many tough days lately. At least construction has finally finished and I'm in the office. George and I ran our first joint meeting as CEO and CFO of the newly joint Hyatt Marks Properties this week. There's a lot to do with the merger including promotions and layoffs. Yesterday, I had to fire three of my own people to make space for new hires. I hate to do it and it's put me in a sour mood.

Worse than that, my mother's condition has only worsened. She's downright depressed. Ben reached out to Dr. Roberts, her old therapist, and she's got an appointment this week. I'm working on trying to get her sister to come to town to visit, but Aunt Mary's a workaholic and can't take a day off.

I invited her to dinner later in the week. She still hasn't seen the penthouse and she's a sucker for a good view, so I hope it will lift her spirits a little. I'm not sure what else to do.

After I finish the salad and pork chops, I dig into the cake — or torte, rather, that Quinn made. It's incredible. I push it away from me, my anger only growing at how good it tastes. After the blowout we had, I expected her to spit in my coffee. Instead, she makes me a three-course meal that rivals some of the best restaurants in the city. Maybe the distance gave her some perspective and she doesn't hate me as much as I thought.

Then I remember the way she looked at the end of our fight. The pain and anger in her eyes.

No, she definitely hates my guts.

When I get home from work, I'm exhausted. The meeting with the architect ended up taking a lot longer than expected. Between that and another round of layoffs, I feel crushed by the weight of my responsibilities. I go straight to the kitchen for a beer and then head towards my room. As I pass by my office, I notice that the door is open, and I can hear shuffling inside.

I push the door open fully and Quinn is leaning over my desk, writing. Her head jerks up at the sound of me entering.

"What are you doing?" I ask.

"Oh, hey. Sorry. I was just leaving a note for you." She drops the pen and backs up from the desk. "I didn't touch anything else. You can pat me down if you don't believe me."

I raise my eyebrows at her suggestion and cock my head to the side, studying her. Realizing the insinuation, she blushes and blinks a few times, avoiding my gaze. The room suddenly feels five degrees warmer.

"I was just leaving a copy of next week's menu." She waves a small piece of paper in her hand. "It's an idea I had. You can fill it out at the end of each week with your choices, that way you can try different things and I'll know when you're going to be out."

I nod and purse my lips. I know I should say something, but I feel aggravated by her presence, and I don't want to snap at her again. I'm honestly sick of fighting. I just want her out of my damn hair.

"Only if you want. If it's too much, I can just forget it. I just thought—"

"It's fine. Leave it there and I'll take a look. Was there anything else you needed?"

"No. That's all. I'll just..." She looks stung by my dismissal and side steps around the desk to walk towards the exit that I'm currently blocking. As she goes to slip past me, my arm shoots out towards hers, stopping her.

She stares up at me with those knockout eyes, blinking. She licks her lips, parting them. I realize my hand is wrapped around her arm again. Does she feel this strange tug between us too?

Get a grip!

I step back into the hallway, releasing her, and turn on my heels to stride back towards my bedroom. I slam the door behind me for good measure. Gulping in a few breaths of air, I try to calm my growing hard-on.

Fuck.

I can't believe it. I'm utterly turned on. I force images into my brain, trying to calm myself: my father playing golf, my grandma's toe fungus.

Come on. Come on.

Realizing my attempts are futile, I go into the shower and step into the running water. I wrap my hand around my cock and start pumping, thinking of Quinn's soft skin and luscious lips. How good it would feel to wrap my hand around the back of her neck and bring her lips to mine. To spread her legs and lay her out like a feast.

I come fast and hard, the water pouring over me. My satisfaction is replaced by shame. I scrub down my body and hang my head with a sigh. What the hell is happening to me?

When I get out of the shower, she's gone, thank God. I go into my office to peak at my desk and confirm that all the drawers are still locked. Sitting on my desk is the menu. I pick it up and study it. It's ornately designed with small checkboxes for different options for each day of the week.

Why is she doing all this? Can't she just clean the place up and be done with it? If she thinks I can't see through this plan, she's wrong. Trying to prove that she's a hard worker, or whatever. Trying to prove me wrong. I toss the menu back onto my desk, frustrated that in fact, Quinn's plan seems to be working.

Because for the rest of the night, all I can think about is seeing her face light up when I return this menu to her with my selections. And that's dangerous. Very, very dangerous.

Chapter 17

Quinn

Things are looking up. Ever since I had the idea to make menus for Wesley, it's reinvigorated me with a desire to prove myself. If I can ignore him and stay out of his way, I can show him what an asset I can be. With each passing day, I'm trying to show my usefulness in the hopes that he won't fire me after our fight. I tell myself that if he were going to fire me, he would have done it already. Right?

I haven't seen Wesley today, but he left the filled-out menu on the kitchen counter for me, so I ordered groceries for what I'll need. I have a meeting with Sharon in a few minutes to check in, so I head downstairs and wait for her in the lobby. Eventually, she brings me into her office.

"I just wanted to check in and see how things are going with Mr. Marks. We do employee evaluations every few months."

I pause before responding. What do I even say to that?

Oh yeah, everything is great with Mr. Marks. Except he thinks I'm a liar and a sellout and hates my guts.

I settle on just the first part.

"Everything is great," I say, forcing a smile that I hope looks genuine. Sharon smiles back at me, so it must be working.

"I'm impressed by your initiative. Ordering flowers, candles, groceries. You've really stepped into the role nicely. I'm so glad Mr. Marks recommended you."

Wait, what?

"Sorry, what did you say?" I ask, thinking that I must have heard her incorrectly.

"You know, when you started, and he had you transferred to the penthouse." Her phone starts ringing and she picks it up, giving me the one-minute signal. She babbles on, but I'm hardly listening. My head is spinning. Wesley had me transferred? Why would he do that? Just to mess with me?

Sharon mouths *I'll email you,* so I give her a thumbs up. I want to ask her about Wesley, but I shuffle out of her office, heading back upstairs.

It's eerily silent when I get back to the penthouse. I hate how quiet it is in here. Reeling from Sharon's revelation, I head into the kitchen to start tonight's dinner, a classic ribeye with truffle fries.

I can't believe that Wesley is responsible for my promotion. Maybe I should have known from the beginning. I guess it was naive to think that it could have just been a coincidence that I ended up here. He not only knew who I was this whole time, but he brought me here for some reason. Probably to torment me. Some sick revenge plan to bring me to my lowest point. Too bad for him — I'm not as weak as he anticipates.

I pound on the raw meat for longer than necessary. As I'm clearing off the counter, I notice an arrow drawn on the menu next to tonight and flip it over. On the back, I find Wesley's neat handwriting.

Cook for two and open the 1999 Cabernet.

A bottle of wine? Steak dinner for two?

Does Wesley have a date?

My anger only grows thinking about some supermodel sitting at the dining room table, gushing over how good *my* steak is. I wonder if he'll claim all the credit for it.

Whatever. Why should I care? He's my *boss* after all. Nothing is going to happen between us and that's a good thing. He's an arrogant asshole and the last complication I need in my life right now. He can't even manage a single please or thank you.

I can't stand the silence, so I connect my phone to the speaker in the living room and play my jams playlist, hoping to improve my mood. I slip the apron on and dance around the kitchen. After boiling the potatoes, I pop the steaks into the frying pan and add butter and garlic. I'm so focused and caught up in the music that I don't hear the elevator doors open.

I turn and scream. The regal old woman standing in the foyer looks at me like I'm insane. I grab my phone, turning the volume down.

"Am I in the right suite? This is the penthouse, yes?" She asks, smiling a little.

"Yes. It is. Sorry, you scared me." I grin sheepishly.

It's silent for a moment.

"Not to be rude, but who are you?" I ask.

"I should be asking you that. After all, you are dancing barefoot in my son's kitchen."

Holy shit.

The woman standing in front of me is Wesley's *mother*. For some reason I thought he spawned from an egg or something. I blink twice, making sure this is real. She's quite pretty, with long, straight silver hair wrapped into a bun and a fur coat wrapped around her shoulders.

"I'm Quinn. I'm Wesley's...maid?"

"Are you sure?" She smirks at me.

"Yes. I am. I do other stuff too, though. Like dinner!" I exclaim, realizing I've left the steaks too long on one side. I run back into the kitchen and flip them, sighing in relief. They're not overcooked.

Wesley's mother takes off her coat and follows me into the kitchen, looking around.

"It's quite nice in here. The food smells amazing," she remarks.

"Thank you," I say. "Would you like a drink?" I gesture towards the bottle of Cabernet.

"Please. That's my favorite wine." She smiles. I open the bottle and pour her a glass, handing it to her.

"I'm Lillian, by the way. I'm sorry that my son didn't mention I was coming by."

I glance over at the kitchen clock. Shit.

"No, no, it's my fault. I'm late. Again. I should be gone by now."

"You won't join us for dinner?" She asks.

"Oh god, no." She looks shocked my outright refusal. "I mean, I can't. I have a frozen pizza calling my name at home."

"I insist. I never get to meet new people and you seem refreshingly fun," she says, sipping her wine.

"I couldn't. There's only food for two and I really should be going."

"Nonsense. There's no way I can eat that whole steak. Split it." Now I know where Wesley gets it from. Her voice is hard as stone, leaving no room for argument. I open my mouth to argue but she lifts her hand.

"Ah ah. None of that. I'll set the table while you finish there. Which drawer?"

Wesley's mother — Lillian — pushes me around the kitchen and sets the table. She pours me a glass of wine, despite my protests. The food is finished, so I plate for two, setting them down.

"Where's your plate?" Lillian's sharp voice chimes in. I look at her, pleading, but she won't let up. She grabs another plate from the kitchen and points to it, crossing her arms.

This woman is like a child! Finally, I give in and make my own plate, sitting next to her at the table.

"Drink your wine." She instructs me and I roll my eyes. "Tell me about yourself, Quinn."

I take a gulp of the wine, glancing towards the elevator doors. I'm absolutely terrified for the moment that Wesley walks through those doors and sees me sitting here. How can I explain this? He'll think the worst, I'm sure.

"Well, um. I'm from Brooklyn. I live in South Slope, have my whole life."

She nods and her eyes bore into mine with an intensity. Like she's really listening. Is it hot in here?

"I'm really passionate about food. I used to work at a restaurant. I like to cook, but my real dream is to open my own restaurant, do more of the business stuff. I don't know. Right now, I'm working and just trying to survive, I guess."

"Tell me about your family."

I don't expect the choking feeling gripping my throat. It almost forces tears into my eyes but I blink them back. My family? Where do you want to start? Disappearing dad or sick mom?

"My mother and I are close. We live together," I say, hoping she doesn't pry any further. This is the last thing I want to talk about.

Ding!

Saved by the bell. Except that Wesley is now striding from the elevator towards the dining room table where I sit across from his mother looking like a Greek god. Lillian jumps up from the table and glides towards him with her arms outstretched.

"Darling!" She chimes affectionately, wrapping her arms around him. The scowl on his face doesn't let up. His eyes are locked on mine.

"What are you doing here?" He nearly growls at me.

"Oh, calm down, I invited her. The poor girl was going to eat a frozen pizza!" Lillian says it like it's as bad as eating human feces.

Wesley doesn't say anything. He strips off his suit jacket and hangs it on the back of the chair at the head of the table and sits down, his eyes boring into mine. Lillian returns to her seat on the other side of him.

God, this is awkward.

"Wine?" I break the silence, lifting the bottle towards Wesley. He gives me a curt nod in response, and I pour a hefty glass, hoping alcohol might loosen up the tension in this room.

"Let's dig in. I don't like cold steak." Lillian lifts her fork and starts eating. I wait for Wesley to start before I touch my fork, but he just stares down at his plate, his brow furrowed. Finally, after what feels like forever, he starts eating, too. I join them, the sound of our forks scraping the porcelain loud in the silent room. It's only broken by what can best be described as a moan coming from Lillian.

"God, that's good," she hums. "Perfectly rare. Nothing worse than overcooked steak."

"Thank you," I murmur.

"I see why you want to open your own restaurant. You're

a natural. If you serve this, I'd come for dinner all the time," she continues.

"You want to open your own restaurant?" Wesley asks, looking directly at me. I expect him to sound judgmental or ridicule me for the idea, but it's that same hard, quizzical look on his face. He doesn't look as angry, just...curious.

"I guess. I don't know, it's just an idea." I wave them both off, hating that the spotlight is on me. "How was your day, Mr. Marks?"

Wesley stares at me like he can see right through me.

"It was good, thank you."

Did he just say thank you?

"And you should call me Wesley."

Am I having a stroke? Who is this man and what has he done with the real Wesley Marks? Is having his mother around all it takes to bring out his pleasant side? If so, I should offer her the guest bedroom. Before I have a chance, Lillian puts her fork down and stands.

"Excuse me. My bladder calls."

She sweeps out of the room, leaving Wesley and I sitting alone. The urge to apologize for encroaching on his space is so strong, I can't contain it.

"I'm sorry for intruding. It wasn't my intention. I tried to say no but she's kind of a force to reckon with."

He cuts into his steak, not looking up. He doesn't say anything, the silence stretching between us. He's pissed. He's definitely pissed.

"I can go. You're probably exhausted from work and I'm the last person you want messing up your evening—"

"It's fine." His voice cuts into mine.

"Are you sure?"

"I just said it's fine," he barks, his dark eyes meeting mine.

I swallow the piece of steak I'm chewing with a gulp. I

don't bother asking him if the food is okay. If he says this steak is *fine,* too, I might lose it. His mother seems to like me, but I doubt she'd like the sight of me screaming at her son, even if he does deserve it.

"Is that why you made the menus?" Wesley interrupts the silence, his eyes meeting mine again.

"What?" I ask.

"Opening your own restaurant. Are the menus for practice?" He clarifies.

"Oh. Yeah, I guess. I just thought it would be fun and maybe make things easier so that we don't have to..." I trail off.

"Interact?" He supplies with a smirk.

I wince. "I just thought you would prefer that."

He nods tightly. "Right."

I take a sip of wine that can hardly be called a sip since I basically down the whole glass. The awkward silence has resumed. Luckily, Lillian returns a minute later, sliding back into her seat.

"So, Quinn, you were telling me about your family?"

The longest meal of my life finally comes to an end about thirty minutes later. Once the plates are clear and Lillian is distracted by her conversation with Wesley, I jump up from the table, busying myself in the kitchen while they talk. I'm finishing up when I hear Lillian saying goodbye.

"Quinn, darling. Lovely to meet you and thank you for humoring me tonight. My son is quite lucky to have you, even if he doesn't say so."

She reaches out, bringing me into a hug that I find myself returning easily. For some reason her approval fills me with a new warmth. She steps back and Wesley walks her to the elevator. I hear the doors open and the *ding*, followed by their hushed goodbyes. Before I know it, Wesley walks back into the kitchen.

We're alone all the time but this feels different. Charged, somehow. I'm done in the kitchen, so I prepare to make my escape.

"Well. I should get going too. Everything's all set here, so..." I trail off. I grab my coat off the coat rack and slip my shoes on, avoiding his eyes. Hopefully I can get out of here relatively unscathed. Only a few more minutes. I'm barreling towards the elevator doors when I hear Wesley call after me.

"Quinn?"

I turn and meet his gaze. He's studying me like he's trying to make a decision.

"Yes?"

I wait for him to speak. He shakes his head a little and breaks eye contact, his hand on the back of his neck.

"Goodnight."

Chapter 18

Wesley

Over the next few weeks, my relationship with Quinn improves little by little. She leaves a menu for me every week and I fill it out and leave it for her. We don't interact that much but occasionally she leaves me little notes with my food, usually with jokes written on them.

This wine is as dry as your sense of humor.

Careful with the hot sauce. On a scale from one to Channing Tatum, this is Magic Mike material.

A burger from the beyond. Haunting not included.

I hate to admit that I've saved all of them in my office desk drawer. Sometimes when I'm on a particularly boring conference call, I'll peak down at them and chuckle to myself.

My mother is absolutely obsessed with her. She comes over all the time now — not to spend time with me, of course, but to chat with Quinn. They've become fast friends and apparently Quinn's even been showing her some recipes. I don't have the heart to tell my mother that Quinn is the reason why dad's story went public. Part of me wonders if Quinn will let her guilt get the best of her and confess to my mother herself. I'd prefer it that way.

I've mostly gotten over it. Stubborn as I am, even I can't hold a grudge forever. It's been months since our night at The Phoenix and since she's started working for me, she's been nothing short of a perfect employee. I keep waiting for her to slip up somehow, but she remains diligent and hardworking and much too charming for her own good. There's no reason I should let her get under my skin so much, yet she still does. I've started going to the gym every day just to burn off some of the buzz I get from being around her.

I made the mistake of talking to Ben about Quinn last weekend. We were running through Central Park early on a Saturday morning when he mentioned her name. My mom spent their last phone call talking his ear off about her new friend.

"Oh yeah, she's my employee, actually," I say without thinking.

"Is she one of the architects on the new project or something?" He asks.

"Not quite." I'm being purposefully evasive, realizing he might pry further. "She's my, ah...maid. And cook, kind of."

He stops running and puts his hands on his knees, heaving in a few breaths of air.

"Your *maid?*" He asks, picking up his pace again. I follow after him, sprinting.

"I live in a hotel. There are housekeepers. And well...she's actually the girl from The Phoenix."

"What girl?"

"You know, the one who leaked the story about dad."

He skids to a stop, putting his hand on my chest to stop me.

"Are you serious?"

"Yeah. Weird coincidence. She got a job at the hotel, so I had her reassigned to the penthouse."

"Why the hell would you do that?" He demands.

"Keep your enemies close." I shrug and start running again. He trails after me.

"I smell bullshit, brother."

I don't take the bait. I've already revealed too much about my bizarre relationship with Miss Taylor.

"Does she know who you are?" He asks.

"Of course. We're at each other's throats." I consider my words. "Well, not as much as we used to. She hates my guts though. The feeling is mutual."

"Yeah, right," he snorts. "Like you're not already half in love with her."

"Excuse me?"

"It's written all over your face. You're into her," he taunts, smirking.

"I am not *into* her. She works for me."

"You're probably turned on by that little maid's uniform. Does she have a feather duster, too?"

"Oh, fuck off."

Thankfully, he dropped the subject and hasn't brought it up since then. Ben has a habit of being wrong. Besides, he's as hopeless as I am when it comes to romance, so he's the last person I'll be taking any sort of advice from. He's working this weekend, so he cancelled our normal weekly run, so I'm currently at the gym, burning off the anger that seems ever-present these days.

I step off the treadmill and wipe off my sweat with my towel. I'm done for today so I head upstairs to my apartment, knowing what's waiting for me will only kick my anger right back up again. I step out of the elevator and beeline towards my bedroom, hoping she won't bother me.

"Wesley?" I hear her call out from the kitchen. Looks like I'm shit out of luck today.

"Yes?" I yell back and she comes from around the corner. *Holy shit.*

She's wearing leggings and a tight tank top. She looks like she's on her way to the gym herself. My eyes wander all the way up her body before I meet her sparkling eyes.

"I hope it's okay I ditched the uniform. I figured you're the only one who sees me anyways," she shrugs.

"Sure. Fine." My eyes are on the floor, looking anywhere but her. "Was there something you needed? I need to shower." I finally meet her eyes and her face is colored pink like she's blushing.

"Yes. Right. Of course. Um."

She glances away from me, seeming to consider something. I blink, waiting.

"Don't get mad, okay?" She shifts back and forth on the balls of her feet, her hands clasped together. "I was getting the trash from your office, and I saw a spreadsheet on your desk. I really didn't mean to look, but there's a mistake on it."

"You were looking through my desk?"

"No! I swear. I didn't mean to read it, really. It was sitting right there!"

"What did I tell you about snooping in my stuff? You aren't going to find your next big story."

Dammit. Stupid of me to leave my stuff out. I've gotten too lax with her around, letting my guard down. Who knows what she might have found if I'd left more valuable documents sitting around? It was a mistake to bring her here at all.

"That's not—" She cuts herself off with a groan. "God, you're so infuriating sometimes!"

"You've already broken my trust once. Are you going for a second time?"

"I was just trying to help! I'm sorry, but whoever your accountant is needs to learn addition and subtraction. It's a small mistake, but—"

"You think you can do his job better than he can?"

"I'm not saying that. I'm just saying there's a mistake. I thought you would want to know. I'm just trying to help."

Just when I think we can finally have a truce, a few weeks of civility, she had to cross the line. Again.

"Well. Thank you so much for the heads up, Miss Taylor. What would I do without you?" I sneer.

She looks livid. If it's possible, she looks angrier than she did after our fight, and she was absolutely seething then.

"From now on, don't go in my office at all. I can take my own trash out."

"Fine. I'll stay far away, Mr. Marks," she snaps at me and turns away, storming back towards the kitchen. I don't want to watch her go but I can't help myself. The miniskirt was safer than those goddamn leggings. In the kitchen, I hear her grumbling under her breath and slamming cabinet doors harder than necessary.

Looks like things are back to normal between us.

* * *

Quinn hasn't uttered a word to me since our argument on Saturday. I know I shouldn't have been so harsh on her, but I can't seem to help it. She sets me off. Gets under my skin.

The worst part is that I checked the spreadsheet, and she was right. There was a mistake in the numbers. I immediately called Enrique, my accountant, giving him a reaming that my father would have been proud of. Twice this week I went to apologize to Quinn, but she was nowhere to be found. Turns out she really was doing extra work, sticking around later than she was supposed to and coming in early. Now she's gone by the time I get home and my food sits on the counter like a reproach.

I can't take it anymore. I intend to apologize tonight. I may be stubborn and damn prideful, but I can admit when I'm wrong. I decide to leave work early and catch her before she leaves for the day. Tomorrow is her day off, so I know it's my last chance before I lose my resolve.

All the way up the elevator, I'm filled with nervousness. I pray she's not wearing those leggings again. I won't be able to take it.

Ding!

I step out of the elevator doors and walk towards the kitchen, but she's not in there. She's in the living room, dancing. She's wearing a long summer dress that fits her perfectly, swaying around her ankles as she moves around the room. She picks up a glass vase, wiping it down as she bops her head. I move closer, getting ready to call her name, when she turns and gasps in surprise at the sight of me, dropping the glass vase.

It shatters all over the floor at her feet.

"Oh my god." She pulls out her headphones and drops to her knees immediately, reaching for the broken pieces. "Oh my god. I'm so sorry."

Before I can even blink, she starts crying. Heaping, uncontrollable sobs. The tears stream down her face as she picks up every piece of glass. I just stand there, frozen in place, not sure what to do. I've never had a woman cry like this in front of me before. My mother has only cried once and it was the steely type of crying where only one or two tears escaped. Not like this.

What do I do?

"I'm sorry. I'm sorry," she mutters through her sobs,

depositing the broken pieces of glass into her palm, despite the small cuts forming on her hand. Finally, I can't take it anymore.

"It's okay. It's just a vase." I drop down towards her, reaching out to stop her, but as soon as I move towards her, she flinches, leaning backwards away from me.

My heart drops.

Does she really think I'd hurt her?

Fuck. A wave of nausea rolls through me.

She blinks a few times and looks at me like she's looking right through me. "Wesley?" She whispers my name like a question.

I have to shake off the feeling of guilt crawling up my throat. I reach for her again and she doesn't flinch this time, so I lift her up with me, both of us standing. She's shaking still and her sobs have stopped, but tears leak from the corner of her eyes.

"I don't—" She looks down at the broken glass like she's just realized it's there. "I'm really sorry. I'll clean it all up."

"I don't give a fuck about the glass, Quinn." My voice sounds harsher than I intended but the sight of her like this is making me feel insane.

She stares down at the broken glass, not looking at me.

"Come here," I say softly, leading her towards the kitchen.

I sit her on one of the stools and run to the bathroom, grabbing my first aid kit. When I return, she hasn't moved from her spot. She's just staring down at the floor. I move towards her slowly and when she looks up at me, tears swim in her eyes. I take her palm gingerly and shake out the small pieces of glass, examining the cuts.

She doesn't say anything as I clean her palm. I swallow, hard, trying to shake off the image of her flinching away from me.

"Does it hurt?" I ask, finally.

She shakes her head.

"Are you sure?"

"It's fine," she murmurs.

I take the last piece of glass out of her hand and apply antiseptic ointment, hoping nothing is infected and the bandages I have will suffice. I cover the wounds with a few band-aids. Maybe I should call Ben and ask Jamie to come over. She's a doctor. She'll know what to do, right?

My frantic thoughts are interrupted by Quinn's soft hand pulling away from mine.

"I'm sorry. That was...embarrassing."

"You have nothing to be embarrassed about."

She turns to look at the broken glass, avoiding my eyes.

"Are you...why did you flinch away from me?" I ask.

She has to know. She has to know that I'd never hurt her. I might be a stubborn asshole, but I can't believe we've taken our feud so far that she's actually scared of me. The thought makes me feel sick.

"I thought—" She's still avoiding my eyes. "Would you excuse me for a minute?"

She hops off the stool and beelines for the bathroom, shutting the door behind her. I put the bandages back into the first-aid kit with a sigh. The time seems to pass impossibly slow as I wait for her to return. Before she does, my phone rings and I pick it up.

"Wes, it's George. I've got accounting on the other line, there's an issue with the latest numbers."

"Again? Jesus Christ." I run my hand through my hair.

"Do you have last quarterly report in front of you?"

"It's in my office. Hold on."

I press the phone to my ear and go into my office, shuffling through my files until I find the report George is looking for.

After a few minutes, the issue is resolved and George agrees to report back to me later with an update, so I hang up.

When I get back into the kitchen, it's silent. A small piece of paper rests on the counter. I pick it up and read it.

Left for the day. Hope you're okay with takeout tonight. I cleaned up the mess. Sorry again.

Replaying today's events, I feel a pit in my stomach. Who has that kind of reaction to a simple mistake? Part of me is scared to find out the answer, but the other part needs to know. I feel this overwhelming need to protect her, like I should run out of this apartment and track her down to make sure she's okay.

Instead, I just stare at the empty room in front of me, replaying the image of Quinn's huddled figure flinching away from me. It plays over and over until I can do nothing but crumple the note and throw it away.

Chapter 19

Quinn

The first time I had sex for money was when I was twenty years old.

Mom had just been diagnosed and lost her job in the same month. She was at an all-time low, and if I'm being honest with myself, I was too. I knew I had to drop out of school because I couldn't afford the classes anymore with mom's medical payments and the amount of loans I'd already taken.

It was in one of my classes when I overheard two girls talking about it — some website where you could find Sugar Daddies. The idea had never occurred to me before. At first, I felt myself judging them, wondering how they could do that. Until I heard one of them say she made $500 in an hour with one guy.

I'd never really been in a relationship before, and honestly, I didn't really get the hype around sex. It was always just okay for me, and I figured if I wasn't going to enjoy sex with men, I might as well get paid for it. Take something of my own. I could finish my degree and figure out my mom's medical payments.

I worked up the courage to talk to the girls in my class and ask them a few questions about the website. After that, I made a profile on Seeking Arrangements. At first, I only went on a couple of first dates, making $100 here and there. Eventually I found a guy who was interested in something more long term. He just wanted to masturbate while I said degrading things to him, and I thought I'd hit the jackpot. I didn't even have to touch him. Unfortunately for me, he broke things off after a few weeks. That's when I found someone else.

His name was Derek, or at least that's what he told me. I doubt it was his real name.

He was one of the more attractive guys I'd seen on the website. I couldn't believe he needed to pay for sex. That should have been the first red flag. If they're handsome, there's something they want to do to you that their girlfriends won't let them do.

Derek had an extreme degradation kink. He warned me in advance the types of things he wanted to do to me, but the money he was offering was more than anyone else had ever given me, and I was lost in it by then, lost in the illusion that I was somehow reclaiming myself, my body. I know it feels that way for some people, but it never felt that way for me. Not really.

So, every few weeks, I'd travel to the Upper West Side and meet Derek at his apartment where we'd have sex, and every time, he'd tell me I was worthless, tell me I was nothing, less than nothing. I realize now I would disassociate while it was happening. I wasn't there, not mentally. Somehow, I would just float away from myself until I could pretend it was happening to someone else.

I thought it was fine. Each time I'd leave his place, a cold sort of numbness would pass over me. I would sit on the train and stare at the faces of the strangers around me, feeling more alone than ever. But then I'd count the bills later that night and a sort of giddiness and shameful pride would overtake me. This cycle would continue for a few months.

We'd been seeing each other for almost six months when it happened. One night he was undressing me and calling me a horrible name when he slapped me across the face. I immediately shoved him away, livid. We had not agreed to that. I scrambled off the bed to leave when he suddenly grabbed me again and shoved me further onto the bed.

I told him to stop, but I felt a shift. I knew. I don't know how, but I just knew then that he wasn't going to stop, that words weren't going to be enough for him. Somehow, I managed all my strength to push him off. When I hurled myself across the room, grabbing my bag in search for my keys and the pepper spray on them, he shoved me into the table and the glass vase next to it shattered next to me on the hard floor, a shard cutting into my leg. I managed to get my pepper spray and ran out of there before it could go any further. After that night, I vowed that I was done.

I didn't tell my mom. I didn't tell anyone. I went to the free clinic at the hospital and got my leg stitched up, making up some lie about tripping with a glass. Wore jeans so my mom wouldn't notice. Buried it deep inside and never touched it again.

I haven't thought about that time in my life or that night in forever, but the remnants of it have stuck with me. Every time I've had sex since, it hasn't been the same. Even when I'm really into the person, guy or girl, I start to disassociate. I can't help it.

Worst of all, it's not the type of thing I'm conscious of in the moment. Casual partners tend not to notice it either and I've been too scared to try any serious dating. After all, sex is a prerequisite for that, and I have all this baggage surrounding it now. Somehow, even when I think I'm ready and enjoying myself, I'm still not really *there*.

Standing on the sidewalk outside of the Hyatt, I try to calm my impending hyperventilating.

Breathe, breathe.

I can't believe I cried like that. In front of Wesley of all people. I'm so embarrassed. How the hell am I going to explain my reaction? He probably thinks I'm crazy. Like, balls-to-the-walls insane. Who turns into a sobbing mess just from dropping a glass?

It's not like I can explain the truth.

Whoops, sorry! A glass smashed the night I was assaulted by my sugar daddy and now the trauma lives inside me where I can't really control how or when I react!

I didn't think I'd be triggered like that, but when the glass shattered, it was like I wasn't in Wesley's penthouse suite. I was a scared young woman who'd allowed herself to be used over and over by men. I actually thought Wesley was Derek before I snapped out of it. It was his face swimming in my vision.

Breathe, breathe.

I feel sick. I can't go back to work. How am I ever going to face Wesley again? This is worse than any argument. He's seen a side of me I swore I would never show. He's seen me vulnerable. He's seen my weakness and now he can exploit it however he wants.

I can't take it. I rush over to the trash can and hurl right into it, the vomit rushing out of me.

"Hey, lady, you alright?" Someone asks from behind me.

I heave again and empty out the entire contents of my stomach. Oh god.

"I'm fine," I groan, waving them to leave me alone.

Thankfully, it's New York, so whoever it is walks away

without further questioning. I think I'm done throwing up, so I sit on a bench with my head in my hands.

My phone buzzes and I look down to see a text from my mom.

> Don't forget to pick up the cake from the bakery! See you tonight. xx

Shit. I completely forgot that tonight is Sheila's going away party at our place. Here I thought the day couldn't possibly get worse. I'm dreading saying goodbye to Sheila. I look up at the cloudy sky with a sigh. Someone up there's really got it in for me.

* * *

Later that night, our apartment is packed for Sheila's party. To be fair, it's a pretty small place, so it doesn't take much to fill it up.

"Everything looks amazing." Sheila smiles, looking around at the decor.

"Wait until you try dessert. Quinn made your favorite." my mom says, pushing Sheila towards the kitchen.

I pour myself a giant glass of wine, wishing we'd gone for the harder stuff. I could use a shot of tequila right about now. Sannika is talking my ear off about how well the candle business is doing and won't stop thanking me for my support.

"It's no problem, really," I mutter, looking around the room for an escape. "Would you excuse me for a minute?"

I beeline for the bathroom, locking the door behind me. I put the seat down and sit on the toilet with a sigh. My phone buzzes in my pocket. When I look at the screen, I read the message almost three times.

I can't believe what I'm seeing.

> Hi Quinn, it's Wesley Marks. I just wanted to make sure you got home okay. Let me know.

I rub my eyes to make sure I'm not imagining the words on my screen. I type quickly in disbelief.

> How did you get this number?

I stare down at the phone. What a dumb question. He probably has a PI on speed dial and elves who do his bidding. My phone buzzes again with his response.

> Sharon at the front desk gave it to me. I hope that's okay.

As I'm trying to formulate some sort of a response, another text comes through.

> Are you alright? You seemed pretty upset earlier.

Oh my god. Why would he bring that up? Doesn't he have the common decency to ignore someone's panic attack? I quickly type out a reply.

I'm fine. Thanks for checking in. See you tomorrow.

There. A polite response, but curt enough to remind him that we are not friends. We work together. The dreaded three dots appear as he types but they disappear and there's no response. I can't stare at the awkward conversation any longer, so I slip my phone into my back pocket and return to the party.

"...thinking maybe it's time for us to move, too. Too many memories in this place." I catch the tail end of my mom's sentence as I walk into the kitchen.

"What did you say?" I interrupt.

"Oh, nothing." My mom pats my arm. "Just telling Sheila that maybe we'll be following in her footsteps."

"I'll never leave New York," I say, my voice harsher than intended.

"I know that. I just meant maybe a new place. Maybe you could even find your own place," my mom replies.

"What are you even talking about? I can't afford to live alone and I'm not going to let you live alone."

"It was just an idea, sweetheart. Don't get defensive."

I grumble and down the rest of my wine.

"Did something happen? You seem off tonight." My mom rubs my arm, concerned.

"It's fine. I'm fine."

That word is starting to sound fake, I've said it so many times. I slip out of my mom's grip and go to the kitchen to refill my glass. I know I'm in a grumpy mood. I can't help it. Between today's freak-out and Wesley texting me, I don't know how I'm going to go back to work tomorrow.

I pour another glass and pull my phone out. My fingers shaking, I type out one last text.

> Actually, I'm feeling kind of sick. I might not make it tomorrow — just a heads up.

I hit send, not waiting for Wesley's reply, and turn my phone off. I put on my biggest smile and lift the stack of paper plates.

"Who wants cake?"

Chapter 20

Wesley

I stare down at the text message from Quinn, not knowing how to respond. Maybe I shouldn't have gotten her phone number from Sharon. She seems upset that I texted her, but I had to know if she was okay. She was so distressed when she ran out of here —what if she's still crying? What if something else happened when she left?

Why do you care?

I shouldn't. I don't. It's none of my business why she was so upset about the glass and it's none of my business if she's still upset now. The wounded doe act is probably part of her plan to bring my walls down and trust her again.

No — I know that's not true. That wasn't an act. If anything that's happened between us has been real at all, it's what happened today.

I run my hand through my hair with a sigh. When the hell did this become my life? Worse, why am I disappointed that Quinn won't be here tomorrow when all I've wanted is her out of my hair? Maybe it's because I know she's avoiding me and feeding me bullshit about being sick.

Frustrated, I call my brother and ask if I can come over.

He asks me to pick up some beers. Pete's off-duty now, so I decide I'll take the train uptown. Give me some time to clear my head. I grab a six-pack of Blue Moons from the corner and hop on the C train, my headphones in.

When I get to Ben's place, Luna is already asleep, so we settle in on the couch.

"What's up?" He asks.

"Clearly not much, since it's a Friday night and I'm here. How are you?"

"I'm fine. Jamie's traveling again." He sips his beer. "Luna has reached the 'why' phase. All she does is ask me why, why, why. I'd like to know myself."

"Me too. Like why Quinn was crying today," I wonder out loud.

"Your sexy housekeeper? You made her cry?"

"No!" I shake my head and suppress a groan. "I mean — maybe. I don't know."

"Whatever it is, just apologize. Always apologize."

"Good advice, coming from a guy who sees his wife twice a year."

"Ouch. First of all, I see Jamie more than twice a year. Don't be a dick. Secondly, we can't all be chronically single bitter assholes."

"Ouch."

We clink our beers together and drink in silence. Seems like I have a few things to apologize for where Quinn is concerned. Maybe one blanket apology will suffice. Too bad for me, I won't be seeing Quinn tomorrow because of her fake illness. So, for now, we drink.

I wake up with a killer hangover. It's my own fault. I should've never convinced Ben to bust out the whiskey we'd confiscated from our dad a few months ago. Vague memories of karaoke in my brother's living room flash through my mind. I pray that was a dream.

Once I'm settled in at my desk, I check my phone. A text from Ben with a video attached:

> Thank God for smart phones, Mariah.

I only watch the video for a few seconds before smacking my forehead in mortification. I respond quickly:

> Show anyone and I kill you.

> Wouldn't dream of it. My eyes only. And maybe the American Idol judges.

I toss my phone on my desk with a groan and pop two Advil with a glass of water. Pushing my drunk mistakes aside, I start on today's work. I glance through an email from my assistant with yesterday's trades highlights. None of them concern me, really, but one catches my eye:

Mason Corp Faces Allegations of Fraud, Embezzlement

I grimace, thinking of the last time I saw Tim Mason. He'd been wasted and high on pills, crying on my shoulder about how his wife slept with their gardener. Classic. I knew Tim was an idiot, but fraud? Really?

For now, I push it to the back of my mind and get to work so I can enjoy the rest of my weekend. I'm finishing up with most of my urgent tasks when my mom calls.

"Darling! How are you?"

"Fine, mom. How are you?"

"Oh, bored as all hell. But guess what? Quinn signed me up for a cooking class and I went last night."

I grumble at the mention of Quinn.

"That sounds nice," I reply.

"The teacher is quite handsome, too."

I laugh. "You're still married last I checked."

"Sure, sure."

We've avoided speaking about my father, but I can't help but feel guilty. The new program is much stricter than the original facility, which means I haven't talked to my dad since the scandal broke. You'd think he'd be able to bribe his way into a phone call, but nothing so far.

"...he even plays violin! Anyway, he invited me to come over and try his new paella recipe."

I snap back to reality, realizing my mom has been talking this whole time.

"What? That sounds like a date."

"It's not a date," my mom insists. "Michaelangelo is just a friend."

"Michaelangelo? Oh, for Christ's sake," I groan.

She hangs up, reminding me to tell Quinn to call her because apparently, they are friends now.

I'm starting to feel too tense, like I could explode from the conflicting emotions within me when it comes to Quinn. Can I trust her? I guess she betrayed us all before she even knew us. Part of me wants to tell her to get out of my life. It's like she's lodged herself right in the center of it. Like everywhere I look, she's there with that perfect smile. I need her to get out. But the thought of never seeing her again causes a twist in my gut.

I push away from my desk with a groan. It's only a matter of time. She can't stay 'sick' forever. Come Monday, Quinn will return, I can get to the bottom of her recent fit of tears, and things will return to normal between us.

Mutual disdain. It's for the best for everyone.

* * *

The weekend passes quickly and unsurprisingly, I get a call from Sharon downstairs informing me that Quinn won't be in today either. I get the urge to text her again, but it didn't seem to go over too well last time, so I stop myself.

By Monday, I'm grateful to be back to work. Anything to distract from my endless thoughts about Quinn and her mysterious illness — if that even exists. I'm starting to worry she might actually be sick. It's not like her to skip out on work and I can't believe she's this devoted to avoiding me.

The day drags by with endless tasks, and I find myself hoping she'll show up tomorrow. The rational part of me knows that she's only here to pick up the laundry, but the irrational side is bustling with something dangerously close to nerves.

I'm finishing up in the late afternoon when I see another email from my assistant with updated trades announcements and notice that Mason Corp is still in the headlines. In a move completely unlike me, I decide to give Tim a call. It rings a few times before his out-of-breath voice greets me.

"Tim? It's Wesley. Wesley Marks."

The shuffling of papers on the other end halts and I think I hear Tim sit down.

"Wesley? Wow. I wasn't expecting to hear from you. How are you?"

"I'm good, I'm alright. I actually was just calling to check on you," I say, hoping it's not awkward.

"I guess you saw the news. Who hasn't, right?" He chuckles with a twinge of self-deprecation.

"You don't have to feel embarrassed. I know how you feel."

"Yeah. I'm sorry about your old man, by the way. I should have called."

"Nah, we've all got our own shit. That's pretty clear," I mumble.

"Swarvoski, man."

"What?"

"Crystal fucking clear."

I chuckle, remembering the hint of the more playful Tim I used to know.

"Listen, man, I appreciate you calling. It's nice to hear from a friend. I know I brought a lot of this all upon myself, but it still sucks," he says.

"So, the allegations are true?" I probe a little.

"FBI probably tapped my phone lines, dude."

"Yikes. Hope they aren't listening to this one. I'm not using my interview voice."

Tim huffs out a laugh that ends into a sigh. "The thing I can't figure out is how the hell the media got their hands on the story. I swear to God, this shit was airtight. Nobody knew about the investigation because they don't have much evidence and we've been cooperating. Then last week I went to The Phoenix for a meeting with my lawyer to discuss my case. The next day I'm on the front page of every newspaper in this goddamn city."

I've mostly zoned out of Tim's rant at this point, because my mind is stuck on one tiny detail.

"Sorry, did you say The Phoenix?"

"Yeah. New York Post must have the place fuckin' bugged or something."

"Or something," I mumble, my head spinning.

It's a coincidence. Just a coincidence.

My mind flickers with the memory of my argument with Quinn, the image of her insisting she didn't leak the story. The raw glimpse of honesty I thought I'd seen in her eyes.

No, no. This can't be happening. Because if someone else, some other employee at The Phoenix is the rat, then that means...

My stomach drops.

"Tim? I'm sorry to rush off but I have to go."

"No problem, bud. Thanks for calling."

I hang up, my body moving rapidly, as if I'm on autopilot. Hands shaking, I dial The Phoenix, needing answers.

* * *

A few hours later, I'm sitting at my desk in the darkness, replaying my conversations with Pierre.

Ian's been maitre-d here for almost 5 years and we've never had any problems.

Rest assured, he will be fired immediately and the situation will be reconciled.

Of course, Miss Taylor can certainly have her job back. I'll be calling her personally with my apologies.

The words swirl together in my brain as I knock back another full glass of whisky. I stopped keeping track a few glasses ago. I don't normally drink like this, but I need to get rid of the feeling that's pooling in my gut and clawing its way up my throat.

I pour myself another glass with shaking hands, attacking myself with my thoughts.

All this time, I've been blaming Quinn. Treating her terribly. Making her cry, making her flinch away from me, making her dread seeing me so much she'd rather call in sick than face me.

A wave of nausea rolls through me. Oh god. Am I going to be sick?

My head is pounding with the painful reminder of our last encounter, as if my mind is tormenting me with every conversation, every jab I threw in her direction.

Do I apologize? Would she even forgive me? Do I even deserve her forgiveness, or anyone's for that matter?

I don't even know.

All I know is I feel so deep in despair, so wracked with guilt, so deeply uncomfortable with the realization that all I've done for the past few weeks is make life difficult for someone who only ever treated me with patience.

I push down the tears threatening to spill over and knock back another glass, praying the whiskey numbs me completely.

Chapter 21

Quinn

My stomach rolls with another wave of anxiety as I ride the elevator up to the familiar penthouse suite. It somehow feels more sinister than ever, like I'm about to confront the final boss at the end of the video game. Honestly, Bowser sounds like a sweet turtle in comparison to Wesley Marks. Every fiber within my being screams *abort mission now!*

I've been dreading this moment for the past two days. In my most childish form, I called out of work all weekend. Sharon told me if I didn't come back soon, they'd temporarily replace me with another housekeeper. I agreed to come by tonight to get the laundry and pick up Wesley's dry-cleaning, hoping that he won't be home.

To make things worse, I have to say goodbye to Sheila tomorrow. I've been avoiding thinking about her departure, but now it's here, and I can't run from it any longer.

Ding!

I step out to the elevator into the dark apartment. It's very quiet.

"Wesley?" I call out.

Nothing.

Thank God.

Wesley has left his suits out in the hallway for dry-cleaning, so I gather the laundry from all the rooms. In and out. I'm almost finished throwing everything into the laundry cart when I hear a sound from Wesley's office.

A warning low in my gut tells me to ignore it, but I don't listen. It sounds like a voice.

Wesley's voice.

He's here!

I make a move to escape before he realizes I'm here, but I stop in my place, listening. It almost sounds like he's...crying?

That's impossible.

My hands moving before my brain can form thoughts, I push open the office door. Wesley sits slumped over his desk, his head in his hands. An empty whiskey glass sits next to him.

"Wesley?" My voice is soft as a whisper.

His head snaps up at the sound, his red eyes meeting mine. My stomach drops at the sight of his teary-eyed face. This is a Wesley I have never seen before, and it fills me with an unexpected dread. He looks completely devastated.

"Are you okay?" I ask. He just blinks back at me as if he can't believe I'm real. The feeling is mutual. If there's one thing I didn't expect to see tonight, it's this.

"Quinn?" His gruff voice breaks off halfway through. "I thought you were sick."

"Sick?" I say without thinking.

Yes, sick, idiot! You told him you were sick!

"Right, yes. I'm feeling much better, thanks." The words spill out and I hope they sound convincing. Wesley just nods like he can barely keep his head up. He stands, rising to his full height, and stumbles over to the bar cart where a near-empty whiskey bottle sits.

"Should you—" I start.

He lifts the bottle but immediately drops it, the glass shattering. I flinch.

Jeez, we really have to stop meeting this way.

Wesley hardly notices the bottle and stumbles back, laughing. I rush over to him.

"Here. Come on." I put some of his weight on my body and start moving out of the office towards Wesley's room.

"What are you doing?" He asks, his words slurred.

"Putting you to bed. Can you help me a little? You're heavy as shit," I groan, leaning against the wall as we stumble through the hallway.

"Shit." He giggles. Giggles! Wesley Marks can giggle! "You said shit. You never curse."

"Around you," I correct him, pushing open his bedroom door.

"Why are you being so nice? You hate me." His voice is tinged with pain and...regret?

My stomach bottoms out again.

"I don't hate you," I say, rushing into his room and depositing his giant body onto the bed.

He rolls onto his back, looking at me. "You should. You should hate me," he whispers, his eyes meeting mine.

"Wesley," I scold him a little, shaking my head.

"I should have—" He breaks off and looks away. His Adams apple bobs unbelievably slow and I should not be so turned on at the sight of messy Wesley. "I should have believed you."

"What do you mean?" I ask.

"Tim Mason told me the truth...shit. Piece of shit."

He's rambling and not making any sense. "Shh, just wait here for a sec. I'll get you some water," I whisper.

I rush into the kitchen and pour a hefty glass of water, hoping he's not currently vomiting in his bed. I wonder if he's the vomiting type of drunk. When I get back to his bedroom, his eyes are closed and he's resting against the pillows, his body angled awkwardly on the bed. He looks so peaceful.

I shake it off and sit next to him on the bed, holding out the glass.

"Here. Drink this, please."

He opens his eyes and looks at me again like he can't believe I'm real. Like he's drinking me in with his eyes. It makes my whole body buzz, like I can feel my skin tingling under his gaze.

He takes a small sip of the water.

"All of it," I say, pushing the glass forward. He chugs the entire glass and slams it onto the bedside table with a little too much force, his glazed eyes coming back to meet mine.

"Why are you drinking like this?" I ask.

"Because of you," he says, his voice unwavering.

"Me?" My voice, meanwhile, could not be shakier. "What did I do?"

"Nothing. You're perfect." The words roll off his tongue. "So perfect, it hurts."

I take in a shocked breath, the gasp loud in the quiet room. Suddenly, I feel the warmth of his hand in mine. I look down and his fingers are wrapped around mine.

"If I said I was sorry, would you believe me?"

When I meet his eyes again, they are wet with fresh tears. Pleading pools of pain, fresh and clear. I blink a few times, struck by the emotion gathering in my throat.

"Because I am. Sorry. I'm sorry." He exhales the words, his head falling forward slightly. He blinks and curls his legs in, leaning to the side. He's falling asleep, I realize. "So sorry," he mutters, his eyes closing. He keeps muttering the word until his breath turns into soft snores.

I blink again, my throat dry. I sit there for a few minutes watching Wesley's chest heave up and down with soft breaths, a strange feeling bubbling and unfurling in my chest.

I pour another glass of water in the kitchen and get some Advil from the medicine cabinet, leaving both on the bedside table for him. Then I untie his shoes one by one and pull his socks off. I decide to leave the pants and swing his body under the covers, tucking him in.

I go back into the living room and stare at the laundry cart and dry-cleaning bags, knowing I should leave now. But for some reason, my mind is filled with concern.

What if he throws up on his back and chokes?

What if he has alcohol poisoning or a concussion?

Glancing at the couch, I groan, cursing my good intentions. I grab my phone and call my mom, leaving a message.

"Hey, it's me. I won't be home tonight. Don't worry, I'm just crashing at a friend's place. I'll see you tomorrow."

I hang up and slip the phone in my pocket, falling onto the couch. I close my eyes and try to ward off the fresh memories swirling through my mind: Wesley's face staring up at me, pure and raw, and the feeling of his hand in mine.

Chapter 22

Wesley

Bright. It's so bright.

I blink through the light with a groan, my head pounding. My eyes finally adjust to the light enough for me to recognize my own bedroom, the curtains wide open. Strange, since I usually close them before I go to bed.

God, I must have drank a lot last night.

I push the covers off and realize I'm still wearing yesterday's slacks and button down, but my socks and shoes are off. That's weird.

I reach for the spot where my water bottle usually is and instead, I find a glass and my Advil pill bottle. That's when it all hits me at once, memories from last night assaulting me head on.

Quinn. In my room. Putting me to bed.

If I said I was sorry, would you believe me?

Oh shit.

I toss a few of the Advil in my mouth and wash it down with the water. At least the worst part is over, right? When Quinn comes back to work, I can explain and apologize properly, like a man instead of a drunk, weepy asshole. That is if she returns to work tomorrow.

I remember with a pang that Pierre said he'd offer Quinn her old job back. It's not like she can stay as my goddamn housekeeper now that the truth is out. What an asshole I am to even put her in this situation to begin with.

I go to the kitchen. I need coffee if I'm going to think through this. The espresso machine starts whirring and I hear the sound of...snoring? Turning to the couch, I see none other than Quinn curled up, her hands resting softly under her chin. I blink a few times, not believing it.

She slept here?

God, she looks beautiful. I want to reach out and find out if her skin is as soft as it looks. I flex my fingers out, suddenly nervous for when she wakes up. What the hell am I going to say?

I don't have much time to figure it out. Suddenly, Quinn stirs, stretches her arms above her head, and blinks. I realize I probably look completely creepy hunched over her as she sleeps but it's too late because she's already looking into my eyes.

"Wesley?" Her voice is as soft as a caress.

"Good morning," I reply, hoping I sound casual.

As if my words shock her fully awake, she sits upright and pushes her legs out, glancing around.

"Thank you for staying over. You didn't need to do that. And you should have taken the second bedroom," I say.

"Shit. I forgot about it, to be honest. I was a little distract-ed," she says and then snaps her mouth shut, her face coloring red. She's *blushing*, I realize with a jolt. The soft pink hue on her cheeks is making me inexplicably turned-on.

"Are you feeling better?" She asks, distracting me again.

I grin a little, half-grimacing at my behavior. "Yeah.

Thanks for the Advil, and for taking care of me. You really didn't need to stay."

"I wanted to make sure you were okay," she says, her eyes twinkling as she blinks up at me.

I want to kiss her.

The thought is so strong, I have to thrust it out of my mind immediately. I look away and clear my throat, my heart racing.

"Listen, about last night." I force the words out quickly. "I was wrong. I didn't explain it or apologize properly, but I'd like to try."

"What do you mean?"

"Has Pierre called you yet?" I ask.

"Pierre?" She blinks. Her eyebrows scrunch in that way when she's confused, so I guess he hasn't yet. I take in a big gulp of air and tap my fist on my chest.

"Last night, he fired Ian Thomas from The Phoenix."

I look up again and meet her eyes, ready to continue, but she interrupts me, her face coloring in angry recognition.

"Oh." She looks away. "I see."

"So, you always knew it was him?" I ask. She shrugs and avoids my gaze still. "Why didn't you say anything before?"

She finally meets my gaze head on, her bright eyes shining. "Nobody believed me, anyway. Nobody ever believes women." Her voice is unwavering, and her words are a warning of something deeper than my mistake.

"I'm sorry."

"Yeah, you said that last night." She smirks humorlessly.

"I should have believed you. I wanted to." I swallow, the desire to avoid these feelings stronger than ever. Quinn rolls her eyes and I take a step closer. "Honestly, I did. I have...trust issues. A lot of people have used me for money and status. Ex-girlfriends have gone to the press with intimate details of our lives and my own father lied to our family for years about his addiction problems."

I take a breath and force myself to meet her intense gaze head-on.

"It's hard for me to trust and I tend to assume the worst of people. Not that any of that is an excuse, because it's not. I'm not trying to...I just wanted to say that I was wrong, and I'm sorry."

We are locked in some sort of staring contest that she finally breaks at the end of my speech, blinking in surprise. Her eyes flicker towards my lips and I know that look. Right? That's a *kiss me* look. I let my gaze fall to her plush lips and when she licks them, I almost lose it right fucking there.

I step closer again, my hand reaching for her impulsively. My hand grazes her arm and we're almost touching. So close.

She stumbles backwards with a gasp. I match her move, taking a full step back. When I meet her eyes again, I swear there's still a hunger there.

"Thank you. For apologizing," she says, and I'm hit with another pang.

You're supposed to be apologizing, not trying to kiss her, asshole!

She squares her shoulders. "I forgive you."

Her words curl around me and bury themselves deep in my chest, warming my whole body. She's perfect. Why didn't I see it before?

"Can I ask you something?" I say, the words spilling out of me. It's like she's opened something inside of me that threatens to unfold completely if I don't find a way to stuff it back inside.

"Sure," she says, a little nervous. I can tell when she's nervous because her eyelashes flutter and she always glances to the left, biting on her lip. She's doing it now, her head cocked to the side.

"On Friday..." I start. "Did you think that I was going to—" I break off. I can't seem to get the words right, the foreign way they feel on my tongue even thinking about it. "Did you think that I'd hurt you?"

"No! No," she says the words abruptly. The silence that follows is heavy and awkward.

"Okay," I say, still confused, but wanting to move on from this conversation. "I just—I wouldn't do that. Ever. And the thought of you thinking that I might—" I break off again, my throat closing. I'm starting to sound like I'm going through puberty. "If I made you feel unsafe at all—"

"You didn't! I don't!" She reassures me, her eyes wide. "Really. I promise. We're good. Let's not mention last night or Friday again. Okay?" She talks quickly, standing up and moving towards the door like she's ready to bolt.

"You're leaving?" I move to stop her without thinking. She can't leave yet. I don't know why but it feels like everything has changed and if she walks out that door now, I won't be able to fix things between us.

"Yeah, I should probably go," she says, pulling her hair up into a ponytail that reveals her long, slender neck.

Since when are necks a turn-on? Jesus.

"Wait!" I almost shout the word. Why am I acting like an insane person? I chuckle and run my hand through my hair. "I was thinking I could take you to breakfast or something. To thank you for last night."

Quinn looks at me like I've grown a second head and I feel like an absolute idiot.

"You really don't have to do that." She tucks a loose strand of hair behind her ear, her eyes flickering away from mine.

"I want to," I insist. She meets my gaze and I hold steady, hoping she sees something that makes her say yes.

"Alright." She nods, putting her bag down. "Okay. Breakfast." She says the word like she's hearing it for the first time. At her agreement, I smile, grinning so hard it almost hurts. I wipe it off quickly.

"Yes. Breakfast." I smirk. "Let me just change really quick," I say, squeezing her arm briefly and walking back towards my room.

I really need to stop touching her.

Breakfast? Where the hell did that even come from? And that almost-kiss. For a second there, I was stupid enough to think she'd want that. She pulled away so fast I would've blinked and missed it. And now we're about to go to breakfast, when what I really need is a cold shower and to get far away from her before I lose myself completely.

Chapter 23

Quinn

Breakfast. Wesley Marks is taking me to breakfast.

My mind has been spinning since I woke up. I seriously should have taken the train home last night. If I'd known I'd wake up to this Wesley — apologetic, sweet, soft-spoken, — I'd have run far, far away. This Wesley is much more dangerous than cold, distant Wesley.

This is your boss, idiot!

Right. Except that it really seemed like he might kiss me at one point there. He looked kind of...well, angry. But he definitely touched me. I don't think I could forget the feeling of his hands on me even if I tried. I wish he'd do it again. My skin is buzzing like I'm waiting for it.

Snap out of it!

I take a deep breath, trying not to remember his deep eyes boring into mine. How troubled and clouded his expression looked when he apologized. I don't know what came over me then. I should have been angry, but it was like I had this need to get that look off his face at any cost.

This is bad.

Despite the voice in my head scolding me, all I can think

about is that *smile*. Seeing it once was not enough. I need to see it again to make sure I didn't imagine the way it spread across his face, creating dimples that lit up his face like magic. If I'm not careful, Wesley's smile will be my new addiction.

"Hey, sorry I took so long. I'm ready." His gruff voice interrupts my spiraling. I turn to face him. He's changed into dark jeans and a white t-shirt, his wet hair hanging in front of his face. He runs his hand through it, tugging the strands out of his face and grinning a little.

I am going to die.

Calm down, Quinn. You've seen attractive men before. You've slept with attractive men before! Why should this one be any different? I can keep it together for one meal.

"Quinn?" Wesley prompts me and I realize I'm just standing there staring at him.

"Yes! Ready."

He nods and we walk towards the elevator together in silence and he pushes the button.

"There's a diner I like in Midtown East. Is that okay?" He pushes his hands into his pockets.

Since when does Wesley Marks ask if something is okay?

"Sure. Sounds great." I expected him to take us to some fancy brunch place in Soho with $25 buttered toast. The elevator doors open right as my phone buzzes. He steps in and I follow, glancing down to see my mom is calling.

"Are you going to answer that?" Wesley asks, pointing to my phone.

"Um." I try to think of some valid reason for why I shouldn't answer the phone, but my brain is just static.

I pick up the phone and press it to my ear. "Hello?"

"Hi, sweetheart! I got your message. Is everything okay? Are you at Sannika's?"

"No, everything's fine. I stayed at a friend's place. You don't know them."

My eyes flicker over to Wesley, who is watching me with his lips slightly curled.

"When will you be home?" My mom asks. "In time to say goodbye to Sheila, right?"

"Yes. Of course. I'll see you at four," I say, hoping it's not obvious that I'm rushing her off the phone.

"Alright. Love you!" She shouts the words at me.

"I love you too. Bye." I slip my phone into my back pocket. "Sorry about that," I say to Wesley.

"No need to apologize," he replies. "Was that your boyfriend?" He avoids my gaze, but I know fishing when I hear it. The forced casualness in his tone. "Or...girlfriend?" He prompts.

I chuckle and shake my head.

"No, it was my mom," I say, letting the words hang between us. He nods, flattening his lips. He's clearly unsatisfied that his not-so-subtle attempt at finding out my relationship status has failed. I sigh. "I'm single. No boyfriend. Or girlfriend."

"Right." He says with a curt nod, unaffected.

"But I am bi."

"Oh. Cool."

Okayyy. This is awkward.

This must be the world's longest elevator ride. The silence between us stretches out louder than ever.

"She's sick." The words spill from me. "My mom. She has cancer."

What the hell are you doing?

He turns towards me, his eyes soft, and traces his palm along his stomach, smoothing his shirt down.

"I'm sorry," he says, and *God* why do those words always

sound so perfect coming from his lips?

The words keep coming. "It's been on and off for a while. She was in remission, but...it came back. And it's worse now. She pretends to be fine, but I know she feels like shit, and I feel like shit because all I do is work trying to afford all our bills, but I never get to see her because of it and..."

I take a deep breath, stopping myself. When I look over at Wesley, he's frowning at my words. I've gone and upset him again, talking about work. I've already said way too much today.

"Sorry. I didn't mean..." I trail off.

Mercifully, the elevator finally stops in the lobby and the doors open. Wesley steps back and gestures for me to go ahead.

"My driver, Pete, is picking us up," he says and before I can respond, his hand is resting on my lower back, guiding me forward.

I have to purse my lips to stop the sound — no, moan — that threatens to escape from my lips. There is no earthly explanation for why my body should be reacting so much to his touch, but here I am. Goosebumps gather on my arms and warmth pools in my stomach. I manage to keep my cool the entire walk out to the sidewalk and thankfully, when we step outside, Wesley removes his hand and walks towards a black town car with a tall Black man standing out front.

Wesley clasps the man's hand into his, shaking it firmly.

"Quinn, this is my driver, Peter. Everyone calls him Pete."

I step forward and shake his hand.

"Nice to meet you, sir."

Pete clasps mine, an easy grin spreading across his face.

"Sir?" He raises his eyebrows. "Oh, I like you. Nobody calls me Sir. Probably for good reason. Just Pete is fine." He nudges me a little with an easy smile.

"Sorry, force of habit. Nice to meet you, Pete," I repeat.

He turns to Wesley with a smirk. "Does she call you Sir, too, boss?"

Wesley looks at me, his eyes darkening.

"No," he says as Pete opens the door and gestures for me to slide in. As I duck my head, I swear I hear Wesley's soft voice mutter. "Not yet."

* * *

When we get to the diner, Wesley is greeted by half the kitchen staff and given his "favorite corner booth."

He's the opposite of everything I expected. Casual clothes, local diner. I hate to think that perhaps I judged him as harshly as he judged me, but it seems we are both proving each other wrong today.

I pick up the menu to study it. The waitress comes by and we both order coffees. She brings them over and we order our food. Now it's just Wesley and me.

"So, I guess you come here a lot?" I ask, glancing up at him. How can someone look so good drinking diner coffee?

He smiles lightly. "My niece, Luna, likes it here. We come by at least once a month."

"That's sweet," I say. "How old is she?"

"Almost six. She's a firecracker, that's for sure. My brother definitely has his hands full with her." He smiles absently again, then reaches for his pocket, glancing at his phone. "Speak of the devil. Excuse me."

He picks up his phone and slides out of the booth, walking towards the exit. I study the checkered print of the table with a slow blink. Closing my eyes, I take a few measured breaths.

Don't freak out. Just be normal.

Wesley returns to the table, sliding back across from me with a scowl on his face. He looks more like himself.

"Bad news. My niece—"

"Luna." I interrupt with a small smile.

"Yeah, Luna." The corner of his mouth tugs slightly upwards and I almost leap for joy. "There's a lice case in her class so they're sending everyone home. Ben needs me to pick her up because he's in court."

"Is he a lawyer?" I interrupt again and Wesley flickers his eyes towards me. I'm annoying him. I can tell.

"Yes," Wesley answers, his words controlled. "I know I said I'd buy you breakfast, but..."

"Oh. No, of course. It's totally fine. I can just get the train from here." I start reaching for my bag, ready to get out of his way.

"Do you have somewhere to be?" Wesley asks, his scowl fading into a soft interest as he looks at me.

"Not until this afternoon," I reply. I don't let myself think about saying goodbye to Sheila in only a few hours.

Wesley looks thoughtful for a moment before he speaks. "Would you like to come with me? I can't promise it will be very much fun, but I'm sure Luna will keep us busy." His eyebrows lift as his offer hangs in the air.

Spend the day with Wesley and his niece? Did I wake up in an alternate reality?

"Okay," I say. "Sure."

And there it is again. That smile. It breaks free from his hard face and fills my stomach with butterflies. It doesn't last long — only a few seconds — but this time I really soak it in. I try to memorize every minute detail of how beautiful he looks. I'm not sure how long this Wesley will last, the one who gives smiles away freely, like they cost nothing at all, and I need to savor all of it while it lasts.

Chapter 24

Wesley

"Uncle Wes! Uncle Wes!" Luna comes bounding into my arms as soon as she sees me walking towards the student pick-up area. Quinn trails behind me, twisting her hands in front of her. I turn back towards her with an apologetic smile, knowing that the rest of the day will likely be overshadowed by Luna and her many demands.

"Hi, Loon." I lean down to hug her, but don't lift her up, and she looks up at me with her face twisted into a scowl that reminds me of my brother. "This is my friend, Quinn. She's going to hang out with us today."

"Hi." Quinn steps forward and waves at Luna. "Nice to meet you, Luna."

Luna blinks up at her. "You're pretty," she says. "Are you my uncle's girlfriend?"

Quinn's eyes widen and her gaze flickers towards me. "No, no. We're just friends."

"Uncle Wes doesn't ever have a girlfriend. He's alone every time I come over," she announces.

I suppress a groan as Quinn smirks from beside me.

"Thanks for that, Loon. You don't have lice, do you?" I pull her backwards, peeling her hair to the side to inspect her scalp, and she pushes me off.

"No. They checked all of us before we left. Maggie is the one with lice and I don't like playing with her because she licks all the toys," Luna says.

"Alright. Let me just check in with your teacher before we go. I'll be right back." I leave Luna with Quinn and jog over to Ms. Hanson. She confirms that Luna is in the clear and gives me her phone number on a slip of paper in case anything changes. When I get back over to Quinn and Luna, they are playing one of the hand-clapping games that Luna loves.

"Quinn said we can go to the carnival!" Luna shouts, jumping up and down.

I quirk my eyebrow at Quinn, and she chuckles. "I said we'd ask you," she corrects.

"Carnival?" I ask.

"She just means Coney Island. I mentioned I used to go there a lot when I was a kid. My fault for bringing it up." Quinn tucks her hair behind her ear, looking apologetic.

"We can go." I shrug. "Nothing else to do, really."

Luna squeals in delight, jumping up and down with even more fervor. I push her forward towards where Pete waits for us and sneak a small smile at Quinn.

"What's that?" She asks, pointing to the small piece of paper pinched between my fingers. I'd forgotten I was holding it.

"Oh. Ms. Hanson gave me her number in case I need it. For Luna," I say.

Quinn nods and hums, hiding a small smile as she glances away, her lips flat.

"What?" I ask. Luna runs ahead to greet Pete, who gets her car seat set up and starts strapping her in.

Quinn shakes her head, brushing me off. "Come on. What?" I ask again, stopping her before she gets to the car.

"She gave you her number, Wesley. I doubt she does that with all the parents. Or Uncles." Quinn's eyes sparkle knowingly as she looks up at me with a soft smile.

She's trying to say that she was flirting with you, dumbass.

"Right," I say. "It's been a while. I've kind of forgotten how to flirt, to be honest."

Quinn makes a face like she doesn't quite believe me, and Luna starts letting out short, loud screams. We all climb into the car and it's a tight squeeze. I can feel Quinn's arm brushing against mine. It's soft. I imagine running the back of my hand up and down it, watching the goosebumps form along her skin.

This is your employee!

I try to lean away from where our arms are touching, but the car suddenly feels incredibly small. I inhale a breath, but instead of steadying me, I'm suddenly filled with the scent of her, a floral, sweet smell. How good would it feel to be surrounded by it? By her?

"Carnival! Carnival!" Luna chants, breaking me out of my reverie.

For the rest of the car ride, Quinn asks Luna questions about school and her life. Each time, Quinn listens thoughtfully, giving Luna her undivided attention. I spend most of the ride on my phone, sending emails and moving today's meetings, trying to distract myself from my growing attraction to Quinn.

When we get to Coney Island, it's somewhat empty, which makes sense since it's almost noon on a weekday.

"It's nice today," Quinn remarks, looking around. She's right. The sky is the clearest of blues, with only a soft chill in the air. It's a perfect spring day, the winter almost entirely behind us. I'm stuck staring at her and the way her eyes look over everything in wonder.

"Do you come here a lot?" I ask.

"When I was a kid. I used to ride the train and hangout here all day." Her eyes crinkle a little and she glances away, clearing her throat.

"Can we get cotton candy?" Luna interrupts, jumping up and down and giving me her best puppy dog eyes.

"Real food first. Hot dogs?"

"Fine." She crosses her arm and grabs my hand, dragging us towards Nathan's. I order three hot dogs, and we wait off to the side while Luna lists off everything she wants to do today. We get our food and walk down the boardwalk, sitting at an empty table.

"You're sweet with her."

I glance over and Quinn is watching me wipe a glob ketchup from Luna's shirt. She's wearing her signature soft smile that I never want to disappear from her face.

"Thanks," I say, rubbing the back of my neck. "Are you close with your family? Besides your mother."

Her smile fades as she glances away, her face clouding over again with that ghostly look in her eyes.

"Not really." She shrugs. "It's just me and mom. And Sheila, my neighbor. She's actually moving today. She's lived across the hall from us since...forever."

"I'm sorry. That must be difficult, her moving away."

She shrugs, her shoulders falling lower than usual. I never noticed it before, the way she forces the soft smile to stay on her face. Like there's a light in her eyes that refuses to dim.

She opens her mouth as if to say something, then stops herself, avoiding my gaze.

I clear my throat. "I was never very close with my parents. My father worked a lot. I'm close with my mom and Ben now but not my dad. We haven't talked in a while. Last time we did, we got in a huge fight, and I just shut down."

I blink a few times, trying not to falter under her gaze. She reaches out and puts her hand over mine, warm and heavy. I can't seem to focus on anything but the feeling of her skin on mine.

For some reason, I keep going. "I'm just angry at myself for not knowing what was going on with him...with the company, the dangerous direction it was headed in. I felt like an idiot."

The moments following my confession are painfully silent. Quinn seems to know that I can't look at her, because she looks away from me and down to where our hands are linked together in my lap.

"My dad left us when I was a kid. I don't really remember him that much. I can't tell if that's better or worse. It's kind of like I never had him at all, but at the same time, I have these glimpses. Like an idea of him, but never the real thing."

"Have you ever thought of looking for him?" I ask.

She shakes her head. "I figure he doesn't want to be found. I don't need him. Mom is enough. She always has been," she says in a wistful tone.

It's quiet for a moment and I'm hit again with that pang, that overwhelming urge to reach out and wrap my arms around her.

"All done!" Luna shouts from next to us, her mouth stuffed with food. I blink. I'd basically forgotten she was here. I look back at Quinn and she seems to be thinking the same thing. She covers her mouth with the back of her hand, hiding a smile. "Can we get cotton candy now, Uncle Wes?" Luna pleads.

I take one last bite of my hot dog and toss it into the

nearby trash can. "Yes, you've been very patient." I glance over at Quinn. "And silent."

She laughs outright this time and it's almost angelic, the way the sound travels all the way through me.

"Cotton candy. Then the roller coaster. Then ice cream," Luna lists off.

"Cotton candy *or* ice cream, Loon. Not both," I remind her, shaking my head.

"How am I supposed to choose? Shit!" She cries.

"Luna!" I use my best chastising tone. "Where did you hear that word?"

"From daddy. He says it when he drops things."

Quinn giggles from next to me and I can't help but groan at this little devil in front of me. I shake my head but shrug. "Well, don't say it again or you'll owe me a nickel."

"What's a nickel?"

"A coin. For the swear jar. If you say bad words, you have to pay up. Those are the rules."

"Are you playing too? And your girlfriend?"

"You bet."

Quinn makes a sound from next to me and I glance at her, where a blush is blooming on her cheeks. A strand of hair has fallen in front of her face and I want to reach out and tuck it behind her ear.

"Should I get ice cream or cotton candy?" Luna asks Quinn.

"Definitely cotton candy. You can get ice cream anytime," Quinn answers with a small smirk. Luna nods, considering her answer thoughtfully.

"Okay! I want the cotton candy. But Ferris wheel first!" Luna announces, grabbing my hand and pulling us towards the ride.

"I hope you aren't scared of heights." Quinn raises her eyebrows.

"Terrified. But I think I'll survive." I give our tickets to the snot-nosed kid working the ride and usher the girls inside, stepping in behind them. "You do realize I live on the 50th floor, right?"

"How could I forget?" She rolls her eyes. "You always have to be on top."

Her words go straight to my dick. Jesus Christ, woman. She glances away as the ride starts, completely oblivious to her effect on me.

"We're moving! We're moving!" Luna cheers.

"Yes, we see that, sweetheart." I smile conspiratorially at Quinn. We're close to the top and she glances around in soft wonder, her hair blowing behind her with the wind.

"Uncle Wes, look! You can see everything from up here!" Luna points around but my eyes are glued to Quinn. I swear if Luna weren't here, I'd reach over and kiss her right now.

Suddenly, the ride jolts and we stop at the top. Of course.

"What's happening?" Luna asks. "We stopped! Uncle Wes!"

"It's okay, they just stop it sometimes."

"I'm scared. I wanna go down," Luna cries, starting to tear up. "I wanna go down now!"

"We'll be down real soon, Luna. I promise." I reach out and console her but she keeps crying, wailing even louder. Her eyes are closed, and her hands are balled into fists as she bounces up and down, shouting.

Quinn reaches out and puts her hand over Luna's. "You know what helps me sometimes when I get scared?"

"What?" Luna sniffles.

"Imagine your happy place. The place where you have

the most fun in the world. Your favorite place in the whole wide world. The place you feel safe."

Luna opens one eye and sniffles again, her tears stopping. "Like Paris? I wanna visit the iPhone Tower."

Quinn chuckles. "The Eiffel Tower? Sure, it could be that. It could be anywhere."

"Or Disneyland. I like Disneyland." Luna says.

The ride jolts, starting again and Luna cheers, but I'm still stuck staring at Quinn, marveling at how effortlessly she handled that. At how warm and comforting her presence feels. At how I can't believe how wrong I was about her. Completely, utterly wrong.

Chapter 25

Quinn

I am on a Ferris wheel with Wesley Marks. Nine words I never thought I would utter in my lifetime. Yet here we are. Wesley has been nothing but a gentleman since I woke up this morning. I feel like I've woken up in an alternate dimension, one where Wesley and I eat hot dogs and share intimate details about our families.

Wesley doesn't seem at all terrified by this development. In fact, he's happy as a clam. Besides Luna's occasional outburst or tantrum, the day has gone smoothly, and Wesley has been close to outright smiling at least four times that I've counted. Every time one dances across his lips, even the slightest suggestion of a smile, I feel like I've won some grand prize.

It's the way his lips tug upward and his white teeth break through his soft lips. I've been trying not to stare at them for this entire ride. Thankfully, it's almost over and I'll have other distractions from Wesley's perfect lips. Like his sculpted torso and his sharp, piercing eyes.

Get it together!

We stop at the bottom and Wesley lifts Luna to climb out.

My face feels warm despite the cool air. I go to climb out after them and Wesley holds his hand out for me to hold on to. Reluctantly, I grab his hand and clammer down the stairs in the least graceful manner possible. Wesley at least doesn't seem to notice — he's busy holding Luna back with his other hand.

I lose my footing on the last step and stumble forward, almost bumping directly into him.

"Sorry." I push myself backwards.

"Are you okay?" He braces his hands on either side of me. More heat rises to my face. "You look flushed," he observes.

Thanks, Captain Obvious! What's next, I have blue eyes?

"I'm fine." I tangle myself away from him and skip towards Luna.

"What do you think? Cotton candy time?" I smile down at her, avoiding Wesley's gaze for fear it will turn me into jelly again.

"Luna, did you know that Quinn is a chef? She could probably make you whatever you wanted," Wesley says, a mischievous smirk playing on his lips.

I roll my eyes. "I'm not a chef."

"Can you make chicken nuggets?" Luna peers up at me.

I chuckle. "Yes, I can make chicken nuggets."

"See." Wesley nudges me. "Chef."

I nudge him back. "I seem to remember a certain someone telling me my cooking was *fine.*"

Wesley gasps in mock horror. "Who would say such a thing?"

"Just this jerk I know."

Wesley barks out a laugh and I try to stamp out the pleased expression on my face at having made him laugh.

"You're right. I was being a jerk." He shrugs. "And I lied.

Your cooking is much better than fine, but I think you know that. At least I hope you do."

His earnestness catches me off guard, but before I have a chance to respond, he's bringing Luna over to the cotton-candy stand and buying her a pink cone. I grab a spot at a nearby table and check my phone. My stomach drops. A missed call from Pierre.

To be fair, Wesley did say that he would call me. Is he going to offer me my old job back? Do I even want that job?

It's not like I'm thriving in my current role. I would at least be closer to the restaurant environment. But still...it doesn't feel right. Sure, I'd love to see Manny again, but after how quickly they threw me out last time, I don't really want anything to do with Pierre or that place.

"I wasn't sure if you wanted some, so, here you go." Wesley stands in front of me holding a blue cotton candy. He raises his eyebrows. "I hope you like pure sugar."

"What's not to like?"

He sits down next to me, placing Luna between us this time.

"What's next?" I ask.

"I want a big teddy bear. You have to win me the big one, Uncle Wes," Luna says, pointing to a shooting game with large stuffed animals hanging all around it.

"Yes, we can get the big bear," Wes agrees and rips off a piece of my cotton candy.

"You're awfully confident in your ability to get the big bear, Wesley."

He stands and pops the cotton candy into his mouth. "What can I say?" He shrugs. "I know how to shoot."

I stand up, raising my chin. "Let's see it then, Eastwood."

"Big bear! Big bear!" Luna chants.

Luna and I stand off to the side as Wesley prepares to

shoot. He glances over at me and starts whistling the tune from *The Good, the Bad, and the Ugly*. I roll my eyes.

This really shouldn't be sexy. It's just a carnival game. It's silly, really. Ridiculous.

Except for what happens next. Wesley looks right at me as he lifts his arm over his head to stretch. His shirt slowly rides up, revealing his lower torso and— oh my god.

It's the V. The dreaded V.

I bite down on the cotton candy, my throat unbelievably dry.

"Watch and learn," Wesley says, yanking the gun out like we're in an old western movie and shooting the bottles. He knocks them out like it's the easiest thing in the entire world, then twirls the gun and pretends to holster it. He's smirking the whole time.

This display of masculinity should bother me, but it doesn't. Desire pools deep in my stomach. Just when I'm thinking he can't get any more ridiculous, he locks eyes with me and winks. He *winks*.

"I'll take the big bear, please," he says to the ticket guy, who reaches out and unclips the pink one, handing it to Wesley.

Luna jumps up and down, reaching for it.

"What do you say, Loon?"

"Thank you, Uncle Wes!" Luna shouts, reaching for the bear. He hands it to her and ruffles her hair as she hugs it tightly. He looks over at me.

"You want one?"

I scoff and shake my head.

"I'm serious. I'll win you one." He suppresses a smile, this one familiar. "Babe," he tacks on with a cheeky grin.

"Oh my god, stop it." I shove him a little, but he doesn't move. God, he's hard as stone. He's like a sculpture.

"I'll take another round," Wesley says, handing the man a few more tickets. Before I can stop him, he's shooting again, knocking down every single bottle with ease.

"Show off," I mutter and Wesley smirks as he points to another big bear. I stop him. "No! I want that one." I point to a smaller stuffed dog.

Wesley quirks an eyebrow at me, and I give him my best pleading puppy eyes.

"Alright, give me the dog."

I try my hardest to stamp out my gleeful expression as we walk away from the stand with our new toys.

"What are you gonna name yours?" Luna asks me. "This is Mr. Thomas." She points to her bear.

I glance at the dog, studying it. "I don't know. What do you think I should name him?" I ask Luna.

"Wes! Like Uncle Wes!" Luna shouts.

I chuckle. "I don't think so."

"Hey! Why not?" Wesley nudges me. "I won it for you. You should name it after me."

"Name my stuffed dog Wesley?"

His gaze turns serious. "No, not Wesley. Wes. You should call me Wes."

I swallow a little too hard.

"I think you should call him Grumpy," Luna announces.

"Great idea. See, now it's named after you." I smile brightly at Wes, petting Grumpy on the head.

* * *

Ben calls after a few hours and says he can come and pick up Luna, so we go down to the beach and wait for him to arrive. We sit in the sand, Luna hardly able to stay still.

I excuse myself to run to the bathroom. Unfortunately,

there's a pretty long line and by the time I return to our spot on the beach, there's nobody there. I glance around the beach. Maybe I'm in the wrong place?

They wouldn't have just left, right? Wesley...he wouldn't do that, would he?

I guess I can just take the train home. It's not that far. And then...what? See Wesley at work? I don't even know where we stand. Did he seriously just leave me here?

"Hey."

I turn and let out a quick breath of relief at the sight of Wes illuminated in the golden light of the afternoon.

"Sorry. Ben was in a rush. I just brought her up to the parking lot. She was pretty upset she couldn't say goodbye to you, but I promised you'd see each other again."

"I thought..." I trail off, looking at him.

"You didn't think I left, did you?"

"No. I don't know. I wasn't really sure."

"I wouldn't do that," he says, his voice warm and firm. "I wouldn't have just left without saying goodbye."

I nod, suddenly feeling very aware that we are alone. No more Luna between us. I have to break eye contact to avoid this intensity rising within me, so I turn towards the water, inhaling.

I close my eyes, smelling in the salty air. It's perfectly crisp as a breeze rustles across the crashing water. I'm trying to keep my hair from flying to no avail when Wesley steps up next to me, his arm too close to mine. I can feel the warmth radiating off his skin.

"Beautiful," he says the word so softly I almost don't hear it over the sound of the wind against my ears.

"Isn't it?" I turn to him now, and his eyes are focused on me. He's not looking at the beach in front of us and I suddenly get the feeling that he wasn't talking about the landscape. I shift under the weight of his gaze.

"I should probably get going," I say reluctantly. Wesley looks at me for a second longer like he might say something else, but then he nods and turns, walking ahead of me. When we get to the parking lot, he stops in front of a Tesla and opens the passenger door.

"What are you doing?" I ask, my eyes wide.

He raises his eyebrows. "Giving you a ride home?"

"Where did that thing come from?" I point to the shiny black Tesla.

"It's mine," he says simply.

"Oh-kay." My mind is moving slowly. "How did it get here? Why did it get here?"

"I asked Pete to drop it off for me because I felt like driving home. Are you satisfied yet or should we continue the interrogation inside the car?"

I roll my eyes and slip into the front seat. He shuts the door behind me and goes around to the driver's seat, sliding into the car.

"Of course it's a Tesla," I mutter.

"What's wrong with a Tesla?" Wesley asks, fiddling with the touch screen in between us.

I roll my eyes. "It's like, the ultimate rich person car."

"It's good for the environment," he replies. "What's your address?"

I tell him and he pulls out of the parking lot, his hand gripping the steering wheel. His very large hand. It suddenly feels very warm in here. Cramped. I stare down at my hands in my lap.

Don't look at Wesley driving. Don't think about Wesley's hands. Think about his stupid Tesla and the likelihood that he evades taxes.

"So, you've always lived in Sunset Park?" Wesley asks, filling the silence in the car.

"It's technically South Slope, but yes." I correct him.

"Oh, right. Do you like it?"

I shrug. "Yeah. I guess I do. Not much to compare it to, really."

It's quiet again.

I'm suddenly aware of how weird this is. Wesley and me being friends. Like, the whole concept of it is ridiculous. We're from completely different worlds.

"I live in Dumbo, actually. Normally, I mean. Before I moved into the hotel for work," he says, shocking me. "Sometimes I go into your area to get stuff from the Japanese market."

"Wow," I say. "I was not expecting that. Is your apartment nice? Is it bigger than the penthouse?" Then I shake my head. "No. No way."

The corners of his lips tug upward, but he still doesn't break. "Yes, it's nice. It's smaller than the penthouse, but I like it."

He pauses for a moment.

"You should come see it sometime."

My stomach flutters with the thought. I don't know why I should be so nervous about the prospect — it's not like I haven't seen his bedroom at the hotel or been in close quarters with him. For some reason, though, this offer feels more...intimate.

"Sure," I manage to squeak out.

He connects his phone to the Bluetooth and asks me about what kind of music I like. We spend a few minutes bickering back and forth about what constitutes classic rock before he finally puts on Tame Impala and we sit quietly, humming along. He gives me his phone to queue up some songs and as I swipe through his Spotify, I'm struck again by how different Wesley is than what I thought.

"Arctic Monkeys? Soccer Mommy?" I try to hide my shock. "I can't believe you listen to like, indie rock and sad girl shit."

He shrugs. "I'm not *that* old. Also, my friend Jake works at Atlantic Records and he's always sending me new artists and playlists."

Dammit. He's supposed to be stuffy and fancy and uptight. He's supposed to eat caviar and listen to Chopin. Instead, he likes hot dogs and listens to some of my favorite bands. This is not good.

We get to my apartment and Wesley pulls over. I gather my bag in my hands and brace myself.

"Well. Thanks for inviting me." I glance away from Wesley. "Luna is really sweet."

"Yeah, she's pretty cute."

Why does it suddenly feel so heavy in here? The weight of my goodbye is pressing against my head.

"I guess I'll see you tomorrow," I say.

"Yeah?" He runs his hand through his hair like he does when he's nervous. I recognize the move by now. "I'd understand if you wanted to quit. I won't be upset or anything."

"Why would I do that?" I grab the door handle. "Bye."

I push open the door and sprint up the steps towards my building, not looking back. I close the door behind me and duck into the window, wave, and turn on my heels to run up the stairs to my apartment, not looking back.

* * *

"I don't want you to go."

I'm pouting. Like a child. I feel about ten years old gripping Sheila's arms and hugging her against me like I'll never let go. She rubs my back.

"I know, baby. But it's time." She steps back from my hug and watches as her son, Darius, picks up the last of her boxes and loads it into the U-Haul. "I'll be back to visit soon. You won't even notice I'm gone, you're gonna be so busy."

I push down the tears threatening to spill over. I will not cry. I will not cry.

My mother comes behind me and puts her arm around me.

"I'll still cut coupons for you. We'll just keep them in a drawer in case you come back," my mom jokes.

A choked sob escapes me, and I try to turn away from both of them, but they wrap me in their arms once more. We hug for a few minutes before Darius calls down to Sheila that they have to get going.

Sheila steps back again and gives me a warm smile, cupping my arm.

"Don't cry now, baby. Good things are coming. You just have to have faith."

She slips something into my hand, squeezes it, and turns to meet Darius as he helps her into the truck. I look down at my hand and it's a rosary. She hasn't given me one since I was a child. My mom told me that the first time Sheila met me, when I was a baby, she had rosary beads in her hands. I took them and just sucked on the beads and never let go.

I look up just in time to watch Darius pull away from the curb and Sheila press her hand to the passenger window and wave, a smile on her face.

My mom's hand comes around my shoulder again and I clutch the rosary beads. Too much has happened today. I feel out of control — like my emotions are all over the place. I feel happy and sad and hopeful and angry and most of all, confused.

"Let's go in. Looks like rain," my mom says, squeezing my shoulder.

I don't know what comes over me then, but I grab her arm and don't let go.

"You're gonna be okay. You have to be okay."

"Of course, sweetheart. I'm going to be fine."

"You can't die. You can't leave me. Do you understand?" I grip her arm even tighter. "You can't."

Her eyes soften and she puts her hand over mine.

"Oh, Quinn," she says. "Let's go inside."

She takes my hand, leading me up the stairs to our apartment. As I pass by Sheila's door, I glance towards it, trying to imagine someone else moving in.

When we get inside, I go straight to my bed. Curling on my side, I lay my head against the pillow, squeezing my eyes shut.

Chapter 26

Quinn

I wake up with a pounding headache. The last thing I want to do is get on the train to Midtown, but I do. On the way, I pop a few Advil and try not to think about the gaping hole that Sheila's departure has opened up in my chest.

Why should it affect me like this? My mom is fine — well, except that I woke up in the night and heard her throwing up. I knocked on the bathroom door to ask if she was okay and she told me to go away. The hurt from that comment lodged itself right inside the existing Sheila-shaped hole.

I know things are bad because I'm not even worried about seeing Wesley. Not really. I may have ran away from his car faster than necessary, but at least things have simmered out between us. Sometime in between fleeing from his Tesla and getting onto the train this morning, I realized that it's stupid of us to try and be friends. We're too different.

I'm not going to take my old job at The Phoenix, but I am going to ask for a raise. I figure Wesley probably still feels bad enough about the whole false accusation thing that he'll agree to whatever number I ask for. Then we can go back to our normal relationship. Boss and employee. Cordial, but distanced. Friendly, with clear boundaries.

Part of me feels bad demanding such a high number for being a glorified maid, thinking of the other employees who don't have the weird leverage over the boss that I do. Is it wrong of me to make more than them?

Then I remember the whopping pile of medical bills and the fact that I woke up to another missed call from Miss Perky about my overdue balance and this being her final warning and on and on and on. So, I'm not feeling that guilty. Mostly just desperate.

I get off the train and go up the stairs to the street when my phone rings with an unknown number. I pick it up.

"Miss Taylor?"

"Yes, who's this?" I press the phone to my ear, shifting my bag over my shoulder.

"It's Hannah, from the hospital."

Dammit. As if this day could get any worse. I somehow summoned Perky just by thinking about my bills. She's like Beetlejuice but more powerful. You don't even have to say her name.

"I'm so glad I caught you. I keep getting your voicemail. I take it you've gotten my messages?"

"Maybe. One or two."

"Great, so you're aware that today I'm officially turning your bills over to a collections agency," she says the words with no emotions, like they aren't going to tear my life apart.

"Yeah. I think I heard that part," I grumble.

"And you're aware that failure to pay within the next six months could result in a potential lien on your assets and properties?"

Joke's on you, Perky! It's a renter's economy. I don't own anything.

"Yes." I'm hissing the word out now.

"I'm so sorry to be the bearer of bad news. You'll be hearing from the agency. Best of luck."

"Thanks. Bye."

I'm standing outside the hotel when I hang up my phone and stuff it into my back pocket, furious. I toss my head back, look up at the sky, and sigh, blinking back tears. I must be PMSing the way I feel like crying at every little thing lately.

What's next, universe?

"Hey."

I'd recognize his deep, soothing voice anywhere, but we're right outside the hotel, so it's no surprise when I turn and see Wesley standing in front of me.

I blink, making sure there's no tears left in my eyes. "Morning. You heading in or out?" I gesture towards the revolving doors.

"Out, actually. I have a meeting downtown," he furrows his brow, staring down at me.

"Cool. See you later." I start moving away from him towards the building.

"Yeah," he mumbles, then turns and reaches out to stop me. "Wait. Did you say goodbye to Sheila?"

My stomach flutters at the physical contact of his hand on my arm, steadying me.

"Yeah. I did." I shrug him off and force a wry smile. "It sucked."

He frowns. "Do you want to talk about it? I can cancel my meeting."

"No, no. Don't do that. It's fine."

He nods, still frowning, but I don't stick around for the rest of his reaction. "I'll see you later."

I rush inside to find Marguerite and apologize for missing so many days. When I finally do, she's not pissed at all, but I have to go see Sharon, too. I spend most of the morning making up fake excuses about my illness until I'm finally upstairs gathering Wesley's laundry.

I print out this week's menu and leave it on Wesley's desk while I wait for the dryer cycle to finish. After that, I scrub down the tub and the bathroom, and clean the kitchen. By the time I finish all that, the laundry is done, so I replace all the bedding and put all the clothes away.

I'm just about to get started on vacuuming when Wesley gets back. He slings his briefcase onto the kitchen counter and pours himself a glass of water.

"Hey," I say to his back. I'm holding the vacuum awkwardly beside me because I don't really want to start it while he's in the room. "How was your meeting?"

He turns and meets my gaze and that feeling bubbles up inside me again. My eyes flicker down to his lips.

"It was good, actually. Thanks for asking." He sets the glass down in front of him. He looks like he's about to speak again when my phone buzzes loudly from the counter. I go over and see Pierre's name flashing on the screen and I quickly silence it.

"Aren't you going to answer that?" Wesley asks. He's staring down at my phone.

"No."

"Why not?"

"Why do you care?" I shoot back.

He looks taken-aback by my animosity. I know I'm being rude. He can probably see the storm clouds building above my head or the steam coming out of my ears.

"I'm curious."

"I'm not answering. I'm not interested in whatever he has to say. Or getting my old job back." I huff out a breath. "Satisfied? Can I get back to work now?"

Wesley just lets a lazy smile spread across his face. He looks almost relieved. He rubs the back of his neck. "It smells nice in here. I like the candles you got."

"Oh. Thanks. They're from my friend's company."

Wesley nods. "Did you want to talk still? About Sheila?"

I don't think I can handle another minute of his presence, so I shake my head quickly. "I should probably finish up here."

He stares at me, something unreadable in his expression. Then he nods sharply. "I'll be in my office if you need anything."

He picks up his briefcase and disappears down the hallway towards his office. I sit down on the couch with a heavy sigh. Things are irreversibly awkward between us. It was almost better when we were fighting. At least I knew where I stood. Now I feel like I'm walking along a balancing beam, just waiting to tip one way or the other.

I'm tired of pretending. Pretending that I'm okay. Pretending that I'm not terrified about my mom and missing Sheila and drowning under the crushing weight of being a broke adult woman. Pretending I'm not attracted to Wesley.

I close my eyes, trying to shake off my thoughts. Unfortunately, my brain is still thinking about yesterday. His boyish smile. His casual charm and disarming kindness.

Yeah. I've got it bad. But what can I do about it? What's a casual way to tell your former enemy turned boss turned friend that you want to jump his bones?

What if...what if I disassociate? My flush of desire sizzles out quickly before I can hold onto it, before I can let myself truly *want.* Even in my fantasies, reality finds a way back in.

What if sex is all he's ever going to be interested in with me? Nobody has ever really wanted anything else from me, but Wesley said he wants to be friends. The idea sends a jolt to my heart, a spot in my chest that seems to be aching with a constant longing lately.

A longing for...more.

* * *

I'm just about to get started on dinner when Wesley emerges from his office, rubbing his eyes. He comes into the kitchen.

"Fair warning. My mother is on the way here with about ten pounds of yarn."

I give him a confused look and he puts on his signature smirk.

"She's learning to knit."

"That's great!" I turn back towards the task at hand. I'm preparing lobster that I got delivered from a specialty market. "I actually knit hats and scarves sometimes in the winter."

"Oh god. Don't tell her that or she'll never leave me alone about you."

I stiffen at Wesley's words, and he seems to realize what he's said, because he chuckles softly.

"I just meant that she likes you a lot. Probably more than me."

That sentence should not make me smile as much as it is. I flatten my mouth, hoping Wesley can't see how pleased I am. For some reason, Lillian's approval feels important.

"Do you mind if I work out here while I wait for her?" Wesley asks.

"As long as you don't mind the smell." I lift up one of the lobster tails and he crinkles his nose and shrugs, opening his laptop. I finish cutting all the ingredients and wash my hands. The sound of Wesley typing rapidly is making me anxious, so I grab my phone to turn on some music.

"Will it bother you if I play some music? I can put on headphones."

"As long as it's not Metallica," he grins at me.

"Not this time."

That earns a chuckle, and my pleased expression only grows. I turn on a jazz cooking playlist and take the baked potatoes out of the oven. A few minutes pass before I hear the *ding!* of the elevator doors and hear some familiar heels clacking across the floor.

"Darling!" Lillian's voice rings out and I turn to see Wesley slide off the kitchen stool, but she's beelining towards me with her arms open. "It's been too long."

"Nice to see you too, Mom," Wesley mutters.

"Oh, hush. I see you nearly every day it feels like." She releases me and goes over to Wesley, kissing him on one cheek and patting the other. "It smells incredible, Quinn. No surprise there."

I try to hide my blush and growing smile.

"Will you be joining us tonight?" Lillian asks. I make eye contact with Wesley, searching his face for some hint of disapproval, but his blank expression is unreadable.

"Not tonight, sorry. My mom is waiting for me," I say, hoping she won't insist again.

She nods and pulls out her knitting gear, sitting at the head of the dining room table. Her blob of fabric doesn't really look like anything, but I have to give her credit for trying something new.

"How is your mom?" Wesley asks.

I swallow. "She's fine. The same mostly." I finish plating the lobster to avoid his gaze. Maybe he can sense that the topic upsets me because he doesn't say anything else.

"You know, I knit hats and scarves. I could show you how if you wanted one day," I offer, changing the subject.

Lillian beams. "That would be wonderful. As you can see, I'm terrible at it."

"You're not terrible, Mom." Wesley shakes his head and closes his laptop. "You're learning."

She rolls her eyes and holds up the shapeless blob of yarn, eyebrows raised. Wesley chuckles a little and I hide a smile. I bring the lobsters, garlic butter, and potatoes to the table and Wesley sits down next to his mother.

"Is there anything else you need before I head out?" I ask.

"No. It looks perfect." Wesley meets my eyes. "Thank you, Quinn."

He really should not say my name. We hold eye contact for a beat longer than normal and Lillian clears her throat.

"Will you be here tomorrow, Quinn?"

"All day."

"Great. I'll come for lunch, and you can help me with this mess." She shoves the knitting back into her bag.

"Alright. See you guys tomorrow." I wave and head towards the elevator. As the doors slide open, I sneak a glance back towards the table. Wesley's dark eyes meet mine across the room and as I step into the elevator, I swear I can still feel his hot gaze on me, filling me up with a terrifying and wonderful warmth.

Chapter 27

Wesley

It's been two weeks since our trip to Coney Island and I've almost forgotten what life was like before Quinn. It's hard to imagine ordering takeout sushi instead of eating her specialty rolls or coming home to an apartment that doesn't smell like the inside of a candle store. It's strange how quickly I've gotten used to her presence in my life.

My mother comes over constantly. It's no surprise that she spends the entire time hanging out with Quinn. Luna is also infatuated with her. Last week when I picked her up from school, she spent the entire ride asking me questions about Quinn, mainly about why she isn't my girlfriend.

I'm forcing myself to accept that Quinn and I won't ever be anything more than friends. The reality is that she just doesn't see me that way. Why would she after all the shit I put her through? I'm grateful she's forgiven me and stuck around despite that, but I'm not stupid enough to ask for anything more.

The only problem is my body doesn't seem to quite get the message. I took a twenty-minute cold shower yesterday.

I've doubled my gym routine and I still can't seem to stop thinking about her. She's *everywhere.*

It's Saturday, so I'm waiting for Ben near Sheepshead Meadow for our weekly run. I see him jogging towards me and he waves.

"Let's hope you can keep up with me today," I say, stepping in time with him as we jog towards the running path.

Ben rolls his eyes. "It's not my fault you're going to the gym like eight times a week these days. Some of us have children and wives to deal with."

"Yeah, well some of us have the pent-up sexual frustration of a ninth grader," I grumble.

"Pretty sure that's just you."

I shove Ben and he stumbles a little to the side and keeps in step with me.

"Please, for the love of God, just sleep with her already."

"I'm not going to do that."

"You're ridiculous. Why don't you call one of your ex one-night stands? I'm sure they'd be more than eager for another round with *the* Wesley Marks," Ben teases.

"Because meaningless sex doesn't satisfy me anymore. I'm not 25, dude."

Ben nods, picking up his pace to keep up with me. "Yeah, I know what you mean. Wasn't it easier back before we developed emotional intelligence?"

I slow down. "I really like this girl. I just don't want to fuck it up more than I already have." Ben puts his hand on my shoulder and we both stop.

"Listen, Wes. I know I give you a hard time, but you're a good guy. Quinn wouldn't have stuck around if she didn't think the same. Alright? Just man up and ask her out."

I consider Ben's words. "I'll think about it."

Ben nods, patting my shoulder. "Good. And I'll come by

this week to finally meet the infamous Quinn." He takes off running and I follow him, shaking my head.

* * *

Ben stays true to his word. It's Wednesday night and Quinn is finishing up dinner when he texts me that he's downstairs. I decide to meet him down there and I find him in the lobby.

"This place is ridiculous," he says as I bring him to the private elevator.

"You say that every time you come over." I shake my head. "What's so ridiculous about it?"

"It's like The Plaza on cocaine. It's too much. The next hotel you build should be simpler. Humble, even."

We step into the elevator. "Listen to me. Don't say anything to Quinn, alright? I'll just introduce you guys and we can hang out in my room or somewhere out of her way."

Ben nods, smiling a little too wide. "Sure, sure."

We step out of the elevator into the suite. Quinn's in the kitchen with her headphones in, so I approach her and put my hand on her shoulder. She jumps and pulls her headphones out.

"Sorry!" She lets out a breath. "I thought you left."

"I was just grabbing Ben downstairs. Quinn, this is my brother, Ben. Ben, Quinn." I gesture between them as Ben walks closer with his hand outstretched.

"It's nice to finally meet you, Quinn. I've heard so much about you," Ben says and my head snaps towards him. He's wearing his award-winning smile, the one he uses in court. Asshole.

Quinn shakes his hand, a little dazed. "Wesley talks about me?" She looks over at me, her eyes sparkling. "All bad, I'm sure."

"Just the opposite." Ben drops his hand and glances over at the cutting board. "What are you making here?"

"Oh." She shrugs and waves her hand. "It's a sweet potato and kale faro bowl with pine nuts. Are you hungry?"

"Sure. Looks good." Ben goes over to the fridge and opens it, grabbing a beer.

I turn to Quinn. "I know it's late, but would you like to join us for dinner?"

She opens her mouth and I already know it's to insist that she can't, so I keep going.

"I'm sure Ben would appreciate it." I pause. "And so would I." Pause again. "But I understand if you can't. Or if you want to go home—"

Quinn cuts me off, mercifully. "I can stay. Let me just call my mom and let her know. Can you watch this for a sec?" She points to one of the pots and slips into the hallway with her phone in hand. I glance over at the stovetop, hiding my smile.

"You weren't kidding. You've really got it bad." Ben comes up behind me and hands me a beer. "I haven't seen you so flustered since you asked out Carrie Lincoln in the eighth grade."

"That was a big moment for me."

Ben chuckles. "Is she leaving?"

I take a long swig of my beer. "No, I convinced her to join us for dinner."

Ben grins and settles into the head of the table with his feet propped up. He sets his beer down and rubs his hands together.

"Let the games begin."

* * *

It turns out Ben was speaking literally. As soon as we finish dinner, he somehow convinces both me and Quinn to take tequila shots. Quinn insisted that we do them properly, fishing out some limes from the pantry and grabbing the salt. Three shots later, Ben starts playing music and then has the marvelous idea of playing Charades.

Which is how I'm standing in front of Ben and Quinn trying to pantomime *The Matrix* and failing miserably. Quinn has given up and is simply laughing at my pathetic efforts. Finally, she stops laughing and her eyes light up as she shouts out the answer.

"Wow. Wes, you are truly bad at this." Ben shakes his head and falls onto the couch next to Quinn.

"Hey, she got it eventually." I settle in between them.

"What are we thinking next? Truth or dare?" Ben wiggles his eyebrows at me.

Quinn sits up. "Time for me to go home. The trains are going to be a nightmare." I look over at the clock. It's past midnight. I hadn't realized how much time had passed once we started drinking.

"You're not taking the train. I'm calling you a car."

"Excuse me?" Quinn snaps her head towards me. "I take the train all the time and it's fine."

"I'm sure it is. And I'll be calling you a car."

She scoffs. "You are so..." She throws her hands up like she's frustrated "...bossy!"

Without thinking, I lean towards her. "I'll show you how bossy I can be." My hand wraps around her wrist and her jaw drops.

"Okay, that's my cue." Ben stands suddenly, stumbling a little. "Want to call me one, too?"

Ten minutes later, the three of us stand on the curb

outside the hotel as Ben's cab pulls up. He hugs both me and Quinn.

"Absolutely amazing to meet you, Quinn. I see many more tequila shots in our future."

His car pulls away and it's just the two of us. A heaviness settles in my stomach as I study her.

"Thanks for calling me a cab."

"Oh, now you're thanking me? Hmm." The corner of my mouth quirks up. "Just ten minutes ago you were angry."

"That's not me angry, Wesley."

My name sounds special coming from her lips. It wraps around me and lodges itself in my chest. It must be the tequila clouding my judgement because my hand reaches up and touches the bottom of her hair, pulling at a few strands. She turns at the slight tug and my hand falls quickly at my side.

Her taxi pulls up and she smiles up at me, warm and hazy.

"Thanks for tonight. I had fun. Ben is pretty funny."

"You should see him in court. He's like that but worse." I shake my head with a small chuckle. "Luna's a chip off the old block, for sure."

The taxi honks, and she glances over at the sound, startled.

"Coming!" She starts towards the car and glances back at me. "Goodnight, Wesley."

She's still smiling softly, a twinkle of laughter in her eye. I can't stop thinking about it as she climbs into the back of the cab.

I spend the rest of the night thinking about that smile.

Chapter 28

Quinn

I haven't seen Wesley since dinner with his brother earlier this week. He's hardly been home and the last two dinners have sat on the counter, uneaten. Yesterday I found a note on the counter in his neat handwriting:

New development has me crazy busy - sorry. Don't worry about dinners for the rest of the week.

I tried not to take it personally. Obviously, he's busy with work. He's a busy guy, running his own company and everything. I don't know why his absence makes me insecure — like he'll decide he doesn't need me anymore in the few days since we've last spoken.

Today is my day off and I'm taking mom in for her chemo treatment. Joe is coming with us this time. My mom's been going over to his apartment much more often these days. She insists it's casual, but I know her better than she thinks.

Joe's brother's treatments are finished and he's in remission. He invited mom and I to a celebration at his brother's house in Long Island this weekend. Mom basically begged me to come — I think she's nervous about meeting his family.

When we get to Brooklyn Presbyterian, we go straight to the treatment center. Joe holds my mom's hand the entire time. She doesn't look great. I know that she's trying to stay strong, but it's impossible to ignore the gaunt, hollow shape that her face has taken on or the way she trembles slightly with every step.

On our way upstairs, we run into Miss Perky because of course we do. I swear the woman arranges her workday around how to best annoy me.

"Hey team," she greets us with a wide smile. "How are you feeling today?"

"I'm alright." My mom tries a smile, but it looks weak on her frail face. "This is my boyfriend, Joe."

I keep my face neutral at the B-word that comes out of my mom's mouth. Last time we talked, she told me they were keeping things casual. Now he's her boyfriend? Why wouldn't she tell me that? She'll mention it to freaking Perky before telling me?

Perky and Joe shake hands and we ride up in silence, my thoughts wandering to the stack of bills hiding in our kitchen drawer. I've tried not to let mom see how they're piling up — she doesn't need anything else to worry about — but they're hanging over my head like a guillotine. Perky's current expression of pity reminds me that I'm not the only one thinking about it.

We get to the treatment center and the nurse sets up my

mom at her station while Joe and I sit on the sidelines, unsure what to do with ourselves.

Joe turns to me. "So, Quinn, your mom tells me you've been struggling at work? Bad boss and all?"

"It's gotten a lot better," I say. "I get to cook in his massive kitchen, which is pretty cool."

"Someday I'm sure you'll have a massive kitchen of your own." He smiles, genuine and surprisingly warm. "Your mom told me about your restaurant idea."

"Oh, yeah, it's kind of silly."

Joe blinks, studying me. "Why do you say that?"

"Oh, I don't know." I shift, feeling self-conscious. "I just mean it's kind of a long shot."

He hums a little in response, not agreeing or disagreeing. My mom calls for him so he goes over to her and wraps his hand in hers, leaning his head in close to hers. I watch as she closes her eyes and rests her forehead against his. It's an intimate moment that I find myself looking away from.

I suppress the feeling bubbling within me — a sense of being left out. The third wheel. With Joe here, it almost feels like my mom doesn't really need me. The thought sends a painful jolt through my spine.

I guess for so long it's just been me and mom. Us against the world. It was hard, but we leaned on each other. It's hard to imagine a world in which we find new people to lean on. I'm happy for my mom, I really am. She deserves this more than anyone. I still remember the weeks after my dad left — how she refused to get out of bed. All she could do was cry. Despite my own feelings of loss, I'd been the one to nurse her back to normal, to get her back on her feet.

In all my preparing for the possibility that I might not have my mom, I never prepared for a future in which she makes it out and I still don't have her. One where she doesn't need me anymore. As I watch Joe stroke her hair lovingly, my stomach bottoms out with a childish and cruel jealousy. What happens when she doesn't need me anymore? What happens when nobody — not my mom, not Wesley — really needs me at all?

* * *

I get to the hotel almost twenty minutes late. Sweating and heaving with exhaustion from booking it up the subway steps, I sneak in the back exit, hoping to avoid Sharon. My plan works and I ride up the elevator in near silence, only the sound of my pathetic gasps echoing back to me.

The elevator doors slide open, and I must be so distracted by my lateness that I don't notice Wesley until I get into the kitchen where he stands. Completely shirtless.

If I weren't already gasping for air like a fish out of water, I might have dropped my jaw on the floor. There's no stopping my eyes as they study every inch of his chiseled chest. Like, seriously. Nobody should look like that. It's rude to the rest of us. He looks like a Calvin Klein model. He looks like a Google image result for *toned*.

I finally force my eyes to stop their perusal when I look up and see Wesley's signature smirk out in full force. He quirks an eyebrow at me. "See something you like?"

I step backwards, snapping back to reality. "What? Of course not." I force my eyes anywhere but on his chest. "You — you shouldn't be walking around like that!"

He raises his eyebrows, incredulous. "I live here. I just finished a workout. Besides, you were running around here in that little maid outfit."

"What?" I rear back. "Those were my *uniform!*"

He shrugs and turns back to the smoothie he's blending,

cranking up the noise. I try to shout over the sound, but he points at it, gesturing that he can't hear me. Fuming, I cross past him and flip the blender off.

"Don't walk around like that when I'm here!"

"Well, you weren't here before. Besides, we're friends, right? Can't friends be shirtless in front of each other?"

He reaches his arm around me and turns the blender back on, not even attempting to stamp out his smug expression. I turn around and flip it off again.

"Oh, really?" I challenge. "So, it wouldn't bother you at all if I took my shirt off? If I decided to scrub the kitchen down in just my bra?"

He swallows, his Adam's apple bobbing up and down. He stares down at me, his expression no longer gleeful. "Of course not. Friend." He tacks on the last word, narrowing his eyes.

"Great. Glad we cleared that up." In one swift move, I pull my shirt off, revealing my black bra underneath. I throw the shirt to the side and strut towards the living room. "I'll be cleaning the bathrooms if you need me!"

* * *

It's not long before Wesley finds me in the bathroom with my shirt in his hand. I'm scrubbing the tub and could not look like more of a mess.

"Put this on." He flattens his lips into a thin line and tosses the shirt in my direction. "Please."

I smirk and glance down at the shirt. "I thought friends could be shirtless around friends?" I swear he lets out a small growl as his eyes wander down to my chest. "Unless you're having trouble...focusing?"

His eyes snap back up to meet mine, but he doesn't say anything. We stay silent for a few moments, a stalemate.

"Fine," he snaps. "If I admit that I find you attractive, will you put the damn shirt back on?"

My jaw drops. I did not see that coming. Wesley Marks finds me attractive. I have no idea what to do with this information. Suddenly nervous and realizing I am, in fact, topless, I pull the shirt over my head and straighten it out.

"Good." He turns and strides out of the room, leaving me gaping after him.

I pull my gloves off and pick up my phone, wanting to text someone and get advice on this Wesley situation. Who do I text? My mind wanders to my mom, but I don't want to bother her. Besides, she still thinks I have the boss from hell.

It's times like this when I wish I had a best friend. Someone to confide in and talk about boys with. During college, there were a couple of girls who I went to the bar with occasionally, mostly the other sugar babies I knew, but none of them were really friends. After that, I threw myself into work and hardly had time for anything else.

What would a best friend tell me to do right now? What would I do if this was an episode of *Sex and the City*? Am I more of a Carrie or a Samantha?

My stomach flutters remembering the way Wesley's eyes felt on me — the heat that pooled in my stomach at the intensity of his gaze. Is he feeling what I'm feeling?

No, no way. Wesley Marks doesn't do *feelings*. He might find me slightly attractive but that doesn't mean he'd act on it. Or that he even cares.

But he must care a little. He seemed pretty fired up about the shirt issue. I wonder how he would react if I touched him. If I trailed my fingers up his chest to touch his face. If I bent over and let his large hands spread my legs open.

Jesus.

I take a deep breath, ignoring the heat pooling in my stomach again.

This is ridiculous to even consider. Wesley is my boss and he's *Wesley* for God's sakes. He's not going to sleep with me — the maid. I swallow, feeling suddenly small sitting in his bathroom. I'm not the girl he can have on his arm at some fancy gala. Pathetic and cliché as it is, I'm the pauper, not the princess.

Still, that doesn't mean I can't have some fun in the meantime.

I think it may be time to start testing boundaries. Let's see how far I can push the stone-cold Wesley Marks.

Chapter 29

Wesley

I am going to die.

I swear. If Quinn keeps testing me, I am going to lose it completely. It's like she's *trying* to turn me on.

Two days ago, she wore the tightest jeans I've ever seen. I mean, ever. I didn't even know they made jeans that looked that good.

That would have been fine and mostly avoidable if she didn't somehow keep bending over to retrieve items right in my line of sight. I swear she's never been so clumsy.

Then she showed up yesterday in her maid uniform. The very uniform I told her she didn't need to wear anymore, mostly because it gave me very vivid fantasies. When I asked her why she had the tiny thing on, she shrugged and smiled innocently.

"I like the way it looks."

Yeah, right. It was only then that I had the thought that she was teasing me on purpose. At first, I denied it. After all, there's no way Quinn would do that. Why would she do that?

It wasn't until she left last night that I realized she was trying to get to me. She stood in the doorway of the elevator and pulled her coat over her. I said a quick goodbye, willing her to disappear so I could jack off for the third time, but she pulled out her lipstick and applied it slowly. Seductively. Her eyes on me the entire time.

I woke up today with a plan. If she wants to tease me, I'll tease her right back. After all, I saw the way she gaped at my chest when I was shirtless. She must have some ideas of her own.

That's why I'm currently shirtless doing push-ups in the middle of the penthouse. She'll be in any minute. I'm worried she might catch on to my obvious plan. After all, I usually go to the gym to work out and I have my runs with Ben. It's not like me at all to lift weights in the living room, but desperate times call for desperate measures. She's obviously at an advantage here.

Ding!

It's go time. I press down, breathing heavily, and push back up. I do this a few times and try not to focus on the sound of Quinn's footsteps crossing the apartment. I'm on my tenth rep when I see her feet in front of me.

I look up and she's standing in front of me with her arms crossed. She looks beautiful, her soft hair falling in waves over her shoulders and her full lips open slightly. Her expression clouds over in suspicion.

"What are you doing?" She snaps.

I pause. "Working out. Obviously." I continue my push-ups as if she's not there, hiding my smile.

"Why? You never work out here."

"I felt like it. Do you have a problem with that?" I pause and turn over, looking at her. "Because if you do, I can go somewhere else. If it's...distracting you."

Her eyes snap up to mine. She must see the challenge

there or hear it in my tone because she swallows and looks away, lifting her chin in the air.

"Not at all. Do whatever you want. I'm doing laundry, so..."

I nod, acting unfazed. "Cool." I go back to my reps, and she huffs, stomping away.

One point for Wesley.

* * *

Unfortunately, work gets in the way of my plotting. I have to meet George downtown for a meeting and Quinn is doing laundry when I leave, so I don't get the chance to say goodbye. The level of disappointment I feel is pathetic, really. I spend the entire meeting with George checking my watch, hoping I can make it back in time to watch Quinn cook.

It's fascinating to watch her in the kitchen. She comes alive in a way I hadn't realized before — it's like she gets into the zone and loses sight of everything else. I noticed it a few weeks ago, the way her soft smile plays on her lips as she dances from the cutting board to the stovetop. She's *fast*, too. I've never seen someone work so quickly and still turn out an incredible meal.

Now that I've noticed it, it's become a strange sort of addiction for me, watching her cook. I've started trying to plan my days around it — ending early so that I can make it back to the apartment in time, working from home and bringing my laptop out into the living room just as she's getting started.

I'm on my way back to the hotel now, hoping she's still there. I have a few more tricks up my sleeves. The push-ups were easy, and likely transparent. It's time to step up my game.

My phone buzzes in my pocket and I look down to see my brother's name flashing on the screen.

I lift the phone to my ear. "Yes?"

"Wow, hello to you too," Ben chuckles.

"What do you want?" I ask, forcing some patience into my tone.

"Why do you always assume I want something?" Ben asks. "Can't a man call his brother just for the hell of it?"

I check my watch again. I bet Quinn's already started on dinner. Dammit. I'm missing it.

"Alright, fine. I need you to babysit Luna on Saturday," he admits.

"There it is."

"Yeah, yeah." I can almost hear him rolling his eyes through the phone. "Can you do it or not?"

"Yes."

"Great." It's silent for a moment. "So, you sleep with her yet? Or is that why you're in such a bad mood? Still playing horny teenager?"

"Fuck off." I growl.

Ben chuckles on the other line. "That's a no, then."

"She's my—"

"If you tell me again some bullshit about how she works for you or how she'd never go for it, I'm going to blow my brains out."

I sigh and shake my head. Ben always did have a flare for the dramatics. I always thought if he wasn't a lawyer, he'd be an actor. Pete meets my eyes in the mirror and nods. We're here.

"I gotta go." I don't wait for a response as I hang up the phone and slide out of the car, heading upstairs.

When I get to the penthouse, Quinn is carefully loading the dishwasher, a plate with a charred steak, mashed potatoes, and a salad sitting on the table. She has her headphones in — I can tell by the way she's swaying as she washes the plates off and slips them into the dishwasher.

I put my briefcase on the counter, and she turns, meeting my eyes. I smile and she pulls out one of her earbuds.

"Hey. Dinner's on the table."

"Thanks. It looks great."

My stomach flutters uncomfortably. Nerves, Wesley? Really?

Somehow, after all this time, she still makes me nervous. Like my skin is buzzing. Like I've come alive.

She's changed clothes from earlier and there's light makeup coated on her face. A tight black dress hugs her body, a light pink cardigan over her shoulders. She looks incredible. More dressed up than usual. Is this part of the game? Did she wear this for me? My heart flutters at the thought.

She unties her apron and turns away from me. "Is it okay if I leave a little early? I have a date."

My stomach drops.

A date?

With who? Where? When did this happen?

That's why she's so dressed up. I can't believe I was enough of an idiot to think any of this was for my benefit.

"Sure. That's fine." I swallow, hard. My voice does not sound like mine. It's strangled like I'm choking on the words.

It's none of my business. None at all. It shouldn't even bother me. Still, I can't help the sinking feeling in the pit of my stomach. I feel like I've been punched in the gut. Repeatedly.

I blink, quickly, and grab my bag.

"Thanks for the heads up. I hope you have a great time." I manage to make my voice sound somewhat positive despite how gutted I feel. "I'll see you tomorrow."

Chapter 30

Quinn

Sitting at a lonely high-top table at a dive bar in the East Village, I stir my gin and tonic in frustration. I probably should have just gone straight home — it's not like Wesley had any idea that my so-called date was complete bullshit.

Still, after his reaction (or lack thereof) I needed a drink. I feel like someone put their hand in my intestines and twisted them all up into a knot.

I can't believe I got dressed up for a fake date just to try and make Wesley jealous. Why would he be jealous? He probably has beautiful women throwing themselves at his feet. Just because he likes the way I look in a short skirt doesn't mean he cares about my love life.

Flames dance on my face as I knock back the rest of my drink. I feel so silly to even think he'd care about whether I had a date or not. Clearly from his complete non-reaction, he doesn't care one bit. The reminder of how easily he dismissed me just fuels the sinking feeling in my stomach. I drop my head into my hands, too upset to care about how dirty this table is.

"Miss Taylor? Is that you?"

My head snaps up and I can't believe what I'm seeing. None other than Miss Perky standing in front of me. She's dressed up too, with dark makeup on her eyes and a few other women flanking her. Of all the luck. God must really have it out for me.

"Oh...hi!" I search my memory. What the hell is her real name? It's not like I can call her Perky.

"Hannah. Hannah Dwyer, from the hospital," she says with a smile, then turns to her friends and waves them towards the bar. "What are you doing here?"

"Oh...you know." I wave around me like it's obvious why I'm drinking alone in this tiny dive. "Just hanging out."

"Right," she says, glancing around. "You know ladies drink free starting at 8? That's why we come here."

"Yes!" I hop on to her words like a life raft. "Yep, that's why I'm here. Ready to get my drank on." I force an excited twang into my voice.

"Would you like to join us? I'm here with some of my friends from college." She gestures over to the group she came in with. "Unless you're waiting for someone?"

I open my mouth to decline her offer. She's just being nice. That's what Perky — Hannah — does. She's nice. But then I remember my earlier promise to myself to try and make a friend. Hannah, slightly annoying as she may be, well, I guess I have to admit that she's been pretty kind to me. Maybe we could be at least...friendly.

"You know what?" I push my empty drink away from me and stand up from the table. "I'd love that."

* * *

Two hours later, I'm completely trashed. My vision is slightly blurry, and I feel amazing. Empty shot glasses litter the bar in front of us as Hannah continues her story about her ex-girlfriend.

"You won't believe it." She laughs through her words, shaking her head. "It's so embarrassing."

"Come on!" I yell, clapping my hands together. The rest of the women around me cheer and shout with me, urging her to continue.

She covers her face with her eyes and shakes her head again. "I come up for air, right? And I look down and there's blood everywhere, so I stopped. Wanted to make sure everything was okay. I'm like, oh shit, Nikki, you must have gotten your period. But it wasn't her period." She drags her hand down her face and looks at us. "It was a nosebleed! I guess we'd been a little bit intense, and she'd rocked against my face too hard. My nose just started bleeding."

At this, the group starts howling with laughter. I can't help but join in at the ridiculous scenario.

"Oh my god. What did you do?" Jess, one of Hannah's friends, asks, leaning forward.

Hannah shrugs. "Tilted my head back and switched." Gasps and chuckles run through the group. "That's it." She drinks the rest of the margarita. "Okay, it's your turn, Quinn. What's your most embarrassing sex story?"

My face colors red and I shake my head. "Jess, why don't you go? I'll get the next round." I push away from our table and go over to the bar, waving the bartender over for another round of shots.

I can't believe that just a few hours ago, I was feeling sorry for myself over Wesley Marks. Who cares what he thinks? He's just some guy. A hot guy, yes. A really hot guy who wears incredible suits, yes. But still just some guy.

I should give him a piece of my mind. Tell him what I really think of him and his stupid abs.

You know what?

I will. I'll tell him right now.

That's the last thing I remember before I blackout.

* * *

The next day at work is terrible. I have a horrible stomachache and I look like a complete mess. Thank God Wesley isn't home all day. It's almost time for me to start dinner and I still feel nauseous. I've hardly eaten all day — I've just been sipping Gatorade and force-feeding myself saltine crackers.

Despite my hangover, I had a fun time with Hannah and her friends. She even invited me to a party next weekend, and she seemed genuine. I feel bad that I dismissed her so quickly.

A wave of nausea rolls through me as I wipe down the kitchen counters. It hits me all at once.

I'm going to throw up. Definitely.

I manage to make it to the closest bathroom and push my head into the toilet bowl. I hurl for a minute, letting out everything in my stomach. It's disgusting and putrid but once I'm finished, I feel a million times better.

Until I glance down at my clothes and realize I didn't quite reach the toilet entirely. Gross. I glance at the clock — I still have an hour until Wesley comes home. I strip my clothes off and quickly scrub them in the sink, hanging them to dry on the towel rod. Then I hop in the shower.

I'm already under the running water when I'm hit with the realization that I am currently in Wesley's bathroom. In his shower. In my fleeing to the toilet, I didn't think to go to the guest bathroom on the far end of the apartment. I look down at the fancy body wash and lift the bottle, popping the cap open, and sniffing.

God. This is weird and creepy and wrong in probably a million ways. But it smells just like him. I'm tempted to lather it all over my body, but I grab a bar of soap and use that instead. Hopefully Wesley won't realize that I've showered at all. Or I can explain that I spilled on myself. Something like that.

I wash off quickly, not wanting to waste any time. I waterfall some mouthwash and swish it around. It's amazing how much better I feel after only a few minutes. Relieved, I step out of the shower and wrap a towel around myself. My clothes aren't quite dry, so I grab the hair dryer off the wall and turn it on, trying quickly to get the wet stains out of my shirt.

The sound of the hair dryer bombards my ears as I flip my hair over and run the nozzle through it. It's so loud I don't hear anything. I don't hear the *ding* of the elevator or the opening of Wesley's door. I'm completely oblivious as I flip my hair back up and turn the hair dryer off.

I step out of the bathroom into Wesley's bedroom, where he stands, gaping at me.

* * *

"Oh my god!"

I pull my towel up higher at an attempt of covering myself, even though nothing is visible. Wesley's eyes are wide, and his jaw is locked tighter than I've ever seen it. He blinks and then turns away, averting his eyes.

"What the hell?" His voice booms. "What are you doing?"

"Oh my god," I repeat. Where are my clothes? Where the hell are my clothes? "I'm so sorry. I got my clothes dirty, and I thought I would have time and oh my god..."

Wesley makes a strangled noise. "Where are your clothes?"

"Hanging. In the bathroom. I'll get them. Right now."

I turn on my heels to flee back into the bathroom, but he stops me, his hand wrapping around my arm. He looks down at me like he's in pain.

I should speak, but I can't. All I can think is how badly I want him to kiss me. How desperate I am for him to press his lips to mine. I let the hope build in my chest as I look into his eyes, but he just stares into mine, searching.

I'm sure he's going to let go and break away, so I turn my head away, but he catches my cheek with his other hand. The movement is surprisingly gentle as he brushes his thumb along my cheekbone.

I suck in a sharp breath, my chest rising and falling with desire.

Will he...?

Finally, after what feels like a lifetime, he presses his lips to mine.

God, yes.

It's soft at first. Like a question — like he's still asking for permission. His grip on my arm loosens as he caresses my arm and his other hand moves from my cheek to the back of my neck, bringing me closer to him. His lips are soft and rugged at the same time as he tugs on my bottom lip with impatience, opening my mouth. I let out an involuntary moan at the movement, needing more, meeting his kisses with an embarrassing eagerness.

The sound of my breathless moan shocks him backwards and for a moment, we're separated. He looks at me like he can't believe what we just did. I can't bare the regret that must be hiding behind his gaze, so I don't give him a chance to voice it. I attach my lips to his again, kissing him wildly. I drag my fingers through his soft hair, loving the way it feels in my hands.

I pull back and meet his scorching gaze again. My eyes flicker back and forth between his, a silent question, a *please* fluttering at my lips. I'm terrified that he'll stop this — let me down easy, turn away from me.

But he doesn't.

He brings his lips back down to mine like he's a drowning man gasping for air. It's not soft this time. His hand tangles in my hair, tugging my head back slightly to give him a better angle. I love it, the possessive way he claims my mouth. I moan again, but this time the sound sends a groan of satisfaction through him. Slowly, he steps forward, guiding me backwards towards the bed.

He breaks off again, but only to pull his shirt over his head and fling it to the side. He dips his head to kiss me again, but I stop him with my hand, sliding it down his abs. I can't help but stare in wonder as I clutch the towel at my chest.

"Wow," I whisper, dragging my hand lower. I want to explore every inch of his perfect body.

His eyes darken. His hand dips under the towel, his thumb circling my inner thigh. It's torturous and teasing and everything I need. "I want to know everything you like. I want to taste every inch of you."

He presses his lips to my neck, sending soft kisses across my chest as his fingers continue their movement. He runs his hand up and down my inner thigh, touching me everywhere but where I need it.

"Yes." I moan. I can't help myself. I need it. I need him.

He looks into my eyes. "Do you want this? Do you want me?"

I nod, eager. I can't believe the fire that is spreading through my body. I've never felt like this before. This aching *need* inside of me. I feel completely present right now. Like everything is brighter, more aware somehow.

"Say it. I need you to say it."

I swallow the lump in my throat. "I want you, Wesley." My lips start to tremble, and I feel suddenly vulnerable with him staring down at me with earnest desire. I swallow and meet his gaze. "I need you."

The words ignite him. He attacks me with his lips again, setting me on fire. Finally, his fingers find me, his thumb circling my clit. I buckle against the movement, pushing against his hand, desperate for more. He rewards me by teasing one finger at my entrance.

"Fuck, yes," he groans. "You're so wet. So wet for me." His husky voice sends another jolt of pleasure through me.

His words only turn me on more. I unclench my hand and let the towel fall with a newfound inhibition. Desperate, I fist my hands into the fabric of the sheets. He leans forward, his eyes darkening as he takes me in. The way he's looking at me makes me feel incredible. A thrill rushes through me as he pins me down with his intense gaze.

"You're perfect," he chokes out, his eyes exploring every inch of me. "So perfect."

His sweet words sent a wave of desire through me. I've never felt so alive as I feel when Wesley looks at me. His fingers continue their soft exploration as he brings my left nipple into his mouth with a groan. I arch my back at his touch, which only fuels him further.

"More," I urge him on. "I need more."

I wrap my arms around his neck and bring his mouth up to mine. We kiss like we're running out of time, like his mouth on mine is the only thing in the entire world. I have no idea how much time has passed — I could spend days, weeks, months with Wesley's lips on mine.

His body pushes forward, and I scoot backwards onto the bed, bringing him completely on top of me.

"Yes." I wrap my arms around him, loving the way his weight feels on me. Like I'm completely engulfed by him. I grind my hips against him, needing to feel more of him, and he groans at the movement.

Suddenly, he grabs my wrists, pinning them over my head. He sits squarely on top of me now and I let out reckless breaths, meeting his gaze.

"What do you like?" He barks out, his voice strained.

I'm so dazed, my brain is moving at a glacial pace. "Like?" I stutter, blinking up at him.

He loosens his grip and runs his nose along my neck, moving lower. He presses a soft kiss in between my breasts, his hot breath fluttering across my chest.

"Tell me what you like." He releases my left hand and brings his hand lower. I gasp again at the contact. "Like that?"

My eyes flutter as his thumb circles me again, bringing me closer. He kisses me again, this time on my stomach, as he moves lower and lower. My head snaps up as I feel his breath on my inner thighs. He's staring down at me with a carnal look in his eyes.

"Can I taste you?" He presses another finger in and I love it. Then he says a word I never thought I'd hear torn from his lips. "Please?"

"Yes," I manage to breathe out.

He brings his lips down to me and I almost see stars. I can't believe how turned on I am. I feel like I'm going to die as he devours me, his fingers and tongue hitting every pleasure point. My moans are turning to screams as he picks up his pace.

"Wesley. Oh my god. I'm gonna—" I gasp.

"Not yet," he says, slowing his pace in the most torturous

way. I exhale in frustration, and he smirks up at me. "Good girl."

He must know his words would be my undoing because he brings his tongue back to that perfect spot and his fingers are pumping and I can't breathe. My entire body shakes as the world around me explodes until I feel nothing but bliss. I manage to lift my head and Wesley stares up at me as he sucks his fingers dry.

Holy fuck.

"Oh my god." I hear myself say. "I can't believe we just did that."

Wesley lifts himself up and leans over me, his elbows pressed on either side. "Did that?" He smirks. "We're just getting started, sweetheart."

Chapter 31

Wesley

I smile down at Quinn as her eyes widen in anticipation. She looks more beautiful than ever — hair everywhere, face flushed. I close my eyes, remembering the look of pure ecstasy on her face. I need to see it again.

"You're wearing too many clothes," she says, tugging at my pants, which are somehow still on. I chuckle watching her struggle with the belt and she rolls her eyes. I gently push her hand back and yank the belt off, pulling my pants and briefs down in one swoop.

Her mouth drops. Normally I might make some arrogant comment, but my mouth is suddenly very dry, watching Quinn watch me. The desire is written all over her face.

I press her backwards, my mouth meeting hers with a shared intensity. I can't believe I get to kiss her. I press soft kisses along her collarbone, touching her everywhere. My hands make it their mission to explore every inch of her perfect skin. It's not long before they find her soft pussy, soaking wet for me. I groan again at the contact, loving the way she feels.

"Oh god," she moans, throwing her head back.

"You like that? Yeah, you like that." I circle my thumb on her clit, teasing her. "I want to feel you come again."

She gasps. "Please." I meet her gaze. "I can't wait anymore."

"Please what?" I almost growl the words, knowing what she needs. "Do you want me inside you, baby?" I rub my nose against her throat, humming against it. Her head falls back, and I gather her hair in my hands. "Tell me what you want." I meet her eyes again.

She blinks, her gaze darkening. "I want you to fuck me, Wesley," she breaks off and bites her lip.

I move faster than I ever have, fumbling for a condom in my bedside table. I grab it and rip the foil with my teeth, pressing it along my length and leveraging myself above Quinn. I hold for a moment, teasing her with the tip, but she grabs my body and pulls it against her.

I almost lose it when I press inside her. There's no feeling like this. It's incredible. I take a deep breath, trying to steady myself. Finally, I thrust into her, slow, shuddering against her.

It's intense, the feeling rushing through me. I wonder if she feels it too.

"Oh god," she moans. "It feels — so good."

I grunt in approval, thrusting harder.

"You're so good." I'm losing it. "So beautiful."

I flip over so she's on top.

"Ride me," I say, twisting her nipple in my fingers. She pushes into me, our bodies meeting perfectly. She's even better than I imagined, and I know, right then, watching her bouncing on top of me, that once isn't enough. I need this again and again and again. I need it forever.

"Wesley," she moans.

"Yes, baby. Say my name." I love the way it sounds on her lips. She screams and clenches around me and it feels incredible. She's close, I can feel it. I flip her over and pump harder, on the edge.

"Look at me," I say, lifting her chin with my hand. Her bright, wide eyes meet mine and I lose it, collapsing into her, flying. Her legs shake and she clenches again as she bites my neck to hold in her screams.

I release a shuddering breath. "I'm close—"

She nods fervently, her eyes still locked on mine. I can't hold it in anymore. I thrust into her once more, coming quickly. It must set her off, because I feel her clench around me and her own release follows as she collapses against me.

Holy shit. The only sound in the room is our heaving breaths.

It's overwhelming, the feeling of her wrapped around me, and I swallow a lump in my throat. I pull out and roll over, tossing the condom into the trash.

I turn around and see her sitting up, reaching for her towel.

"What are you doing?"

She glances at me, a flash of something behind her eyes. "Oh. I don't know. I was going to..." She gestures towards the door.

I tug her towards me, laying down. I wrap my arms around her and press my nose into the back of her neck, pulling the blankets over us.

"What are you doing?" She repeats my words back to me.

"Shh. Just lay here for a minute." I nuzzle her closer, loving the way her body feels wrapped around mine. I close my eyes and it's quiet for a few minutes.

"But shouldn't we talk about what just happened?" She whispers. "We just had sex!"

I chuckle against her. "Yes, I know. I was there."

I feel her stiffen against me. "I don't know. Maybe I should go. I really feel like maybe I should go?"

I loosen my grip and lift up to my elbows, turning her to look at me.

"I want you to stay."

The words are meant to be simple, but they sound intense. She seems to consider them for a moment before nodding up at me.

"Yes? You'll stay?" I press.

"Okay."

I chuckle and lay back down with her, tugging her close to me again. I inhale her scent and feel her warmth and it's perfect. I suddenly remember her late-night call last night and chuckle to myself.

"What?" Quinn whispers, turning to face me. We're almost nose-to-nose now as she looks into my eyes.

"Mmm." I trail my fingers along her legs and up to her stomach, flattening my hand against her. "Just remembering your very feisty phone call last night."

She shoots up. "What? What phone call?" Her wild eyes study me.

"Calm down." I pull her down again, missing the feeling of her in my arms. "You didn't say anything new, really. Arrogant jerk, entitled asshole...great butt. Actually, I think the word you used was 'firm'."

She gasps. "I didn't!"

"You did."

She buries her face into the pillow, groaning. "Oh my god." She shakes her head against it and I pull her closer with a soft chuckle.

"I can't believe I actually talked to you while that intoxicated." She peeks up at me, her eyebrows scrunched.

"Actually, it was a voicemail," I murmur, brushing my

hand on her stomach again. I'm not in the mood to talk about phone calls. Not at all. In fact, I'm ready for another round, but she won't relent.

"What?" She sits up, holding her hand out expectantly. "Let me hear it."

I fall back against the pillow, pinching the bridge of my nose. "Are you sure about that?"

"Yes. Give it to me."

I roll over and grab my phone from the bedside table, searching for her message. I click on it and the sound of her voice fills the room.

Hey, you. Mr. Marks. I bet all the secretaries at your job call you that. Mr. Markssssss.

I glance over at Quinn and her entire face is red. She's completely still as we listen to her slurred voice.

You know something? I want to tell you what I really think, Mr. Meanie Marks. I think that I do not understand you! One day you are rude, the next you're nice! One day you act like an arrogant jerk, insulting me, making me feel so...small.

I glance away, pained by the vulnerability in her voice, swallowing the lump in my throat. I'd forgotten about that part. My eyes flicker over to her, searching for a reaction, but her face gives nothing away.

Then the next day you're being all friendly and being cute with your niece and telling me we are friends. Well — I don't want to be

friends with you or your firm butt. Even if it is a great butt...GUYS! It's a firm butt. A yummy butt—

She yelps and reaches out and grabs my phone, turning the sound off. "That's enough. Where's the delete button on this thing?" She's blushing more than I've ever seen her.

I grab the phone from her hands and slip it into the top drawer of my bedside table. "Don't you dare. I'm keeping it forever."

She drops her head into her hands and groans. "That is so embarrassing. I can't believe I called you."

I pull her into my arms again, wanting her close. There's a need to make her feel better clawing its way up my throat, like I'm in pain seeing her in distress.

"Don't be embarrassed." I nudge her. "I think your butt is much more than yummy." I drag my hand down and smack her ass lightly, wrapping her closer to me. "I'm sorry I didn't answer. I didn't see the message til later and I was worried about you getting home."

"I don't normally drink like that. This was a special occasion."

"Oh yeah? Your hot date?" I press a soft kiss on her neck. "How did that go, by the way?"

She groans again and nuzzles into my chest. "You're the worst. How did you know I was lying?"

"I didn't." I smirk, quirking an eyebrow at her as she turns away and buries her face further into the pillow. "Though I was wondering why you'd be drunk-dialing me if you were on a date."

I run my fingers along her spine, watching goosebumps form slowly on her arm. "Why did you lie, sweetheart?"

"You know why."

"Hmm." I continue tracing circles on her back. "Our little game."

She turns back towards me quickly and peers right into my eyes. "So you admit it! You were trying to seduce me!"

I chuckle and wrap my hand around her waist. "Well, apparently it worked. Can we rest now? Or do you have more questions?"

"Only like a million." She snuggles closer and closes her eyes, finally. I tighten my hold on her, listening closely to the sound of her breaths until she falls asleep in my arms.

Chapter 32

Quinn

I wake up feeling very warm and soft. Like I'm sleeping on a cloud. I snuggle tighter, pulling my pillow closer, and inhale. My pillow smells amazing — it smells like Wesley, actually.

Wait — Wesley.

My eyes fly open as the events of last night tumble through my mind. Wesley kissing me. Wesley coaxing orgasm after orgasm from me. Wesley's wild thrusts, the feeling of his hard body rocking into mine.

Oh my god.

That was real. That was real, right? I pinch myself to make sure I'm not dreaming Nope — nothing. Rubbing my eyes, I glance around to register that I am in Wesley's bedroom. In Wesley's bed. Alone.

I pull the blankets over my chest, feeling suddenly nervous in this empty bed.

Where is he? Did he leave?

Well, it is a Wednesday morning. Who knows what time it is? I glance around at the messy room, at Wesley's strewn clothes on the floor. I should probably clean that up. Right?

I sit up, wrapping the blanket around myself, and try to make a mental game plan.

Put my clothes on, then get out of here faster than the speed of light and immediately quit?

That feels unlikely. Okay —first step. Get my clothes.

Oh god. My mom is probably worried sick. I can't believe I didn't call her and tell her that I was staying the night out. Shit.

Focus, Quinn.

I glance over at the bedside table for a note from Wesley, anything, but there's nothing. Maybe he sent me a text and I just haven't seen it. I need my phone. Game plan: clothes, phone, evaluate.

I grab my now-dry clothes from the bathroom and slip them on quickly. I tiptoe into the living room and cross towards the kitchen when I see Wesley, standing shirtless in front of the stove, his back to me. He's holding a spatula and has an apron — the pink one I usually wear — wrapped around his waist.

I clear my throat and he turns at the sound.

"Good morning." He reaches for a coffee mug and places it in front of me. "I thought you were still sleeping."

"I thought you left." I take a sip of the coffee.

He puts the spatula down and comes around the island, stepping towards me. He takes the coffee from my hands and sets it back on the counter, then lifts me up next to it as if I weigh nothing.

"You're always thinking I'm going to leave you." He presses a soft kiss on my lips. "You can't get rid of me that easy." His mouth dips lower, his warm breath dancing against my neck.

I'm putty in his hands, melting for his touch. It's scary

how much I can get used to this — waking up to Wesley in the kitchen, wrapping my legs around him on this counter every day. My heart gallops in my chest at the thought, a wild, fluttering feeling.

I pull back and press my hand against his chest, avoiding his eyes. If I look into his eyes, I'm doomed. "I need to find my phone and call my mom. She's probably worried."

He steps back. "Good idea. Breakfast will be ready soon." He rounds the island back to the stovetop.

I quirk an eyebrow. "Oh? You're cooking?"

He must hear the smirk in my voice because he turns back with a hand on his hip. "Yes, I'm cooking. I can cook, you know. Just not nearly as well as you."

I smile at his compliment and go to the laundry room to gather my clothes. I slip them back on and go back into the living room to search my bag for my phone. When I find it, there's three missed calls from my mom. Shit.

I dial back and she answers right away, sounding out of breath.

"Quinn! Where are you? Are you okay?"

"I'm fine! I'm so sorry. I didn't have my phone and I completely forgot to call you."

My mom sighs on the other end. "Sweetheart. C'mon. You can't worry me like that. I almost called the police."

"I know, I know. I really am sorry. It won't happen again, I swear."

I feel like a teenager, getting scolded by my mother for staying out too late. But I know it's my fault — I know how she worries, and I really should have remembered to call.

I change the subject as I pad into the dining room to see Wesley setting the table, a small grin on his face. "How are you feeling?"

"Pretty good, actually. Joe is coming over later and we're going to the movies."

"Any nausea today?"

I can almost hear her eye roll through the phone. "No, sweetheart. I'm fine."

"Alright. I'll call you later. Love you."

"I love you too."

I hang up the phone and slide it into my pocket, coming over to meet Wesley at the table where he's laid out a beautiful breakfast spread. He comes up behind me and wraps his arms around my waist, pressing a soft kiss to the back of my neck.

"How's your mom?" He asks, tracing his hands along my hips.

I turn around and press my hands against his chest, meeting his eyes. "She's fine. A little upset that I forgot to call. She gets worried." I press my head against his hard chest, loving the way I feel wrapped in his arms.

I turn back towards the food. "This looks incredible." There's a whole spread of breakfast food including french toast, bacon, and fresh fruit.

He slides out a chair and gestures for me to take it. Sitting across from me, he starts loading food onto our plates. "I hope you're hungry."

"Always."

We eat in silence for a few moments. Pouring syrup over my French toast, I feel suddenly nervous again. Is this the part where we talk about what happens next? Is this just a casual thing? Has he done this sort of thing before — sleeping with his enemy-turned-employee-turned-friend?

Does he want to keep things casual or is this something else? I'm not even sure what I want anymore. My head feels like a jumbled mess — probably from the multiple orgasms.

"What are you thinking over there?" Wesley's voice interrupts my spiraling.

"I guess I'm freaking out a little. I work for you and you're you and I'm me and I thought you hated me and what are we doing here?"

My rambling does nothing to extinguish the fire in his eyes. He doesn't say anything. Instead, he takes a few more bites of his food, and I do the same. The silence is killing me and he still hasn't answered my question. Finally, he wipes the corners of his mouth and throws his napkin onto his plate, pushing back to stand. He pulls at my hand, bringing me with him, and pressing me against the kitchen island.

"First of all, I could never hate you," he hums, brushing his nose against my cheek. "Would it help if I told you I don't know either?"

He presses soft kisses to my neck, and I let out a breathy moan.

"All I know is I want to do this. All. Day. Long." He growls and lifts me into his arms, his hands gripping my ass firmly. As if I weigh nothing, he carries me back towards the bedroom.

He lowers me down to the bed, pressing his lips to mine with a groan. I love the feeling of his hard body pressed into mine and I wrap my arms around him, tugging him closer.

He chuckles against my mouth. "So impatient."

All thoughts have evaporated from my mind. There is nothing but Wesley and the way his hands feel roaming my skin. Before I realize it, the clothes that I just put on are being stripped away by his exploring hands.

I smirk against his lips, pulling back. "Now who's impatient?"

He groans into my mouth. "You're right. I've been thinking about this all morning."

He kisses me again and the intensity of it almost knocks me backwards. It's a kiss that brands me and makes me entirely his. It's like he's trying to communicate something urgent, delicate and wonderful with his lips and I match him for every word.

He moves his lips lower, taking my nipple into his mouth and thumbing the other with soft circles. I love how big his hands are, how my breast fits perfectly into his palms.

"So soft." He continues circling my nipple with his thumb, the movement sending a wave of pleasure up my spine. "You feel so fucking amazing, it's unbelievable."

His dirty talk is going to be my undoing, I swear. The husky edge to his voice as he dips his hand lower, telling me how every inch of me feels, how soft, how perfect, how ready for him I am.

He dips a finger into my waistband, finally where I need him most. He groans at the contact.

"You're so wet for me, aren't you?" He circles my clit with his thumb, the movement slow and torturous.

I try to hold in a whimper as he lifts his head up and meets my gaze. "There's so much I want to do with you, I can't decide." He holds my gaze as he dips a finger inside me.

"What do you like? Be specific." He nearly growls the words out, watching me intently. "You didn't tell me last night."

I try to hide my blush. "The...way you talk. Dirty talk. I like that."

"I know you do, baby. What else?"

"Well..." My head feels dizzy, and my mouth is dry. "What do you want to do?"

"I want to fuck you from behind while we watch in the mirror at how beautiful you look. I want to tie you up and tease you for hours. I want you to come when I tell you to and not a second earlier."

Pleasure explodes inside me at his words and before I can stop myself, I'm thrusting against his hand, an orgasm ripping through me.

He lifts his fingers to his lips and slips them inside his mouth, sucking in a way that has me ready to go again.

"Should I take that as a yes?" He cocks his head, watching me.

I heave out a breath. "Yes. Please."

"Good girl." He pulls his pants down, already hard in his hand. He moves towards me, kissing me again, and my whole body is on fire where we meet. Feeling bold, I move my hand down his body and wrap my hand around him.

He lets out a strangled sound that makes me feel incredible. Like I can make him feel as good as he makes me feel. Better, even.

I push him backwards and move lower, settling myself in between his legs. Slowly, softly, I open my mouth and lick along the tip, opening my mouth for him. I lower my head entirely and flicker my gaze up to meet his, where he watches.

"Quinn." He chokes the word out, his hand fisting the sheets. "God, you can't look at me like that. I'm gonna fucking lose it."

I steady my gaze, taking all of him in my mouth as he rests a hand on the back of my head, steadying me. I quicken my pace, thrusting against him and he wraps his hand tighter, fisting my hair.

"Oh, fuck. Baby."

His words only fuel me as I slacken my jaw and go deeper. He groans, letting out another moan of pleasure that I love. I flash a wicked gaze back up to his eyes.

"Fuck — I'm gonna — Quinn —" He tugs my hair back slightly in warning, but I run my tongue along him, relentless.

I never thought I'd feel so powerful on my knees. I always felt the opposite. But with Wesley, somehow, with the way he's looking down at me, it's like *I'm* the one in control.

He gasps as he releases into my mouth and I swallow every drop, smirking as I gaze up at him, matching his breathlessness.

"You are perfect."

He looks at me with such a sharp affection in his dark eyes that I lift myself up and cradle his chest just to look away, but he doesn't let me. He lifts my face to his and kisses me again, this one soft and delicate. He's holding my face like I'm something precious. Then he wraps his arms around me, his hands gliding up my back. He's hugging me. We stay like that, wrapped around each other, for a few silent moments.

I can't believe I get this piece of Wesley. It feels like a gift to have my arms wrapped around his strong, broad torso. I pull back to look at him, running my thumb along his chin with a soft smile.

The corner of his mouth ticks up. "Lost in thought again?" He asks, somehow knowing.

I lay my head on his chest, listening to his heartbeat.

"What did you think of me the first time you saw me?"

"Is this a test?" He chuckles and I can feel the sound vibrating in his chest. "I thought, fuck, she's beautiful."

I nearly snort, rolling my eyes. "Oh, come on. What did you really think?" I run my fingers along his chest, tracing lines across his abdomen. He lifts up, nudging me to look at him.

He furrows his brow. "Is that so hard to believe?"

"I don't know." I shrug.

He shakes his head and meets my gaze. "There wasn't a

single moment when I wasn't looking at you and thinking how energetic, how expressive, and how breathtaking you are. And how all I wanted to do was kiss you." He caresses my cheek.

He smirks, that signature quirk in his mouth that I want to kiss. "You infuriated me, that's for sure. Got under my skin. I couldn't stand it. Couldn't bare it — the way you made me feel. Make me feel."

A burst of feeling swells in my chest and sets my heart racing. I reach for him, bringing his lips to mine, and kissing him in earnest. I send all of his loving words back to him with my lips before he pulls back lightly.

"Ah — what about my turn? What did you think when you first saw me?" He raises an eyebrow, smirking.

"Oh, don't make me say it, you egomaniac." I paw against his chest, rolling my eyes, but he tightens his grip.

"Me? Ego?" He feigns offense. Suddenly, he flips me over onto my back, resting on his elbows above me. "Never."

I lick my lips. "I thought 'I'd like to know the color of his sheets.' This was much more what I had in mind than washing them."

I expect a low chuckle at my attempt at humor, but Wesley stiffens above me, his face twisting. He flips over and rests his elbows onto his knees and tucking away from me.

I reach for him absently. "Wes." I swallow, feeling his absence. "I was joking."

"Yeah, I know." His voice is hard.

"I'm s—"

"Don't apologize! Fuck." He still won't look at me, but I can imagine the pained expression on his face, that haunted, guilty look in his eyes. I can't stand it.

I reach for him, forcing him to look at me. "It was a dumb joke. I shouldn't have said anything."

"You were just telling the truth." His voice is flat.

I sigh and meet his gaze head-on. "Listen to me. I don't want this to be a thing between us. I like my life, and I work hard. Do I make as much money as I wish I did? No. But that's just the way it is. I'm fine with it. You need to be, too."

Something flickers in his gaze. I press my palm to his chest, leaning closer. "I want this. I want you." I press my forehead against his and wrap my hands around his neck. "Please."

He wraps his arms around me, rubbing circles on my back, but his eyes are still pained. I lift my leg, crawling onto his lap, and grind into him.

"Please." I press into his chest, arching my back. "Wesley."

His eyes darken, flames rising in his gaze.

I lean back from him, resting on my heels. Slowly, I bring my hands down and slip my fingers inside of me, my gaze never leaving his. He groans, the sound nearly a growl as he watches me, his eyes dropping.

I circle my clit slowly, bringing my other hand up to my nipple and twisting it in my fingers. I moan and continue circling, letting out breathy, choked sounds of pleasure.

"Quinn, fuck." Wesley watches me and I can feel his hardness growing underneath me. It makes me feel bold. I've never been very good at dirty talk, but I want Wesley to know how turned on I am.

"Wes. I want your hand. Your cock." I slip two fingers inside with a gasp. "I want you to feel how wet I am for you. Please?"

Before I can say anything else, he attacks me with his mouth, kissing every inch of me hungrily. He takes his cock into his hand, moving it towards me, pressing the tip into me.

"Is this what you want, baby?" He pulls my hair back to

meet his hungry gaze and I love it, being totally under his control.

"Yes, please, please."

And for the rest of the day, we don't leave the bed.

Chapter 33

Wesley

Hours later, we're still in bed, eating Thai takeout and watching a True Crime series. I'm hardly paying attention because I'm so focused on Quinn, her body curled up next to me. I somehow convince her to stay for dinner, selfishly taking every minute I can get with her. Part of me is terrified that once I let her out of my sight, she'll leave forever.

For now, it's just us. In this room. No family pressures, no business to deal with, no secrets and lies. Just us.

She pops a piece of edamame into her mouth and holds one out for me to do the same, letting me suck on it until she pulls the shell out of my mouth. The gesture sees a strange tingle in my stomach.

"Tell me about your restaurant."

She gets that little crinkle between her eyes, looking at me. "What do you mean?"

"Your restaurant. Your dream."

She's quiet for a long time. So long that I'm sure she's ignored me, that she won't answer at all. But then her soft voice cuts through the heavy silence.

"My mom taught me a love for food, and that good food can be found anywhere. We both used it as an escape, I think. Just from life. I feel like cooking kind of lost all joy for her when my dad left. Cooking was a love language for her, same way it is for me, and I think when he left...well, she lost a lot.

"But when we went to the diner, it felt like a lot of that stuff fell away. That first bite of pie, a late-night breakfast platter. Nothing can stop that feeling of pleasure, of trying something new. I just knew that I wanted to somehow *make* other people have that feeling. I love comfort foods, good old diner foods, that kind of stuff. My idea is to do a more elegant twist on classic dishes, a sort of elevated diner concept. I guess I dream of making a place that has that special feeling — of home, of comfort. I'm not sure about the full menu yet, but I know I want to name it after my mom. I just hope she's around for it."

I hear the sniffle in her voice, and I wrap my arms around her, inhaling her floral scent. The warm feeling in my chest grows, crashing over me like a wave.

"That's a beautiful dream. I hope she's there for it, too."

* * *

A couple of hours later, we're both dressed and standing near the elevator. My hands are in my pockets, because I know if I touch her, I'll never let her go.

Quinn is buzzing. She's looking anywhere but me, her eyes studying every inch of the elevator door as if she hasn't stood in front of it every single day for the past few months. I can't help but smile down at her, wishing she could stay longer. Unfortunately, I have work to do and she has a life of her own. One that I want to know everything about.

"Well," she says, shifting. "This was fun! I'll be back tomorrow reporting for duty!"

"Listen." I take a deep breath, trying to figure out the right move. "Why don't you take tomorrow off? We can talk on Friday morning when you come, please? About what's next. And text me that you're home safe tonight too?"

Her eyes are almost as wide as saucers as she takes in my words. "Right. Yes. Okay."

I suppress a chuckle and lean in, kissing her softly, exploring her lips with mine. She moans against my mouth and the sound goes straight to my dick.

I step back. "If you keep on with that, I'll never let you leave."

She stamps down her grin at my words and nods, pressing the elevator button. I feel a pang in my stomach at the thought of her leaving — like this place feels empty without her. I try to blink it back, feeling overwhelmed.

"Are you sure you can fend for yourself tomorrow? We left your room in quite a mess," she smirks.

"I'll survive," I chuckle, reaching for her hand and rubbing soft circles on the back of it.

It's quiet for a moment, save for the faint city sounds from the ground below.

"I had a really nice time." She avoids my gaze, her signature blush growing on her cheeks.

I brush my thumb along the soft pink hue. "Me too. I can't wait to see you again soon."

Ding!

The elevator doors slide open, and she steps inside, giving me a little wave, still blushing. I hold the doors with my hand, leaning against the frame.

"Friday night, I'm taking you out on a real date. In case you need to bring something to change into."

Her eyes widen as I step back and send her a wink, letting the doors close in front of me. When she's gone, I lean against the doorway for far too long, waiting for the lump in my throat to go down. I step back and inhale. It still smells like her.

I go straight to my office, and I have 37 missed calls. I call my assistant and she gives me the important messages — mainly that George has called three times with updates on the Park Ave project. You'd think the man could handle running our company for a single day, but apparently not.

My phone rings with a call from my mother. I'm nervous to answer it because I know she's going to ask me about Quinn, and I have no idea what to say to her. Lillian Marks can sniff out a lie faster than anyone I know. I don't have time to debate the subject any longer, so I answer the phone.

"Hello, mother. To what do I owe the pleasure?"

My mother huffs. "You're awfully formal today, *son*. What are you hiding?"

I rub my hand on my forehead, leaning back in my chair. How does she already know? "Nothing. But I'm a very busy man. Running the family company and all," I say, like I haven't been completely AWOL from work since I tasted Quinn.

"Yes, yes. You're very important." She clicks her tongue. "I'm only calling to let you know that we're driving up to see your father next Saturday."

My stomach bottoms out.

"What?" I force the harsh word out.

Memories from the last time I saw my father, the last time I spoke to him, assault my mind. That dreadful day when I'd gotten Quinn fired from The Phoenix. When my father checked himself out of rehab and showed up at my office as if nothing had changed — as if he hadn't nearly lost everything. I can still picture him standing in front of me, running his hand through his graying hair and scowling at me.

"You really think you can run this company?" My dad looks around at what used to be his office with a sneer. "Hardly a week on the job and you've already fucked up."

I force my face into a neutral mask, trying not to show how his latest insult lands. "Yeah, this was a mistake. I admit it. But we wouldn't be in this position at all if you hadn't shown up to a board meeting completely wasted."

"I'm sick." He always does this. I know that it's not his fault that he has a disease, but so does he, and he weaponizes it every chance he gets. He turns his scowl into a well-rehearsed pout. "I'm getting the help I need and then I'll be back on my feet."

"I don't think so." I turn towards the window, looking out at the skyline.

"What the hell does that mean? You think you can run my company better than I can?" Dad sneers from behind me.

I turn back to face him. "It's not your company anymore, dad. I'm the one who negotiated this merger. It's Hyatt Marks Properties and I'm the CEO. You should focus on getting the help you need and being a good husband to mom."

I'm being harsh. I know how much the company means to my father — it's everything to him. The truth is that he always cared more about business than family and now he's losing both. I can see the twisted fury on his face as he calculates his next move. He took it too far when he showed up drunk at work, when he showed up at mom's birthday party sporting a black eye, completely drunk.

His mask of anger gives way to harsh amusement as he sits down and props his feet on my desk. He cocks his head to the side.

"Finally grow some balls on you?" He chuckles darkly. "I remember when you pissed the bed, when you ran crying about monsters in the closet. You always were a weak little boy. Pathetic. Always crying about something. Like a little wounded deer."

I clamp my mouth shut, not saying anything. I know he's just getting started.

"I thought if I taught you the business, if I took you under my wing and showed you, that one day you would takeover. Silly me," he smirks. "Should've seen my own son waiting to stab me in the back and take me down. Turns out the baby deer is a shark."

I cross over to the desk, sitting across from him. "It's not like that—"

He cuts me off. "You got lucky, didn't you, boy? If I weren't a goddamn drunk, you'd have to wait another 15 years for your big-boy-suit and big-boy-office."

He puts his palms on the desk, leaning towards me. "Go ahead and ship me upstate, son." He sneers the word like it's disgusting. "I'll be watching your inevitable downfall from afar."

I inhale, trying to calm my racing heart. "Is that all?" I feign indifference as I glance towards my computer. "I have things to do."

His eyes flash with anger and he stands abruptly. "Sure, that's all."

I can't stop myself. "What about mom? Did you talk to her? Because she was pretty upset this morning when I spoke to her."

My father turns and his cold eyes meet mine. "Don't you worry about her. Or Bennie. They'll be fine. We'll all be fine." He turns his eyes towards the window, the city outside.

"Worry about this shitty deal you've gotten yourself into.

Worry about your inevitable failure. You worry about that, son."

Before I can say anything else, he turns on his heel and sweeps out of the room, leaving me alone in his office. My office.

I smooth my shirt out, my hands shaking. He's good, my father. Very good. He accomplished his mission simply and effectively. I glance around the office I used to love, remembering how I'd beg my dad to let me come to work with him. How I admired him, wanted to be like him, despite his constant belittling, his never-ending jabs at me. Looking around at it, I feel nothing.

Nothing at all.

"Wesley! Are you even listening to me?" My mother's voice interrupts the assault of memories flashing through my mind.

I press the phone against my ear. "Sorry, what did you say?"

My mom huffs, annoyed at repeating herself, I'm sure. "I said the car is booked and Ben and I will be in the lobby of my building in the morning. We'll see you then."

To go visit dad. Right.

I clear my throat. "Alright. I'll be there." I hope she can't hear the dread in my voice.

"Sweetheart. I know you and your father have a difficult relationship, especially now with the company."

That's putting it lightly.

"He's not happy about stepping down, but it's for the best. He'll see what an incredible job you're doing."

"Yeah, because he was always so good at handing out praise," I mumble.

"Just play nice, please."

"Why are you telling me? He's the one who's always picked on me. Relentlessly. I don't know why you expect me to put up with it." I rub my hand against my forehead.

She sighs. "I know, and I'm sorry. I should have stood up for you boys more when you were growing up—"

"That's not what I mean—" I interrupt her. I don't want my mom to feel guilty about my dad's actions.

"No, you're right. I heard the things he said to you and I..." She cuts off, sounding choked up, and I suddenly regret saying anything at all. "He's difficult, your father. I thought that maybe he'd ease up on you once you took an interest in the business...and then once he started drinking..."

"It's fine," I say. "Forget I said anything. I'll see you next Saturday. I have to go."

I hang up before she has a chance to say anything else, hating the swirl of emotions building in my stomach. I lean back in my chair, tired. Just a few hours ago, I was riding high, elated, feeling Quinn's gorgeous body in my hands.

I check my phone and see a text from her:

Home!

That's it? What do I say to that? Should I even text her back or just ignore it? Maybe I should call her?

After a few minutes of panicking, I settle on a safe reply:

Great, thanks for letting me know. Can't wait for our date on Friday.

I float my thumb over the screen for an embarrassing

amount of time before finally pressing send. Once I do, I stare at the messages, waiting for those dreaded three dots, but nothing comes. I put my phone on the desk face-down.

It's time to buckle down on this project and get the ball rolling. I'm sick of waiting around for George to get his shit together. I'm the boss now and it's time to start acting like it.

Chapter 34

Quinn

It's my day off from work and I am buzzing with energy. After my incredible two days with Wesley, I came home and broke down to my mother about everything. I told her about The Phoenix —the real reason I was fired, how Ian leaked the story and blamed it on me, how Wesley found out and I ended up working for him. And how I've fallen for him in the worst way.

We sat up for hours eating Rocky Road and shuffling between crying, laughing, and stuffing our faces with food. She told me all about Joe and how much she likes him, and we commiserated about our mutual lovestruck foolishness.

I'm glad I finally told my mom about Wesley — even if I did have to listen to her lecture me about him for 45 minutes. Between the two of us, we've got enough trust issues to last a lifetime, so her lecture isn't really necessary, but she gives it to me anyway. Given how Wesley and I met, she's probably right for me to be cautious, but some part of me knows it's already too late for me.

The truth is it's been a steady fall. From the first time I saw Wesley, I've been slipping and slipping further into his orbit. Maybe if I had stayed away, if I had never known what he felt like inside of me, I'd be able to resist him. But not anymore. Not now that I know how soft and wicked he is, how he makes me feel things I've never felt before.

Our date tomorrow night swirls through my mind, sending my nerves off. I have no idea what a real date with Wesley Marks implies. Sure, we got half a breakfast and rode a ferris wheel, but something tells me this might be the Wesley I always imagined. The Wesley that wears expensive suits and orders the most French-sounding bottle of wine on the menu.

I turn over in bed and decide to do something with all my pent-up energy besides stressing about my date with Wes. For me, that something means a baking fest. Luckily my mom is spending the day with Joe, so I have the apartment to myself. Our kitchen is tiny, so I make a mess of ingredients in the living room as I mix the dough for muffins.

I'm popping the last batch into the oven when my phone buzzes with a text from Wesley:

Thinking of you. Can't wait for tomorrow night.

Butterflies dance in my stomach and I want to smack myself for the giddy feeling spreading through me at the simple text. I type out a few different messages, fiddling with my fingers as I finally settle on something.

Me too. Is it weird for me to ask what to wear? I don't want to be overdressed.

I stare at the screen, feeling like an idiot. It's probably not very smooth of me to ask, but I'd rather feel embarrassed now than show up in the wrong thing later. I clean up the kitchen while I wait for a response that finally comes a few minutes later.

> Whatever you wear will be perfect. But since I know that's a non-answer…semi-formal?

I smile down at the words, hearing his smirk in them. Semi-formal? So jeans are out, I guess. Another text buzzes.

> A cocktail dress. Something I can peel off you easily ;)

A blush grows on my cheeks, and I bite my lip to stamp out the smile growing at his promise. I type out a quick response and check the oven, but the muffins still need more time. I wipe my hands off and almost skip to my closet to search through my clothes. I only really have one dress that will suffice. Almost all of my clothes are thrifted, but I have a few dresses leftover from my time at The Phoenix.

The oven beeps and I take out the muffins and leave them on the counter. Waiting for them to cool, I take out my phone and dial an unexpected number.

"Hello?" Hannah's bright voice rings out from the other line.

I trudge through my anxiety at even making this call. "Hey, Hannah. It's Quinn." I pause. Should I say my last name? "Quinn Taylor, from the other night, and from the hospital—"

"Quinn, hey! What's up? Did you get home alright the other night?"

I switch the phone to my other ear. "Yeah, totally fine." Oh god, this is so weird. "Listen, I was wondering if you have plans tonight?"

"No plans. Just a tentative date with my Netflix account."

I chuckle at that and take a deep breath. "Well, I was wondering if you wanted to come over. I could use some fashion advice and some girl talk, to be honest."

"Where do you live? I'm not commuting to Bushwick, sorry."

I smirk. "I'm in South Slope."

"Sweet, I'm in Prospect Heights. Text me your address and what time to come. I'll see you later!"

Before I can reply, she hangs up. Despite the abruptness, I can't help the smile spreading across my face. Who would've thought that Wine Night with Hannah would make me this excited? I guess I've been needing a friend more than I realized. Maybe expanding my life beyond just work and my mom is a good idea.

A few hours and three muffins later, Hannah texts to let me know she's on the way to my place. I clean up my room since it's kind of a mess and light some candles, feeling suddenly self-conscious about having a new friend over. My stomach clenches nervously.

The buzzer goes off and I let her up, glancing down at my sweats and stained Yankees sweatshirt. Should I have changed into something nicer? Why didn't I think of this until this exact moment?

A knock at the door interrupts my thoughts and I answer it.

"Hey!"

Hannah smiles and lifts two bottles of red wine, stepping past me easily.

"The store had a deal if you got two, so we're getting drunk I guess." She shrugs her coat off and glances around.

"Welcome. This is my apartment," I say, gesturing out at the small room that is basically the whole place. She nods and moves towards the kitchen. She starts opening drawers, searching.

"By all means, make yourself at home." I smirk, leaning against the wall.

She shoots a smile back at me. "Bottle opener?"

"To your left."

She waves it around like a madwoman, turning to face me directly. "So, what's this womanly advice you so desperately need?"

"I think that conversation might require wine first." I hope she can't tell how I'm suddenly stalling about talking about Wesley. He doesn't feel real. Our whole situation doesn't really, so it's strange to talk about. "How was your day?"

She rolls her eyes. "Budget cuts mean I have to share an office now. Which would be whatever, except that Terry is the most annoying person possibly ever. He eats tuna every day. Every day, Quinn." She gives me the most serious expression that I can't help but bark out a laugh.

I pull two glasses out of the cabinet and Hannah passes me the wine bottle to pour. I pour and wave her to the living room, where we settle in the couch with the bottle between us.

"Chugging contest?" She asks, lifting her glass.

I chuckle. "Not with wine, please."

She shrugs and takes a large gulp of hers. "Okay, just spill, would you? I took the train here to hear all about your drama just to hopefully feel better about my own weird situationship."

I sip my wine and lean forward. "What do you mean?"

"Oh, just my ex who wants to get back together all of a sudden. It's weird and I'm not sure how I feel about it." She frowns, twisting her necklace. "Laura is...I don't know, I just don't know if she's changed."

I consider her words. "Well, I guess you can't know if she's changed until you find out, right?"

She nods. "The last time we dated, she was so insecure that it made her jealous and just mad all the time. No matter how much I'd tell her we were good, she was always so anxious that I would leave. It started to make me think she didn't love me like I loved her, if she could believe that I'd just fuck off and disappear."

I'm quiet at her words, thoughtful. She shakes her head and chuckles. "Anyway, why are we talking about me? We came here to talk about you."

"You came here to hang out with me, actually," I correct her, raising my eyebrows. "And that really sucks. I'm sorry you felt that way, but maybe she's worked on it. I don't know a lot about the situation, but I think people deserve a second chance."

She smiles softly. "I guess you're right. I just don't know if I'm trying to get hurt again right now, getting back into all that."

"Yeah." I nod, looking down at my mug. "But you know what they say...better to have loved and lost than never loved at all."

"Oh my god. You're not like, a romantic, are you?" She groans and I hide a smile, which just makes her groan further.

"What do you mean? I thought you were the most smiley person I'd ever met when we first met." I tell her with a smirk.

She shrugs. "That's my work persona, obviously. I'm all smiles there. But I've always been a hater deep down."

"Wow." I shake my head at this revelation. "Can I admit something you might get mad at me for? I thought you were so annoying when we first met. I called you Miss Perky in my head."

It's quiet for a moment that I think I've offended her, but she surprises me by bursting into laughter.

When she finally stops laughing, she shrugs. "That doesn't surprise me. I'm pretty different at work. I guess I'm a people pleaser in that way."

She lifts the bottle and tops off our mugs. "Now. Okay. Can I please hear the drama? Please?"

I pause, unsure where to start. How to even explain our whole situation and how much I should explain.

"Hello. Anytime now?" She waves her hand at me.

"I'm trying to figure out where to start! There's a lot. Don't rush me."

"Start at the beginning."

* * *

Two hours and bottles of wine later, I'm finished telling Hannah everything. Afterwards, she just leans backwards and exhales, her eyes wide.

"Wow. That is some story. Very *Fifty Shades*." She shakes her head. "Well, okay. Alright. So, what's the problem?"

"I'm sorry, did you not just hear everything I just said?"

"Right." She nods. "I do see your point."

At that, I start giggling, and so does she. I'm starting to think we're a little too drunk to be dissecting this right now, but it feels good to gush a little bit.

"Here's what I think. Never trust a man." Her words are slurred, and she points towards me.

I laugh. "You're just saying that because you're gay."

"Hey! You could be too if you committed." She raises her eyebrows suggestively and I shove her, both of us giggling.

Our hands graze and I blink. "We're not going to hook up," I say.

She stares blankly at me. "I know."

We both burst into laughter again.

"No, but seriously, I think I like you and what's his name? Walt?"

I giggle at the thought of Wes being called Walter and correct her. "Wesley. Wes." His name tastes good — I want to say it again, but I don't.

"Right, Wesley. Yeah, I like it. I love an enemies-to-lovers vibe."

I scoff. "Wesley and I were not *enemies*." I shake my head.

"You totally were." She sips the last of her wine and puts the mug down on the table. "He like — wrongly suspected you or whatever, didn't like you or thought he didn't like you. And you didn't like him in turn because he was a bag of dicks to you."

"Okay, yes, we had some misunderstandings—"

"Enemies! To lovers!" She chants until I beg her to stop.

For the rest of the night, we chat back and forth about relationships and work and life. Eventually, she announces that she's going to head home. I make her promise to text me when she gets home and walk her to the subway station despite her protests. We're standing at the subway entrance when she wraps her arms around me in a warm embrace.

"Thanks for inviting me over. I needed this, too." Hannah smiles and shuffles towards the stairs. "Next time, you can come to mine. I have a bidet!"

I barely have the chance to ask what a bidet is before she disappears down the subway steps, leaving me chuckling after her.

* * *

It's Friday morning — the day of my highly anticipated date with Wesley. I'm on the train on the way to the hotel, my black dress folded neatly in my canvas bag. I managed to fit my overly large makeup bag in there, too, and even snuck in my toothbrush just in case I end up staying the night. Maybe I'm being too hopeful.

I'm hit with a pang at the thought of seeing Wesley again. Somehow, even though it's only been two days, I've missed him. I close my eyes, picturing his broad shoulders, or how he rubs his hand over his clenched jaw when he's frustrated.

I see Sharon at the front desk on my way in and throw her a little wave. She waves me over with a smile and I'm hit with a wave of nervousness as I approach her.

"Quinn! How's it going?" She types rapidly at her computer, sending me a side glance.

I shift. "Good. All good. What's up?" Does my voice sound normal? I've always been a terrible liar.

"Nothing. Just wanted to check in. Mr. Marks left you a glowing review, so I assume all is well."

I balk at that. "Review? What do you mean?" Wes didn't mention anything about a review — when did he fill it out?

She waves me off. "It's not a big deal, just a check-in we do with VIP guests. There's a comment section that most people just leave blank, but Mr. Marks mentioned that your talents were being wasted in cleaning services, that you'd be better suited in a culinary position."

My mouth is opening and closing but no words come out. Sharon just goes on as if I'm hardly there.

"Anyway, congratulations. I know you've only been here a little while, but I have a feeling that upwards movement is in your future," she says. "Whatever you're doing for Mr. Marks is working!"

She laughs but the sound lands hollow in my stomach. I think I manage a nod and choke out something close to a thanks before I stumble to the private elevator. I lean a hand against the wall, bracing myself.

Whatever you're doing for Mr. Marks is working.

My stomach turns at her phrasing — the suggestion and the memories it triggers. Am I imagining the implication?

The thought that us having sex somehow had some bearing on Wesley's remarks on my professional performance makes me feel sick. Like I'm sleeping my way to the top. Like I'm back to the days where my body was a commodity.

Ding!

The elevator doors slide open, and I step out in a daze. The familiar smell of the place assaults me and I'm hit with a double pang of guilt and desire. I cross into the living room and put my bag down with a heavy sigh.

"Quinn."

I look up at the sound and Wesley is crossing the room towards me, the corners of his mouth ticked upwards. I push down the bubble of warmth at the sight of it — how incredible that little upwards twitch makes me feel — and stand abruptly, putting my palm out to stop him from touching me.

"Did you tell Sharon about us?"

His face scrunches in confusion. "What?"

"Sharon." My voice sounds hard. "At the front desk. What did you say to her?"

His confusion gives way to slight irritation. "What are you talking about?"

I throw my hands up, frustrated. "Sharon told me about the review you wrote! You can't just say nice stuff about me just because we slept together. I don't want any favors in exchange for sex, that's not what I'm doing."

"What the hell are you talking about?" He rears his head back, his jaw clenched. "I wrote that stupid thing two weeks ago, and my opinion is the same now as it was then. You are much too good to spend your time washing my fucking sheets and we will find you something better. Whether we're intimate or not, that doesn't change."

His chest rises and falls with the end of his speech, his dark eyes burning into mine. I step backwards and look away from him, needing relief from the intensity of his words.

"Oh," I finally manage to say. "Okay. Thank you. I'm sorry."

He nods once, a sharp, simple movement, an acceptance of my apology. It's quiet again.

He clears his throat. "I wanted to talk to you more about it tonight. If you'd still like to get dinner with me, that is."

"Of course," I say, a little too quickly. My past anger quickly gives way to excitement. "I brought a dress. A short one."

His eyes darken and he meets my gaze, quirking an eyebrow. "Is that so?"

I nod, a slow smile spreading across my face. He almost lets a full smile peak out, but he presses his lips into a line.

"I'm leaving for the day, but I'll be back around six to pick you up. Can you meet me downstairs?"

"Sure," I agree easily, hoping my face doesn't look too eager. He nods again and glances towards the elevator, shifting on his feet, hesitating. He looks back at me, his brow furrowed.

"Can I kiss you?"

My legs turn to jelly. I breath out something close to a yes, my heart in my eyes as he crosses towards me and reaches for my face. His lips descend onto mine with a perfect warmth, his hands holding the side of my face. He deepens the kiss and runs his tongue along mine, circling his thumbs against my face.

He pulls backwards and I stumble towards him, still reaching out for more. He chuckles and presses his forehead to mine, his breath warm against mine.

"Perfect," he murmurs, then pulls back and smooths out his tie, running his hand over his torso. "I'll see you later."

I can't even form a response before he strides swiftly towards the elevator. He throws me a smile I've never seen from him — something close to playful — before he gives a small wave and exits.

For the rest of the day, I'm thinking about that little smile and wave and how they feel like they are just for me. My little piece of Wesley.

* * *

By the time 5 o'clock rolls around, I'm almost giddy with anticipation. I've finished cleaning — there wasn't really much to do, anyways — so I give myself the hour to get ready and do my makeup.

I slip my work clothes off and change into the small black dress, the deep swoop leaving my back exposed. I take my braids out and squeeze some product into my hair, tossing my curls to add volume. Then I apply a light contour and a smokey eye, finishing off with mascara and a soft lipstick. I look good. Really good.

The elevator ride down to the lobby feels endless. My stomach flutters as the doors slide open and I cross the room to the exit. I step out into the cold air and suddenly feel like I've lost my breath. Wesley is leaning against his car, the Tesla he drove me back from the beach with, his hands folded across his chest. He looks incredible. I wish I were an artist so that I could paint him.

Without thinking, I move towards him, needing to be closer. His eyes seem to burn as he takes me in, scanning his eyes across my body.

"Hi," I breathe out, stepping in between his legs.

He straightens and peers down at me, blinking. "Hi." The word is almost a whisper. Then, louder. "You look incredible."

I make no attempt to hide my blush. "So do you."

The air between us feels charged with electricity. I want him to kiss me again. I want him to kiss me forever.

"No Pete tonight?" I ask lightly, glancing towards the Tesla.

He shakes his head and steps backwards, opening the passenger door. "It's just you and me tonight." I slide into the seat and he shuts the door softly behind me, rounding the front to take his place in the driver's seat.

I fiddle with the bracelets on my arm, twisting them a few times as Wesley starts the car. He braces on the seat between us, and I jostle my knee, tapping my foot on the floor softly. Wesley turns to me, his gaze sharp as ever.

"What's wrong?"

I peek a glance at him. "Nothing."

"Quinn." He says my name knowingly and puts his hand over where I'm still twisting my bracelets, letting his gaze fall to my jostling knee. I stop on both accounts and let out a breath.

"I'm just a little nervous, I guess."

As soon as I say the words, I regret it. Why would I tell him that? I should have played it cool. I should have said something witty and cute.

He furrows his brow like he doesn't quite understand. "You have nothing to be nervous about. It's just us. Getting dinner."

It's just us, he said.

"You're right," I nod, giving him a reassuring smile. He takes his hand off mine and peels the car away from the curb into traffic, watching the road steadily.

I glance out the window at the passing lights. "Where are we going? Can I ask?"

"Yes, you can ask." His mouth ticks up and my heart leaps in my chest. "It's actually an Italian spot that I'm a part-owner of as of recently. It's in Soho."

I smile. "I can't wait. I love Italian."

"Good."

His eyes are on the road so I can examine him freely — the lights and shadows dancing along his striking jaw, set firmly in place. I want to reach out and stroke it, but I force my gaze away from my gawking, worried he may notice me staring at him. I let my eyes wander to the passing lights of the city as we head downtown, willing my racing heart to calm in my chest.

Chapter 35

Wesley

As I drive down 6th Avenue, Quinn slips her hand away from mine and settles her palms in her lap, still playing lightly with the bracelets hanging on her arm. All I can focus on is the way her black dress is riding up her leg, revealing another inch of the soft skin of her bare thigh. An image flashes in my mind of my hand dipping past that skirt and feeling her bare underneath, ready for me.

I clench my jaw and focus on the road, the minutes ticking by in endless silence. Why am I not saying anything? Why isn't she saying anything? I should be making first date small talk, not fantasizing about taking her in the backseat of my car.

I clear my throat, needing to say something. Anything. "I guess we're both a bit nervous. Luckily, I happen to know that someone gets very talkative after a few glasses of wine."

She turns, gaping at me. "Excuse me? Are you saying I talk too much?"

I smirk. "I wouldn't say 'too much' but..."

She scoffs. "Of course, you'd say that. Mr. Dark and Brooding over here can barely string together a full sentence."

I blush at her words. I didn't realize how transparent my nerves were. I try for earnest, shooting her a smile.

"What can I say? You leave me speechless." She rolls her eyes and I'm frustrated that she never trusts my sincerity, so I double down. "It's true. When I'm with you...there are no words."

It's quiet and I manage a glance in her direction to see her staring down at her hands, looking deep in thought.

"Which is good, because you've got enough for the both of us." I grin wolfishly, bringing us back into safer territory. She scowls but laughs, and we settle into a conversation about the restaurant, how I got involved with it, and other properties I'm thinking of buying or co-owning.

When we get to the restaurant, I pull the car over and give the valet my keys, coming around to open the door for Quinn, but she's already clamoring out and smoothing her dress out.

I reach for her arm and lean down to murmur in her ear. "You're supposed to let me be a gentleman, please."

"I don't know. I think caveman might be more your style." She shoots me a grin, but settles into my embrace, letting me guide her towards the front. She doesn't protest when I open the door for her and gesture for her to enter gallantly, or when I place my hand on the small of her back to guide her.

I lean down again to her ear. "You're playing nice now."

She looks up at me. "It feels good," she says.

I pull Quinn's chair back for her and let her sit, then settle across from her, smoothing my tie down. She glances around at the restaurant with a glowing smile.

"Wow," she says, softly. "It's beautiful here."

"I'm glad you like it. This is actually only my second time here. I only recently got involved. My friend Jackson is the owner, and he needed some help as he plans to expand his brand. Plus, you know me, keeping busy with work."

She nods and smiles a little. "I'm always impressed when I get glimpses of it. You must work so hard, running an entire company."

I shake off her compliment. "I really don't believe I work any harder than you or anyone at my company or the waiter serving us, for that matter."

She nods thoughtfully at my words. "I have to admit I don't really understand all that you do — the business of it, I mean." Her smile fades a little as she looks around. "I guess that's why my restaurant idea feels like a pipe dream. I wouldn't know how to navigate any of that."

I nod, thinking of how to respond. How close she's hinting at some ideas I've had, but I don't want to scare her off.

"You don't necessarily need to know all of it. The basics, sure, and maybe you could take an intro business class, or just have a business partner who handles that, someone you trust, and you can worry about the food."

"Taking a class would be nice," she says, a little wistful.

I glance down at the menu. "Do you prefer red or white wine?"

The corner of her mouth ticks up as she answers. "My wine usually comes in the $10 variety, so I'm sure whatever you choose will be wonderful."

I smile at that. Her open playfulness is one of the many things I adore about her. The waiter approaches and introduces himself as Jacob. I order a Cabernet Sauvignon that I'm familiar with, choosing one that I know isn't too ridiculously priced. Usually I wouldn't care about that, but I don't want Quinn to feel weird about anything tonight. Jacob comes back quickly and pours our glasses, leaving the bottle between us.

I lift my glass.

"A toast? To you, Quinn Helena Taylor. Thank you for

your forgiveness, and for giving me a chance to take you out, to get to know you. I am more grateful than you know."

She raises her glass to mine, her eyes meeting mine with reluctance. "You have got to stop using my middle name," she says, utterly serious. I let out a laugh and she watches me, her eyes sparkling. Finally, we both drink, effectively finishing our glasses. I quickly pour us both refills.

"Thank you," she adds with a smile. "For inviting me." She looks down at the menu, studying it for the first time. "So, what's good here?"

I glance down at the menu, but before I can read it, a hand falls on my shoulder. I look up and Jackson is standing over me, a smile spread across his face. "Wes. You trying to hide from me?"

I clasp his hand into a shake, smirking. "Only because I knew you'd completely embarrass me in front of my date. Jackson, this is Quinn. Quinn, Jackson." I gesture to Quinn, who is eyeing us with a small smile.

Jackson steps forward and puts his hand out. She goes to shake his hand, but he lifts it to his lips, planting a soft kiss on the back of her hand. "Enchanté."

She giggles and I want to burn that hand. "Nice to meet you, Jackson. Your restaurant is beautiful."

"You're very kind. Did Wesley tell you he's a part owner now?" He gestures towards me as I shake my head.

"He did mention that." Quinn flattens her lips into a line, hiding a smile.

"He's usually too humble about these things," Jackson explains. "So we have to brag on his behalf."

"He's sitting right here," I grumble and Quinn's smile only grows along with Jackson's. "You can run along now, you've said your hello."

Jackson feigns offense. "Can you believe how rude he is? I

can't believe I ever had a crush on him," he conspires with Quinn and she raises her eyebrows.

"In college," I clarify.

Quinn nods. "You two go that far back?"

"Unfortunately," I quip, and Jackson rolls his eyes. "You should have seen Wesley in college. A skinny little thing and much too smart for his own good. A total nerd. But the ladies still loved him."

Quinn chuckles. "I bet he was breaking hearts left and right."

"Mine included," Jackson agrees and they both giggle together.

"Yes, yes, it's all hilarious." I shoot daggers at Jackson. "Would you just send us some free food and get out of here?"

"Of course, my liege. Nothing less for you, sir." He salutes me and walks away, sending Quinn a wink before he does.

She chuckles as she watches him go. "He's quite a character."

"He's annoying," I correct her.

She smiles. "I'm trying to imagine you in college, but I can't. What did you study?"

"Music at first. But then I switched to a double in Business and Psychology when my father threatened to stop paying for my education."

She frowns at that. "Do you play an instrument?" She asks, her brow furrowed.

I swallow. "Piano. I used to."

"Why did you stop?" She asks. My first instinct is to shut her and this entire conversation down, but when I look at her, her face is open. Curious.

"I guess...I don't really have a good answer. Something stupid about my dad sort of ruining my love for it." I shrug. "When my dad gave me the ultimatum about my major, he basically told me I wasn't any good at music, nothing special, that kind of thing. *Painfully mediocre* were his exact words. Every time I sat down to play after that, it's like I just kept playing those words in my head, and I couldn't play."

A wave of anger rises in me at the thought, and I clench my wine glass a little tighter. Taking a deep breath, I force myself to look back at Quinn and shake it off. "Anyway. It's kind of stupid."

She shakes her head. "I don't think it's stupid at all. The same thing happens to me sometimes. That voice in your head that tells you you're worthless...sometimes that voice comes from somewhere."

Her words are heavy, and I feel a wave of anger at the thought of someone saying that to Quinn. She reaches for me and puts her palm over my hand like she did in the car, the familiar gesture sending a comforting warmth where she touches me.

"For what it's worth, I bet your dad was completely wrong about your music. Everything you do is incredible, Wes, and I'm sure this is no different. I'd love to hear you play some-time, if you ever wanted to."

She squeezes my hand and pulls back. As soon as she does, I miss the warmth. I want her hand back on mine imme-diately, but just then, our waiter and Jackson arrive with a few appetizers. Quinn's eyes go wide as Jackson explains what everything is and rushes off, not bothering to tease me further.

She looks down at the food, her eyes still wide. "We didn't even order this!" She whisper-yells at me.

I smile. "I tried to hide us from Jackson so we could order our food and try to be normal, but now that he's seen us, get ready. This is only the beginning. We're going to be stuffed when we leave here."

She smiles and grabs her fork. "Fine by me."

* * *

A few hours later, I've stayed true to my word. Quinn and I have to beg Jackson to stop bringing us food and he relents. He still brings us a small soufflé for desert that we manage a few bites each of.

When we stumble from the restaurant, we're both completely full and Quinn is decently tipsy from what I can tell. She's leaning into me, groaning about how she'll never eat again. The valet sees us, but I hold my hand up to him.

"Do you mind if we walk for a bit?" I ask Quinn. It's a rare warm spring evening and neither of us needs a coat.

"Sure," she agrees, and I tell the valet we'll be back in a few minutes to get the car. "Are you okay to drive?" She asks me.

"Yes. I only had two glasses, but thank you for checking." I reach for her hand, intertwining our fingers, and the movement sends my heart racing. She beams up at me. "Is this okay?"

"More than okay."

I step closer to her and snake my other arm around her. "This okay?"

She gazes up at me, her lips parting. "Yes, it's okay."

I lean down and brush her hair to the side, pressing my lips to her neck softly. "This?"

She lets out a moan of agreement that sounds close to a yes, but I can't wait any longer. I wrap my hand around the back of her neck and bring her mouth to mine. I let my tongue explore her mouth, loving the feeling of her wrapped around me. As I deepen the kiss, she moans again, the sound going straight to my cock.

I pull back to ease up but she reaches for me, capturing my mouth again and taking control. She rolls against me and I groan. She pulls back this time, leaning her forehead against mine. "Wesley."

I groan and shift away from her. "You *cannot* say my name like that. Not here." I chuckle and let out a pained breath.

She smiles. The little vixen — she knows exactly what she's doing to me. I shake my head, distracted. This isn't why I wanted to take this walk, dammit. I see a bench nearby and move towards it, bringing her over. I sit down and settle her next to me.

"Okay. I wanted to talk to you about something."

She shifts, looking nervous now. "Okay. Is it something bad? Because I've had a really great night and if you're going to ruin it can we maybe just wait until tomorrow?"

I want to reach for her, but instead I bring my hand to the back of my neck. "I don't think it's bad. The last thing I want to do is upset you. I don't know."

She groans and runs her hand down her face. "Oh god. The anticipation is worse. Just get it over with, whatever it is."

I intertwine our fingers again, tracing my thumb over the back of her hand. "I've been thinking...about your job."

She pales. "You're firing me?" Her voice shakes.

"What? No. No." I grip her hand tighter. "I was thinking maybe the restaurant at the hotel. I spoke to the chef and she's open to having you start as a line cook, training under her. If that would interest you."

She pulls her hand away from mine and looks away. Shit, no. She's upset. Shit, shit, shit.

"What? What did I say wrong?" I ask, panicking.

She sighs. "That is — Wesley, you can't do that." She shakes her head.

"Do what?"

"Do favors for me because we're sleeping together! I already told you that can't happen," she says, her voice rising.

I shake my head. "That's not — I just thought you would like that kind of work more, and then you and I wouldn't be working together so closely."

She rears back like she's been struck. "You don't like working with me?"

"No!" God, why is everything coming out completely wrong? "No, that's not what I meant. I just mean...can't you understand why it's difficult for us, you working for me? As my..."

"Maid." She deadpans. "You can say the fucking word. You're the one who made it happen."

I flinch. "I'm sorry. I really didn't want to upset you. I thought you would be excited."

She softens. "I am, Wesley. That sounds like a dream to me. But I have to get it because I deserve it, not because you pulled some strings and made it happen. No."

I feel a swell of anger that she doesn't believe she deserves this. "You *do* deserve it. I didn't just snap my fingers and get you a job, Quinn. I gave your resume to the head chef and explained all about your restaurant idea and she said you sounded really passionate and she'd be happy to interview you. It's just an interview, and it has nothing to do with our relationship. Nothing."

It's quiet for a few moments.

"Okay," she says, finally, her voice firm.

"Okay?" I repeat back at her. "Are you upset with me?"

She shakes her head. "No. Thank you for getting me an interview."

I reach for her, needing her close to me again. "You're welcome. I just want you to be happy, Quinn. I want to help make you happy in any way I can."

"You really want to make me happy?" She asks me, tilting her head up to meet my eyes. Her warm smile smolders into something deeper.

"Yes," I breathe out, taking her in.

She licks her lips, her eyes darkening. "Then take me home."

Chapter 36

Wesley

We stumble into the apartment, wrapped up in each other. I want to touch every inch of her. My hands roam freely as she grips my hair, and I kick my shoes off and rip off my suit jacket, throwing it to the side. I move to do the same to hers, frantic, desperate to touch her, and she chuckles against my mouth, stepping back.

"Feeling impatient again?" She grins.

I scoop her up in response, carrying her to the bedroom and laying her on her back softly on my bed. I pull back and stare down at her, drinking her in, but she reaches for me and brings me down to her soft lips. So soft.

Everything in me is screaming to take her now, but I force myself to slow down, matching the pace of her exploring mouth. She pulls me down to her, but then surprises me by pushing me to the side and lifting her leg over mine and settling in my lap on top of me.

I let her take the lead, resting my palms on the bed behind us as she kisses my neck, teething at it in a way that I know will leave a mark.

"Feeling territorial?" I smirk, lifting her chin to meet my

gaze. She doesn't back down. Not at all. Instead, her hand travels to my pants, unbuckling my belt and touching me where I need her most.

I moan and she takes me out, drawing her hand up and down my length with wicked slowness.

"Faster," I choke out.

She grins and obeys, quickening her pace as she continues to stroke me. She brings her lips down to mine again, kissing me as she jerks me, her fingers tightening around me. I can't help but thrust into her hand, needing more. I move to flip us but she pulls her hand away and pushes my chest down, straddling me, her eyes flashing in warning.

Understanding spreads through me and I take a deep breath. "Quinn. I need it."

She smirks. "Need what, Wesley?" Her hand travels back down to me and traces down my length again.

I buck my hips and groan. "Please baby, let me fuck you."

I've barely let the words out when she stands up completely, leaving me lying on the bed, my pants pooled at my ankles. I watch as she turns and unzips her dress, her hands traveling slowly down her back. She steps out of the dress, standing in front of me in a matching red lace set.

"Quinn," I half-choke the word, taking her in. She smirks another wicked grin and reaches behind her, unclasping her bra and letting it fall to the ground in front of her. My chest rises and falls as I watch her hook her fingers around the sides of her panties and slowly — God, so slowly — she lets them fall around her ankles and steps out, completely naked.

I reach out to touch her and she grabs my hands and presses them on either side of me, straddling me again. I never thought I'd be so turned on by a woman taking the lead like this, but I want to obey every word that Quinn tells me. I love watching her straddle me and take control.

"No touching," she whispers, her tone scolding as she rubs her clit up against me, sending me into a frenzy. I groan at her instructions and how badly I want to touch her.

"Let me make you feel good, baby."

She shakes her head, her eyes darkening, and keeps my hands pinned at my sides. "No touching," she repeats, then releases my hands and shifts so she's aligned right with my cock. Then, slowly, she lowers herself onto me and lets me fill her completely.

"Fuck," I hiss out the word and twist my hands into the sheets, watching her. She arches her back and lowers herself all the way and I fill her completely. "Fuck, Quinn." I'm not capable of saying anything else.

"Wesley," she moans to match me and brings her hand up to her nipple, twisting it in her hands. "Do you wish you could feel this?" She moves her hand down to her clit. "How wet I am for you."

She presses down on me again, riding me with a slow rhythm now. "God, baby, this is torture." I watch her fingers play with her clit and I can see how soaking she is from here.

"It feels good." She lets out a breathy moan as she fucks me. "Almost as good as your cock feels, filling me up." I thrust my hips up, driving into her and her mouth falls open with surprise. She smirks down at me in permission, so I thrust again, and she moans at the contact.

"Please, baby, let me touch you." I can't stand it another minute. "I'm begging you."

Her smirk grows at my words, and she meets my thrust again and leans down, pressing a kiss against my mouth. "You can touch now."

I don't wait a single second. My hand moves down to her clit, and I take her nipple into my mouth, swirling my tongue over her and circling my thumb over her clit. She moans at the contact, and I lose all control, sick of playing her game. I flip her over and thrust further into her.

She gasps at the movement, but I thrust again, pressing against her, needing to feel every part of her. I reach for her clit again. I'm going to make her come so many times she forgets her name.

"Oh, god. Fuck. I'm close. Wesley." Her breathy moans fill my ears and send another wave of pleasure through me. I slow my pace and slowly bring my mouth back down to her nipple, taking her in my mouth, delaying her. "Wes. Please." She whines and I grin down at her.

"Who's begging now?" I growl into her ear.

I thrust again, brushing her clit once more, and that simple movement sends her over the edge. She screams and I keep going, meeting her for every movement. I feel her clench around me, and I love it, the feeling of her milking my cock.

"Wes," she whispers. "Are you close?"

A shudder goes through me as I thrust into her again. "Yes," I manage through my breaths.

She brings my head down, forcing me to look at her. She meets my eyes and steels her gaze. "Not yet."

I thrust again, teetering on the edge, my eyes going wide as I drink her in, the sight of her staring at me. She bites her lip and blinks, her eyes not leaving mine. "Not yet, Wesley."

I groan and gasp, so close. "Oh, fuck. Baby — I can't. I need to —"

"Not yet, Wesley. I need more." Her soft voice is somewhere between scolding and begging. "More."

I obey, my eyes never leaving hers. Our gazes melt together as I beg once more, needing release, needing her so badly.

"Now, Wesley. Come. Come for me."

I spill into her, finally getting my release, thrusting against her wildly, completely out of control, like I've never been before. Finally, I come back down to reality. I soften and fall against her, completely spent.

She meets my gaze and presses a soft kiss to my mouth. "Perfect," she whispers. I pull out of her and collapse on the bed next to her, pulling her against me automatically.

"Fuck, Quinn. That was so hot. Oh my god." I still feel like my head is spinning.

She turns and buries into me. "Yeah? I wasn't sure if you'd like it, me taking control, but I thought about what you said... about making me beg to finish, and it made me really hot thinking about it." She sounds adorably shy admitting it.

I press a soft kiss against her mouth. "I fucking loved it. But next time you'll be the one begging me, baby. We'll see how you like it."

She grins wickedly, reaching for me. "I don't think I'll like it," she smirks. "I think I'll love it."

* * *

Sunlight pours into my room the following morning. Quinn's soft body is nestled into mine and it feels incredible. I blink a few times and stretch my arms up, exhausted. Glancing down at Quinn's sleeping figure, I reach my hand towards her, caressing her cheek. I could get used to this — going on dates, spending the whole night together, waking up next to her.

I check my phone and see a text from Ben confirming that I'm watching Luna tonight, as well as a few emails from George that I really don't want to deal with. In fact, I can't bring myself to care about work at all, not with this beautiful woman in my bed.

Quinn stirs next to me and yawns, waking. I try not to make it too obvious that I've been watching her as she sleeps.

She blinks a few times and rubs her eyes, looking up at me with a lazy smile.

"Hi," she whispers, and I bring my lips down to hers in response.

"How did you sleep?"

She stretches her arms, mimicking my earlier movement, and rolls her shoulders back. "Okay. It takes some getting used to for me, sleeping with someone else. You're like a furnace."

I snuggle closer to her. "You love it." I nudge my nose into the crook of her neck, inhaling her perfect scent. "I slept like a rock, personally."

I can almost feel her roll her eyes against me. "Do you have work to do today?"

I groan and fall onto the pillow. "Unfortunately, yes." I curl my hand around her stomach and press her closer to me again. "Not yet. Five more minutes."

Pressing Quinn close to me, I kiss her again. She meets me with every stroke of her mouth against mine, the taste of her filling me with a familiar warmth.

Eventually, she pulls back, half-gasping for air and giggling against me. The breathy sound goes straight to my dick as she sits up and stretches, nudging against me. "Come on, get up, boss-man."

"Don't call me that."

"You don't like boss man? What about...Sir?" Her eyes darken on the word. "I'm sure you've got a lot of work to do, Sir. I wouldn't want to distract you from that." She bites on her lip.

I roll my eyes. Swinging my legs over the side of the bed, I cross over to the bathroom, turning to find her watching me. I quirk an eyebrow at her, but she just shrugs. With a low laugh, I walk into the bathroom and turn the shower on. I meet her eyes in the mirror as she stands in the doorway, the blanket wrapped around her.

"Yes?" I prompt her. I'm still completely naked and she clearly notices from the way her gaze falls down to my bare ass.

She shifts on her feet. "Aren't you going to ask me to join you?" She comes closer and drops the blanket, wrapping her arms around my torso and running her hands along my chest.

I turn and kiss her again. "Are you expecting shower sex? Because I hate to disappoint, but I really should work at some point."

She smirks up at me and grabs my hand, pulling me towards the steaming stream of water. "No, not shower sex." She guides me to stand underneath it and I close my eyes, releasing a sigh of relief at the feeling of the warm water cascading down my skin. When I open my eyes, Quinn is just standing against the wall, watching me.

"I just want to watch you," she admits, biting her lip.

I pull her towards me and kiss her again, the water tumbling over both of us. I step back and lather shampoo in my hair as she cleans herself off, running her hands up and down her body. I know she doesn't mean for the motion to be so teasing, but fuck. I feel myself growing hard the more I watch her soap down her wet, naked body.

We switch places again so I can wash my hair out and as soon as I'm done washing my body, I slip out of the shower and will my dick to calm down. I head into my bedroom and pick out one of my suits, laying it on the bed as I get dressed.

I'm sitting on the edge of the bed in my slacks and gray button down, cuffing the sleeves, when Quinn comes out of the bathroom with one towel wrapped around her body and a second in her hair.

"You okay?" She asks me, reaching for her bag on the table

and pulling out clothes of her own. "You practically ran out of the shower. I thought you were going to slip."

"If I spent one more minute watching you lather soap all over your perfect body, I'd be taking you up against that wall right now."

Her mouth forms a perfect *o* as she nods, her eyes darkening as if she's imagining the scene I've described. As if she wants it as much as I do.

"Too bad," she says eventually, dropping her towel and dressing in front of me, her eyes on me as she slips into a soft blue sundress.

I'm struggling with my gold cufflinks when she steps in between my legs and smiles down at me. "Let me." She says, taking my wrist in her hand. I stare up at her, mesmerized. This simple activity should not be setting my heart racing, but for some reason, it does.

When she's finished, she steps back and reaches for my suit jacket, gesturing for me to stand. When I do, she slips it over my arms and turns us towards the mirror, smoothing her hand over the front of the jacket.

I stare at our reflections in the mirror, my tall, hard body next to her small, soft one.

"We look good together," I say, hoping I'm the only one who can hear the hint of vulnerability in my voice — the question of whether she's thinking the same.

Her soft smile grows. "My favorite picture." She turns and grabs her bag, lifting it over her shoulder.

I want to ask her what she means by that, but I don't. She's already moving to the living room, so I follow her, grabbing my phone off the nightstand. I already have a million notifications. Even my assistant has been asking why I'm more absent than usual. The answer is currently standing in my kitchen.

Quinn turns to me. "I cleaned the whole place yesterday. All I really have to do is order some stuff for the place if that's okay? What do you think about getting smart lightbulbs or something? You could be like 'Hey, turn the lights on' and they'd turn on." She smiles at the idea.

I can't help but chuckle. "Sure. Whatever you want. I have to go. I have a meeting in a few hours and to be honest, I have a lot to catch up on."

She frowns, but nods. "I understand." She shifts on her feet again, one of her telltale signs of nervousness. "I'm going to a barbecue thing tomorrow with my mom and her new boyfriend. With his family in Long Island. Would you maybe want to come?"

It's the way she asks it, the hopeful twinge in her voice at the end. How her eyes meet mine with such an earnest expression. It sends something into my chest, some painfully beautiful wave that feels an awful lot like...

"What am I thinking? You probably have work. You must be busy. It's totally fine. I just thought it would be weird meeting his family and—"

I reach for her, wanting to kiss her, but force words out instead. "I'll go. I'd like to go. Thank you for inviting me."

She nods, a jerky movement, her eyes wide. Relief in her features. I press my lips to hers, needing to taste her again. I break away and press the elevator button, out of breath.

"What time should I pick you up tomorrow?"

"Noon?"

The elevator doors slide open, and I shoot her a smile. "It's a date."

Chapter 37

Quinn

It's Sunday morning and I'm still reeling from Friday night as I get dressed for Joe's party. My mom left a few hours ago to help set up, looking more dressed up than I've seen her in a while. She looked beautiful. The bandana wrapped around her head matched her red dress and lipstick.

It's past noon when my phone buzzes with a text from Wes:

I'm downstairs. Can I come up?

I cringe at the thought of Wesley seeing my tiny apartment.

Be right down!

Slinging my bag over my shoulder, I grab my keys and

slide my phone into my pocket. I stumble down the stairs and out the door, seeing Wesley's town car. As usual, Pete and Wesley are standing outside waiting for me.

I skip over to them with a smile.

"Hi, Pete."

He nods at me. "Miss Taylor."

My smile turns into a scowl. "Pete..." My tone is a warning.

He rubs the back of his neck. "Sorry. Quinn." He opens the door and gestures for me to enter. My gaze slides to Wesley. He's looking more casual than usual in a black t-shirt and jeans and the sight is utterly swoon worthy. Wes wears casual just as well as a hand-pressed suit.

"You look incredible," Wes says softly, reaching for my hand and intertwining our fingers.

I smile, trying to hide my blush, but he runs his thumb along my cheekbone in a warm gesture that only causes the pink hue to grow.

"How are you?" I ask as he opens the door for me and gestures for me to slide in.

In the backseat, he settles in right next to me, close enough that our bodies are touching. "Better now." He smirks. His hand is still in mine and he's rubbing soft circles on my knuckles. "And you?"

"I'm good. Excited to meet Joe's family. And a little nervous. He's been really good for my mom lately."

"You have nothing to be nervous about," he murmurs, pressing his lips to the back of my hand with a soft kiss and I can't help the smile that spreads across my face. I feel giddy with Wes by my side like this.

Pete continues forward and Wes makes a motion to him. A few seconds later, he closes the divider, sealing us in the back.

"Craving some privacy, Mr. Marks?" I lean into him, pressing my hand against his chest.

The corners of his mouth tilt up. "Do you only call me Mr. Marks when you're horny, then?"

My mouth drops. "Wesley!"

He presses his mouth against mine, his tongue pressing against mine softly. He tastes like mint and smells musky, like sandalwood and pine. He chuckles against my mouth. "See? Back to Wesley already."

He pulls back and intertwines our hands again. "Can I come over after the party? I'd like to see your apartment."

My smile falters. I hope he can't see the fear growing in my eyes as I glance away, but it's too late. "What? What's wrong?" He says, reaching for me.

I shake my head. I know I'm being dramatic. It shouldn't be a big deal, but for some reason the thought of him in my tiny hole of an apartment makes me nervous. I know he won't judge me or think lesser of me, but still...

"Quinn." His flat voice interrupts my spiraling trail of thoughts. I glance back at him and my heart falls at the earnest expression of irritation etched into his features. It's so perfectly him that my chest aches.

"Nothing," I say quickly, rubbing my thumb across his knuckles as he does for me, hoping the gesture brings him a similar comfort. "I just got nervous about you coming over. My apartment...well, it's not very nice."

"Quinn," he breathes out. "I wouldn't care if you lived in a shoebox. I just want to see all the parts of you. I don't want you to hide any of yourself from me."

His words pierce me somewhere unexpected. Simple, beautiful words that make my heart swell in my chest. I press my forehead against his, our breaths mingling. "I know. I don't want you to hide from me, either."

He looks at me, his gaze drinking me in, and there's such plain adoration on his features that I can't help but bring my lips to his. Then we're kissing. Really kissing this time. It's like we're both starved for each other. His hand fists into my hair, bringing me closer, impossibly close, and I can't help but mimic his movements.

He groans against me as he deepens the kiss. Seconds or minutes or hours could have passed but all I can feel is this kiss. All I can feel is Wesley.

"How about this?" He pulls back. "I'll show you mine if you show me yours."

"Wesley! How scandalous."

He chuckles and shakes his head. "I meant my apartment. If I can come over to your place, you can see mine."

I furrow my brow, considering his words, how this feels like a trap somehow. After all, he is a businessman. "What's so special about your place? I've already seen the penthouse."

"Ah, but this isn't the penthouse. This is *my* place. As for what's special about it, well, I guess you'll have to come over to find out." His grin is teasing. "Or maybe you'll never know..."

I roll my eyes. "Alright, fine. You have a deal, Mr. Marks." I hold my hand out for a handshake. With a smile, he slips his hand into mind and shakes it firmly.

"You have a deal, Miss Taylor."

* * *

Deep breaths. It's just a party. Just a normal, friendly gathering. Not like I have anybody to impress, not really. Right?

"You still with me over there?" Wesley's voice breaks me out of my spell. We're standing in front of Joe's house. It's a

267

lovely place with a lush garden out front, a winding stone path leading towards the red front door.

I turn towards Wesley. "I don't know why I'm making such a big deal of this. Getting myself all worked up over nothing."

He wraps his arms around me easily, tugging me towards him. "You're allowed to feel however you feel. You're not 'getting yourself worked up' just because you're feeling nervous," he says simply.

I reach up for him, pressing onto my tippy toes so that I can reach his lips with mine. "When did you get so wise? You're supposed to be the stubborn and obstinate one, not me."

He chuckles against my mouth. "I like you, Quinn Taylor. Stubborn and all." He pulls back with a warm smile, our foreheads resting against each other.

My stomach drops at his words. Sweet, adoring words that I never imagined I'd hear from Wesley. This strong, brooding man is standing in some stranger's driveway in Long Island for me. All for me.

A rush of fear crashes through me. What does this mean? We've only been on a couple of dates, but it feels like everything is moving so quickly. Like there's an intensity pulsing between us.

"I really like you, too, Wesley Marks."

We approach the front door, our hands intertwined. The feeling of Wesley's warm hand in mine makes me feel stronger somehow. Like I can conquer anything with him by my side.

"Wait." I pull up abruptly at the front door and turn to him, entirely serious. "What's your middle name?"

He smirks, his eyes soft in the midday light. "Is this very important?"

"Of course! You've known mine since we met. It's only fair."

He considers my words and nods, leaning against the doorway. "Alright. Guess, then."

I cross my arms. "Give me a hint at least."

"It starts with the letter J."

"Jack?"

"Nope."

"No, no, not Jack. John."

He shakes his head, suppressing his growing smile.

"Oh, god. Don't tell me it's something awful like Josh or Justin? Or worse...Jason." I shudder like I'm imagining something truly terrible.

Wesley throws his head back and laughs — really laughs, that full, belly sound that reaches all the way down to my toes. I can't help but smile with him, my hand reaching for him again, wanting to touch him.

He reaches out and captures my hand again. "It's James."

My smile grows. "Wesley James Marks."

The door swings open and my mom stands in the doorway, relief coloring her features. "Good. You're here. I'm dying without you."

I chuckle lightly. "Hello to you too. You're in a very good mood."

"Oh, hush. You know how nervous I am and—" Her eyes widen as her gaze flicker to Wesley, as if she only just noticed the towering man standing over me.

Wesley sticks his hand out, smoothing his shirt down with the other hand and quirking his lips up. "Hello, ma'am. I'm Wesley Marks. It's a pleasure to meet you."

My mom's jaw nearly drops, and I imagine she's having a similar reaction as I did the first time I saw Wesley. Her eyes are as wide as saucers as she stares down at his outstretched hand.

She bursts into laughter. "Oh, dear." She looks right at me, shaking her head. "You are in trouble, all right."

She puts her hand into his and looks right into his eyes. "I've heard a lot about you and let me tell you — not all of it has been good. If you hurt my daughter, I don't care who you are. I will string you up by your balls."

"Mom!" My face turns completely red.

Wesley just nods, taking it all in stride. "You're absolutely right, Ms. Taylor. I have made some mistakes, but really, all I'd like now is a chance to show your daughter and your family how much she means to me."

My mom nods sharply and they release their hands. "Well, then. Call me Mel," she says to Wes. "Welcome to the party! Come, let me introduce you to everyone."

I reach for Wesley's hand again and squeeze it, smiling up at him, hoping the gesture communicates how happy I am to be here with him. He squeezes back, the corners of his lips ticking upwards, and we follow my mom into the backyard.

The next few hours are a whirlwind of introductions and small talk. My mom introduces us to Joe's brother and sister, as well as his father and uncle. I'm terrible with names, but Wesley remembers every single one and whispers in my ear helpfully throughout the day. Eventually, I leave him with the guys while I go into the kitchen with my mom.

"Will you let me do that, please? You shouldn't be fussing around." I take a casserole dish from her hands and push her towards the dining room table.

She rolls her eyes. "I feel fine. I'm stronger than you give me credit for."

"You're the strongest person I know," I say, putting the

dish into the open dishwasher. "But you can let me do the dishes."

She hums in agreement and turns to the window, looking out. "He's won everyone over, it seems."

"Why are you being so weird about him?" I ask. "I really like this guy. Do you even realize what a big deal that is for me?"

"It's your fault for telling me how awful he was to you."

"But—"

"I'm looking out for you. Somebody has to. You're too trusting, too forgiving sometimes."

"I'm not that forgiving. I haven't forgiven Dad for leaving." I'm scrubbing the plate in front of me with such ferocity I hardly notice my mom next to me until her hand closes over mine.

"I think..." She trails off and glances out the window to where Joe stands, in front of the grill, laughing. "I think I hadn't forgiven him either until I met Joe. It's like I didn't know I was drowning until I met him and finally came up for air.

"You don't ever have to forgive him. That's your choice. But don't ever let his mistake infect you. The best revenge is for you to be happy." She brushes my hair back with a soft smile. "What do the kids say? Live your best life."

I turn around and wrap my arms around her in a hug, not caring that my hands are still wet. She pulls back from the hug and looks back out the window. "As for tall, dark, and brooding..." She smiles and I follow her gaze to the backyard, where Greg's daughters seem to be turning Wesley into a toilet paper mummy.

"Good luck."

* * *

It takes us nearly an hour to escape my mother's clutches once we announce we're headed back to the city. She insists on packing me a hefty bag of leftovers despite my protests. Greg's daughters are so enamored with Wesley that they cling onto his legs as we inch towards the front door, surrounded. Finally, hands clasped together, we shuffle out into the front yard, sighing in relief.

"Well. I thought we'd never make it out of there," he jokes, shrugging into his jacket.

I shake my head. "I'm sorry. That was a lot. More than I was expecting—"

He reaches for my arm. "I'm kidding. Don't apologize. I had a really great time." He ducks down and brings his lips to mine, capturing me in a kiss that takes my breath away. My eyes flutter closed and my whole body feels lighter with his lips on mine.

"I've been dying to do that for hours," he murmurs against my mouth.

I smirk. "I'll have to get in line behind Greg's daughters," I chuckle. "I thought I had it bad for you, but those girls put me to shame."

He leans back slightly, his eyes boring into mine. "Oh? You've got it bad for me?"

I freeze, realizing what I said, and force a laugh. "We should get going, huh? City traffic and all that!" I skip towards the car, keeping my voice light. Wesley chuckles darkly from behind me, and I know, somehow, without looking back at him, that his hand is rubbing the back of his neck.

We slide into the car and Wesley nods in Pete's direction. "We're headed back to Quinn's place for a bit, then to my apartment in Dumbo. Can you call Federico and let him know we're on the way?"

"Sure thing, boss." Pete starts the car and Wesley walks us

to the backseat and we both slide in. The dividend is still up and it's quiet as we pull away from Joe's house.

"Thanks again for coming with me. It kind of helped, having you by my side, and my mom just seemed good today. Happy." My voice sounds wistful even to my ears and maybe Wesley notices as he slips his hand in mine.

"I can't take credit for that, but I am glad to hear it." He flips my hand over, running his thumb on the inside of my wrist. "It's only fair. You've met my family, and now I've met yours."

"It's strange to think of them as my family," I admit. "My mom said she's staying there for the week to help Joe with some stuff. I just feel like..."

I look at the window, away from Wesley's intense gaze, his open, steady expression. He circles my wrist again, as if he knows the small movement brings me comfort.

"Watching her in that house, with Joe's family...she seemed so at peace. Like she'd finally come home. Found her place, or something." I swallow the lump forming in my throat as my voice drops to a whisper. "I'm so selfish."

Wesley gathers my hands in his and pulls me lightly, forcing me to look towards him. "Hey, hey. Why are you saying that?"

I swallow the tears threatening to spill over. "She's my best friend. She's all I have and now she's found this big, wonderful family to be happy with and I'll have no one."

Wes pulls me closer, wrapping his arms around me in the warmest embrace. "So, I'm no one, then?" I groan against his chest, but he continues. "I'm serious. First of all, your mother isn't going to up and abandon you just because she's dating someone new. You know that." He smooths my hair over with his hand. "And if somehow, by some stretch of the imagination, that happened, you wouldn't be alone. I'd be there."

Before I know what's happening, he's kissing me and oh *god* I never want him to stop. All my fears seem to melt away with his lips on mine and all I can feel is *him* and how wonderful it is to be in his arms. How right it feels.

I'm trembling as he pulls away and leans his forehead against mine, both of us gasping for air. I don't realize we're outside my house until the corners up his mouth tick up and he reaches for my hand.

"Come on."

Chapter 38

Wesley

I follow Quinn up the stairs to her apartment, hiding a grimace. The last thing I want to do is act like a snob. I'm grateful that she's letting me into this part of her life, meeting her family and showing me her home. Still, when we got out of the car and she told me the subway was a fifteen-minute walk, I couldn't help but imagine her walking all that way in the middle of winter.

When we get to her apartment, she slides the key in the lock and jingles it for a few moments too long. She sends me a sidelong glance. "It hates me."

She opens the door, letting me in behind her.

It's a small room with a couch, TV, and a kitchen tucked into the wall on our left. Quinn drops her bag on the floor beside me, next to an overflowing coat rack and what appears to be a chair covered in clothes. The place is...messy.

"My room is this way," she says and moves down the hall as I follow behind her, craning my neck to look around.

There's a small bathroom and two bedrooms. She pushes open the right door and I stand in the doorway as she goes into her room. The walls are covered in collage cut-outs from magazines and a few posters.

She sits on the bed and puts her hands in her lap, twisting her fingers. "So, yeah. This is it." I look around the room again and after a few moments of perusal, move to the bedside table and look at her books, picking up *The Bell Jar* and flipping through it before placing it back on the table and sitting next to Quinn on the bed.

She stares at me. "Say something! Oh my god."

I chuckle. "What would you like me to say?"

She throws her hands up. "Literally anything is better than the silence!"

I reach for her hand, my smile growing. "It's great. Thank you for showing me." I run my hand up her arm to her face, pressing my thumb against her lips. "Now, why don't we see how quiet you can be, hmm?"

Her mouth opens slightly, and I see her eyes flare with a mixture of excitement and anticipation. Fuck, she looks beautiful. I can't help but lean closer and capture her mouth in mine. She tastes sweet, like cherries or peach, something incredibly edible, a taste that makes me dizzy.

I let my hands travel further, thumbing down to the sides of her breasts and kissing her deeper. I feel her moan against me as I tease closer and closer to her nipple and I tsk her slightly, moving her shirt lower to expose her to me.

"Better stay quiet, princess." I murmur against her and take her into my mouth, circling her nipple with my tongue, tasting all of her. I drag my hand down her shirt, needing more. "Lie back. Take this off," I growl the words against her.

Quinn doesn't waste any time. She grabs her shirt and tears it off. Then she reaches behind her, unclasps her bra to free herself completely and lays back on the bed, watching me. I pull back and stare at her, drinking her in. She goes to unbutton her pants, but I grab her hands and pin them above her head, floating over her.

"Allow me." Keeping her arms pinned with one hand, I pull her pants down, revealing her lace panties. I tease my fingers against the soft fabric. "Oh, you're so wet. What should I give you? My fingers, my mouth, or my cock?"

Her eyes flare and she lets out a whoosh of air. "I want—"

I move quickly, pressing a finger against her mouth and cutting her off. "What did I say about being quiet?" She shudders, her eyes wide, and I press on her lips with my finger as she opens up for me. I add another finger, pressing both into her mouth as she swirls her tongue around them.

"Good girl."

She squirms and my smile darkens at the movement. "Hmm. So impatient." I press my fingers deeper into her mouth, gagging her, and she bucks again, a breathy moan coming out of her. Finally, I move my fingers lower, playing at the edge of her panties again.

The sight of her squirming beneath me is making me impossibly hard, but I want to watch her first. I swirl my finger against her panties, still not moving the fabric, and Quinn lets out a frustrated grunt. I chuckle and hook my fingers on the lace and drag it down her legs, baring her completely. She's almost shaking as I drag my hand up her legs to her inner thighs.

She moans again, quietly, but she thrusts towards my hand, perhaps involuntarily. Finally, I run my finger along her slit and slip one inside her. As soon as I do, she lets out another moan. I slip another finger in, spreading her legs open for me, and she exhales again, a choked breath escaping her.

"Tsk tsk. Do I need to gag you, princess? Or should I just punish you?" She whimpers and I watch her take her hand and clasp it over her mouth.

Rubbing my thumb on her clit, I press my head in between her thighs and replace my thumb with my tongue. She tastes so fucking good, I can't help but quicken my pace, feasting on her. I work my fingers deeper inside her and I hear her moan against my hand. Soon enough, her hand is in my hair, clasping down on me, and her legs are shaking.

"Wes." She exhales my name as I slow my pace, lifting my eyes to meet hers. Her hair is a mess and I look down, watching her wetness drip down her legs.

"I'm not done with you yet." I bring my fingers back to her lips and spread them, pushing my fingers inside her mouth so she can taste herself. "I think you want to be punished. Don't you?"

Her eyes widen, but there's clear excitement as she nods, swirling her tongue on my fingers again. I'm so hard I feel like I'm going to lose it, and I can't keep teasing her because I need it – need her wrapped around me. I need it now.

"Turn around. Hands and knees." I command her and she moves swiftly into position. She's fucking perfect. "Just like that. Lift your ass up for me, baby."

She listens and I spread my palm against her ass, rubbing soft circles. "Do you want your punishment? Yes or no?"

"Yes. Yes, please," she chokes out. She's shaking again as I bring my hand down on her bare ass, the sound of the smack ringing in the air. I don't wait for her moan. I smack her again, then slip my fingers back into her, feeling her tight, wet pussy clenching against my fingers.

"Oh, god, Wes," she moans, and I don't care that's she's not being quiet anymore. I want to hear her screams as I slam into her over and over.

I move quickly, pulling my pants down and freeing my cock. I pull her back by her hair, lifting her up to her knees.

"Are you ready for me, baby? How do you want it?"

"Hard, please, Wes. Please."

There's a sharp vulnerability behind her begging and I slow down, moving my hands from her hair towards her throat, softly brushing against her neck.

"You are so beautiful. So perfect," I whisper in her ear, letting my hands fall to her nipples, softly circling them. "I want this all the time. All the time. Forever."

I push into her, and she falls forward onto her hands, arching against me. It's incredible, how good she feels. Even better than the last time, somehow, like I've forgotten how sweet and tight she is, how complete I feel inside her.

I thrust into her, hard, again, and again, until I hear her saying my name, louder and louder until I'm sure she's screaming it. I can hardly breathe as the world explodes and I lose myself completely in her, in this feeling, in the beauty of her writhing beneath me.

"Fuck," I sputter out. "Yeah, you're taking it so good, like a good little slut."

She goes suddenly still below me, and it takes me a moment to realize she's not saying my name anymore, not pressing into me like she just was. It's as if she's withdrawn completely.

"Quinn?"

I hear the sharp intake of breath and a choking sound. Something is happening. I pull out and turn her shoulder to see tears streaming down her face.

"Quinn, whoa. Hey, what's wrong? What happened?"

She shakes her head and moves away from me, more sobs wracking through her. The movement, the sound cracks through my chest, splitting me open. I keep my distance, resting a hand on her leg.

"I'm sorry. I just...can you not call me that? That word."

My heart drops.

I swallow, hard. "Of course. I mean, no, fuck. I'm sorry. I shouldn't have just said that. I don't think that. At all. I just got caught up in the moment and the dirty talk."

She wipes at her face and shakes her head. "No, it's okay. Really. It's just a specific thing for me."

An awkward silence settles over us and I move slowly closer to her, needing to hold her closer. Thankfully, she lets me. Her tears have stopped and she's just taking some gasping breaths.

"Quinn. Talk to me. What just happened? I won't ever say it again, I swear, but can you tell me why?"

She shakes her head, and her pain seems to swell as another round of tears starts. I squeeze her closer, hating this, that I'm somehow responsible for her feeling this way.

"I don't want you to think of me differently," she whispers, so quiet I can barely hear it.

"That will never happen," I promise her, thumbing her cheeks and wiping away a tear that threatens to fall.

She gulps and I feel the moment when she turns away from my gaze. "I used to have sex for money for a little while when I was younger."

Her words hit me square in the gut. All the air leaves the room.

"There was this one guy...Derek. He had a degradation kink. He used to say things to me. Let's just say they weren't the best for my self-esteem."

I go completely still against her. "What kinds of things?" I grit out.

She shakes her head. "You know, like, you're ugly, you're worthless, only good for sex, cum slut, fuck doll. Just like, porno script shit. I don't know. I try not to think about it."

I can't breathe. Can't think.

"There was one night when we were together at his place

and he...hit me. We hadn't agreed on that so I tried to leave, but he wouldn't let me. I knew he wasn't going to take no for an answer. I managed to get away, but there was this glass that crashed and sliced my leg. That's what happened that day when you surprised me at the penthouse...I guess the glass breaking just kind of triggered me. I don't know."

The silence in the room is overwhelming. The rage and helplessness clawing up my throat is uncontrollable. I want to find the bastard who did this to Quinn and kill him. Watch him bleed as I beat him senseless.

"Are you gonna say something?" Quinn's soft voice breaks me out of the red I'm seeing.

I take a deep, steadying breath and wait a few moments before I'm sure I can speak. "Thank you for telling me." I swallow the lump in my throat. "I'm so sorry. I don't know what else to say. It hurts so fucking badly to think of you like that. I want to kill him."

Her eyes widen and she lets out a sound somewhere between a sob and a laugh. I squeeze her closer to me.

"You are beautiful, Quinn. You are smart, loyal, passionate, and *kind*. I am constantly in awe of you and I don't ever want you to believe a single word of whatever that asshole said to you."

She sighs into my arms. "Wes."

"I mean it. I'm sorry that I said that or if anything I've done has reminded you of those memories. Don't ever be afraid to tell me to stop if I cross a boundary, please. I need to know that you feel safe in everything we do."

She nods. "I do. I do feel safe with you. I've never told anyone about that night. Not even my mom." The sharp vulnerability in her voice makes my chest ache.

"Thank you for trusting me with that. Thank you."

She settles into me, our bodies curled together. I run my

thumb along her back, brushing softly along her spine. "You're not..." I swallow the lump gathering in my throat. "You're not doing that anymore, are you?"

She shakes her head fervently. "No. I haven't in a while. Years before I met you. After that night, I swore I was done, that I'd figure out some other way to make money."

I inhale a shaky breath. "I know you don't like to talk about money, but can you just please promise me that if you're ever in a bad situation and you need help, you'll come to me first? That you won't put yourself in harm's way because of your pride."

She's quiet for a moment. "I don't know. I don't know if I can promise that."

The ache in my chest intensifies. Someone hurt her. Someone told her she was worthless. Helplessness crawls up my throat and I have never felt so out of control, so out of my depth.

My voice drops down to a whisper. "Please. I won't ask anything else of you. Just please promise me this one thing. I need you safe."

Finally, she nods against me. "Okay. I promise."

My sigh of relief settles over both of us. The silence in the room is heavy with the weight of our confessions. Quinn nudges against me, pushing her ass into me. "I really do love it when you take control."

I wiggle my eyebrows, feeling lighter. "Oh, so you like it when I order you around?"

She swats my arm, rolling her eyes. "In the bedroom only. Don't get any ideas."

There's only one problem. When it comes to Quinn, I have lots of ideas. Too many. Ones of us together, in the future, something close to forever. Ones where she is mine — truly mine. An image of hope forms in my mind and just for a moment, I let myself hold on to it. I close my eyes and savor the taste of it, sweet and delicious and completely out of reach.

* * *

We don't stay at Quinn's long. We're both emotionally drained from that conversation, and I think we just need to rest and decompress. Still, she's eager to hold up my end of the bargain and go see my apartment in Dumbo, so she packs a bag while I wait in the living room. It's not until we're saying goodbye to Pete for the night and heading towards the front door of my building that my stomach drops with a wave of nerves.

Nobody has seen this place. It's been my secret corner of the city and the thought of someone seeing it — or worse, judging it — has my stomach fluttering with nerves. But after all we've said tonight, I feel safe with her.

Letting her into this part of my life feels like a big step. I don't know if she realizes how much it means to me, and right now I'm feeling too raw to tell her. Better to just rip the band aid off.

I guide us inside to the elevator and we're quiet on the ride up. I so desperately want to know what she's thinking.

"You're staring," she smiles at me, twirling her hair with one finger.

Instinct tells me to look away, but I don't. I hold her gaze, letting my own smile loosen. "You're beautiful."

The elevator doors slide open, and I clasp her hand in mine and step into the open room, bracing myself. I hadn't been coming here much, but yesterday after Quinn left, I felt the tugging urge to return. I told myself it was just to check on the place, but I knew the truth.

It was our conversation about piano. Yesterday, for the first time in years, I sat down at that grand piano in the corner. I didn't play. I just sat there and ran my fingers on the keys, letting myself feel the guilt and anguish and fear that crept up from the bench, from the instrument itself.

I don't know if I'll ever be able to play again, to put myself through those feelings again, but having Quinn by my side, getting even a glimpse of her fierce belief in me, makes me feel something I'd scarcely let myself feel these days. Hope.

"Wow." Quinn's voice breaks into my thoughts as she tears her hand from mine and walks over to the windows. "It's incredible."

Her face lights up as she takes in the view of the bridge and skyline behind it. I watch her scan the exposed brick wall next to her and then turn, taking in the rest of the room. She runs her fingers along the bookshelves that cover the far wall, examining the titles, and after what feels like an eternity, she finally turns to me, her eyes glowing.

"It's perfect. It's exactly the type of place I would choose if I could afford it. I love it."

My heart stutters at her words and there's some kind of swelling in my chest that I can't seem to swallow.

She continues moving through the room. "Did you do the interior design?"

I shake my head, trying to choke down the growing feeling inside me. "I helped, but no, I hired someone much better at design than me. Though all the books and art pieces are mine."

She seems to notice the piano as I speak and I watch as she approaches it and sits on the bench, dropping her bag on the floor beside her. She runs her fingers along the keys, the same repetitive movement that I did yesterday. She looks thoughtful and peaceful and somehow, having her here just feels...right.

The feeling in my chest seems to grow in intensity as she taps one of the keys, the sound of it hitting me in the gut. Suddenly, I blink, and something very important seems to shift inside me. A realization rising like a tide inside me and crashing over everything.

I'm in love with her.

I almost stumble backwards, the thought jolting me in my place. For a moment, a flash of fear rushes through me at the realization, but almost as soon, it's replaced by a sort of rightness, a warm feeling pooling in my stomach.

I don't know how I didn't see it earlier. Ben was right — I've probably been falling for her since I met her. But I'm done being in denial. Done pretending like she isn't the best thing that ever happened to me. The best thing in my life.

I love her. Every part of her.

Now all I have to do is figure out how the hell to tell her.

Chapter 39

Quinn

It's been a month since I visited Wesley's apartment and since then, things have been good. Almost...too good. Last week, he officially asked me to be his girlfriend. Well, if I'm being accurate, he *told* me I was his girlfriend. We were laying on the couch in his apartment one Sunday afternoon when for some reason, I opened my mouth and asked the dreaded question: what are we?

Wes stared down at me, his expression hard as stone. "What do you mean? You're my girlfriend."

I let out a strangled laugh, choking on it halfway and coughing a fit. "Oh, am I? I must have missed the memo. Let me check my work email."

He rolled his eyes and must have realized I was being serious about my question, because he nudged me to face him. "You're my girlfriend. We're exclusive. There's nobody else for either of us. You're mine."

The words probably should have freaked me out, but instead, they landed in my chest and filled me with a giddy, warm feeling.

"So bossy," I murmured.

"Do you disagree?" At least he had the decency to look somewhat unsure.

I shook my head. "No. I agree." A smile peeked out from my serious expression, and he kissed me, a twinge of satisfaction in his features.

"Good. You aren't getting rid of me anytime soon."

I also started my new job at Le Petit Fleur, the restaurant in the hotel lobby. I had my interview a few days after seeing Wesley's apartment, which has become my new favorite place in this city, if only because it feels like a secret that Wesley and I share. Even though staying at the penthouse is much more convenient, we often have Pete drive us out to Dumbo to watch the sunset over the downtown skyline together.

The head chef, Rita, told me that she's taking a chance on me because of Wesley's recommendation. Even though I didn't have any direct experience working in a kitchen, she's hiring me as part of a training internship of sorts. My pay hasn't changed very much from what I was making with Wesley, but instead of cleaning sheets, I get to shadow Rita in a real kitchen all day long. It's incredible and I've managed to quell my remaining guilt about whether I deserve this opportunity and simply accept that I am here and going to prove my worth the best I can.

Wesley has been busy with work and the new development has finally gone into construction, but he still finds time to come down to the restaurant at least once a day to say hello. Rita refuses to let him in the kitchen even though he insists that he technically owns the place. He's right, but I do love to see Rita knock him down a few pegs.

Mom spends a few nights a week at Joe's place. He's also been taking her to chemo so that I can work more hours at the restaurant, which I'm grateful for. Still, I can't help but miss her and the nights we used to spend eating ice cream on the couch.

"Where are those scallops?" Rita's urgent voice breaks me out of my thoughts.

I spin on my heels. "Sorry! Right here, chef."

She waves me over and I help her finish plating a few dishes as Annette, one of the servers, grabs two prepared plates and skips out of the kitchen.

"Here, watch this," Rita snaps towards me and I point my eyes at the plate she's decorating. She finishes with a flourish, and it looks incredible, a visual masterpiece on a plate. Annette arrives swiftly and Rita nods for her to take it.

I'm still in awe — The Phoenix had a cool atmosphere and I liked hanging out with Manny, but I never thought the food was anything to write home about. It's clear that Rita has her sights set on greatness when it comes to the culinary arts.

"Some guy is here to see you," Annette jerks her head towards me as she enters the kitchen, two other servers trailing behind her.

I furrow my brow. "Me?"

"Yes, you. He's standing out front looking weirdly suspicious. In a trench coat and sunglasses and everything." Before I can ask for more information, Annette sweeps back into the dining room.

I shoot Rita a pleading glance and she waves me out, giving me permission, so I untie my apron and cut through the restaurant to the front.

Annette's right. There's a man standing in front of the hostess stand — tall, brunette by the looks of it, though it's hard to tell under the baseball cap and raised collar of his coat. He's wearing dark sunglasses and shifting on his feet, glancing left and right.

I approach him, leaving a good amount of distance between us.

"Hello?" I say, half-question. The man rips his sunglasses off and it's—

He grabs my arm and jostles me towards the corner, where we're slightly hidden by a curtain.

"What are you doing? Let go of me," I rip my arm from his grip.

"Oh, calm down. You're fine."

I look him up and down. "What the hell are you wearing?"

Ben just smirks down at me, a devious grin spread over his face. He looks just like Wes when he smiles. "I'm incognito. Don't want my brother spotting me."

"Why? What's the big secret?"

"It's Wesley's birthday this weekend."

I rear back, my mouth dropping. "What? When? Why wouldn't he tell me?"

"Because he hates his birthday." Ben glances around the corner dramatically and I have to stop myself from rolling my eyes. "Blame our dad. He's to blame for pretty much everything."

I blink, still processing that Wesley's birthday is only a few days away. "Okay, well, thank you for telling me. When is it?"

"Saturday. May 19th."

"He's a Taurus?" I realize. "How did I not know that? It makes so much sense. Oh shit. I have to figure out what to get him."

Ben snaps his fingers in my face. "Spiral about that later. I came here to tell you that we're throwing him a surprise party."

I raise an eyebrow. "You just said he hates his birthday."

Ben just shrugs. "Oh, come on, it'll be fun. We'll toast to Wesley, you can meet his friends, I can meet your friends. It's a party!"

I deaden my expression. "I don't have any friends."

"I knew you and Wesley had a lot in common."

"This really doesn't sound like a good idea."

Ben just smirks at me again, a glint in his eye that must be a family trait. "Too bad. You're going to help me plan it."

* * *

I am terrible at keeping secrets, which is why Ben's plan has made it nearly impossible for me to be around Wesley. I've spent this whole week avoiding him and I'm pretty sure he can tell.

The worst part about the plan is that it hinges on my execution of it. I've already laid the groundwork with Wesley by convincing him to bring me to his apartment where everyone will be waiting for us.

Even though it was Ben's idea, party planning is clearly not his area of expertise. He handled the guest list while I did everything else: food, decorations, and most importantly, getting Wesley to show up.

I'm standing outside the hotel, more nervous than ever. I close my eyes and inhale to steady myself for the night ahead.

I feel a hand snaking around my waist and my eyes fly open in time to see Wesley leaning into me before our lips touch. His kiss is demanding, more than expected, like he needs something from me, from this moment. I'm gasping as he pulls back and rests his forehead on mine.

"Hey," he says.

My smile grows. "Hi," I whisper back and bring my hands up to his shoulders. "Are you okay?"

His whole body is buzzing with tension. Anger is written all over him, but he nods sharply and steps back, smoothing the front of his button-down. He's not wearing his jacket and the buttons of his shirt are undone, revealing a tiny glimpse of his chiseled chest below.

"Yeah. I'm fine. Just a tough day." He glances away from me, his eyes distant. "Come on."

He takes my hand and leads me towards the car. When we get inside, Pete and I exchange pleasantries. The car ride is nearly silent. I glance over at Wesley and he's clutching a folder to his thighs, his knuckles tight. Something is definitely wrong.

I grasp for something, anything to say. I gesture towards the folder, trying for a joke to lighten the mood. "Talk about bringing work home with you." He doesn't crack a smile. "Wes?"

His eyes meet mine and there's a flare of something — fear? — but he blinks, and it's gone.

He shrugs and leans forward, sliding the folder into the back of Pete's seat. "It's confidential work stuff." His voice is rough, almost strained.

I blink and look away, taken-aback. Confidential? Does he still think I'd look through his shit? It's not like I actually care, but what the hell?

The silence in the car is suffocating me. I'm desperately searching for something to say to curb his obvious bad mood. I lean into him and force a brittle smile. "Happy Birthday."

He stills against me. "How did you know?"

"A little birdie told me."

His face hardens. "Ben. Ben told you." I nod and he grimaces, shaking his head.

I roll my eyes and nudge him. "Oh, come on, don't be dramatic."

He grumbles nonetheless, crossing his arms over his chest. "I can't wait for this day to be over. The last thing I want to do right now is think about, or celebrate, my birthday."

Shit.

I meet Pete's eyes in the rearview mirror, my panic spiking. He knows about the party since I invited him a few days ago, and my guess is he's thinking the same thing as me: this is a terrible idea.

It's too late to do anything. Pete's already exiting the bridge towards Dumbo and my phone buzzes with a text from Ben that I sneak a peek at.

All set. ETA?

My fingers trembling slightly, I text Ben that we're five minutes away and slip my phone into my purse.

Wesley sighs from beside me and I feel him wrap his hand in mine, tugging my attention back to him. "I'm sorry," he breathes out. "I'm not trying to be a dick. I've just had a rough day. All I want is to spend a quiet evening with you. No more pouting, I promise."

He presses his lips to the back of my hand and my stomach drops even further. Oh god. Guilt is crawling its way up my throat. Why do I feel like throwing Wesley this birthday party is akin to ripping his heart out of his chest? Is it too late to call Ben and clear the place out?

I never should have let Ben talk me into this. It's too soon for me as his girlfriend to be doing something like this — throwing him a surprise party with his friends and family. I should have known that it's exactly the type of thing that Wes would hate.

The car idles and I realize we're outside the building. Pete's voice interrupts my spiraling. "Here we are, boss."

"Thanks, Pete. We'll see you tomorrow."

"If not sooner," Pete mutters under his breath as Wes steps out of the car.

We walk past the doorman to the elevator and I'm nearly shaking. Wes runs his hand up and down the length of my arm. He's holding that folder in his other hand. "I love this dress. These shoes. All dressed up for me?" He groans and tugs me closer. "I can't believe you're mine."

He lowers his lips to my neck, pressing openmouthed kisses along my naval. I gasp at the contact, and he brings his hand up to my hair, running his fingers through the threads as he presses our lips together.

The elevator doors slide open, and he walks towards his door with urgency.

"Wait!" I shout as his hand touches the handle. I brush past him, knocking his hand from the door. He looks at me like I'm insane as I block the doorway.

I take a deep breath. "I just want to say...I care about you. A lot." I twist the door handle, my heart pounding. "And I'm sorry."

His confusion deepens. "Sorry for what?"

I swing the door open, and a barrage of cheers assaults us. "Surprise!"

Wesley's face is as red as a tomato. I've never seen him look so shocked. His face is usually a mask of his emotions with the occasional icy glare peeking out from his signature stony expression, but right now, he looks utterly thrown.

Ben clasps his hand on Wesley's shoulder as Lillian runs up and throws her arms around her son, hugging him. Other people I don't know float behind them, smiling and chatting amongst themselves.

I meet Wesley's gaze over his mom's shoulder and his eyes flare with a warning. It's a look that says one thing: *what the fuck?*

To his credit, he manages a smile as he steps back from his mother. He looks around at everyone. "Wow, what a surprise. Good job, guys." He forces a chuckle, and I can see the effort it's taking for him to stay pleasant. "Now, let's get a drink!"

Everyone cheers. I grip Ben's arm, pulling him towards me. "This was a huge mistake. He's pissed. Really pissed."

Ben raises his eyebrows innocently. "What do you mean? He looks happy to me." He gestures over to where Wes stands with two friends from grad school, a pleasant expression plastered onto his face. I roll my eyes and go to argue with Ben, but he's already slipped away towards the kitchen.

I go over to Wesley and press my hand on his arm. "Here, let me take your stuff." I gesture towards the folder and his jacket.

"I'm good," he says brusquely.

I blink and smile awkwardly at his two friends. Is he seriously this mad about the party? I shake my head. "Would you just give me your stuff and go get a drink, you grump?"

His friends are looking at him with identical expressions, as if silently saying: *bro, give her the jacket.*

Finally, Wes hands his stuff over. "Just put them in my office."

I roll my eyes and bring his stuff into his office. I put the jacket on the back of his chair and as I'm about to set the folder on the table, something slips out the bottom, falling to the floor. I pick it up, and it's a photo.

A photo of me and my mother, sitting on our stoop outside our apartment, sharing a joint.

What the hell?

My brain is moving slowly, forming both a million questions and no thoughts at all at the same time. Some part of me is warning me, screaming at me not to open the folder. That I don't want to know. That I shouldn't be snooping in Wesley's things. That it's nothing.

But the other part of me, the part now in control of my movements, reaches for the folder and opens it, sprawling the truth on the desk in front of me.

As I take in the sight of it, the words and photos staring up at me, my entire world turns upside down.

Chapter 40

Wesley

I hate my birthday. I'm sure I'm not the only one and it's melodramatic and brooding of me to lament about it every time it comes around, but the fact remains that I can't stand it. The day is a reminder of everything I've tried to forget.

When I turned 10, my father forced me to sit at the piano for hours without standing up. I begged to be allowed to use the bathroom or stretch my legs, but he refused until I finally pissed my pants.

When I turned 14, my father dropped me off at an arcade in Brooklyn and forgot about me. The owner closed the place, and it was nearly two in the morning when one of his drivers finally showed up and found me asleep on the curb.

When I turned 18, my father introduced me to his business associate, Mr. King, who took us both to a gentleman's lounge in the meatpacking district where he introduced me to a woman named Candy and sent us to a private room.

Last year, my father said nothing. If I had to guess, I'd say he was drunk somewhere. Maybe he forgot what day it was. Maybe he simply didn't care.

The day is already off to a rough start when my assistant Beverly tells me she's quitting. It's a disappointment, but nothing I can't handle by finding a new assistant. A pain, sure, but easily remedied.

My family knows well enough not to send me any birthday messages, so luckily my phone remains silent except for the usual emails. It's not until I'm about to leave to pick up Quinn that my phone rings with a number that I dread to see. Still, I pick up.

"Son."

One simple word and my spine feels as though it's made of steel and ice. He sounds exactly the same — that gravelly, tired voice that haunts me in my worst moments.

"Dad. What a surprise. I didn't know they let you make calls," I say, my throat dry.

He chuckles darkly, devoid of humor. "It's rehab, son, not prison. You might know if you ever gave your old man a visit."

He's angry that I didn't show up to see him when my mom went to visit him. I was supposed to. Told my mother that I would, too. But when it came to the day, I just couldn't get myself to give enough of a shit to drag my ass all the way upstate just to be some fake version of myself.

"Is that what this is about? My parental neglect?"

"Not quite. I wanted to call you, obviously."

I'm quiet for a moment. He can't be calling to wish me a happy birthday. It's not possible. I let myself hope, for a brief moment that he's changed—

"Your mother and I are officially getting a divorce. I thought you should hear it from me first. You know how she has a tendency to exaggerate things in her favor."

I don't move. The only thing I can hear is the pounding of my heartbeat, and a ringing in my ear.

I've known this was coming. My mother has been dating

and there's no love left between her and my father — if there ever was any to begin with. I'm happy for her, that she can get a chance to try again, to be with someone who deserves her.

I realize my father is still speaking on the other line, his sneering, pompous voice breaking through my panic.

"...of course, property issues to discuss and dividing the assets and such, so I may need your brother to look over everything before it's finalized. I assume you can inform him."

"Leave Ben out of it. Find another lawyer to look over your shit."

He just chuckles again. "Alright, son. That's all."

I grind my teeth. "Yeah? That's all? Nothing else you wanna say?"

"Goodbye, Wesley."

He hangs up.

Somehow, I know that he remembers. He knows it's my birthday. He wants me to know that he doesn't care. Each word is deliberate. Intended to hurt me.

I feel empty. My hand reaches for my phone to call Quinn, like maybe if I could just hear her voice, I won't feel so hollowed out inside. But I can't shake the sense that she's avoiding me, and I don't know why. Is she second-guessing us? Does she want to end things?

The thought sends a painful jolt through me. Glancing at the clock, I realize I need to get going to pick Quinn up. I leave my office and run into George on the way out. He's in much too good a mood as he follows me to the elevator bank.

"Wesley! Just the man I wanted to see."

We step into the elevator and I'm counting the seconds until this interaction with him is over. I've managed to communicate mostly through third parties and assistants with George since the project construction began.

George pulls out a folder, smiling widely. "Happy Birthday, Wesley."

I look down at his outstretched hand and take the folder from him. "What is this?"

"A while back, I found out who screwed us over with the story. Who leaked to the press. Anyway, I did the normal shit, you know, PI, ruin the life, yada yada. All the info is in there for you to do whatever you want."

I open the folder. A photo...no, photos...of Quinn. Quinn and her mother. Her apartment. A letter to her landlord threatening legal action against her...eviction? I'm flipping through it, but none of this makes any fucking sense.

"No better gift than ruining the life of some scum who deserves it, right?" He grins.

I don't breathe. I don't blink. I hardly register my own movements as I haul George by the collar, throwing him against the wall of the elevator and crushing him in an iron grip.

"Don't ever fucking talk about her like that again. Whatever this shit is, reverse it, get rid of it. I don't care what you have to do, just do it." I inhale, trying to force myself to calm down. "If you have any fucking sense, George, avoid me for a while."

His eyes are wide as I release him and stumble out of the elevator. Pete's waiting and I'm still holding this fucking folder in my hands. I can't bring myself to look at it.

I settle into the back of the car, my heart still racing. I'm pumped up on adrenaline, I think, because my hands are still shaking. Maybe it's just rage.

"You good back there, boss?" Pete asks, eyeing me in the mirror.

"Yeah. Fine." I grip the folder tighter. I should just throw it away, but I can't. Not yet. Not until I can figure out exactly what the fuck George has done and how far it's gone and fix it.

I clench my fist, rage bubbling within me. I need to get back in control of the situation. I can feel it slipping away from me, and my chest clenches uncomfortably at the thought. I have to fix this. I have to take care of her.

My jaw hardens and I grind my teeth, anxiety rising in me. "Just drive."

* * *

"Surprise!"

I should have known. I sensed something was off with Quinn all week, but I had no idea it was this. Why would she do this? Why would she invite them all *here?*

Ben is talking, but I barely hear him. I'm stuck looking past him, towards the hallway that Quinn disappeared down to my office. I'm sweating. What's taking her so long? She didn't open the folder, did she?

A pang of guilt hits me.

Trust. I'm supposed to trust her. She wouldn't look through my personal files. She wouldn't do that.

"Are you even listening to me?" Ben waves his beer in front of my face.

"Not really." I take a sip of my beer. "Why are we doing this? A party? Really?"

He sighs. "There's not one part of you that likes this? Seeing me? Mom? Your friends? Quinn? All together in one place, celebrating you."

"Well. I don't like you, and I don't have friends." I glance over to where my mother is currently chatting with two older men. "Who even are those guys?"

"I think mom's boyfriends." Ben finishes his beer and gestures to my half-full bottle. "Want another one?"

I shake my head. He goes into the kitchen, and I yell after him. "Boyfriends? Plural?"

I take another pull from my beer and glance back towards the hallway. What is taking so long? I look around and everyone has broken off into conversations. The song changes to something upbeat and luckily nobody is pulling me aside for birthday wishes, so I slip out of the room and down the hall.

I press open the door to my office, but it's empty. "Quinn?" I call out, checking my bedroom, but she's not there either.

That's when I see the bathroom light is on. I approach the closed door and knock twice. "Quinn? Baby?"

She finally answers a few moments later. "Yeah?"

"You okay? You've been gone for a while."

"I'm—" She breaks off and I wait. "I'm not feeling very well. I think it must have been the takeout I got for lunch."

My heart drops. She's sick? I jiggle the door handle. "What's wrong? I'll get you some water and take care of you."

"No! No. Pete is waiting for me downstairs. I'll just head home. Go enjoy your party."

I growl against the door. "No. I don't even want—"

The door swings open. Her face is pink and splotchy as if she's been...

She brushes past me before I can say anything. "Please tell Ben I'm sorry."

"Wait. Quinn." I grab her arm, pulling her back to face me, but she keeps her head down, avoiding my gaze. "What is happening right now?"

She yanks her arm out of my grip, still not looking at me. "I'm *sick*. I gotta go."

I follow her dumbly, stumbling after her and repeating her name, louder each time, but she's too fast. There's nothing I can do to stop her, and all I can do is stare as she walks out the door.

* * *

Needless to say, the party doesn't last very long. Ben stays the longest, helping me clean up and asking me questions about Quinn that I'm wondering myself and don't have an answer to. Questions like why did she leave? Is she okay? Is she upset? There's one question, though, at the front of my mind. One that Ben wouldn't think to ask.

Did she open the folder?

I tell myself again that she wouldn't do that. That I trust her. I really do. I refuse to believe that she would read through it. Even if she did, there's no way that she would believe that I would do such a thing, and then lie about it and tell me she's sick.

Yeah, because she's never lied to you before about that to avoid a conversation.

Shit. I should have gone after her. Instead, I had to pretend to enjoy talking about sports and the stock market with my "friends" — most of whom I see once a year if I'm lucky.

"That's the last of it." Ben ties a trash bag and throws it with the other. "I'll bring them down when I leave if you want."

"Okay," I say, looking around at the empty apartment. The dusty piano in the corner staring back at me. Taunting me.

"You good?" Ben clasps his hand on my shoulder. "Seriously, what is going on with Quinn?"

302

"She said she was sick," I bark the words out like a robot, knowing they feel wrong.

Ben rolls his eyes. "She seemed fine to me. Sure you didn't piss her off somehow?"

I'm silent for a moment, debating asking Ben for advice. Then again, he usually gives good advice. "There might be something. It's a long story, but basically George from work looked into the leak and found out it was Quinn, or *thought* it was Quinn, so he... "

I shake my head, bringing my hand to the back of my neck. "I don't know the details, but it seems like he hired a PI, tried to get her evicted, a bunch of fucked up stuff."

Ben shakes his head along with me. "Jesus."

"It gets worse. Apparently, he thought I'd be fucking over-joyed about it, and showed all of it to me for my birthday. Gave me this folder with everything in it. Photos, letters..."

Ben grows still beside me. "Wes."

"I told her it was confidential. Private business stuff. She wouldn't look at it. Not after everything that happened."

He just shakes his head again and looks at me with his lips flattened. "Maybe it's nothing. Maybe she really is sick."

We both know he's lying. Eventually, he moves his hand away from my shoulder, grabs the trash, and leaves. He must sense that I need to be alone.

It's almost 1 a.m. and I'm dead tired from the day I've had, but I send one more text to Quinn to match the five others that have gone unanswered.

Please call me in the morning.

I toss my phone on my bedside table with a little too much

force as I fall onto my bed. It feels cold without her here. The bed is almost too big for just me, like I need her here beside me to feel...complete.

Fuck.

I fall against my pillow with a sigh, willing sleep to come.

Chapter 41

Quinn

My first thought is *there must be a mistake.* Followed by others like it. You know, *this can't be true, this isn't right,* on and on until I finally wrap my head around the contents of the folder I just had in my hands. I don't have time to process it. Almost as soon as I register what I'm seeing, my head is in the toilet and Wesley's concerned face is all I can see. Before I know it, I'm in the backseat as Pete drives me back to my place.

I've been gasping for breath for the past few minutes. Pete already asked me twice if I'm okay, and he's eyeing me in the mirror with concern.

"Are you sure you're alright?" He asks again, glancing back at me.

"Fine," I grit the word out. "Remember what I said, don't—"

"Say anything to Wesley, yeah, yeah. What's the big secret from him? He'd want to know what's upsetting you."

He's upsetting me. *He's* the reason I'm on the verge of sobbing in the back of this car. I've managed to keep it together so far. I just need to get out of this car, into my bedroom where I can let myself break. A humorless laugh erupts out of me at how we've somehow come full circle. How this all started with a folder and now it ends with one.

My phone rings with a call from my mom and I ignore it. I can't handle her soothing voice right now. She'd probably say it was a misunderstanding and that I should talk to Wes, which is the last thing I want to do right now. My shock from the whole situation seems to be wearing off as the magnitude of this betrayal rocks through me again.

I just don't understand. Why would he do this to me?

He probably realized how pathetic you really are. Probably just wanted an easy lay.

The cold words taunt me, sending a jolt to my chest. I shake my head.

No.

No, Wes isn't like that. He wouldn't use me like that.

Maybe the documents are old. I guess if it was something Wesley did months ago, before we got together, I could understand that. Maybe it is just a misunderstanding, and I shouldn't have run out of there. Don't I at least owe him the chance to explain?

My phone rings again with another call from my mom. It's not like her to call twice. I press the phone to my ear with a heavy sigh.

"Hello?"

"Quinn, it's Joe. Listen, I'm at the hospital with your mom. Everything is fine, but you need to come right away. Your mother..."

Everything fades into the background as Joe speaks. I don't hear the whooshing of the bikers passing beside us, the honking of the taxis trying to merge lanes, or the soft sound of Pete tapping his fingers against the steering wheel. It all disappears. All I can hear is the sound of Joe's voice as he tells me the news that will shatter me completely.

I finally break down, sobbing, the wretched sobs bursting out me. I cry and cry and cry until there's nothing left inside me at all.

* * *

Pete drops me off at the hospital. I feel far away from myself as I walk through the halls. I hear myself asking the nurse which room my mother is in. She must tell me, because my legs start moving, carrying me towards the ICU.

I see Joe first. He's sitting, his hands clasped in front of him, his head down. I realize with a jolt that he's praying.

"Joe," my raspy voice breaks out as I stumble down the hall to meet him, glancing around. "Where is she? Is she okay?"

He wraps his arms around me. "She's fine. She's stable. They're waiting on the results of the MRI and CAT scan before they decide if she needs surgery."

I step back, glancing around at the too-empty hallway. "Can I see her? Where's the doctor?"

Joe sits back down in his chair. "He said he'd be back shortly with an update and we could see her then. He's on the phone with Dr. Emmanuel getting up to speed on her case."

Reluctantly, I sit next to Joe. My hand is tapping on my leg impatiently. I need to do something. Talk to the doctor, see my mom. Something.

"Explain the surgery to me again."

Joe repeats again what he told me on the phone. My mom was in the shower when she passed out and hit her head. It's only a mild bump and luckily, she doesn't have a concussion, but they realized that she had internal bleeding when she arrived. It turns out her liver is leaking blood or something, so they need to do surgery to repair it. Joe does his best to explain it to me, but all I know is that it sounds bad. Really bad.

"I don't understand. If she has breast cancer, why is she having issues with her liver?"

Joe exhales and meets my eyes. "It's metastasis. The cancer has spread to her liver now. Maybe other places."

"But..." I shake my head. "No, she was getting better. She said she's been feeling a lot better."

Joe flinches slightly, pity in his eyes. "You know your mother. She's too strong for her own good." He shakes his head. "I noticed a few weeks ago she looked a little yellow, but she insisted everything was fine."

I swallow the lump in my throat. She's been lying, downplaying how bad it's been. She's been trying to be strong, to protect us from how bad she feels. I feel...angry. Mad at her for keeping this from me. She should have told me.

If you were around more, maybe she would have.

Guilt claws its way up my throat as I blink back a round of fresh tears. This is my fault. If I'd been paying more attention, spending as much time with my mom as I used to, I would have noticed that something was wrong. We could have done something earlier.

My phone buzzes against my pocket. It's Wesley, calling for the fifth time since I left his place. I can't think about him right now. Can't let myself spiral into the depths of his betrayal. I turn my phone off.

I need to focus on my mom. Nothing else matters.

After what feels like an eternity, a doctor strides down the hallway towards us. Joe shoots to his feet and I follow. The doctor reaches his hand out to shake mine.

"Hi, I'm Dr. Brooks. I'm in charge of your mother's case. I just got off the phone with Dr. Emmanuel to update him on your mother's results, which we've just received. She's awake and we can all go discuss the results together, if you'd like."

I nod and follow Dr. Brooks and Joe into the room at the end of the hall. My heart is beating rapidly against my chest as I take another rattled breath, trying to prepare myself. But nothing can prepare me for the sight in front of me.

My mother is a jumble of wires and machines. Her face looks crumpled and hallowed out, a faint yellow tint under her skin. It's too much, the sight of it. I can feel nausea swirling in my gut as I blink again, willing myself not to cry. I have to be strong for her.

A nurse flutters next to her bed, fiddling with the computer that my mom is hooked up to.

"Ms. Taylor?" Dr. Brooks rests a gentle hand on my mother's shoulder, and she stirs, opening her eyes. "Your family is here. I've got news to share with all of you."

My feet are moving on their own and suddenly I'm beside her, my hand in hers.

"Mom," I choke out.

She pats my hand, another tentative smile. "It's okay." She looks at Dr. Brooks and nods.

"First things first, we need to get the internal bleeding under control, which means getting you into surgery right away. Vera is going to take you into prep shortly, once we get all the paperwork signed. It's a fairly simple procedure to repair the liver damage caused from your breast cancer metastasis."

I blink, trying to take in his words. Nodding along.

"Now the surgery won't actually cure the metastasis. I've spoken to Dr. Emmanuel about the spread of the cancer and assuming all goes well with the surgery, we'll need to run some more tests to figure out the next move after that. It could mean increasing chemo treatments."

I can feel myself shaking. My mom squeezes my hand reassuringly and I hate that *she* is comforting *me*. I need to get it together.

"The good news is that we've caught this fairly early. The cancer hasn't spread beyond the liver and if we're lucky, we can stop it from spreading any further."

"The surgery." I can't help but interrupt. "Is it...like, what are the odds? The risk level?"

"Sweetheart," my mom says in a chiding tone.

Dr. Brooks looks at me. "All surgeries carry some risk level. While this type of surgery has very high positive outcomes, the CT scan alone can't give me a full sense of what her liver looks like. There is a chance of finding more tumors than expected."

"What happens then?" I ask, my voice shaking.

"We can't know for sure. I know that's not the answer you want, and I'm sorry, but I can assure you that I'm a skilled surgeon. Your mom is in good hands."

Dr. Brooks smiles tightly and tucks his clipboard under his hands. "I'm going to get you the paperwork and book us an OR. I'll be back shortly if you have any questions."

It's quiet when he leaves. I'm still holding my mom's hand and Joe is sitting on the other side of the bed, his hands folded in his lap.

"Well," my mom croaks. "Not the best Saturday night I've had."

I shake my head. "Don't do that."

She pats my hand. "I'm sorry I didn't tell you. It wasn't that bad before, really. It's okay."

"No, Mom, it's not okay. You can't keep downplaying how you feel. You have to tell us the truth about your symptoms." I hate that I sound angry. "Just...don't shield me just because it sucks. We don't do that."

"You're right." She sits up a little higher and grimaces. "I'm sorry, baby. I just that you've seemed so happy lately. I didn't want to take that away from you."

My stomach bottoms out and I try not to flinch. It is my fault. If I hadn't been so caught up in Wesley, in whatever game he's been playing, she would have been honest with me.

"What? Did something happen?" My mom asks, eyeing me. She must be able to read the heartbreak written all over my face.

"Nothing. We need to focus on you, on getting through the surgery. Are you scared?"

"Fucking terrified," she admits, her shaky voice betraying her real fear underneath all her bravado. "I'm not done yet. I still have more to do."

My blood goes cold. "It's gonna be fine. You heard the doctor. Everything's going to be fine."

I squeeze her hand, not sure who I'm trying to convince more: myself, or her.

* * *

My mom has been in surgery for the past three hours. It's the middle of the night. Joe left to pick up some of my mom's things for when she wakes up. I've been sitting on this chair, wide-awake, watching the fingers on the clock tick slowly by. Time has never moved so slowly.

I feel exhausted, down to my bones, but I can't sleep. When I close my eyes, all I can see is my mom's crackled, stained skin, that scared look in her eyes before they took her into surgery. She is so strong all the time, seeing the fear plainly there in her eyes almost broke me entirely.

Someone sits next to me, and I glance over, my eyes half-open.

"If this is a financial visit, I will kill you."

Hannah chuckles and slips her hand into mine. "It's a friend visit."

I sigh and sit back. "How did you know?"

"I shared an elevator with Dr. Emmanuel on my way out of the hospital. He was on the phone, and I am a top-tier eavesdropper." I try to laugh, but it sounds all wrong to my ears. Hannah sighs and squeezes my hand. "You should have called me."

"So you could tell me the cost of the surgery down to the penny? I already have enough to deal with the chemo costs."

Her brow furrows. "What do you mean? All that debt was paid weeks ago."

"What?" I rear back. I must be so tired that I'm hearing things. "What did you just say?"

"I thought you knew. I assumed Joe told you. He came to me a few weeks back, said he'd found out about a grant that your mom qualified for, and paid the whole thing off."

My brain must be fried from everything that's happened today. Maybe I'm hallucinating from tiredness. I try to soak in Hannah's words, but nothing is really happening in my brain. I just nod. I'll have to ask Joe about it when he returns, but the thought of not having to worry about paying those bills feels like a weight lifted off my shoulders.

Hannah looks around. "Where's Wes? I thought I'd find him by your side when I got here. Did I just miss the sexy hunk, because I've really been dying to meet him—"

"He isn't here. He's not...I don't know. We're...I can't think about him right now." Hearing his name hurts. My hands start shaking and I try to breathe through the panic rising within me, the heartbreak still so fresh.

"What happened?" Hannah asks, her expression saddening further.

I shake my head. "I don't want to talk about it." I can't. Physically can't. I look at the clock again. Is it supposed to take this long?

Hannah stays for almost an hour by my side, until I basically force her to leave. Once she's gone, I turn my phone back on to send a text with Joe asking how long until he's back. As soon as I do, I see the notifications from Wesley rolling in. A few missed calls, and a series of texts increasing in frustration.

Did you get home okay?

How are you feeling?

Quinn.

Are you ignoring me?

What's wrong? If you're upset, please just talk to me.

At least just let me know you're okay.

> Please call me in the morning.

He's been calling and texting me all night? Couldn't he just wait til the morning? I have too much to be dealing with right now.

He doesn't know that, a voice reminds me. For a moment, I consider calling him and explaining what's going on with my mom. Our issues would take a back seat and he'd be here by my side, and even though I'm angry and confused…part of me wants nothing more than to have his warm, comforting arms wrapped around me.

The sound of footsteps from behind me signals Dr. Brooks walking towards me and I slip my phone in my pocket, stumbling to my feet.

"What happened? Is she okay?"

Dr. Brooks puts a gentle hand on my shoulder. "Your mother is fine. She's back in her room and you can go see her. The surgery was successful, and I'll be in shortly to explain more in detail."

I let out of sigh of relief, tears prickling at my eyes. She's okay.

"Is she awake?"

"Not yet. It could be a couple of hours. You can sit with her if you'd like, but if you'd like to go home—"

"No, no. I want to be here when she wakes up."

Dr. Brooks nods and I follow him back to my mom's room. She's asleep, hooked up again with wires. She looks…peaceful. Luckily, the doctor doesn't linger. I pull a chair up next to her bed, taking her hand in mine. I hear the door shut behind Dr. Brooks, leaving us alone in the room.

I breathe out and the dam breaks. Sobs wrack my body as I grip my mother's hand tightly. Everything from the past twelve hours comes crashing down over me. The folder. My mom. The surgery. The debt being paid. I try to breathe, sucking in a few ragged breaths. She's okay. She's going to be okay.

The door opens and Joe slips inside, carrying a duffel bag. I sniffle and rub my face on my sleeve.

"What's happened? Is she okay? What did the doctor say?" Joe asks, moving to the other side of the bed, his eyes scanning my mom's face, his expression one of plain adoration and concern.

"He said it was a success. He said it was good." I sniffle again. "He'll be in shortly to explain it all."

Joe nods, relief coloring his face. He drops down into the other chair, scooting up and grabbing her other hand. "Will she wake up soon?"

I yawn and wipe my face again. "He said it could be a few hours."

"You should go home, Quinn." I shake my head and go to insist, but Joe cuts me off. "Just for a few hours. Try to sleep, take a shower. I'll stay here."

"But—"

He gives me an insistent look. "I know you want to be there for your mom, and the best way you can do that is taking care of yourself first. Just go for a few hours. She'll probably still be sleeping when you get back."

I nod. Laying down and taking a shower sounds incredible right now and I don't know how much longer I can sit here waiting to talk to her again. I pick myself up and trudge towards the door. I turn to Joe.

"Oh. Um. Did you pay my mom's medical bills? Hannah said you got some grant or something."

Joe's eyes widen. He nods. "Right. The grant." He stares down at my mom, avoiding my eyes.

"Joe?"

He meets my eyes again. "Yeah...I..." He rubs his hand on the back of his neck, looking away again. "He asked me not to say anything. I wasn't sure if you knew, but I kind of had a feeling you didn't and well, I didn't want to get in the middle."

I shake my head. "What are you talking about?"

"The grant money was from Wesley. He pulled me aside at the barbecue and explained it, said it was a foundation or something he was involved in. I didn't really understand, but he basically gave me a giant check."

I must have reached my limit because the revelation washes over me with a cold sort of numbness. I don't say anything to Joe. I just leave quietly, stumbling down the dark hallway and calling myself a car. The whole ride back to my place, I stew silently, unbelieving.

Why the hell would Wesley do that? And why would he keep it from me? How much is he keeping from me?

I hate secrets, and it feels like I've learned more than enough about Wesley tonight. This...paying for my bills, invading my life like that, and keeping it from me. Trying to get me evicted? For what? Is this all some giant manipulation, to make me dependent on him, and then what?

I told him. I told him that I didn't want money to be a thing between us, and he ignored me. Went behind my back and paid for me.

Paid for me.

My heart wrenches with a lurch. I thought, hoped, maybe, that the apathy had gripped me enough so I wouldn't feel this searing pain, this unbelievable hole in my chest where my feelings for Wesley once lived. The car pulls over and I thank the driver, stepping out onto my empty street.

Only it's not empty. Wesley is sitting on my stoop, his head in his hands.

Chapter 42

Wesley

I couldn't sleep. No matter how hard I tried.

After firing off a series of texts and calls to Quinn that all went unanswered, I tossed and turned for most of the night. It was past midnight when I decided I couldn't take it. I had to call Pete to check in. It was much later than I usually bothered him, but I couldn't find it in me to care. I'd give him an extra Christmas bonus this year.

He answers on the first ring, his voice groggy. "Hello?"

"Pete, it's Wesley. Sorry to call so late, but I wanted to make sure Quinn got home okay. She's not answering my calls or texts and you know I tend to worry about these things."

"Uhh." A rustling on the other end interrupts him. "Yep."

Something in his voice sounds off. "Yes? You dropped her off at home and watched her go inside?" I confirm.

It's quiet for a moment before Pete speaks again. "How about we talk in the morning, boss? I'll come first thing."

Something is off. I can feel it from the way my defenses are starting to rise, familiar walls at the ready. "What's going on?"

He sighs, a resigned sort of sound. "She asked me not to say anything."

I'm hit with a pang. She's avoiding me on purpose. Ignoring my calls. "Peter," I growl, losing my temper at this endless bullshit of a day. "She doesn't sign your checks. I do, and if you want me to keep signing them, you'll tell me where she is. Now."

It's quiet again before he speaks, and when he does, I almost regret forcing him to tell me.

"I dropped her off at the hospital."

* * *

I've been sitting on Quinn's stoop for almost an hour when a car pulls up in front of me. She steps out, her arms wrapped around herself, and the sight of her threatens to send me to my knees.

"Quinn," I exhale, taking in the sight of her.

She looks like she's been through hell. Her face is red and splotchy, dried tears on her cheeks. When she finally sees me, her expression deadens. I can see the fight going out of her, but I have to know what's going on, if her mom is okay.

I just want to be here for her, to hold her and tell her that it's going to be okay. To make it okay for her, somehow.

I stumble towards her, needing her in my arms. "Is your mom okay? Are you okay? Pete told me, and don't be upset with him, I forced it out of him. Why didn't you call me?"

She steps back. Away from me.

The movement stops me in my tracks, a tiny crack forming in my chest. I swallow, my mouth suddenly dry and achy.

"I can't do this right now," she croaks out, not looking at me.

"But—" I stutter. "What is happening? Why didn't tell me about your mom?"

"Yeah? Like you told me about paying her medical bills? Going behind my back with Joe to pay for it and pretending like it's some fucking grant?" She snaps, her expression darkening.

Fuck.

No, no. The timing is all wrong. I'd planned to tell her about it myself...eventually.

"I should have told you, and I was going to." She shakes her head and goes to move past me, but I hold my hand up. "I was just worried that you would be upset with me, like with the job, and I was waiting for the right moment—"

"I *am* upset. You *lied* to me. Would you have even told me about it if I hadn't found out on my own?"

She shakes her head and sighs. "You don't care about me. You just want to control me, just want someone to take care of, to rely on you, so you fucking made me rely on you."

"No, Quinn, that is not it. I do want to protect you and take care of you, but it's not about that."

"It is." Her voice quivers and I step towards her, wanting so badly to take the pain out of her voice. "Everything..." She slumps her shoulders. "You ruined everything."

"Don't—" I choke on my own words. "Don't say that. Whatever I've done wrong, I want to fix it. I want to be there for you, whatever is happening with your mom—"

She stiffens suddenly and whips her head towards me. "I saw the folder, okay? You can stop pretending. Stop manipulating me. Stay the fuck away from me and stay out of my life."

I stumble back. Her words feel like a physical blow. Manipulating her? Pretending? I don't...the folder.

No, no, no.

I can't believe it. I can't believe this is happening. "You read it? I told you that was confidential—"

She cuts me off, seething. "Don't do that. Don't turn this around on me. A photo of *me* fell out of it, so I looked. I can't believe I thought..." She breaks off and pushes past me and goes for the door with her keys.

I follow her, trying to get her to look at me. If she would just look at me, I could explain. I could fix this.

"It's not what you think. Let me in, and we can talk. I don't want you to be alone right now."

She just shakes her head. "I really can't. I need to sleep and shower and go back to see my mom and I just can't handle this." I go to speak again but she turns to me, her eyes cutting and sharp. "Just go, Wesley."

"But—" I have to say it. I know it's the wrong time, all wrong, but she has to know. I have to get the words out. She has to hear them. "Quinn, I lo—"

Her icy eyes meet mine again. "Go, and do not come back. I mean it, Wesley. We're done." She turns the lock, slides inside, and slams the door in my face, leaving me standing on her stoop with my heart in my hands.

I try to inhale. Try to breathe, but it feels wrong somehow. My heart is racing, her words echoing, rattling in my head.

We're done.

I press my hand against my chest, rubbing the center, hoping that I can get rid of this feeling. This sinking, endless, *hurt.*

She didn't mean it. Her mother is sick, and everything that happened tonight upset her. She's been up half the night and the folder...

My stomach lurches. She really believes I'd do that? One letter, some photos, and she doesn't think to give me the benefit of the doubt? To let me explain?

A sinking feeling settles inside me, a taunting voice repeating a chorus in my head: *she doesn't trust you, she doesn't trust you, she doesn't trust you.*

Why should she? She's always been too good, much too good for me. Maybe she's finally realizing that the perfect Wesley Marks is nothing but a disappointment. Like my dad always said. I'm nobody. Nothing.

The thought settles somewhere familiar inside me, lodging itself there.

I am nothing.

* * *

It's been three days.

Three days since I've left my apartment. Three days since my world ended. Three days since I lost her.

Beverly called me about a hundred times before I finally answered.

"Mr. Marks. Are you okay?"

I didn't even have the energy to lie.

"No," I said, my voice devoid of any emotion. Then I hung up.

It's the only word I've spoken since I saw Quinn.

Just thinking her name is physical pain, so I don't think of it. Don't think anything. Instead, I keep all the curtains closed, the whole apartment covered in a cloud of darkness, and I hardly leave this spot on my bed, except to get food from the delivery guys or get a new bottle of liquor to knock back.

I'm almost through my second bottle of scotch, the brown, scorching liquid making my head pound uncontrollably at this point. But I can't stop. Stopping means thinking. Thinking means...thinking about her.

I throw another shot back, my stomach rolling. I haven't

had much of an appetite, but I managed to swallow down a piece of pizza or two yesterday. I think that's the last time I ate, but I can't remember. I should probably shower, but I can't bring myself to make it the short distance to the bathroom right now.

It would be better if I could cry. I almost wish I would. Wish there was something, anything, to release this endless pit of despair inside me.

I grip the scotch bottle, the brown liquid sloshing over the side and spilling onto my sheets.

"Fuck," I mumble and put the bottle on the bedside table. I force myself out of bed when I see one of my dresser drawers open, color peeking out of it.

I stumble over to it and between my blurry vision, I can make out two wrapped gifts, with a note on the top with my name. I open the note and read it twice before the words sink in:

To Wesley.
Thank you for making my life better every day. Happy Birthday.
Yours, Quinn

The words are like knives. I feel bile rising in my throat, like I might throw up right here. I swallow and blink back the wave of emotions threatening to spill over.

Not yours anymore.

I shouldn't open them. I should just leave them or give them back to her at some point. I don't know, but it feels like they aren't for me anymore. Not really.

Still, my hands grab at the wrapping paper, tearing the first gift open. It's a framed photo of us. I rack my mind, trying to remember when she took it, when I realize. It's from one of our Friday night dates, after we'd gone to see a Broadway show. She'd snapped a selfie outside the theater. Both of us are smiling widely, hints of laughter on both our expressions. We look so happy.

I put the photo down, my throat tighter than before. Tears are strolling down my face and I can't stop them. I thought it would feel good to cry but it feels terrible. I can't stop it.

My hands unwrap the second gift, knowing I'm making a mistake, but I can't seem to stop myself. It's two books. The first is what looks like a self-help book, titled *Finding Your Way: A Guide to Healing Through Music*. The second is a songwriting music book. Next to both of them, a small, hand-written note:

I hope one day we can share in your music together.

I can't breathe. There is nothing but this pain. This endless, empty despair. The tears are falling in earnest now and I don't bother trying to stop them. I wrench myself away from my room, needing to get away from the trace of her.

Everything starts to go black as I see the vase full of flowers on my table. The flowers she likely bought. I grab the vase and throw it against the wall.

The crash sounds good. It sounds like me.

So I do it again, and again, and again.

* * *

When I wake up on the couch, I hear a banging and Ben's voice calling through the door. I ignore him. Whatever the hell he needs, he can wait. Unfortunately for me, my brother has never listened to me in his entire life.

"Fuck off," I yell through the door, not moving from my spot on the couch.

He bangs on the door again. "Watch your language. There is a child present."

I groan. He brought Luna? Why the hell would he do that? The last thing my niece needs to see is me in this state. I don't want to see her either. Just the thought of her tiny fucking fingers and sweet voice causes a swell of feeling in my stomach, one that I immediately push down.

"Open the door, Wes. I'll break it down if I have to," Ben threatens.

"Why are you hitting the door, Daddy? Are you mad at it?" I hear Luna's high-pitched voice from outside.

Ben really is stubborn, and I can't just let them stand out there while he knocks on my door. I groan again and grab a shirt from the ground, sniffing it. Not great, but it'll do.

"Wes, I just took the subway all the way here from uptown with a 5-year-old. If you don't open this door—"

I swing the door open. Ben's eyes widen at the sight of me, and I don't look at Luna as I leave the door open and stalk back inside, throwing myself onto the couch. They can come in, but I don't want to talk.

"Uncle Wes looks ugly," Luna whispers loudly to Ben and he chuckles.

"Why don't you go play in Uncle Wesley's office, Luna? Remember the games he has in there?"

He's talking about the poker chips and chess board, neither of which Luna actually knows how to play.

She must leave because Ben settles into the chair in the living room, frowning. "Luna is right. You look like a mess and so does this place. I mean, Jesus, Wes. It's trashed in here. What the hell is going on?"

"How did you know I was here?" I grumble.

"Beverly," he says. "So? What's wrong?"

"Nothing. You've done your brotherly duty. You can leave now." I turn away from him, facing the ceiling, my anger brewing.

"It's clearly not nothing, and it's clearly about Quinn. I take it you talked to her?" Ben presses.

I growl. "I don't want to talk about it."

Ben slaps my legs and sits next to me on the couch, forcing me to move. "Well, too bad. Cause we are."

I say nothing. Ben says nothing. He just looks at me expectantly, as if to say: *I'll wait all day if I have to.*

I sigh and roll my eyes. Why did I even let him in?

"Fine. I called Pete to make sure she got home okay, and he told me that he dropped her off at the hospital and something had happened with her mom. She's sick. I waited for her at her place and when I got there, she told me we're done."

"That's it?" Ben asks. I'm silent again and he scoffs. "Sounds like you're leaving a lot out."

"She read the folder. She thinks I betrayed her, and she found out that I paid her mom's medical bills—"

"You did *what?*" He slaps his hand to his head. "Wesley."

"Don't fucking lecture me about it," I growl, anger replacing the well of hurt inside me. "Her mom's boyfriend Joe spent half an hour telling me about how Quinn's been basically paying the bills off herself, and it's still not enough, how stressed they've been with money. What was I supposed to do? Just let her carry that shit alone when we have more money than we know what to do with? Just because she's too proud to admit when she needs help?"

Ben shakes his head, his expression softening. "No, Wes. It's very admirable that you want to help her with the situation, but you should have talked to her about it first. Talked to her mom. It's not really your business."

"She is my business! She is—" I break off. Fuck. I wasn't supposed to do this. I wasn't supposed to think about her. "Whatever. It's already done, and I'd do it again if I could."

He sighs and shakes his head. "Alright then. What about her mom? Is she okay?"

I shake my head, feeling even worse. "I don't know. She wouldn't tell me. Just kept telling me to leave."

"Did you explain to her about George and the folder?"

"No. I tried to. She wouldn't listen."

It's quiet. From my office, I think I can vaguely hear Luna playing with the chess pieces. Ben leans forward on his knees.

"Well, bro, I think you need to try a little harder. You need to sober up, shower, and go see her mom. Make sure everything is okay. Then talk to her. Explain again and do a better job this time."

I exhale, my voice shaking. "It's not that easy."

"Never said it would be."

"You don't get it. I've fucked it up. She was the best thing in my life. The only good thing in my life, and I ruined it. Like I ruin everything."

Ben doesn't let me wallow. He quirks an eyebrow, his expression still playful. "Only good thing, huh?" He rolls his eyes and calls out to his daughter. "Luna! Come in here!"

Luna runs into the room, a wild smile on her face. She bounds towards us and launches herself onto the couch between us, cuddling close to Ben.

"I have a question and if you answer, there may be chocolate in it for you," Ben says and Luna's face lights up like a Christmas tree. "What's your favorite thing about your Uncle Wes?"

"Ben—" I start to protest.

He shoots me daggers. "I believe I asked Luna, not you. Didn't I?"

Luna nods eagerly. "It's my question, Uncle Wes. You can't have it."

I huff out a sigh, feeling like an absolute child, and wanting them both out of my apartment. Now. As if things can't get any worse, Luna reaches her small hand towards me, her face thoughtful.

"I can't pick one. Is that okay?" She looks at Ben like she's worried she won't get it right, but she keeps going. "I like that he always gives me presents and takes me to get pancakes. He's really funny and tall. He won me Mr. Thomas at the carnival. He picks me up from school and has nice friends. He's my favorite uncle."

My heart aches. I have to look away from her at the swell of emotion growing inside me. I can't handle this. Anything but that. Anything but that...innocent adoration.

Ben gives Luna a tiny high-five. "Good job, Luna. That was a perfect answer," he whispers.

"Candy, please," she demands. He slips a mini-Hershey's bar out of his pocket and gives it to her. A wide smile spreads across her face. "You can go back to playing," Ben says, and Luna skips away from us, not a care in the world.

It's quiet again and Ben turns to me, studying my face. He knows all my fucking weak spots, Luna being the main one. He knows how much I love the little weirdo.

"Sounds to me like you've still got one good thing, at the very least."

I say nothing, keeping my gaze trained on the floor, refusing to look at him. He doesn't let it go. He stands up and holds his hand out, as if waiting for me to take it. Waiting for me to get up.

Reluctantly, I press my hand into his and he tugs me to a standing position. He pats my shoulder with his hand.

"Now, you gonna get her back, or what?"

Chapter 43

Quinn

I am so cold. Ever since I left Wesley standing on my front stoop, no matter what I do, I can't get warm. Even now, days later, sitting by my mother's hospital bed, I feel a shiver traveling down my spine.

He looked so...defeated. I wasn't prepared to see him. Not after the horrible day I'd had, feeling so exhausted and broken. All I wanted was to launch myself into his arms, for him to hold me and tell me that everything was going to be okay.

Instead, I told him to leave. Told him that we were over. I want to cry now thinking of it, remembering the shock and disbelief that colored his features, the way they changed, fading into a plain, raw pain.

Part of me wishes he were here, fighting for me. It was almost too easy for him to accept that we were done. He didn't say anything, or maybe I hadn't given him the chance to. Either way, I haven't heard from him since that day, and I can't really blame him. All he did was follow my instructions.

Another wave of cold blankets me. Even the warmth of my mother's hand in mine can't seem to push this feeling down. I squeeze it, hoping she will wake up soon. She fell asleep a few hours ago after we talked to the doctor. The surgery was successful in stopping her internal bleeding, but they still need to deal with the spread of the cancer and keep monitoring her liver.

If they can't stop it from spreading further...I can't think about that.

Joe and I have been taking shifts here. Earlier, I spent three hours on the phone with Sheila, explaining everything to her. She wanted to get on a plane and come back here, but I insisted she stay right where she is. As much as I'd love to see her, my mom isn't in any shape to see people. She spends most of her time sleeping.

She's supposed to be released in a few days, according to Dr. Brooks. Dr. Emmanuel is going to take over her case again and they're going to increase her chemo treatments. I'm terrified. Every minute of my life since Saturday night has been clouded by fear, its awful grips digging deep into my heart.

My mom stirs, waking a little. She blinks up at me and tries a soft smile. "Hey," she croaks out and I reach for her cup of water, bringing it to her lips for her to sip. "Thanks."

"How you feeling?" I ask.

She sits up. "Still exhausted. You'd think I've slept enough by now," she jokes, jostling me.

She's been trying to get me to smile since she woke up. I've been trying, really. For her sake, I've pretended to be positive, agreeing with her that everything is going to be fine. In reality, I feel devastated. Hopeless. Like I've lost Wesley and I'm slowly losing her too.

"Where's Joe?" She asks.

"He went home to sleep for a bit. I just talked to Sheila. She says get well soon or she'll kick your ass. Her words."

My mom chuckles and then coughs a few times. It's not a

good sound. It sends another icy chill down my body. The door to my mom's room opens and I expect to see Dr. Brooks or the nurse coming in to check in on my mom.

Instead, my heart drops and a sudden heat rushes through me. I feel like I'm standing on the edge of a cliff with no safety net.

"Wesley," my mom croaks and smiles at the sight of him.

I can't believe he came here. After I explicitly told him to leave me alone, he comes to my mom's hospital bed? His eyes flicker towards me briefly, a flash of pain behind his eyes, but he recovers quickly and moves towards my mom.

"Ms. Taylor. I was so sorry to hear that you were in the hospital." He presents her with a bouquet of beautiful flowers that he sets on the table with the others from Joe and Hannah. "How are you?"

She shrugs. "I've been better. Quinn's been taking good care of me, though." I can feel him looking at me, but I refuse to meet his eyes. Can't. Instead, I keep focused on my mom, smiling tightly, hoping she can't tell how tense I am.

"Haven't seen you around here as much as I was expecting," my mom says, a hint of accusation in her voice. It's more meant for me than him and I suppress the desire to roll my eyes.

"Yeah, well..." Wes mutters, trailing off.

It's so awkward. So quiet. I hate him for coming here. I haven't said anything to my mom about my break-up with Wesley. She's got enough going on without worrying about my relationship status. But the tension in here is thick enough to cut with a knife and my mom isn't stupid.

I finally force myself to look at his face. "Can I talk to you outside for a minute?" I say, moving towards the exit. "Now."

"Yeah," he agrees, lingering for a moment. "I hope you get

well soon, Ms. Taylor. Please let me know if you need anything at all."

I try to hide my grumble as I leave, not waiting for Wesley to follow me, but he does, and closes the door behind us. He stares down at me, his gaze as intense as ever. I can't look at him. Don't look at him.

"It was nice of you to bring flowers, but you need to go," I say, willing my voice to sound firm and not as unsteady as I feel.

He shakes his head. "Not until you've heard me out. Can we go somewhere more private?" He glances around the busy hallway, at the doctors and nurses and other visitors passing us.

I want to object, but I want this conversation over and done with so I can get back to my mom, so I nod. We walk outside, towards the empty smoker's area of the hospital. We stand a few feet from each other, awkwardness in the air.

I stare at the wall. "Fine. Let's get this over with. Say whatever it is you have to say."

"Will you at least look at me?" He says with a small bite to his tone.

I take a deep breath and close my eyes. I can do this. I won't cry. I won't cry. I won't cry. With another deep breath, I open my eyes and look at him. Really look at him.

He looks tired. Exhausted, actually. There's a red rim around his eyes and the bags beneath them are more pronounced than usual. Worst of all, there's sadness plain in his eyes now. I blink, trying to focus.

"Are you going to say something or what?"

He clears his throat. "Right." He takes a deep breath, like he's preparing. "First off, the folder—"

I shake my head, my whole body stiffening at the reminder of his lies. "I don't want to talk about it."

"What you saw was a mistake. After that night at The Phoenix, when the story broke, I told our CFO, George, about what had happened, or what I thought had happened. I explained that an employee at The Phoenix had leaked the information, but that she'd been fired. Apparently, that wasn't enough for him. He hired a private investigator to find you and sent that letter to your landlord trying to get you evicted. He gave the folder to me as some sick, twisted gift. Said it was for my birthday. I told him to stay the fuck away from you and reverse whatever damage he'd done, or I'd kill him."

His voice is fierce, and his fists are tight at his side. My legs wobble beneath me. Oh god. It wasn't Wesley. It was someone else, and he tried to stop it. Tried to protect me.

"I know I fucked up in the past and said a lot of unforgivable things, but I thought you trusted me, Quinn. You just saw that stuff and immediately assume the worst? Do you know how shitty that makes me feel?"

"Wes—" I start, but he cuts me off.

"No, let me finish. I need to say this." He inhales raggedly and runs his hand through his hair, looking more frantic by the minute. "I'm sorry that you saw that. I didn't want that to happen, and it must have been really...scary and confusing to find that. I wish you would have come to me, but I understand why you didn't. I'm sorry that I didn't make you feel like you could talk to me about it.

"Now, about the medical bills. I shouldn't have done that behind your back. I see that now. I just thought you'd be too stubborn and proud to take my help if I offered it, and when Joe told me at his party how much you guys have been struggling...I just feel like you don't talk to me about that stuff because you're worried about upsetting me, or talking about money, but I want to be able to help you. I *want* to take care of you. It feels awful knowing I have plenty to spare and that you don't have enough. I *hate* it."

At this, I can't help but interrupt him. "You think I don't? You think I like living like this? Seeing how the other half lives and coming home to my shit?" I scoff, shaking my head.

He shakes his head. "No, of course not. But I can't change the way things are. I can only try to do the right thing where we're concerned, and I'm sorry that I misread the situation. It must be even harder for you, and I understand why you're hesitant to share this stuff with me."

My jaw tightens. "Yeah, because you don't respect my decisions. You just get me nepotism jobs and pay my family medical bills without telling me. It's not okay. Where does that leave me once you're gone? Jobless? Homeless?"

He clenches his jaw. "Why do you keep saying that shit? Why do you think I'm gonna leave you?"

I say nothing.

He sighs, his hand rubbing the back of his neck. "I'm sorry. Next time, we'll make decisions together. I won't make them for us again. I swear."

A shiver rocks through me. "I told you I didn't want money to be a thing with us. After everything that's happened to me...why couldn't you just respect that?"

He blanches, his face etched in disbelief and horror. "Fuck. I didn't...I didn't think about that. I was just trying to help. I'm sorry. I'm so sorry, Quinn."

It's quiet as his words settle between us and I can't help but soften at his apology.

"I'm sorry, too," I choke out. "I'm sorry for what I said to you on Saturday. I was angry and exhausted, and I thought my mom was going to die. I was really scared. I'm sorry that I hurt you just because I was hurting."

Wesley's frown seems to lighten. It definitely does as he

steps towards me, relief coloring his features, his arms reaching for me.

I step back. Again. Away from him.

As much as I believe Wesley's words and his heartfelt apology, I can't do this. It hurts too much. I thought I was ready, but I'm not. When I thought he'd betrayed me...it felt like I was cracking in two. Like I was dying.

He hasn't done anything wrong. I see that. I'm the wrong one. I'm not strong enough for this, for the pain that comes along with whatever it is we're doing here. Wesley deserves better. He's standing here, open, communicating, trusting, and all I can give him is shitty apologies.

It's better this way. Better that I walk away now before I fall for him even more. Before he realizes how broken I really am. He'd just leave eventually, and it would hurt even more than this.

"What?" He asks, confused. He reaches for me again, but I shake my head. "But — are you still mad about the grant thing? Or the..." He swallows. "What George did?"

I shake my head again, a coolness settling inside me, replacing the burning. "I'm not mad anymore."

"Then—" He blinks, still not understanding, and I swear my heart breaks right then. Just splits down the middle. It feels like I'm being ripped apart.

"I understand why you did what you did and I'm not mad, but I think it's best if we take some time. Apart."

"No—"

"It's too much." I have to keep it together. I can't cry. Just a few more minutes. "When I thought..." I can't get the words right. It hurts too much. "I can't do this. I just can't. It's too much. I'm sorry."

He moves towards me and grabs my hands, shaking his head frantically. "Quinn, we can figure this out."

"No, we can't," I insist, pulling my hands away from him.

"Quinn—"

I squeeze my hands together. "Please, *please*, if you care about me at all, just go." My voice cracks at the end and I can't bear to look at him a second longer, but whatever he saw in my eyes must have convinced him.

Because he doesn't say anything else. He stands there in front of me, as beautiful as the first time I saw him, and I can see, clear as day, that his heart is breaking with mine. His chest rises and falls, and he clenches his jaw, anger radiating from him.

I open my mouth to speak, to offer some comfort even though this is my fault. All my fault.

Worthless.

Derek is here. Of course he's here.

My voice cracks out, but I'm too late. "Wes—"

He blinks, and suddenly, it's gone. The heartbreak, the pain that was just so plain in his expression has disappeared, leaving his expressionless mask looking down at me. A face I haven't seen on him in months. I realize with a pang that I've taken his openness for granted. These past few months with me, he's let me in, and now, being on the other side of that cold, hard mask feels like a punch to the gut.

He turns on his heel and does exactly as I asked. He leaves, and when he finally does, I stumble backwards against the wall of the hospital and let myself crumble into a thousand pieces.

Chapter 44

Quinn

The cold has settled deep into my bones. I hardly notice it anymore, the dull throb of pain that accompanies me everywhere I go. It's become a companion of sorts, something I can rely on when all else fails. If I have nothing else, I have the cold.

Wes has visited my mother twice since that day. I know because he brought flowers both times and my mom has innocently pointed them out, her eyebrows raised at me. It was her way of saying: *what the hell are you doing?*

My mom was discharged yesterday, but the good news stops there. Her most recent scans show that she needs another surgery, one that we've scheduled for two weeks from now. As much as I hate to admit it, I owe Wesley more than I can fathom for paying for my mom's medical bills. We checked out with another whopping bill for her brief stay, but with our current balance at zero, it could certainly be worse. Her next surgery will be expensive, but Joe has promised that he's got a solution, one that doesn't involve Wesley.

Which is why I'm currently standing next to my mom at City Hall as she signs marriage papers to Joe.

At first, I was totally against the idea. I never imagined my mom would get married again. My mom was even more surprised than me. Then, of course, she was livid. "This is how you propose to me, Joseph? No ring, no romantic gesture?" She'd screeched when he took her hand in the taxi ride back to our apartment and flat out told her that they should get married.

Luckily for Joe, he's more than proven his love and devotion for my mom in the past few weeks. He's been by her side just as much as I have, if not more. You'd have to be a fool not to see the love between them.

So, when my mom stormed up the stairs to our apartment (even though she isn't supposed to be on her feet unsupported) and flung herself onto the couch in anger, I crept to my room where I listened to Joe's real proposal through the door. While he admitted he thought of it so that she could be on his health insurance, he also swore that he knew from the moment he saw her that he wanted to be with her forever.

I wanted to keep listening, to cherish this moment with them, but it hurt too much. Hearing the joy in his words and remembering the stricken look on Wesley's face...I hated the jealousy and pain that rose up in me.

But now, as Joe slips a ring onto my mom's hand and they make out like horny teenagers, I can't seem to find the cold. I try to muster as much enthusiasm for my mom when she turns to me with a wide, amazing smile.

"I'm married! Can you believe it?"

I force my best smile. "I'm so happy for you guys."

Joe bristles and nudges my mom. "The real wedding will be later this year, after the surgery, when you're better." There's not an ounce of doubt in his words and a twinge of sorrow sparks in my chest.

I'm on a 'break' from work. I explained my mom's situation to Rita and basically begged for two weeks off to take care of her. She agreed, but it's unpaid. It's for the best. I can take care of my mom and find a new job, one where I won't run into Wesley.

My mom giggles and wraps her arms around Joe, murmuring something into his lips. It's so intimate, I have to look away. We walk down the steps to the sidewalk when I decide I can't spend another minute in the presence of this love fest.

"I'm gonna go. I'll see you guys tonight? At the apartment?"

My mom's smile falters, and I feel a pang of guilt. "Actually, we thought we'd start moving my stuff slowly to Joe's with his truck. Do you want to help?"

Right. Another change. My mom is moving to Joe's house in Long Island. She begged me to move with them, but I refused. As much as it breaks my heart to think of us leaving our place, the only home I've ever known, I can't hold her back from her future.

Still, that apartment is home. It's the place I've spent my whole life. It's the only thing that is truly ours. I can already feel everything slipping away. The only thing left at the end of it all is me. Alone.

I swallow the lump in my throat, blinking back tears that always seem at-the-ready these days. "I forgot." It's a lie, and she knows it. "I just need a few hours. I'll come later."

She nods and pats my shoulder. I know she's trying to hide the pity in her expression but she's doing a terrible job. It's written all over her face.

"Baby. Just talk to him."

A shudder rolls through me. I don't even bother trying to argue with her. She does this every few days and every time I shut her down.

I can't. Can't think about him. Can't think about myself, who I am, who I've let myself become. This...nothingness.

"Love you," I say, my voice flat. I don't wait for her response before I turn and walk away.

I wander around until I find myself walking towards Prospect Park. It's a warm day and the streets are littered with the joy of spring everywhere I look. I wish it were winter again. I wish I could bundle myself away from the world. Hibernate. Wish everyone else could feel the cold steel in their bones.

I try to steady my mind with a sigh. I need to figure my life out. I realize I've spent the last few years just...floating. Waiting. Waiting for my mom to be okay. Waiting for my restaurant dreams to somehow magically come true. Waiting for my life without realizing it's been passing me by this whole time.

Now, my mom is married and moving to Long Island. I'm alone and probably about to be homeless. Wesley is gone because I pushed him away. Because I'm not strong enough. Not good enough. What was I thinking? Why would anyone be interested in me for anything but sex? I'm clearly not capable of handling an adult relationship. Stupid of me to even try.

I don't think I've felt this emptiness in a while. Since after Derek, probably. It's like everything I was scared of is happening and there's nothing I can do to stop it. Like I can close my eyes and almost imagine the life I dream about: my mom healthy; me, in my own apartment, running a successful restaurant. But no matter how hard I try to erase it, to imagine some other future, the dream always includes Wesley by my side when it happens.

I stop walking and sit on a bench, rubbing my hands on my arms to try and ground myself. My shaky inhale is interrupted by my phone ringing in my pocket. Filled with a mixture of hope and dread, I glance at the name, expecting to see Wesley's name flashing on my screen. Instead, it's Sheila. She's Facetiming me.

I force my mouth into something that resembles a smile and answer the call.

"Sheila?" I blink at the blank screen in front of me. "Are you there?"

Her familiar raspy voice greets me. "How does this thing work? Can you see me?"

I shake my head. "No, your screen is blank. Are you in the FaceTime app?"

"Yeah, that's what I did. I FaceTime called you."

I suppress a growing smile, despite my mood. "No, click into the app, and hold the phone up in front of your face."

Sheila's face appears on the screen. She's leaning away from the phone, staring at it like a foreign object.

"Can you see me now?"

"Yeah. Can you see me?"

She scrunches her nose and peers closer. "Oh! There you are. Stupid thing never does what I want."

"How are you? How's Vegas?" I ask.

She scowls. "Who cares about Vegas? It's exactly what you'd think — lots of strippers and gambling. Don't change the subject on me."

"Subject? We just started talking."

Her scowl only deepens. "So, you have no idea why I'm calling? There's nothing going on with you that might require some insightful advice from a wise old lady?"

I shake my head. "If this is about my mom..."

"Nah, I talked to her earlier. She'll be fine. She's a fighter. Now I thought you were one too, but now I'm hearing that apparently you wanna be a coward all of a sudden."

Ouch.

Leave it to Sheila to take absolutely no prisoners when it comes to calling me out.

"Great talk. Thanks for calling. Always great to hear from you," I deadpan.

"Come on. What are you doing? The girl I knew would run headfirst into the life she wanted the first chance she got."

"It's not that easy. You know it's not."

She rolls her eyes. "It ain't difficult either. You wanna know difficult? Try walking a day in your mom's shoes. You don't see her running scared from her boyfriend. So you got dealt a bad hand, and another, and then another. Sounds to me like you got a winning card in that deck, but you wanna keep playing the fool."

"See? Poker metaphors? Vegas is changing you," I try for a joke. I'm hoping to steer the conversation into simpler territory, but Sheila can see my deflection from a mile away.

"Quinn, take it from me. Life is short. Don't waste it being scared. Call me in a week if you've sorted your shit by then."

Before I can say anything else, her face disappears. She's hung up on me.

Jeez. I didn't expect a verbal lashing from Sheila. It's been a few weeks since we've talked and I haven't been properly scolded by her since she moved away. I didn't realize I missed it.

She's right. I am scared, and I don't know how to get over it. How to loosen the grip of fear that seems to surround me all the time.

Eventually, I find my way home, where I find Joe loading up his truck with one of my mom's suitcases.

"Hey," I call to him with a wave. "Need some help?"

He wipes the sweat off his brow and looks at me with a

steady gaze. "I'm good. Your mom probably needs help upstairs. She can't decide what to take with her."

I manage a smile. "Sounds like her."

When I get upstairs, my mom is sitting in the living room, surrounded by heaps of clothes and furniture.

"Wow," I try for a joking tone. "You really hurricaned through here. Plan on leaving anything for me?"

She throws her hands up and gestures to the mess around her. "I don't know how this happened. I was doing really well, and then suddenly, I found my high school diaries, and started reading them, and then I started crying..."

I drop my bag and cross the living room, wrapping her in my arms. "I'm here now."

She must hear the sadness in my voice because she hugs me back, her grip tightening around me. "I love you, baby," she whispers against me.

I want to say it back, but the emotion in my throat threatens to overwhelm me. I swallow it back and nod, pulling back from her. "Come on, let's get you moved out."

Chapter 45

Wesley

"**G**et me a private line. Now."

I bark the words at my new assistant whose name I don't know. Beverly left a few days ago with some heartfelt goodbye and a damn bouquet of flowers to "thank me." Since then, I decided I don't need to be involved in my assistant's life anymore. At all.

Business has never been better. I am finally focused on what I should be focused on: expanding the Marks empire. Nothing else matters. The only time I've left the office is to sleep and twice, to visit Quinn's mother. It's difficult to be reminded of her when I go there, but I've managed to entirely compartmentalize it so I almost never have to think about her.

It's better this way. I'm finally back in control and taking care of the business and my family like I should have been focused on from the beginning.

Since I put my nose to the grindstone, we're close to acquiring two other real estate companies, one in London and one in Berlin. It's the first step in expanding our global empire, in bringing the Marks name across the ocean and beyond.

Ben has called me six times. He must be too busy to show up in-person again, because I haven't seen him. My mother, too, has called at least twice.

The truth is I just don't want to talk to them. I should just focus on my role in the family: to keep the company going. I don't want to see the disapproval, or worse, pity in their eyes when I tell them that I let her go.

That I lost her. For good.

My assistant knocks twice and pokes her head through the doorway. "Mr. Marks, George is on line one."

My hand curls into an involuntary fist. The last thing I want to do right now is talk to that bastard, but the fact that we run this company together means I have to answer his calls.

"Fine. Put him through," I growl.

With an inhale, I reach for the phone and pick it up. My jaw is grinding as I bark out a hello to George

"Wesley. So sorry to bother you." Ever since I reamed him out in the elevator, he's been treading lightly around me. As he should. "Just wanted to let you know I sent you the final contract for the London deal and also...the thing from the other week, uh, it's all fixed. Reversed. Nothing to worry about."

"Is that all?" My voice is hard as stone.

"No. I mean, yes, there's nothing else."

I hang up without a goodbye, sick of hearing his voice.

My cell rings and I glance down at who's calling my private line. It's Ben, again. He's nothing if not persistent and I'm not sure how much more I can avoid him before he comes around again with Luna, guilting me into making another stupid mistake like putting my heart on the line.

I can't believe the words I almost let leave my mouth. I'd

almost told her I loved her. How fucking embarrassing to get rejected moments after confessing your love for someone.

Rationally, I know I shouldn't blame Ben for how the conversation went. He probably thought I'd be able to win her back somehow. I'm sure he's figured out by now that my ridiculous attempt at vulnerability and romance was a complete failure.

With a sigh, I answer the call. There's no point in avoiding it any longer. I'll have to face him eventually.

"Yep?" My voice makes it clear that I'm in no mood to talk.

"Wes?" Ben's exasperated voice comes through the phone. "I've called you like, ten times. The only reason I know you're alive is because your new assistant told me."

"Closer to six," I correct him.

"Oh? So, you did get my calls, then? You're just deliberately ignoring me?"

I swirl my chair towards my desk, glancing at the email from George. "Pretty much."

Ben sighs. "You know what? You're a fucking dick. I can guess by now that the talk with Quinn didn't go very well, and instead of, I don't know, talking to me about it, you ice me out and act like you're fine?"

"I am fine. I don't need you to call me every day, okay? I'm a big boy. Besides, things are great. Business has never been better."

Ben laughs without a trace of humor. "Yeah, I'm sure you're really fulfilled by that. Idiot. If you want to treat me like shit when I've tried to support you through this, go ahead. If you want to give up on the woman you obviously love, be my guest. Just don't forget to pick up Luna from school on Friday like you said you would, and if you can spare a moment for anyone besides yourself, give mom a call. You aren't the only one going through something."

His words hit their intended target, landing in my stomach like lead. I breathe heavily, ragged and raw. It's why I didn't answer the phone earlier. He always knows how to hit me where it hurts.

I think he's hung up on me, but I hear his soft breathing on the other line, like he's waiting for me to respond. I clear my throat. "I'll be there on Friday, and I'll call mom."

"Great talk. Bye."

The call ends and I feel worse than ever.

Ben is right, yet again. He's been nothing but supportive of me and my relationship with Quinn. I owe him an apology, and some sort of explanation, but the thought of trying to explain everything I'm feeling causes a swell in my chest that is too dangerous to allow. I push it down with another ragged breath.

I should call my mom, but I'm too raw right now to handle her getting emotional on me. It's probably about the divorce going through. I've been so focused on avoiding Quinn at all costs, I've forgotten about my family.

Shame claws up my throat at the mounting failures around me, the sinking feeling that never seems to go away no matter what I do. No matter how many deals I make.

My phone rings again, another urgent call from some associate. I don't know who it is, but the energy and fervor I had just minutes ago has dissipated into a familiar emptiness.

The urge for a drink rushes through me, but I breathe through it. I've managed to avoid spiraling into a drunken haze again.

Any similarity to my father is something I hate about myself.

I pick up the phone, aggravated that my assistant didn't tell me who is calling. "Wesley Marks."

"I heard congratulations are in order." My father's voice turns my blood cold. As if this day couldn't get any worse, somehow thinking of the man has summoned him.

"What do you want?" I bark out.

"Like I said, to congratulate you. I saw the announcement about the expansion and your recent acquisitions. You're doing much better than I expected."

Perhaps the closest thing to a compliment he's ever given me.

"I see you're finally putting your energy where it belongs. Not quite at my level yet, son, but you're getting there."

I can't do this right now. Can't listen to his voice. Can't breathe through the burning rage that threatens to erupt if he says another word to me.

The words are coming before I can stop them. "Listen to me. Do not fucking call me again. I have zero interest in having any sort of relationship with you on any level. I'm buying you out of your shares of the company unless you want a never-ending legal nightmare with me, and when you get out of rehab, don't even think about contacting me, or I will get a restraining order against you."

My chest is rising and falling with an intensity I can't seem to control. All I can hear is my dad's dark chuckle from the other line.

"Wow. Nice speech." He laughs again like he's genuinely delighted by my words. "Practice that one in the mirror this morning? Finally figured out how to fit into your big boy pants?"

I practically growl. "I'm not fucking around. Never call me again. Name a number and I'll pay it, so long as you never contact me, mom, or Ben. Ever. Again."

It's silent for a moment before he speaks, his voice serious again. "I'll get back to you."

"Did you not hear me? *Don't fucking call me again.* You can go through my assistant." I hang up the phone, my heart racing. Adrenaline is pumping through my veins, and I can feel my hands shaking.

I should feel...something. Relieved? Upset? All I can feel is the cold press of anger against my ribs. How long have I wanted to tell my father exactly what I think of him, right to his face, and instead, when I finally worked up the courage, all I wanted was for him to disappear. To never have to hear his voice again.

My head drops into my hands, heavy and resigned. What I wouldn't give to feel Quinn's hand wrap around the back of my neck, to feel her fingers twirling through the tips of my hair. But that's not going to happen. She's not here. She's gone.

* * *

I finally work up the courage to go visit my mom after Ben's phone call.

When I get to the Soho apartment, I can already tell something's up. It's not until I step inside that I realize the walls are bare. My mother sits in the middle of the room, her feet propped up on a box.

I glance around at the half-empty room. "What's going on?"

My mother just shrugs. "I sold the apartment. I got it in the divorce but to be honest, there's nothing here but memories. I'm going to France."

"You sold the apartment?" I can't believe it. "Wait, France?"

She smiles softly. "I met a woman at the knitting store who has a house there. She agreed to rent it to me for six months. I'll figure the rest out."

I shake my head, processing what's happening. "I talked to Dad. He's gone for good this time. He won't be bothering you or Ben anymore."

She stands and crosses to me and before I can move, her arms are circling around me in a hug. I let myself wrap my arms around her, cherishing this embrace. We haven't hugged in a long time.

"Oh, Wes. I'm so proud of you. I know I don't tell you enough, but you've done such a good job taking care of us. Taking care of the family, the business."

She pulls back from me and there are tears gathering in her eyes. "I'm sorry I didn't protect you from your father. I was blinded by love and greed and...well, there's no excuse. You're my son and I should have been there for you."

I shake my head. "You were. You are."

"No, I let him bully you. Bully all of us." She shakes her head, regret clouding her features. "But darling, you've turned out better than I ever could have imagined. You never once let his ugliness infect you. You've stayed my bright spot through it all."

I blink back the wave of emotions crashing through me. Fuck. Did Ben tell her to say this shit?

"I know you want to take care of everything, Wesley, and you have." She glances around at the empty room, the place we both called home for so long. "But sometimes love means letting go."

* * *

"Uncle Wes!" Luna comes bounding towards me, her arms outstretched. The other children from her class stumble out of the school towards their families.

I scoop her up and twirl her in my arms. "Hey, Loon." She giggles and I put her down, slipping her tiny backpack through my arm.

"Uncle Wes, can I have my juice box?"

I shake my head. "Not until we get to your dad's place." She crosses her arms and huffs, but I just roll my eyes, nudging her towards my car, where Pete waits.

When we climb in, he flickers his eyes towards me from the driver's seat. "Where to, Mr. Marks?"

I try not to grimace at his words. Ever since I threatened his job and forced him to tell me about Quinn, he only addresses me as Mr. Marks and hasn't said a word about anything else. Not about his family, not about his fantasy football league he's always talking my ear off about. He just drives in silence.

Add his name to the growing list of apologies I need to make. Best to get started.

"Pete." His eyes meet mine warily, but his gaze is steady, unblinking. "I want to apologize for...threatening you. I was scared of losing Quinn and well, turns out I did anyways." I shake my head, getting off course. "That's not the point. The point is I was disrespectful to you and to our friendship and I'm sorry."

He blinks a few times in the silence and then nods, a quick movement, his eyes softening. "Thanks, boss. Don't worry about it. Water under the bridge."

The car pulls away and I tell Pete to take us to Ben's apartment. Luckily for me, he won't be home until later this evening, so I have a few hours to prepare for the next leg of my apology tour.

After my conversation with my mom last night, my head has been a jumble of thoughts. Do I need to let Quinn go? Does she deserve better than me? Or do I need to let go of myself? Of my own fears and need for control holding me back?

Luna's voice interrupts my thoughts, her hand hitting my arm. "Why did you say sorry to the driver man?" She whispers, but from Pete's small smile, I know he can hear her.

"His name is Peter, and I apologized because I wasn't very nice to him. I said something hurtful."

"Why?" She blinks up at me, her eyebrows furrowed in confusion.

"Why did I say something hurtful?" I clarify, and she nods eagerly, waiting for my answer. I suppress a sigh and consider how to answer. "Because I was hurting, too. Sometimes when people are feeling hurt or angry, they say things they don't mean."

"Is he okay?" She asks, her eyes widening.

"Why don't you ask him?" I tell her, knowing Pete can hear everything we're saying. She taps her finger to her chin, looking thoughtful.

"Mr. Peter?" Her quiet voice pipes up.

"Yes, Miss Luna?"

She glances at me, her expression pleading, but I just shrug. She looks back at Pete. "Are you going to be okay?"

My heart aches at the innocence in her question. Something about her just makes me emotional. I take a deep breath, my chest rising and falling in the quiet car.

"Your uncle is one of the best men I've ever met. I'm going to be just fine, Miss Luna." His words send another jolt through me. I want to tell him he's wrong, but he just turns his head to look at Luna. "Don't you agree?"

She looks over at me and wrinkles her brow, frowning. "I

guess. He's weird," she says definitively, eliciting laughs from Pete and me.

The rest of the ride is quiet. When we finally get to Ben's apartment, Pete opens our doors and helps get Luna unbuckled from her car seat. I ask the doorman to bring her up to the apartment for me. Once she's out of sight, I turn to Pete.

"Thank you. You really didn't have to say that."

"Meant every word, boss."

Perhaps he can sense my frayed emotions, the knife-edge balance of emotions bubbling up in me, because his tone turns joking. "I used to be a taxi driver. If I quit every time someone threatened me, I'd be broke as hell."

* * *

Later that night, I hear Ben letting himself into the apartment. Luna fell asleep two hours ago after guilting me into not one, but two bedtime stories. After countless pages about a nasty troll and a valiant knight, I finally heard her soft snores and closed the book.

In the foyer, Ben peels his coat off and drops his bag on the floor. He goes straight to the fridge, grabs two beers, and flops onto the couch next to me, handing me one of the open bottles.

"If you're about to start a fight, don't bother. I'm fucking exhausted," he says, letting his head fall back. He closes his eyes and takes a deep breath and I feel another pang of guilt hit me in the chest. He's stressed and trying to take care of his family and I'm acting like — well, a shitty brother.

"Don't worry. I left my weapons at the office." I take a sip of my beer. "You too tired to hear an apology?"

"Maybe. Depends how good it is," he grumbles, lifting his head. His expression is a scowl. "Everything fine with Luna?"

"Yeah, all good." I suppress another dramatic sigh. "I talked to Mom. Did you know she's moving to France?"

"Yep. She told me she'd send a postcard."

I chuckle darkly. If he can sense that I'm working my way up to an apology, he doesn't let on.

"I'm sorry for ignoring your calls. It had nothing to do with you. I just...had nothing to say. It's just been a shitty few weeks." I swallow, blinking back another round of fresh tears. Why am I suddenly turning on the waterworks every two seconds?

"Do you want to talk about it?"

I shake my head. "I don't know if I can. It really fucking hurts."

Ben shrugs. "Want to try?"

So, I do. For the second time, I explain everything to Ben. The conversation outside the hospital. How Quinn forgave me but broke things off. I talk for what feels like forever and when I'm finished, my shoulders sag with the weight of all I've been carrying. I feel a little lighter.

"I don't know what to do. Some days, I give up and tell myself it's over and I need to deal with this new shitty reality. Other times, like today...I think I have to get her back no matter what it takes. Even if she keeps pushing me away, even if she hates me, I have to figure out some way to get her back. I just can't imagine my life without her."

Ben nods, his thoughtful, open expression unwavering. I expect him to jump into his advice, but he just points to the empty bottle in my hand. "Want another beer?"

"Sure."

He comes back from the kitchen with two bottles and

hands one to me. He takes a long pull from his and then sets it on the table and turns to me.

"Alright. I have an idea." Ben smirks, an expression I have come to learn means nothing but trouble. This cannot be good. He licks his lips and clasps his hand on my shoulder.

"How do you feel about one more grand romantic gesture?"

Chapter 46

Quinn

Today's the day. My mom is moving out of the apartment we've shared our entire lives. I thought I'd be able to keep the place for a few months without my mom, but I can't afford to drain my savings, so I'll be on my way at the end of the month.

Looking around at the half-empty apartment, it looks like a shell of what it once was. I told myself I wouldn't get emotional today. I'm pretty sure even Joe is sick of my moping and sulking even if he hasn't said anything.

I'm trying to move on. With everything.

A few days ago, I went to the hotel restaurant to give Rita my two weeks' notice. I talked to Pierre and he's willing to give me my old job back and I figure it's better than running into Wesley every day, even if it was a dream job. The only problem is that Rita essentially refused my resignation.

I wasn't sure how to handle it until she called me yesterday and told me she's willing to accept my resignation if I agree to interview for a different position with one of her old friends. So tomorrow I have a job interview in the West Village.

My mom has been helping me search for a new apartment, but I can't afford any studios, so I need to find a roommate. Hannah is letting me crash on her couch if I haven't found a spot by the end of the month, but I'll probably have to find some random online to live with. My mom continues to insist I should move into Joe's place with her. There's enough space for all of us comfortably but I can't help but feel like this is an important step for my mom and me. Part of moving on.

"Feeling nostalgic?" My mom asks from behind me, leaning against the door frame. She's looking a lot better these days, even with the threat of another surgery hanging over her head.

"How'd you know?"

She pushes off the wall and wraps her arms around me. "I know you." She leans back and looks into my eyes. "Which is how I know you aren't happy."

I push slightly away from her. "Mom—"

"No, don't say it's nothing. I've been trying to give you your own space because it's clear you don't want to talk about it, but no more. Talk to me. Tell me what's going on."

I shake my head, already feeling overwhelmed at the direction this conversation is going. This is exactly the thing I can't handle. It's too much.

"I'm fine. I really don't want to talk about it."

"Quinn Helena Taylor."

I know she doesn't mean for the words to crush me entirely. She's always scolded me by using my full name, ever since I was a kid. But the memory of my name on Wesley's lips, of the first time we met, has the tears I've been pushing down for weeks spilling over and running down my face.

"Baby." My mom wraps her arms around me. "Talk to me."

Another sob cracks through my chest and I start talking

through the tears, retelling fragments of what happened with Wesley. By the time I finish, we're sitting on the floor with boxes around us, my tears drying.

I take a shaky breath and blow my nose into a tissue. "I just miss him. A lot. I know I told him to leave, and I know it's for the best, but I guess I thought he would fight for me. That's stupid, and unfair, and he deserves better, he deserves someone to fight for him, too, and I just can't but...I still feel so alone."

My mom rubs soft circles on my back, whispering soothing words until I finally stop shaking. I take a few more deep breaths before I feel steady, and shoot her a soft, embarrassed smile.

She waits for a moment before she speaks. "You know, you've always been guarded. Even when you were a kid, I always swore you were my superhero, not the other way around. So strong." She brushes my hair back behind my ear.

"But sometimes being strong means allowing yourself to be weak. To fall down. Love means giving someone the power to hurt you. And he will hurt you, Quinn. You'll hurt him. But he'll also love you."

Her words hang in the air between us. She must sense that they've hit me some place deep because she squeezes my arm and presses her lips to my forehead.

"You just have to ask yourself: will the love be stronger than the hurt?"

* * *

The first night alone in my apartment is a hard one. After my mom leaves with Joe, I spend the remainder of the night drinking wine and stuffing my face with Chinese food. It doesn't make me feel any better and even my third Amanda Bynes movie can't cure the loneliness coursing through me.

Will the love be stronger than the hurt?

I keep replaying my mom's words over and over in my head like a mantra. I just don't know how to handle the fear that comes with all of this. I'm scared enough of losing my mom and already she's slipping away from me. What if I lose Wesley? What if I already have? What if I'm too late, if I've hurt him too much?

I scoop a mouthful of cookie dough ice cream into my mouth with a sigh. I never thought of myself as a coward before, but that's what I am. A complete and utter coward. Too scared to really try things with Wesley. Too scared he'll hurt me again, or walk away, or somehow, somehow it won't work out.

Because it never has before.

I never really gave dating a chance when I was younger. I was too focused on making money. Trying to keep our bills paid. Nothing else really mattered to me. Making friends, dating, following my dreams — they all took a backseat to surviving.

But the last few months...everything changed. *He* changed everything. Somehow, along the way, I found Hannah, and a job where I really got to develop my skills as a chef. Finally the life I'd always dreamed about was within my reach. And what did I do?

I ruined it. By not trusting Wesley. By letting my fear control me. By convincing myself, yet again, that it was too good to be true. Why? Why is it so hard to believe that maybe things would work out?

Because you don't deserve it.

Derek's voice calls the words out from within me, and they settle in my chest like they're right. They feel right. So...

familiar. A shudder rocks through me and before I know it, tears are slipping down my face. Because I am so *sick*, so *tired* of hearing his voice in my head. All I want is to be free of it.

When I was doing sex work, I told myself it was just work and nothing more. But the truth is that his words and what happened that night and all the nights before it have haunted me for too long. Every time we'd have sex, he'd find another cruel way to tear me open, but the worst was when he said I deserved it. I deserved to be degraded, to be hurt.

I'd be lying to myself if I said it didn't feel like that. Like it doesn't still feel like that sometimes. Because why would it have happened if I didn't somehow deserve it? If it wasn't somehow my fault for putting myself in that position to begin with?

Otherwise, there would be no meaning in it at all. No reason. Isn't that worse somehow?

I take a gasping breath, my tears coming harder. Squeezing my eyes tight, I imagine, for a moment, what Wesley would say if he were here. How his arms would wrap around me and protect me somehow, even if just from myself, from the unkind words bubbling inside me. I can almost hear his no-nonsense voice, the soft brush of his words against my neck.

A fresh wave of wanting rushes through me as images of us together assault me, unrelenting and out of reach. It would be so easy to fall back into his arms if he'd let me. But then what? Another few months pass until something happens and I go running for the hills again? Or worse, I find some way to sabotage us, all because deep down somewhere I don't think I'm worthy? Because I don't think I deserve to be happy?

If I let myself keep going on this cycle, keep believing that I don't deserve good things, the bastard who tried to hurt me wins. A fresh wave of anger resurfaces at the thought.

I can't let that happen. I can't.

Taking a deep breath, I steady myself, wiping away the last of my tears. My mom was right. This hurts. It hurts so much, and the truth is, it's probably going to hurt some more. Right now, I'm alone with it, and it feels endless and impossible to overcome, but maybe...maybe if I had someone to share the hurt with, it wouldn't be so bad. Maybe I could eventually be happy.

And maybe, just maybe, I'm ready to let myself.

* * *

It's a struggle to drag myself out of bed the next morning. Despite my newfound resolve, I'm exhausted. The past few weeks have been a nightmare, one that I feel like I'm only starting to wake up from. The last thing I want to do is meet Rita's friend for my job interview, but I promised her I would, so I go.

On the train ride, I try to think of a plan for reaching out to Wesley again. Just the thought of seeing him brings a fresh wave of fear to the surface, but I breathe through it, telling myself that I'm strong enough, that I can do this.

It's a warm, rainy day. The walk from the subway to the address Rita gave me isn't long, but when I arrive, I have to check my notes three times to make sure I'm at the right place. The building in front of me is empty, with a For Rent sign hanging in the window.

I glance around, confused, but nobody pays me any attention. Pressing my face against the glass, I try to peer inside, but all I see is the empty space. I lean against the wall and take out my phone, dialing Rita's number. She answers with a little too much pep in her voice.

"Rita? I'm here, but I think you gave me the wrong address. It's an empty building."

"Yep! There's a key in the mailbox. Just let yourself in."

"But—"

Before I can say anything else, she hangs up. I shake my head and stuff my phone in my pocket, confused. What kind of job interview is this?

Suppressing an eye roll, I search in the mailbox and find the key. I slip it into the lock and turn, letting myself into the empty building. It's a narrow space, with a bar on the left side and some corner booths left over from what must have once been a restaurant.

I'm about to call Rita again when a figure pops out from behind the bar, causing a scream to erupt from my lips. I press a hand against my chest, steadying my breath, unable to open my eyes.

Wesley.

This isn't happening.

He can't be here. Why is he here?

A breathless laugh escapes me. "Jesus Christ. You scared me."

It's quiet for a moment before Wes speaks, a slight smile in his voice.

"Sorry. Not my best opening. I was supposed to say 'Welcome, can I take your order?' Or something. I can't really remember now. You weren't supposed to scream."

My eyes open and I take him in. He's behind the bar, leaning on his forearms. His sleeves are rolled up, exposing his bare arms and I swear I feel my knees go weak at the sight of him. When I finally let my eyes wander to his face, his gaze is locked onto me, his eyes blazing with an intensity that causes my heart to lurch.

He looks better than the last time I saw him. More...alive.

Is he doing better without me? I guess I just assumed he's been suffering as much as I have these last few weeks, but what if he's here to tell me he's moved on?

I shake my head, feeling suddenly exhausted and very, very nervous. "What are you doing here?"

A small smile plays on his lips. "Isn't it obvious? I'm winning you back."

My jaw practically unhinges itself. The gears in my head are malfunctioning, I think, because I can't seem to form a single thought. I step backwards, stumbling a little, and he takes a step towards me, his face turning serious.

"Don't leave until I've said my piece. Okay? I'll sit all the way over there if you want me to." He points to the only remaining bar stool at the counter. "Or you know what? You sit. You sit and I'll stand."

I roll my eyes. Where did this fumbling, nervous version of Wesley suddenly come from? Where's the brooding billionaire I've come to know and—

"Here." Wesley guides me over to the empty stool and sits me down at the counter. "Sit."

He steps back from me, running his hand through his hair, and looks towards the window. "This really is not going how Ben said it would."

I wait expectantly, taking him in. My heart aches at the sight of him. His nervous smile, the way his fingers are palming his thighs. Watching him, hope swells within me. He said he wants me back.

It's not too late.

"Shit. I'm messing this up." He shakes his head and runs his hands through his hair again.

My heart stutters again and I want so badly to reach towards him, to ease his nerves somehow. Instead, I look around and try for a less intense subject.

"Where are we?"

His gaze meets mine and his eyes light up. "Right. That's a good place to start." He exhales. "This is an empty restaurant space for rent. I thought maybe, it could be your restaurant. If you like it."

I go to protest, but he cuts me off. "Wait. Before you say no, this isn't me trying to buy the space for you. Everyone has agreed to pitch in for the security deposit and even the first month's rent. Nothing has been signed or settled yet because I wanted you to see it first. It's your decision. Your choice."

I close my mouth, stuttering. "What do you mean, everyone pitched in?"

"Your mom, my mom, Joe, Ben. Even Pete and Rita insisted on chipping in, and Hannah suggested starting a GoFundMe to raise the rest of the funds, so the rest of the world can share in your dream and help it come true."

I shake my head in disbelief. "I don't...I don't understand."

Wes takes a step closer to me and I'm overwhelmed by the closeness of him, his familiar luscious scent of pine and sandalwood surrounding me.

"If you don't like it, we can find a different space. But I want you to have your dream, Quinn," he says. "Even if I'm not the one by your side when you get there. Anything you want, I'll do it. I just want you to be happy, even if...even if that means I have to let you go."

Tears are forming in my eyes, but I can't do anything. I can't even blink them back. All I can do is stare at him. At this beautiful, generous man in front of me. He meets my gaze again, steady and unyielding.

"I know you said before that it was too much. Us, being together. I know probably nothing has changed for you and...if you don't want this...don't want me anymore, I understand."

He breaks off and looks away from me.

"It will be hard for me, but I still want to help support you with the restaurant, and your mom, if you'll let me. I'll take any piece of you I can get, Quinn. Any of it is a gift."

The tears are falling in earnest now and I can't stop them. Wes steps forward, his expression twisting in anguish. He reaches for me, then pulls his hand back and brushes it through his hair.

"Please don't cry."

I finally manage to speak. "I'm sorry. I'm sorry."

His throat bobs and the agony in his face only grows. I don't know if I'm reaching for him, but he doesn't hold back anymore, wrapping his arms around me, his lips soft on the top of my head.

I fall into his arms, wrapping myself around him, clutching him to me. This is what I needed. What I'll always need. It feels so...*right* to be in his arms again.

"Quinn." He runs a soothing hand on my back. "Baby. What's wrong?"

"I'm sorry," I repeat, a sob cracking out of me again.

He pulls back slightly, just enough to tuck a strand of hair behind my ear. "Why?"

I take a few gasping, deep breaths, trying to stop the tears from flowing. Wes just holds me, waiting, nothing but patience in his expression.

"I don't deserve all this, Wesley."

His expression darkens. "What do you mean, you don't deserve it?"

I swallow the growing lump in my throat. "I was scared, and I walked away when you needed me. When you were ready to be vulnerable with me and...I wanted that so badly. I think I was just really scared of being hurt again, and there's part of me that just feels like, maybe I don't deserve good things. Like the bad things in my life are my fault like maybe I just...deserve to be hurt."

Wesley grips my arm, his eyes wide, holding my gaze with an intensity I've never seen from him. "Please don't say that. I hate hearing you talk like that. It's *bullshit*."

I take a deep breath, pushing forward.

"I should have trusted you, but instead, I ran away. I think deep down I was just looking for some excuse, just waiting for me to fuck things up somehow, and for you to leave, so instead of waiting around for you to leave me, I left."

I shake my head, feeling confused by the whirlwind of emotions rushing through me. Guilt, shame, fear, pain...but stronger than all of it, pulling me towards Wesley like a rope...

Love.

I love Wesley.

I love him.

A burst of laughter breaks through my tears and Wesley stares at me like he's completely confused by my reaction.

"I'm sorry." I sniffle. "I think I'm going crazy."

He brings his hand up to my cheek, brushing the dried tear marks with his thumb. The movement sends a shudder of pleasure through me.

"I'm going crazy, too. At least, I have been without you. I know that you're scared. I'm scared, too. I'm fucking terrified that I'm going to mess this up again, or that I'm not enough for you—"

"You are enough. Wes, you have to know. I'm the one—"

His expression darkens again as his grip on me tightens. "If you say one more negative thing about yourself, I will kill you."

Another laugh bubbles out of me.

Wes brings his hand around the back of my neck, looking into my eyes. "Whatever that voice is saying, it's wrong. You are everything I have ever wanted, Quinn. You are amazing in every single way."

His words, his touch, everything about this moment fills me with this unbelievable warmth. I look around at the space and feel a sense of wonder rising within me. I turn back to Wes, and let myself truly take him in.

This man. This man who was willing to do anything to get me back. Who listened to my dreams and found a way to make them come true. Who makes me feel alive and deserving for the first time in my life.

I don't wait another second. I wrap my hands in his hair and pull him closer to me, pressing my lips against him. I can sense his surprise, but it melts quickly as he realizes what I'm doing and kisses me back, his tongue exploring my mouth. He gasps against me, deepening our kiss, his hand cupping the back of my head with fervor.

He breaks away with a gasp, his eyes studying me, a question on his lips, but I just lean closer to him and stare deep into his bright blue eyes.

"I love you, Wesley."

His whole body stiffens, and he pulls back further, staring down at me. He blinks. Once, twice.

"Say it again."

I smile softly. "I love you."

The smile that breaks out over his face is incredible. It's breathtaking, the joy in his eyes and the curve of his lips. He pulls me into him again, enveloping me in another kiss, this one deeper than the last. I groan into his mouth, feeling him everywhere. It's like I'm on fire.

He pulls back, his lips mere inches from mine. "I love you. I love you so much."

His words fill me with a rich warmth that spreads all the way to the tips of my fingers and toes. His hand curls in my hair again, pulling my lips back down to his and enveloping me in another intense kiss.

I lose myself in the feel of him, the taste of him. Eventually, he pulls back and we're both gasping for air in the empty room.

A wild laugh escapes me, joy coursing through me. My hand is fisted in his shirt like I'm gripping it for dear life. I shake my head and let go.

"I can't believe you found this space. It's perfect."

"You like it?"

His finger twirls in my hair and I trace the back of his hand with my thumb. I never want to stop touching him.

"I love it." I smile widely, "I love you."

His mouth descends on mine again. "Let's never fight again," I murmur jokingly against his lips. He chuckles and the sound reverberates through his chest.

"Unlikely." His smile fades slightly as his eyes flicker across my face. "We're gonna fight, baby, but no more running. We don't walk away from each other. Deal?"

"Deal." I quirk an eyebrow at him, smirking. "As long as you promise to stop giving me things. I can't handle any more generosity, I swear. I'll pass out."

Wes rolls his eyes and intertwines our hands, running his thumb along the back of my fingers. "Drama queen. Most women would be thanking me, not making me swear to stop."

He wraps his arms around my waist, pulling me closer. "Fine. I won't give you anything else. With one exception."

"What would that be?"

His eyes flicker briefly towards the open window where pedestrians are passing by on the street, then back to me. Slowly, he lowers himself, pressing kisses on my stomach, his gaze dipping lower as his hand dips into my pants.

I smirk in realization. "I think I can allow that exception. But just for you."

His hands press against my thighs as he meets my gaze with a soft, wicked smile. "Damn right. You're mine."

My heart swells at the words. I am. His. Completely. I am his, and he is mine, and strangely enough, I'm not scared anymore. I'm not scared at all.

I'm ready.

Epilogue

Quinn

Tonight's the night. My stomach is fluttering with nerves as I wrap my coat tighter around me to shelter from the cold. Stepping into the front room, I can't help the broad smile that spreads across my face despite my nerves.

"Welcome to Mel's, can I take your coat?" The hostess, Emilia, greets me with a knowing smirk.

I roll my eyes at her, but slip out of my coat nonetheless, letting her take it. She nudges my shoulder. "You're fashionably late, aren't you?"

I shrug. "I insisted on taking the train."

Emilia pulls back the velvet curtains and lets me into a dream.

My dream, to be specific.

It's been two years since I stood in this empty room and told Wesley I loved him for the first time. Now, what was once a dilapidated diner is my very own upscale restaurant. With Wesley's help, I was able to become friends with other restaurant owners in the city to learn the ropes. I kept working for Rita part-time while I spent the last two years getting the restaurant built and hiring people. It was a lot of work, but we managed to get it all together. Best of all, Manny agreed to join as my head chef. I realized that while I love cooking, I enjoy managing all the workings of the restaurant, not just the kitchen. So, I leave the cooking to Manny.

Wesley finally moved out of the hotel and back to his place in Dumbo and eventually convinced me to move in with him. It took a lot of arguing before I agreed — I'd insisted for a while that it was too soon, but I couldn't really afford to keep my own place and truthfully, I was sick of hearing him nag me about it.

Another thing he convinced me to do was start therapy. Our fight made me realize that my time as a sugar baby had really impacted my self-esteem. As I started to remember that time and work through it, certain uncomfortable memories came back to me. It was hard, but Wesley was by my side every step of the way. We even did a couple of joint sessions. He's working on listening better when I share my feelings about that time instead of getting angry and overshadowing my own emotions. We both have a long way to go, but I feel grateful to be on this journey with him.

Glancing around at the grand room, I feel a sense of calmness. Rightness. Like I'm exactly where I need to be.

The familiar scent of pine and sandalwood surrounds me as a pair of soft hand circle around my waist.

"How do you feel?" Wes murmurs, pressing into my back. His breath is soft on my neck as he curls his hand tighter around me.

Breathless, I turn to him. "Terrified. Excited." I run my hand along his jawline. "Grateful. Horny."

He chuckles and presses a soft kiss just next to my mouth, the type of kiss that always leaves me wanting more. "I am so proud of you. Everything looks amazing."

"I couldn't have done it—"

He presses another kiss to my mouth, silencing me. I groan against it, suddenly wishing we were in private. He tastes like peppermint. "Nope. You get all the credit tonight, baby."

He steps back and twists away from me. When he turns back, he somehow produces two full champagne flutes and hands one to me. "To you. I love you."

I clink my glass against his and we both knock back a gulp, our eyes locked over our glasses. I lick my lips afterwards and his eyes dart to the movement, his expression darkening.

He steps closer to me and drops his voice to a whisper, his breath hot on the side of my neck. "You look absolutely delicious. I am having all sorts of inappropriate thoughts. Mostly of abandoning this night completely so I can spread you out like a feast."

I knock back the rest of my champagne and ignore the shiver of delight rushing through me. He can always sense how his words affect me, because he slides his fingers along my thigh, teasing at the hem of my dress.

"I bet you'd like that, wouldn't you?"

I take a full step back and shoot him my best scolding glare, but he just chuckles and plucks my empty glass out of my hand. "I'll get you another, but don't let me carry you home tonight, yeah?"

He's gone before I can roll my eyes at him, quickly replaced by Ben, Lillian, and Lillian's boyfriend, Mathieu.

"Quinn! Congratulations. We're so excited for you, darling," Lillian says. She's much tanner than she was, now that she splits her time between St. Barths and the city. After meeting Mathieu on her vacation in France, they've been inseparable ever since.

"C'est incroyable, Quinn. Very beautiful." Mathieu chimes in from beside her.

Ben congratulates me too and I can't help but glance around at the room with a large smile. I never imagined that so many people would be here to support me.

Wes returns with our drinks and slips his hand around my waist effortlessly. I beam up at him. "Thank you."

He nudges me lightly. "Go on, enjoy your big night. I'm going to hang with Luna. She's the only one who likes me anyways."

"I'll be right over." I press a quick kiss to his cheek as he slips out of my arms and crosses to the corner of the room where Luna has her face pressed into her iPad, which is typical for her these days.

After shaking hands with a few more people, I catch my mom's eyes from across the room. She's standing with a glass of wine in her hand and a wide smile on her face, Joe by her side. It's a relief to see her looking so healthy. Better than that. Alive. Her second surgery was a success and she's been in remission ever since.

I cross the room to meet her. When she sees me coming, she shoves her wine glass into Joe's hand and throws her arms around my neck.

"Sweetheart! I can't believe it. This is incredible. You look so beautiful."

She gestures to my tight red dress and heels. "So do you," I whisper back to her. "And you, Joe."

Joe chuckles and raises his glass. "Congratulations, honey. How do you feel?"

I shake my head, dazed. "I'm in awe. I can't believe everything came together and how many people are here. I honestly was worried that nobody would show."

My mom rolls her eyes. "You've always been much too

humble. Good thing Wesley has enough ego for the both of you."

I can't help but laugh at that, but my mom takes my hand, her expression suddenly serious. "I've got a surprise for you."

My brow furrows in confusion, but before I can ask, suddenly Sheila is standing in front of me.

"Sheila!" I wrap my arms around her, bringing her into a hug, and she returns it. I haven't seen her in over a year, since Mom and I went to visit her for a weekend. "What are you doing here?"

"You thought I'd miss your big night? Child, don't be ridiculous." She slaps my arm, and I can't help the laugh that escapes my lips. She came all this way for me. We catch up for a bit before she tells my mom she wants to go sit down for a bit.

Joe leads her over to one of the booths while my mom clasps my arm and meets my gaze. "Enjoy your night, sweetheart. It's a big one."

I duck into the kitchen to find Manny prepping for a busy kitchen. He greets me with a kiss to the cheek and a twirl. Then, we go over everything again; we created the menu together with final approval going to my mom since all of this was inspired by her.

"Alright, now get out of here and enjoy your night. You deserve it, QT."

I hug Manny again and head back out to the main room, where guests are starting to disperse towards their seats.

I lift my champagne glass and tap a spoon against it, silencing the room. With a wide smile, I look around and find Wesley in the crowd, shooting him a glare that says *get the hell up here!* He smirks back at me and makes his way through the crowd, joining me at my side and clasping his hand in mine.

"Thank you so much, everyone, for joining us for the

Grand Opening of Mel's. I feel so incredibly blessed to be here. Opening my own restaurant has been a dream of mine, one that I never thought would be possible."

I take in a deep breath, feeling unsteady on my feet all of a sudden. As if he can sense my unease, Wes squeezes my hand and rubs his thumb on the back of my hand, soft, comforting circles.

"This wouldn't have been possible without some amazing, incredible people that I want to mention. Lillian and Benjamin Marks, two of our incredible benefactors."

I pause for applause and smile widely at Ben and Lillian across the room, lifting my glass towards them.

"Our amazing head chef, Manuel Gonzalez, our entire team in the kitchen, and our PR and marketing team behind the scenes." More applause scatters through the room. "And of course, the man standing by my side, Wesley Marks."

He grins down at me and squeezes my side, tucking me closer to him.

"Last but not least, the woman who I wouldn't be standing here without, and the namesake of this place, my mother, Mel."

Everyone claps and my mom meets my gaze with a steady, wide smile. I feel so lucky, such an incredible rush of joy coursing through me that I've made it this far.

"Thank you all for coming. Let's eat!"

The applause scatters and as folks settle into their seats, Wesley steps next to me and clinks his glass, raising attention.

"Excuse me, just one more thing."

What the hell is he doing?

I send him daggers with my eyes, but he seems to be ignoring me completely.

"I'm sure you're all eager to get started and I don't blame you. Quinn has created an incredible menu. We're here tonight not only to celebrate the opening of Mel's, but also to celebrate my amazing, incredible, beautiful partner Quinn. Let's give her another round of applause."

"What are you doing?" I whisper under my breath, my eyes widening. He's not supposed to make a speech.

He finally locks eyes with me and his lips quirk upwards. "Remember when I stood in this spot two years ago and promised never to give you anything again?"

I glance around at the silent people watching us: food critics, chefs, influencers, and my closest friends and family. What is he up to?

"Yes, I remember. What does it matter?" I mutter, grumbling.

"I lied."

Before I can think of a response, Wesley is dropping down to one knee, his hand sliding to his jacket pocket. I vaguely register the sounds of gasps and whispers. I think my mom is crying. Or is that Lillian?

Oh.

My.

God.

"Quinn Helena Taylor."

A choke laugh escapes me. I can't believe it. He opens the ring box and I stare at the magnificent diamond that I can't wait to get on my finger. Thankfully, Wes opts out of a big speech, and instead, he just meets my gaze, his eyes so full of warmth and hope and love that I have to blink back tears.

"Will you marry me?"

Then there's nothing left to say but yes. Nothing left to do but throw myself into his arms as cheers envelop us. A bottle of champagne is popped, and Wesley is scooping me up in his arms and I know this is one of those moments I'm going to remember forever.

I close my eyes, breathing in this feeling, wanting this moment to last forever, but then I feel my hand being lifted and my eyes fly open. Wes slips the gorgeous ring onto my finger and lifts my hand to his mouth, pressing a kiss to it.

I steal my hand back and stare at the beautiful piece of jewelry on my finger and what it means.

Forever.

I look up and meet Wesley's loving gaze, his bright eyes fixed on me in awe. It's everywhere, the love I have for him, warm and full and taught between us like a string. I reach for him again and fall into his arms, holding on tight to this moment and our promise of forever.

Acknowledgments

Writing a book is no easy feat but in the case of LOVE MARKS, it was an absolute blast. To my family: thank you for always supporting my dreams and encouraging my creativity. To my beta readers and editors Sarah, Madison, Jessica, Heather, Maddy, Roxana, and Caroline: none of this would have been possible without you all on my team. To my incredible Booktok and Bookstagram community: thank you for your endless support! And lastly, to my 14-year old fanfiction obsessed-self: thank you. Here's to all of us finding our way back to our inner child, and falling in love with love.

About the Author

Rachael Harriet is an independent author making her publishing debut with LOVE MARKS. She is a Wellesley college graduate and has been writing for over two decades (if you count her third grade diary). In her free time, Rachael is a member of an all women's improv group and a voracious romance reader. She currently resides in Brooklyn, NY where she can occasionally be seen carrying stacks of (probably smutty) books through Prospect Park.